don't close your eyes

ALSO BY LISA McMANN

Cryer's Cross

Dead to You

Crash
(Visions Book 1)

Bang
(Visions Book 2)

Gasp
(Visions Book 3)

FOR YOUNGER READERS

The Unwanteds

The Unwanteds: Island of Silence

The Unwanteds: Island of Fire

don't close your eyes

WAKE · FADE · GONE

LISA McMANN

SIMON PULSE
NEW YORK LONDON TORONTO SYDNEY NEW DELHI

This book is a work of fiction. Any references to historical events, real people, or real locales are used fictitiously. Other names, characters, places, and incidents are the product of the author's imagination, and any resemblance to actual events or locales or persons, living or dead, is entirely coincidental.

SIMON PULSE
An imprint of Simon & Schuster Children's Publishing Division
1230 Avenue of the Americas, New York, NY 10020
First Simon Pulse bindup edition December 2013

Designed by Karina Granda
The text of this book was set in Janson.
Manufactured in the United States of America
2 4 6 8 10 9 7 5 3 1
Library of Congress Control Number 2013948304
ISBN 978-1-4424-9913-3
These titles were previously published individually.

CONTENTS

WAKE

This one is for you,
Toots

ACKNOWLEDGMENTS

To my amazing in-home cheerleaders, house cleaners, and editors—Matt, Kilian, and Kennedy—you rock. There would be no Janie without your love, help, patience, and support.

Special thanks to Dr. Diane Blake Harper, my dear friend and Google-monkey; to Dr. Louis Catron for your kind, priceless critiques; to Ramon Collins for your years of support; and to Tricia, Chris, Erica, Greg, Dawn, Joe, David, Jen, Lisa, Andy, Matthew, Linda, Andie, and Ally for your generous assistance.

Finally, warmest gratitude to my fantastic agent, Michael Bourret, who believed in Janie and in me, and great praises for a most terrific team at Simon Pulse—Jennifer Klonsky, Caroline Abbey, Michael del Rosario, and all the others who help make dreams come true.

SIX MINUTES

DECEMBER 9, 2005, 12:55 P.M.

Janie Hannagan's math book slips from her fingers. She grips the edge of the table in the school library. Everything goes black and silent. She sighs and rests her head on the table. Tries to pull herself out of it, but fails miserably. She's too tired today. Too hungry. She really doesn't have time for this.

And then.

She's sitting in the bleachers in the football stadium, blinking under the lights, silent among the roars of the crowd.

She glances at the people sitting in the bleachers around her—fellow classmates, parents—trying to spot the dreamer. She can tell this dreamer is afraid, but where is he? Then she looks to the football field. Finds him. Rolls her eyes.

It's Luke Drake. No question about it. He is, after all, the only naked player on the field for the homecoming game.

Nobody seems to notice or care. Except him. The ball is snapped and the lines collide, but Luke is covering himself with his hands, hopping from one foot to the other. She can feel his panic increasing. Janie's fingers tingle and go numb.

Luke looks over at Janie, eyes pleading, as the football moves toward him, a bullet in slow motion. "Help," he says.

She thinks about helping him. Wonders what it would take to change the course of Luke's dream. She even considers that a boost of confidence to the star receiver the day before the big game could put Fieldridge High in the running for the Regional Class A Championship.

But Luke's really a jerk. He won't appreciate it. So she resigns herself to watching the debacle. She wonders if he'll choose pride or glory.

He's not as big as he thinks he is.

That's for damn sure.

The football nearly reaches Luke when the dream starts over again. *Oh, get ON with it already,* Janie thinks. She concentrates in her seat on the bleachers and slowly manages to stand. She tries to walk back under the bleachers for the rest of the dream so she doesn't have to watch, and surprisingly, this time, she is able.

That's a bonus.

1:01 P.M.

Janie's mind catapults back inside her body, still sitting at her usual remote corner table in the library. She flexes her fingers painfully, lifts her head and, when her sight returns, she scours the library.

She spies the culprit at a table about fifteen feet away. He's awake now. Rubbing his eyes and grinning sheepishly at the two other football players who stand around him, laughing. Shoving him. Whapping him on the head.

Janie shakes her head to clear it and she lifts up her math book, which sits open and facedown on the table where she dropped it. Under it, she finds a fun-size Snickers bar. She smiles to herself and peers to the left, between rows of bookshelves.

But no one is there for her to thank.

WHERE IT BEGINS

EVENING, DECEMBER 23, 1996

Janie Hannagan is eight. She wears a thin, faded red-print dress with too-short sleeves, off-white tights that sag between her thighs, gray moon boots, and a brown, nappy coat with two missing buttons. Her long, dirty-blond hair stands up with static. She rides on an Amtrak train with her mother from their home in Fieldridge, Michigan, to Chicago to visit her grandmother. Mother reads the *Globe* across from her. There is a picture on the cover of an enormous man wearing a powder-blue tuxedo. Janie rests her head against the window, watching her breath make a cloud on it.

The cloud blurs Janie's vision so slowly that she doesn't realize what is happening. She floats in the fog for a moment, and then she is in a large room, sitting at a conference table with five men and three women. At the front of the room is a tall, balding man with a briefcase. He stands in his underwear, giving a presentation, and he is flustered. He tries to speak but he can't get his mouth around the words. The other adults are all wearing crisp suits. They laugh and point at the bald man in his underwear.

The bald man looks at Janie.

And then he looks at the people who are laughing at him.

His face crumples in defeat.

He holds his briefcase in front of his privates, and that makes the others laugh harder. He runs to the door of the conference room, but the handle is slippery—something slimy drips from it. He can't get it open; it squeaks and rattles loudly in his hand, and the people at the table double over. The man's underwear is grayish-white, sagging. He turns to Janie again, with a look of panic and pleading.

Janie doesn't know what to do.

She freezes.

The train's brakes whine.

And the scene grows cloudy and is lost in fog.

"Janie!" Janie's mother is leaning toward Janie. Her breath smells like gin, and her straggly hair falls over one eye. "Janie, I said, maybe Grandma will take you to that big fancy doll store. I thought you would be excited about that, but I guess not." Janie's mother sips from a flask in her ratty old purse.

Janie focuses on her mother and smiles. "That sounds fun," she says, even though she doesn't like dolls. She would rather have new tights. She wriggles on the seat, trying to adjust them. The crotch stretches tight at mid-thigh. She thinks about the bald man and scrunches her eyes. *Weird.*

When the train stops, they take their bags and step into the aisle. In front of Janie's mother, a disheveled, bald businessman emerges from his compartment.

He wipes his face with a handkerchief.

Janie stares at him.

Her jaw drops. "Whoa," she whispers.

The man gives her a bland look when he sees her staring, and turns to exit the train.

SEPTEMBER 6, 1999, 3:05 P.M.

Janie sprints to catch the bus after her first day of sixth grade. Melinda Jeffers, one of the Fieldridge North Side girls, sticks her foot out, sending Janie sprawling across the gravel. Melinda laughs all the way to her mother's shiny red Jeep Cherokee. Janie fights back the urge to cry, and dusts herself off. She climbs on the bus, flops into the front seat, and looks at the dirt and blood on the palms of her hands, and the rip in the knee of her already well-worn pants.

Sixth grade makes her throat hurt.

She leans her head against the window.

When she gets home, Janie walks past her mother, who is on the couch watching *Guiding Light* and drinking from a clear glass bottle. Janie washes her stinging hands carefully, dries them, and sits down next to her mother, hoping she'll notice. Hoping she'll say something.

But Janie's mother is asleep now.

Her mouth is open.

She snores lightly.

The bottle tips in her hand.

Janie sighs, sets the bottle on the beat-up coffee table, and starts her homework.

Halfway through her math homework, the room turns black.

Janie is rushed into a bright tunnel, like a multicolored

kaleidoscope. There's no floor, and Janie is floating while the walls spin around her. It makes her feel like throwing up.

Next to Janie in the tunnel is her mother, and a man who looks like a blond Jesus Christ. The man and Janie's mother are holding hands and flying. They look happy. Janie yells, but no sound comes out. She wants it to stop.

She feels the pencil fall from her fingers.

Feels her body slump to the arm of the couch.

Tries to sit up, but with all the whirling colors around her, she can't tell which way is upright. She overcompensates and falls the other way, onto her mother.

The colors stop, and everything goes black.

Janie hears her mother grumbling.

Feels her shove.

Slowly the room comes into focus again, and Janie's mother slaps Janie in the face.

"Get offa me," her mother says. "What the hell is wrong with you?"

Janie sits up and looks at her mother. Her stomach churns, and she feels dizzy from the colors. "I feel sick," she whispers, and then she stands up and stumbles to the bathroom to vomit.

When she peers out, pale and shaky, her mother is gone from the couch, retired to her bedroom.

Thank God, Janie thinks. She splashes cold water on her face.

JANUARY 1, 2001, 7:29 A.M.

A U-Haul truck pulls up next door. A man, a woman, and a girl Janie's age climb out and sink into the snow-covered driveway. Janie watches them from her bedroom window.

The girl is dark-haired and pretty.

Janie wonders if she'll be snooty, like all the other girls who call Janie white trash at school. Maybe, since this new girl lives next to Janie on the wrong side of town, they'll call her white trash too.

But she's really pretty.

Pretty enough to make a difference.

Janie dresses hurriedly, puts on her boots and coat, and marches next door to have the first chance to get to the girl before the North Siders get to her. Janie's desperate for a friend.

"You guys want some help?" Janie asks in a voice more confident than she feels.

The girl stops in her tracks. A smile deepens the dimples in her cheeks, and she tilts her head to the side. "Hi," she says. "I'm Carrie Brandt."

Carrie's eyes sparkle.

Janie's heart leaps.

MARCH 2, 2001, 7:34 P.M.

Janie is thirteen.

She doesn't have a sleeping bag, but Carrie has an extra that Janie can use. Janie sets her plastic grocery bag on the floor by the couch in Carrie's living room.

Inside the bag:

a hand-made birthday gift for Carrie

Janie's pajamas

a toothbrush

She's nervous. But Carrie is chattering enough for both of them, waiting for Carrie's other new friend, Melinda Jeffers, to show up.

Yes, that Melinda Jeffers.

Of the Fieldridge North Side Jefferses.

Apparently, Melinda Jeffers is also the president of the "Make Janie Hannagan Miserable" Club. Janie wipes her sweating hands on her jeans.

When Melinda arrives, Carrie doesn't fawn over her. Janie nods hello.

Melinda smirks. Tries to whisper something to Carrie, but Carrie ignores her and says, "Hey! Let's do Janie's hair."

Melinda throws a daggered look at Carrie.

Carrie smiles brightly at Janie, asking her with her eyes if it's okay.

Janie squelches a grin, and Melinda shrugs and pretends like she doesn't mind after all.

Even though Janie knows it's killing her.

The three girls slowly grow more comfortable, or maybe just resigned, with one another. They put on makeup and watch Carrie's favorite videos of old comedians, some of whom Janie's never heard of before. And then they play truth or dare.

Carrie alternates: truth, dare, truth, dare.

Melinda always picks truth.

And then there's Janie.

Janie never picks truth.

She's a dare girl.

That way, nobody gets inside.

She can't afford to let anyone inside.

They might find out about her secret.

The giggles become hysterics when Melinda's dare for Janie is to run outside through the snow barefoot, around to the backyard, take off her clothes, and make a naked snow angel.

Janie doesn't have a problem doing that.

Because, really, what does she have to lose?

She'll take that dare over giving up her secrets any day.

Melinda watches Janie, arms folded in the cold night air, and with a sneer on her face, while Carrie giggles and helps Janie get her sweatshirt and jeans back on her wet body. Carrie takes Janie's bra, fills the cups with snow, and slingshots them like snowballs at Melinda.

"Ew, gross," Melinda sneers. "Where'd you get that old grungy thing, Salvation Army?"

Janie's giggles fade. She grabs her bra back from Carrie and shoves it in her jeans pocket, embarrassed. "No," she says hotly, then giggles again. "It was Goodwill. Why, does it look familiar?"

Carrie snorts.

Even Melinda laughs, reluctantly.

They trudge back inside for popcorn.

11:34 P.M.

The noise level in the living room of Carrie's house fades along with the lights after Mr. Brandt, Carrie's father, stomps to the doorway and hollers at the three girls to shut up and get to sleep.

Janie zips up the musty-smelling sleeping bag and closes her eyes, but she is too hyper to sleep after that exhilarating naked snow angel. She had a fun evening despite Melinda. She learned what it's like to be a rich girl (sounds nice for about a day, but too many stinking lessons), and that Luke Drake is supposedly the hottest boy in the class (in Carrie's mind), and what people like Melinda do four times a year (they take vacations to exotic places). Who knew?

Now the hushed giggles subside around her, and Janie opens her eyes to stare at the dark ceiling. She is glad to be here, even though Melinda teases her about her clothes. Melinda even had the nerve to ask Janie why she never wears anything new. But Carrie shut her up with a sudden exclamation: "Janie, you look simply stunning with your hair back like that. Doesn't she, Melinda?"

For the first time ever, Janie's hair is in French braids, and now, lying in the sleeping bag, she feels the bumps pressing against her scalp through the thin pillow. Maybe Carrie could teach her how to do it sometime.

She has to pee, but she is afraid to get up, in case Carrie's father hears her and starts yelling again. She rests quietly like the other girls, listening to them breathe as they drift off to sleep. Melinda is in the middle, curled on her side facing Carrie, her back to Janie.

12:14 A.M.

The ceiling clouds over and disappears. Janie blinks and she is at school, in civics class. She looks around and realizes she is not in her normal fourth-period class, but in the class that follows hers. She stands at the back of the room. There are no empty seats. Ms. Parchelli, the teacher, drones about the judicial branch of government and what the Supreme Court justices wear under their robes. No one seems surprised that Ms. Parchelli is teaching them this. Some of the kids take notes.

Janie looks around at the faces in the room. In the third row, seated at the center desk, is Melinda. Melinda has a dreamy look on her face. She is staring at someone in the next row, one seat forward. As the teacher talks, Melinda stands up slowly and approaches the person she's been staring at. From the back of the room, Janie cannot see who it is.

The teacher doesn't appear to notice. Melinda kneels next to the desk and touches the person's hand. In slow motion, the person turns to Melinda, touches her cheek, and then leans forward. The two of them kiss. After a moment, they both rise to their feet, still kissing. When they part, Janie can see the face of Melinda's kissing partner. Melinda leads her partner by the hand to the front of the room and opens the door of the supply closet. The bell rings, and like ants, the students crowd at the door to leave.

The ceiling in Carrie Brandt's living room reappears as Melinda sighs and flops onto her stomach in the sleeping bag next to Janie. *Cripes!* thinks Janie. She looks at the clock. It's 1:23 a.m.

1:24 A.M.

Janie rolls to her side and she's walking into a forest. It's dark from shade, not night. A few rays of weak sunlight slip through the tree cover. Walking in front of Janie is Carrie. They walk for what seems to be a mile or more, and suddenly a rushing river appears a few steps in front of them. Carrie stops and cups her ear, listening for something. She calls out in a desperate voice, "Carson!" Over and over, Carrie calls the name, until the forest rings with her voice. Carrie walks along the high bank and stumbles over a tree root. Janie bumps into her, falls, and then Carrie helps her up. She gives Janie a puzzled look and says, "You've never been here." Carrie turns back to her search for Carson, her cries growing louder.

There is a splash in the river, and a little boy appears above the surface, bobbing and moving swiftly in the current. Carrie runs along the bank and cries, "Carson! Get out of there! Carson!"

The boy grins and chokes on the water. He goes under and resurfaces. Carrie is frantic. She reaches out her hand to the boy, but it makes no difference—the bank is too high, the river too wide for her to come close to reaching him. She is crying now.

Janie watches, her heart pounding. The boy is still grinning and choking, falling under the water. He is drowning.

"Help him!" screams Carrie. "Save him!"

Janie leaps toward the boy in the water, but she lands on

the bank in the same spot she took off from. She tries again as Carrie screams, but the results are the same.

The boy's eyes are closed now. His grin has turned eerie. From the water behind the boy, an enormous shark bursts above the surface, mouth open, hundreds of sharp teeth gleaming. It closes its mouth around the boy and disappears.

Carrie sits up in her sleeping bag and screams.

Janie screams too, but it catches in her throat.

Her voice is hoarse.

Her fingers are numb.

Her body shakes from the nightmare.

The two girls look at each other in the darkness, while Melinda stirs, groans, and goes back to sleep. "Are you okay?" Janie whispers, sitting up.

Carrie nods, breathing hard. She whisper-laughs, embarrassed. Her voice shakes. "I'm sorry I woke you. Bad dream."

Janie hesitates. "You want to talk about it?" Her mind is racing.

"Nah. Go back to sleep." Carrie rolls to her side. Melinda stirs, rolls a few inches closer to Carrie, and is quiet again.

Janie glances at the clock. 3:42 a.m. She is exhausted. She drifts off to sleep. . . .

3:51 A.M.

. . . she is jolted awake when she falls into a huge, beautiful bedroom. There are framed posters of *NSYNC and Sheryl Crow on the walls. At a desk sits Melinda, doodling on the edge of her notebook. Janie tries to blink herself out of the room. She feels herself sit up in the sleeping bag, but her motions don't affect what she sees. She lies back down, resigned to watch.

Melinda is drawing hearts. Janie walks toward her. She says, "Melinda," but no sound comes out. When someone knocks on the bedroom window, Melinda looks over and smiles. "Help me open this window, will you?"

Janie stares at Melinda. Melinda stares back, then points to the window with a jerk of her head. Janie, feeling compelled, stumbles over to the window next to Melinda and they open it. Carrie climbs in.

She is naked from the waist up.

And has breasts the size of watermelons.

The breasts sway from side to side when Carrie scrambles over the sill.

She walks through Janie and stands shyly in front of Melinda.

Janie tries to turn away, but she can't. She waves a hand in front of Carrie's face, but Carrie doesn't respond. Melinda winks at Janie and folds Carrie into her arms. They embrace and kiss. Janie rolls her eyes, and suddenly all three are back in Ms. Parchelli's civics classroom. Once again, Melinda is embracing someone in the aisle. It's Carrie. She leads Carrie to the front of the room. Janie can see that no one else in the class gives an ounce of notice to the naked Carrie and her enormous breasts.

Janie sits up in her sleeping bag again and shakes her head wildly. She feels the ends of her braids slap the sides of her cheeks, but she is unable to remove herself from the classroom. She is forced not only to be there, but also to watch.

Melinda glides to the supply closet and leads Carrie in there with her. Janie, against her wishes, follows. Melinda closes the door once Carrie and Janie are inside, and Melinda starts kissing Carrie on the lips again.

Janie lunges in her sleeping bag blindly.

Kicks Melinda, hard.

And Janie is back in Carrie's living room.

Melinda sits up, hair disheveled, and scrambles around to look at Janie. "What the hell did you do that for?" Melinda is furious.

Feigning sleep, Janie peers out of one eye. "Sorry," she mumbles. "There was a spider crawling over your sleeping bag. I saved your life."

"What?!"

"Never mind, he's gone."

"Oh, great. Like I'm gonna get back to sleep now."

Janie grins in the darkness. It's 5:51 a.m.

7:45 A.M.

Something nudges Janie's legs. She opens her eyes, wondering where she is. It's pitch dark. Carrie turns the sleeping bag flap off Janie's head. "Wake up, sleepyhead." The sunlight is blinding.

"Mmph," Janie grunts. Slowly she sits up.

Carrie is balancing on her haunches, eyeing her, one brow raised.

Janie remembers. Does Carrie?

"Did you sleep well?" Carrie asks.

Janie's stomach twists. "Um . . . yeah." She gauges Carrie's reaction. "Did you?"

Carrie smiles. "Like a baby. Even on this hard floor."

"Ah, hmm. Well, that's great." Janie scrambles to her feet and untwists from her nightgown. "Where's Melinda?"

"She left about ten minutes ago. She was acting weird. Said she forgot she had a piano lesson at eight." Carrie snorts. "Duh."

Janie laughs weakly. She's starving. The two girls fix breakfast. Carrie doesn't appear to remember her nightmare.

Janie can't forget it.

As they munch on toast, Janie steals a glance at Carrie's chest. Her breasts are the size of half an apple, each.

Janie goes home, falls into bed, thinking about the strange night. Wondering if this ever happens to anyone else. Knowing, deep down, it probably doesn't.

She falls into a hard sleep until late afternoon.

Decides sleepovers are not for her.

They'll never be for her.

JUNE 7, 2004

Janie is sixteen. She buys her own clothing now. Often she buys food, too. The welfare check covers the rent and the booze, and not much else.

Two years ago, Janie started working a few hours after school and on the weekends at Heather Nursing Home. Now she works full-time for the summer.

The office staff and the other aides at Heather Home like Janie, especially during school holidays, because she'll pick up anybody's shifts, day or night, so they can take a last-minute sick day or vacation. Janie needs the money, and they know it.

She's determined to go to college.

Five days a week or more, Janie puts on her hospital scrubs and takes a bus to the nursing home. She likes old people. They don't sleep soundly.

Janie and Carrie are still friends and next-door neighbors. They spend a lot of time at Janie's house, waiting for Janie's mother to pass out in her bedroom before they watch movies and talk about boys. They talk about other things too, like why Carrie's father is so angry all the time, and why Carrie's mother doesn't like company. Mostly, Janie thinks, it's just because they're grouchy people. Plain and simple. Whenever Carrie asks if she can have Janie sleep over, her mother says, "You just had a sleepover on your birthday." Carrie doesn't bother to remind her that that was four years ago.

Janie thinks about Carson and wonders if Carrie really is an only child. But Carrie doesn't seem to talk about anything with sharp edges. Maybe she's afraid they might poke into her and then she'd burst.

Carrie and Melinda are also still friends. Melinda's parents are still rich. Melinda plays tennis. She is a cheerleader. Her parents have condos in Vegas, Marco Island, Vail, and somewhere in Greece. Melinda mostly hangs out with other rich kids. And then there's Carrie.

Janie doesn't mind being with Melinda. Melinda still can't stand Janie. Janie thinks she knows the real reason why, and it doesn't have anything to do with having money.

JUNE 25, 2004, 11:15 P.M.

After working a record eleven evenings straight, and being caught by old Mr. Reed's recurring nightmare about World War II seven of those eleven evenings, Janie collapses on the couch and kicks her shoes off. By the number of empty bottles on the ring-stained coffee table, she assumes her mother is in her bedroom, down for the count.

Carrie lets herself in. "Can I crash here?" Her eyes are rimmed in red.

Janie sighs inwardly. She wants to sleep. "'Course. You okay with the couch?"

"Sure. Thanks."

Janie relaxes. Carrie, on the couch, would work fine.

Carrie sniffles loudly.

"So, what's wrong?" Janie asks, trying to put as much sympathy in her voice as she can muster. It's enough.

"Dad's yelling again. I got asked out. Dad says no."

Janie perks up. "Who asked you out?"

"Stu. From the body shop."

"You mean that old guy?"

Carrie bristles. "He's twenty-two."

"You're sixteen! And he looks older than that."

"Not up close. He's cute. He has a cute ass."

"Maybe he plays Dance Dance Revolution at the arcade."

Carrie giggles. Janie smiles.

"So. You got any liquor around here?" Carrie asks innocently.

Janie laughs. "There's an understatement. Whaddya want, beer?" She looks at the bottles on the table. "Schnapps? Whiskey? Double-stuff vodka?"

"Got any of that cheap grape wine the winos at Selby Park drink?"

"At your service." Janie hauls herself off the couch and looks for clean glasses. The kitchen is a mess. Janie has barely been here the past two weeks. She finds two sticky, mismatched glasses in the sink and washes them out, then searches through her mother's stash for her cheap wine assortment. "Ah, here it is. Boone's Farm, right?" She unscrews the bottle and pours two glasses full, not waiting for an answer from Carrie, and then puts the bottle back in the fridge.

Carrie flips on the TV. She takes a glass from Janie. "Thanks."

Janie sips the sweet wine and makes a face. "So what are you gonna do about Stu?" She thinks there's a country song in that sentence somewhere.

"Go out with him."

"Your dad's gonna kill you if he finds out."

"Yeah, well. What else is new?" They both settle on the creaky couch and put their feet on the coffee table, deftly pushing the mess of bottles to the center of it so they can stretch out.

The TV drones. The girls sip their wine and get silly. Janie gets up, rummages around in her bedroom, and returns with snacks.

"Gross—you keep Doritos in your bedroom?"

"Emergency stash. For nights such as these." *Since Mother can't be bothered to buy any actual food at the grocery store when she goes there for booze*, Janie thinks.

"Ahh." Carrie nods.

12:30 A.M.

Janie is asleep on the couch. She doesn't dream. Never dreams.

5:02 A.M.

Janie, forced awake, catapults into Carrie's dream. It's the one by the river. Again. Janie's been here twice since the first time, when they were thirteen.

Janie, blind to the room her physical body is in, tries to stand. If she can feel her way to her bedroom and close the door before she starts going numb, she might get enough distance to break the connection. She feels with her toes for the bottles on the floor, and goes around them. She reaches out for the wall and finds her way into the hallway as she and Carrie are walking through the forest in Carrie's dream. Janie reaches for the door frames—first her mother's bedroom (hush, don't bump the door), then the bathroom, and then her room. She makes it inside, turns, and closes the door just as Carrie and Janie approach the riverbank.

The connection is lost.

Janie breathes a sigh of relief. She looks around, blinks in the dark as her eyesight returns, crawls into bed, and sleeps.

9:06 A.M.

When she wakes, both her mother and Carrie are in the kitchen. The living room is cleared of bottles. Carrie is drying a sink full of dishes, and Janie's mother is fixing her homemade morning drink: vodka and orange juice on ice. On the stove is a skillet covered by a paper plate. Two pieces of buttered toast, two eggs over easy, and a small fortune of crisp bacon rest on a second paper plate, next to the skillet. Janie's mother picks up a piece of bacon, takes her drink, and disappears back into her bedroom without a word.

"Thanks Carrie—you didn't have to do this. I was planning on cleaning today."

Carrie is cheerful. "It's the least I can do. Did you sleep well? When did you go to bed?"

Janie peeks in the skillet, thinking, discovering hash

browns. "Wow! Um . . . not long ago. It was close to daylight. But I was so tired."

"You've been working ridiculous hours."

Janie. "Yeah, well. College. One day. How did you sleep?"

"Pretty good . . ." She hesitates, like she might say something else, but doesn't.

Janie takes a bite of food. She's famished. "Did you have sweet dreams?"

Carrie glances at Janie, then picks up another dish and wipes it with the towel. "Not really."

Janie concentrates on the food, but her stomach flips. She waits, until the silence grows awkward. "You want to talk about it?"

Carrie is silent for a long time. "Not really. No," she says finally.

AND PICKS UP SPEED

AUGUST 30, 2004

It is the first day of school. Janie and Carrie are juniors. They wait for the bus on the corner of their street. A handful of other high school kids stand with them. Some are anxious. Some are terribly short. Janie and Carrie ignore the freshmen.

The bus is late. Luckily for Cabel Strumheller, the bus is later than he is. Janie and Carrie know Cabel—he's been trouble in school since ninth grade. Janie doesn't remember him much before that—word was that he flunked down into their grade. He was often late. Always looked stoned. Now, he looks about six inches taller than he did in the spring. His blue-black hair hangs in greasy ringlets in front of his eyes, and he walks with shoulders curved, as if he were more comfortable being short. He stands away from everyone and smokes a cigarette.

Janie catches his eye by accident, so she nods hello. He looks down at the ground quickly. Blows smoke from his lips. Tosses the cigarette down and grinds it into the gravel.

Carrie pokes Janie in the ribs. "Lookie, it's your boyfriend."

Janie rolls her eyes. "Be nice."

Carrie observes him carefully while he's not looking. "Well. His pox-face cleared up over the summer. Or maybe the new fancy 'do hides it."

"Stop," hisses Janie. She's giggling, and feeling bad about it. But she's looking at him. He's got to be about as dirt poor as Janie, judging by his clothes. "He's just a loner. And quiet."

"A stoner, maybe, who has a boner for you."

Janie narrows her eyes, and her face grows sober. "Carrie, stop it. I'm serious. You're turning mean like Melinda." Janie glances at Cabel. His jeans are too short. She knows what it's like to be teased for not having cool clothes and stuff. She feels herself wanting to defend him. "He probably has shitty welfare parents, like me."

Carrie is quiet. "I'm not like Melinda."

"So why do you hang with her?"

She shrugs and thinks about it for a minute. "I dunno. 'Cause she's rich."

Finally the bus comes. The ride is forty-five minutes to school, even though the school is less than five miles away, because of all the stops. Juniors like Janie and Carrie are considered by the unwritten bus rules to be upperclassmen. So they sit near the back. Cabel passes by and falls into the seat behind them. Janie can feel him push his knees up against her back. She peers through the crack between her seat back and the window. Cabel's chin is propped up by his hand. His eyes are closed, nearly hidden beneath his greasy curls.

"Fuck," Janie mutters under her breath.

Thankfully, Cabel Strumheller doesn't dream.

Not on the bus, anyway.

Not in chemistry class, either.

Or English.

Nor does anyone else. Janie arrives home after the first day of school, relieved.

OCTOBER 16, 2004, 7:42 P.M.

Carrie and Stu knock on Janie's bedroom window. She opens it a crack. Stu's dressed up, wearing a thin, black leather tie, and Carrie has on a slinky black dress with a shawl and a hideously large orchid pinned to it.

"I saw your light on in here," explains Carrie, regarding the unusual visit. "Come to the homecoming dance, with us, Janers! We're not staying long. Please?"

Janie sighs. "You know I don't have anything to wear."

Carrie holds up a silver spaghetti-strap dress so Janie can see it. "Here—I bet this'll fit you. I got it from Melinda. She'll die if she sees you in it instead of me. And I've got shoes that'll go with it." Carrie grins evilly.

"I haven't washed my hair or anything."

"You look fine, Janie," Stu says. "Come on. Don't make me sit there with a bunch of teenybopper airheads all night. Have pity on an old man."

Janie smirks. Carrie slaps Stu on the arm.

She meets them at the front door, takes the dress, and heads over to Carrie's ten minutes later.

9:12 P.M.

Janie drinks her third cup of punch while Stu and Carrie dance for the billionth time. She sits down at a table, alone.

9:18 P.M.

A sophomore boy, known only to Janie as "the brainiac," asks Janie to dance.

She regards him for a moment. "Why the fuck not," she says. She's a head taller than him.

He rests his head on her chest and grabs her ass.

She pushes him off her, muttering under her breath, finds Carrie, and tells her she has a ride home and she's leaving now.

Carrie waves blissfully from Stu's arms.

Janie attacks the back door of the school gym and finds herself in a heavy cloud of smoke. She realizes she's found the Goths' hangout. Who knew?

"Oof," someone says. She keeps walking, muttering "sorry" to whomever it was she hit with the flying door.

After a mile wearing Carrie's heels, her feet are killing her. She takes off the shoes and walks in the grassy yards, watching the houses evolve from nice to nasty as she goes along. The grass is already wet with dew, and the yards are getting messier. Her feet are freezing.

Someone falls in step beside her, so quietly that she doesn't notice him until he's there. He's carrying a skateboard. A second and third follow suit, then lay their boards down and push off, hanging slightly in front of Janie.

"Jeez!" she says, surrounded. "Scare a girl half to death, why don't you."

Cabel Strumheller shrugs. The other guys move ahead. "Long walk," says Cabel. "You, uh"—he clears his throat—"okay?"

"Fine," she says. "You?" She doesn't remember ever hearing him speak before.

"Get on." He sets his board down, taking Janie's shoes from her hand. "You'll rip your feet to shreds. There's glass an' shit."

Janie looks at the board, and then up at him. He's wearing a knit beanie with a hole in it. "I don't know how."

He flashes a half grin. Shoves a long black lock of hair under the beanie. "Just stand. Bend. Balance. I'll push you."

She blinks. Gets on the board.

Weird.

This is not happening.

They don't talk.

The guys weave in and out the rest of the way, and take off at the corner by Janie's house. Cabel pushes her to her front porch so she can hop off. He sets her shoes on the step, picks up the board, nods, and catches up with his friends.

"Thanks, Cabel," Janie says, but he's gone in the dark already. "That was sweet," she adds, to no one.

They don't acknowledge each other, or the event, for a very long time.

IN EARNEST

FEBRUARY 1, 2005

Janie is seventeen.

A boy named Jack Tomlinson falls asleep in English class. Janie watches his head nodding from across the room. She begins to sweat, even though the room is cold. It is 11:41 a.m. Seven minutes until the bell rings for lunch. Too much time.

She stands, gathers her books, and rushes for the door. "I feel sick," she says to the teacher. The teacher nods understandingly. Melinda Jeffers snickers from the back row. Janie leaves the room and shuts the door.

She leans against the cool tile wall, takes a deep breath, goes into the girls' bathroom, and hides in a stall.

Nobody ever sleeps in the bathroom.

FLASHBACK—JANUARY 9, 1998

It's Janie's tenth birthday. Tanya Weersma falls asleep in school, her head on her pencil box. She is floating, gliding. And then she is falling. Falling into a gorge. The face of a cliff streams by at a dizzying speed. Tanya looks at Janie and screams. Janie closes her eyes and feels sick. They startle at the same time. The fourth graders all laugh.

Janie decides not to hand out her precious birthday treat, after all.

That was after the train ride and the man in the underwear.

Janie's had only a few close calls in school before high school. But the older she gets, the more often her classmates sleep in school. And the more kids sleep, the more of a mess it makes for Janie. She has to get away, wake them up, or risk the consequences.

A year and a half to go.

And then.

College. A roommate.

Janie puts her head in her hands.

She leaves the bathroom after lunch and goes to her next class, grabbing a Snickers bar on her way.

For two weeks afterward, Melinda Jeffers and her rich friends make puking noises when they pass Janie in the hall.

JUNE 15, 2005

Janie is seventeen. She's working her ass off, taking as many shifts as she can.

Old Mr. Reed is dying at the nursing home.

His dreams grow constant and terrible.

He doesn't wake easily.

As his body fades, the pull of his dreams grows eerily stronger. Now, if his door is open, Janie can't enter that wing.

She hadn't planned for this.

She makes an odd request on every shift. "If you cover the east wing, I'll take the rest."

The other aides think she's afraid to see Mr. Reed die.

Janie doesn't have a problem with that.

JUNE 21, 2005, 9:39 P.M.

Heather Home is short-staffed. It's summer. Three patients on the cusp of death. Two have Alzheimer's. One dreams, screams, and cries.

Someone has to empty bedpans. Hand out the night meds. Straighten up the rooms for the day.

Janie approaches with caution. She stands in the west wing, looking into the east wing, and memorizes it. The right-hand wall has five doorways and six sets of handrails. The last door on the right is Mr. Reed. Ten steps farther is a wall, and the emergency exit door.

Some days, a cart stands between doorways three and four. Some days, wheelchairs collect anonymously between doorways one and two. A stretcher often rests in the east wing, but usually it's on the left side. Janie would have to get a glimpse before entering the hallway, no matter the day. Because some days, most days, people travel up and down the hallway without pattern. And Janie doesn't want to run into anyone in case she goes blind.

Tonight, the hallway is clear. Janie noted earlier that the Silva family came for a visit in the fourth room. She checks the record book and sees that they signed out. There are no other visitors recorded. It grows late. For Janie, it's either get the work done, or get fired.

She enters the east wing, grabs the hall bar, and nearly doubles over.

9:41 P.M.

The noise of the battle is overpowering. She hides with old Mr. Reed in a foxhole on a beach that is littered with bodies and watered with blood. The scene is so familiar, Janie could recite the conversation—even the beat of the bullets—by heart. And it always ends the same way, with arms and legs scattered, bones crunching underfoot, and Mr. Reed's body breaking into tiny bits, crumbling off his trunk like cheese being grated from a slab, or like a leper, unraveling.

Janie tries walking normally down the hallway, gripping the handrail. She cannot concentrate enough to remember her count of doorways, the dream is so intense. She keeps walking, reaching, walking, until she hits the wall. She's losing the feeling in her fingers and feet. Wants to make it stop. She backs up eight, ten, maybe twelve steps, and falls to the ground outside Mr. Reed's door. Her head pounds now as she follows Mr. Reed into battle.

She tries to find his door so she can close it. She tries, and she can't feel anything. She doesn't know if she's touching something, or nothing. She is paralyzed. Numb. Desperate.

On the bloody beach, Mr. Reed looks at her and beckons her to come with him. "Behind here. We'll be safe behind here," he says.

"No!" she tries to scream, but no sound comes out. She can't get his attention. *Not behind there!* She knows what will happen.

Mr. Reed's fingers drop off first.

Then his nose and ears.

He looks at Janie.

Like always.

Like she's betrayed him.

"Why didn't you tell me," he whispers.

Janie can't speak, can't move. Again and again, she fights, her head feeling like it might explode any moment. *Just die, old man!* she wants to yell. *I can't do this one anymore!* She knows it's almost over.

And then, there is more. Something new.

Mr. Reed turns to her as his feet break free from his ankles and he stumbles on his stilty legs. His eyes are wide with terror, and the battle rages around them. "Come closer," he says. Fingerless, he shrugs the gun into her arms. His arm breaks off his shoulder as he does it, and it crumbles to the beach like powder. And then he starts crying. "Help me. Help me, Janie."

Janie's eyes widen. She sees the enemy, but she knows they can't see her. She is safe. She looks at the pleading eyes of Mr. Reed.

Lifts the gun.

Points.

And pulls the trigger.

10:59 P.M.

Janie is curled on a portable stretcher in the east hallway when the roaring gunfire in old Mr. Reed's dream stops abruptly. She blinks, her vision clears slowly, and she sees two Heather Home aides staring down at her. She sits up halfway. Her head pounds.

"Careful, Janie, honey," soothes a voice. "You were having a seizure or something. Let's wait for the doc, okay?"

Janie cocks her head and listens for the faint sound of beeping. A moment later, she hears it.

"Old Mr. Reed is dead," she says, her voice rasping. She falls back on the stretcher and passes out.

JUNE 22, 2005

The doctor says, "We need to do some tests. Do a CAT scan."

"No thank you," Janie says. She is polite, but firm.

The doctor looks at Janie's mother. "Mrs. Hannagan?"

Janie's mother shrugs. She looks out the window. Her hands tremble as she fingers the zipper on her purse.

The doctor sighs, exasperated. "Ma'am," he tries again. "What if she has a seizure while she's driving? Or crossing a street? Please think about it."

Mrs. Hannagan closes her eyes.

Janie clears her throat. "May we go?"

The doctor gives Janie a long look. He glances at Janie's mother, who is looking down at her lap. Then looks at Janie again. "Of course," he says softly. "Can you promise me something? Not just for your safety, but for the safety of others on the road—please, don't drive."

It won't happen when I'm driving, she longs to tell him, just so he doesn't worry so much. "Sure. I promise. We don't have a car, anyway."

Mrs. Hannagan stands. Janie stands. The doctor stands too. "Call our office if it happens again, won't you?" He holds out his hand, and Janie shakes it.

"Yes," Janie lies. They walk back to the waiting room.

Janie sends her mother outside to the bus stop. "I'll be right there."

Her mother leaves the office. Janie pays the bill. It's $120, pulled out of her college stash. She can only imagine how much a CAT scan would cost. And she's not about to spend another cent just to hear somebody tell her she's crazy.

She can get that opinion for free.

Janie waits for her mother to ask what that was all about. But she may as well wait for flowers to grow on the moon. Janie's mother simply doesn't care about anything that has to do with Janie. She has never really cared.

And that's fucking sad.

That's what Janie thinks.

But it sure comes in handy, sometimes.

JUNE 28, 2005

There's something about a doctor telling a teenager not to drive that makes it so important to do so. Just to prove him wrong.

Janie and Carrie go see Stu at the body shop. He sees them coming. "Here she is, kiddo," Stu says. He calls Janie "kiddo," which is weird, since Janie is two months older than Carrie.

Janie nods and smiles. She runs her hand over the hood lightly, feeling the curves. It's the color of buttermilk. It's older than Janie. And it's beautiful.

Stu hands Janie the keys, and Janie counts out one thousand, four hundred fifty dollars cash. "Be good to her," he says wistfully. "I started working on this car when she was seventeen years old and I was thirteen. She purrs now."

"I will." Janie smiles. She climbs in the '77 Nova and starts her up.

"Her name's Ethel," adds Stu. He looks a little embarrassed.

Carrie takes Stu's oil-stained hand and squeezes it. "Janie's a really good driver. She's driven my car a bunch of times. Ethel will be fine." She gives Stu a quick kiss on the cheek. "See you tonight," she says with a demure smile.

Stu winks. Carrie gets into her Tracer and Janie slides behind the wheel of her new car. She pats the dashboard, and Ethel purrs. "Good girl, Ethel," she croons.

JUNE 29, 2005

After the incident with Mr. Reed, the Heather Home director made Janie take a week off. When Janie shuffled and hemmed about taking that much time off, the director promised her shifts on July 4 and Labor Day, where Janie gets double pay. She is happy.

Janie drives her new car on her first day back to work. She gives sponge baths and empties a dozen bedpans. For entertainment, she sings a mournful song from *Les Misérables*, changing the words to "Empty pans and empty bladders . . ." Miss Stubin, a schoolteacher who taught for forty-seven years before she retired, laughs for the first time in weeks. Janie makes a mental note to bring in a new book to read to Miss Stubin.

Miss Stubin never has visitors.

And she's blind.

That just might be why she's Janie's favorite.

JULY 4, 2005, 10:15 P.M.

Three Heather Home residents in their wheelchairs, and Janie, in an orange plastic bucket chair, sit in the dark nursing home parking lot. Waiting. Slapping mosquitoes. The fireworks are about to begin at Selby Park, a few blocks away.

Miss Stubin is one of the residents, her gnarled hands curled in her lap, I.V. drip hanging from a stand next to her wheelchair. All of a sudden, she cocks her head and smiles wistfully. “Here they come,” she says.

A moment later, the sky explodes in color.

Janie describes each one in detail to Miss Stubin.

A green sparkly porcupine, she says.

Sparks rising from a magician’s wand.

A perfect circle of white light, which fades into a puddle and dries up.

After a brilliant burst of purple, Janie jumps up. “Don’t go anywhere, you three—I’ll be right back.” She runs inside to the therapy room, grabs a plastic tub, and runs back out.

“Here,” she says breathlessly, taking Miss Stubin’s hand and carefully, gently, stretching out her curled fingers. She puts a Koosh Ball in the old woman’s hands. “That last one looked just like this.”

Miss Stubin’s face lights up. “I think that’s my favorite,” she says.

AUGUST 2, 2005, 11:11 P.M.

Janie leaves Heather Home and drives the four miles to her house. It's wicked hot out, and she chides Ethel mildly for not having air-conditioning. She rolls the windows down, loving the feeling of the hot wind on her face.

11:18 P.M.

She stops at a stop sign on Waverly Road, not far from home, and proceeds through the intersection.

11:19 P.M.

And then she is in a strange house. In a dirty kitchen. A huge, young monster-man with knives for fingers approaches.

Janie, blind to the road, stomps on the brake and flips the gearshift into neutral. She reaches to find the emergency brake and pulls, before she becomes paralyzed. This is a strong one.

He pulls a vinyl-seated chair across the kitchen floor, picks it up, and whirls it around above his head.

But it isn't the emergency brake. It's the hood release.

And then he lets go of the chair. It sails toward Janie, clipping the ceiling fan.

Janie doesn't know it's the hood.

She looks around frantically to see what it will hit. Or who.

Janie is numb. Her foot slides off the brake pedal.
Her car rolls off the road.
Slowly.

But there is no one else. No one else but the monster-man with finger-knives, and Janie. Until the door opens, and a middle-aged man appears. He walks through Janie. The chair, sailing in slow motion, grows knives from its legs.

The car misses a mailbox.

It strikes the middle-aged man in the chest and head. His head is sliced clean off and it rolls around on the floor in a circle.

The car comes to rest in a shallow drainage ditch in the front yard of a tiny, unkempt house.

Janie stares at the large young man with knives for fingers. He walks to the dead man's head and kicks it like a soccer ball. It crashes loudly through the window and there is a blinding flash of light—

11:31 P.M.

Janie groans and opens her eyes. Her head is against the steering wheel. She has a cut on her lip that is bleeding. And Ethel is decidedly not level. When she can see clearly, she looks out the windows, and when she can move again, she eases her way out her door. She walks around the car, sees that it is not injured, and that she is not stuck. She shuts the hood gently, gets into the car, and backs up slowly.

When she arrives in her driveway, she breathes a sigh of relief, and then memorizes the exact location of the parking brake by feel. She sees the keys dangling from the ignition. *Duh*, she thinks.

Next time, she will be ready.

Maybe she should have bought an automatic.

She hopes to God it doesn't happen on a highway.

12:46 A.M.

Janie lies awake in bed. Scared.

In the back of her mind, she hears the distinct sound of knives sharpening. The more she tries not to think about whose dream that might have been, the more she thinks about it. She can never drive that street again.

She wonders if she will end up like her friend Miss Stubin from the nursing home, all alone.

Or dead in a car crash, because of this stupid dream curse.

AUGUST 25, 2005

Carrie brings in the mail to Janie's. Janie is wearing a T-shirt and boxer shorts. It's hot and humid.

"Schedules are here," Carrie says. "Senior year, baby! This is it!"

Excitedly, they open their schedules together. They lay them side-by-side on the coffee table and compare.

Their facial expressions go from excitement, to disappointment, and then excitement again.

"So, first period English and fifth period study hall. That's not terrible," Janie says.

"And we have the same lunch," Carrie says. "Let me see what Melinda has. I'll be right back." Carrie gets up to leave.

"You can call her from here, you know," Janie says, rolling her eyes.

"I-I would, but—"

Janie waits for Carrie to explain. Then it dawns on her. "Oh," she says. "I get it. Caller ID. Sheesh, Carrie."

Carrie looks at her shoes, then slips out.

Janie checks the freezer for ice cream. She eats it out of the carton. She feels like shit.

SEPTEMBER 6, 2005, 7:35 A.M.

Carrie and Janie drive separately to school, because Janie has to work at 3 p.m. Janie waves from the window when she hears Carrie's car horn beep. *This is it*, she thinks.

Janie is only mildly excited to start her senior year of high school. And she is not at all excited to have study hall right after lunch.

She brushes her teeth and grabs her backpack, checking the mirror briefly before heading out the door. She is stopped by the flashing red lights of her former bus, and she smirks when she sees the noobs all climbing the steps to board it. Most of them are dressed in the styles of five years ago—hand-me-downs, or secondhand thrift clothing. "Get jobs, and get the hell out of South Fieldridge," Janie mutters. At least there's strength in numbers.

Ethel purrs.

Janie continues when the red lights stop. A block before the "bad" house on Waverly Road, she turns to take a detour. She's not taking any chances. She slows as she sees someone walking toward her along the road, wearing a ratty backpack. At first, she doesn't recognize him.

And then, she does.

He looks different.

He's not carrying a skateboard.

"You missed it," Janie says through the open window. "Get in. I'll drive you."

Cabel eyes her warily. His features have matured. He's wearing eyeglasses, the new cool rimless kind. His jaw is decidedly angular. He looks both thinner and more muscular at the same time. His hair, wavy at shoulder length, is layered slightly, no longer blue-black or greasy, but golden light brown. His long bangs that hung in his eyes last year are tucked behind his ears this year. And it looks freshly washed. He hesitates, and then opens the passenger door.

"Thanks." His voice is low and gruff. "Jesus," he remarks as he tries to fit his knees inside.

Janie reaches down between her legs. "Grab yours too," she says.

He raises an eyebrow.

"Your seat adjustor, you ass. We have to pull them together. It's a bench seat. As you can see." They pull, and the seat moves back a notch. Janie checks the clutch to make sure she can still reach. She shifts into first as Cabel shuts his door.

"You're on the wrong street," he remarks.

"I know that."

"I figured you were lost or something."

"Oh, puhleeze. I-I take a detour. I don't drive on Waverly anymore. I'm superstitious."

He glances at her and shrugs. "Whatever."

They ride in awkward silence for five minutes, until Janie rolls her eyes inwardly and says, "So. What's your schedule?"

"I have no idea."

"Okaaay . . ." The conversation fizzles.

After a moment, he opens his backpack and takes out a sealed envelope. He rips it open as if it's a chore of great difficulty and looks over his schedule.

"English, math, Spanish, industrial tech, lunch, study hall, government, P.E." He sounds bored.

Janie cringes. "Hmmm. Interesting."

"And yours?" He says it too politely, as if he is forced to chat with his grandmother.

"It's, ah . . . actually . . . ," she sighs, ". . . pretty similar to that. Yeah."

He laughs. "Don't sound so fucking excited, Hannagan. I'll let you cheat off my papers."

She smiles wryly. "Yeah, right! Like I'd want to."

He looks at her. "And your GPA is?"

"Three point eight." She sniffs.

"Well, then, of course you don't need help."

"What's yours?"

He shifts in the seat and shoves his schedule into his backpack. "I have no idea."

That was the most Cabel Strumheller had ever spoken to Janie in all the years she'd known him. Combined. Including the three miles on the skateboard.

12:45 P.M.

Janie meets up with Carrie in study hall. Seniors have study hall in the library so they can access the books and computers and hopefully do actual work rather than sleep. Janie hopes for the best and finds a table in the far corner of the room.

"How's it going?" Janie asks.

"Decent," Carrie says. "The only class I have with Melinda is English. Hey, did you see the new guy?"

"What new guy?"

"In English class."

Janie looks puzzled. "I didn't notice."

Carrie looks around sneakily. "Oh, shit!" she whispers. "Here he comes."

Janie glances up. Carrie is staring at her, not daring to turn around again. He nods in her direction. Janie waves her fingers at him. To Carrie, she says, "Oh, you mean him?"

"You did NOT just wave to him."

"To who . . . er, whom? Yeah, that's it. Whom?"

"The new guy! Aren't you listening to me?" Carrie bounces in her chair.

Janie grins innocently. "Watch this." She gets up, walks to the table where the new guy sits, and pulls up a chair across from him so she can see Carrie watching.

"I have a question for you," Janie says.

"I thought you didn't need my help," he replies, rummaging through his backpack.

"It's not that kind."

"Go ahead, then."

"Are you getting a lot of strange looks today, by any chance?"

He pulls his notebook out of his backpack, takes off his outer button-down shirt, leaving on a loose, white T-shirt. He folds the button-down haphazardly, sets it on top of his backpack, scoots his chair back, and lays his head on the shirt. His newly muscular arms reach around this makeshift pillow.

"I hadn't noticed," he says. He takes off his glasses and sets them off to the side.

Janie nods thoughtfully. "I see. So . . . you don't know what classes you have, you don't know your GPA, you don't notice all the girls drooling over your new look—"

"That's bullshit," he says, closing his eyes.

"So what do you pay attention to?"

He opens his eyes. Lifts his head from his pillow. He looks at Janie for a long time. His eyes are silky brown. She's never noticed them before.

For a split second, Janie thinks she sees something in them, but then it's gone.

"Pfft. You wouldn't believe me if I told you," he says.

Janie flashes a crooked smile, shrugs, and shakes her head slightly, feeling warm. "Try me."

Cabel raises a skeptical eyebrow.

"You know . . . sometime," she says finally. She picks up his shirt and refolds it so the buttons turn in. "So you don't get a button impression on your face," she says.

"Thank you," he says. His eyes don't leave hers. He's searching them. His brow furrows.

Janie clears her throat lightly. "So, uh, shall I break the news to Carrie that you're not a new guy?"

Cabel blinks. "What?"

"Half the girls in the school think you're a new student. Cabel, come on. You look a lot different from last year. . . ."

The words trail off her tongue and they sound wrong.

He gives her a confused look.

"What did you call me?"

Janie's stomach lurches. "Um, Cabel?"

He isn't smiling. "Who do you think I am?"

Maybe she's in somebody's weird dream and she doesn't know it.

She panics.

"Oh, God, no," she whispers. She stands up abruptly and tries to get past him. He catches her arm.

"Whoa, time out," he says. "Sit."

Tears pool in Janie's eyes. She covers her mouth.

"Jesus, Janie. I'm just playing with your mind a little. I'm sorry. Hey," he says. He keeps hold of her wrist, lightly.

She feels like a fool.

"Come on, Hannagan. Look at me, will you? Listen to me."

Janie can't look at him. She sees Carrie, half-standing, peering over the bookshelves, a concerned look on her face. Janie waves her away. Carrie sits down.

"Janie."

"What, already," she says, growing hot. "And will you please let go of me before I call security?"

He drops her wrist like a baked potato.

His eyes widen.

"Forget it." He sighs. "I'm an asshole." He looks away.

Janie walks back to her table and sits down miserably.

"What was that?" Carrie hisses.

Janie looks at her and summons a calm smile. She shakes her head. "Nothing. The new guy just told me . . . that . . ." She stalls, pretending to search for a pen. "That, uh, I'm doing the advance math equations completely wrong. I . . . you know me. I hate to be wrong. Math's my best subject, you know." She pulls out a sheet of paper and opens her math book. "Now I've got to start all over."

"Sheesh, Janie. You looked like he just threatened to kill you or something."

Janie laughs. "As if."

1:30 P.M.

Cabel tries to catch Janie's eye in government class. She ignores him.

2:20 P.M.

P.E. It's coed this year. The students play rotating games of five-on-five basketball. Guys against the girls.

Janie commits the most egregious foul Fieldridge High School has ever seen. When he is able, the new guy stands up and insists it was his fault.

The P.E. staff confer, and decide girls versus guys is not a good idea for contact sports. Coach Crater gives Janie a hard look. She returns it, with interest.

2:45 P.M.

Janie dries off hurriedly after her shower and slips into her scrubs for work. The bell rings. She takes her stuff and jumps in her car so she's not late for work.

8:01 P.M.

Life is blissfully calm at Heather Home tonight. Janie finishes her paperwork and her other duties on the floor early, so she goes to see Miss Stubin. She shuffles her feet and clears her throat so Miss Stubin knows Janie is there.

"It's me, Janie. Are you up for a few chapters of *Jane Eyre*?" Janie asks.

Miss Stubin smiles warmly and turns her face toward Janie's voice. "I'd love it, if you have the time."

Janie pulls the visitor chair closer to the bed and begins where they left off last time. She doesn't notice when Miss Stubin drifts off to sleep.

8:24 P.M.

Janie is standing on a street called Center in a small town. Everything is in black and white, like an old movie. Nearby, a couple strolls arm and arm, window-shopping. Janie follows them. The store windows are filled with simplicity. Saws and hammers. Yarn and material. Baking sheets and metal tins. Dry goods.

The couple stops at the corner, and Janie can see the young woman has been crying. The young man is wearing a military uniform.

He pulls the young woman gently around the corner of the building, and they kiss passionately. He touches her breast and says something, and she shakes her head, no. He tries again, and she moves his hand away. He pulls back. "Please, Martha. Let me make love to you before I go."

The young woman, Martha, begins to say no. Then she turns, and looks at Janie with complete regret in her eyes. "Not even in my dream?" she says.

Martha waits for Janie to respond.

Janie looks at the young man. He is frozen, momentarily,

gazing adoringly at Martha. Martha pleads with her eyes locked on Janie. "Help me, Janie."

Janie, startled, shrugs and nods, and Martha smiles through her tears. She turns back to the young man, touches his face, his lips, and nods. They walk through the alley, away from Janie. Janie takes a step to follow them, but she doesn't want to see any more of this dream—it's too intimate. She grips the chair in Miss Stubin's room with all her might, concentrates, and pulls herself back into the nursing home.

It's 8:43 p.m. Janie shakes her head to clear it. Surprised. Slowly, a grin spreads across her face. She did it—she pulled herself out of the dream. And she's not getting sucked back into it. Janie chuckles quietly to herself.

Miss Stubin sleeps peacefully, a smile on her thin, tired lips. It must be nice for poor old Miss Stubin to have a good dream.

Janie leaves the book on the table and exits the room quietly. She turns off the light and closes the door, giving Miss Stubin some intimate time alone with her soldier.

Before he dies.

And she never has the chance again.

SEPTEMBER 9, 2005, 12:45 P.M.

"Why didn't you tell me the new guy was Cabel Strumheller?" Carrie demands.

Janie looks up from her book. She sits in the library at their usual table. "Because I'm an asshole?" She smiles sweetly.

Carrie tries to hold back a laugh. "Yes, you are. I see you're driving him to school."

"Only when he misses the bus," Janie says lightly.

Carrie gives her a sly smile. "Yeah, well. Anyways, I made yearbook staff, so I'll be gone a lot during study hall, okay? I gotta go there now for the first meeting."

Janie waves, distracted by the play she's reading for English. "Have fun. Play nice." She slides down in her seat and plops her feet on the chair opposite hers. She's reading *Camelot* in preparation for next month's senior English trip to Stratford, Canada.

Every now and then she peers over the bookshelves to see if anyone is looking sleepy nearby. She figures she can handle anything outside a twenty-foot radius, unless it's a nightmare, and then the distance jumps dramatically. Luckily, most school-day dreams tend to either be the "falling" dream, the "naked presentation" dream, or something sexual. She can usually get a handle on those without doing a full pass-out-on-the-floor reaction.

It's the paralyzing, shiver-and-shake nightmares that are killing her.

12:55 P.M.

The book disappears in front of her. Janie sighs and sets it on the table. She lays her head in her arms and closes her eyes.

She is floating. *Not the falling dream again,* she thinks. She is sick to death of the falling dream.

The scene changes immediately. Now, Janie is outside. It's dark. She's alone, behind a shed, but she can hear muffled voices. She's never been alone before, and she doesn't know how people can have dreams that they are not in. She is curious. She watches nervously, hoping this isn't somebody's nightmare about to explode through the wall of the shed, or from the bushes.

From around the corner comes a hulking, monstrous figure, outlined by the moonlight. It thrashes its arms through the bushes and lifts its hands to the sky, letting out a horrible yell. Janie feels her fingers going numb. She tries to get out. But she can't.

The figure's long fingers glint in the moonlight.

Janie leans back against the barn. She is shaking.

The grotesque figure sharpens his knife-fingers on each other. The sound is deafening.

Janie, against the barn, squeaks.

The figure wheels around. He sees her.

Approaches her.

She has seen this character before.

Right before she and Ethel ended up in a ditch.

Janie stands up, tries to run. But her legs won't move.

The figure's face is furious, but he has stopped sharpening his knives. He's five feet away, and Janie closes her eyes. *Nothing can hurt me,* she tries to tell herself.

When she opens her eyes, it is daylight. She is still behind the barn. And the horrid, menacing figure has turned into a normal, human young man.

It's Cabel Strumheller.

A second Janie steps out from Janie's body and walks to Cabel, unafraid.

Janie stays back, against the barn.

Cabel touches the second Janie's face.

He leans in.

He kisses her.

She kisses him back.

He steps out of the embrace and looks at the Janie against the barn wall. Tears fall down his cheeks.

"Help me," he says.

1:35 P.M.

The bell rings. Janie feels the fog lifting, but she cannot move. Not yet. She needs a minute.

1:36 P.M.

Make that two minutes.

1:37 P.M.

When she feels the hand on her shoulder, she jumps.

A mile, a foot, an inch . . . she doesn't know.

She looks up.

"Ready?" he says. "Didn't know if you heard the bell."

She stares at him.

"You okay, Hannagan?"

She nods and grabs her books. "Yeah." Her voice is not completely back yet. She clears her throat. "Yes," she says firmly. "Are you? You have a dent in your cheek." She smiles shakily.

"Fell asleep on my book."

"I figured."

"You too, huh?"

"I, uh, must've been really tired, I guess."

"You look freaked. Did you have a bad dream or something?"

She looks at him as they walk through the crowded hall to government class. He slips his hand onto the small of her back so they stay together as they talk.

"Not exactly," she says slowly. Her eyes narrow. "Did you?" The words come out of her mouth like gunshots.

He turns sharply into the doorway as the bell rings and he sees the look on her face. He stops in his tracks. His eyes narrow as they search her face. She can see his eyes are puzzled. His face flushes slightly, but she's not sure why.

The teacher comes in and shoos them to their seats.

Janie looks over her shoulder, two rows back and toward the middle of the room.

Cabel is still staring at her, looking incredibly puzzled. He shakes his head just slightly.

She looks at the chalkboard. Not seeing it. Just wondering. Wondering what the hell is wrong with her. And what is wrong with *him*, that he has dreams like that. Does he know? Did he see her in that one?

2:03 P.M.

A wad of paper lands on Janie's desk. She jumps and slowly looks over to Cabel. He is slumped in his seat, doodling on his notebook, looking a little too innocent.

Janie opens the paper.

Smooths it out.

Yeah, maybe . . . (?)

That's what it says.

SEPTEMBER 29, 2005 2:55 P.M.

Leaning against the hood of her car is the lanky, long-haired figure of Cabel Strumheller. The one who dreams about monsters, and kissing her all in the same dream. His hair is wet.

"Hey," Janie says lightly. Her hair is wet too.

"Why are you avoiding me?"

She sighs. "Am I?" She knows it sounds fake.

He doesn't answer.

She gets in the car.

Starts the engine.

Pulls out of the parking space.

Cabel stands there, looking. Arms folded across his chest. His lips are concerned.

She leans over and rolls down the window. "Get in. You've missed the bus by now."

His expression doesn't change.

He doesn't move.

She hesitates, one more minute.

He turns and starts walking toward home.

She watches him, sighs exasperatedly, and guns it. Her tires squeal around the corner. *Idiot.*

OCTOBER 10, 2005, 4:57 A.M.

On a thin piece of paper in the cave of her own dream, Janie writes:

I keep to myself.

I have to.

Because of what I know about you.

And then she crumples it up, lights a match, and turns it into ash. The charcoaled remains shrivel up and the wind takes them down the street, across the yards. To his house. He steps on them as he saunters to catch the bus. The ash is softer than the crisp Halloween leaves that gather and huddle around the corners of his front step. Under the weight of his footstep, the ash disintegrates. The wind swallows it. Gone.

7:15 A.M.

Janie wakes up, running late for school. She blinks.

She has never had a dream before—not that she can remember.

She only has everyone else's.

At least she can sleep during hers.

She gives her straight dirty-blond hair a lesson with a wet comb, brushes her teeth at top speed, shoves two dollars in the front pocket of her jeans, and grabs her backpack, searching wildly for her keys. They are on the kitchen table. She grabs them, saying good-bye to her nightgowned mother, who stands at the sink eating a Pop-Tart and looking aimlessly out the window.

"I'm late," Janie says.

Her mother doesn't respond.

Janie lets the door slam, but not angrily. Hurriedly. She climbs into the Nova and zooms to Fieldridge High School. She's ten long strides from her English classroom when the bell rings, just like half the class. Sliding into her desk, the back seat in the row nearest the door, she mouses unnoticed through the class, except for a sleepy grin from Carrie. Janie stealthily finishes her math assignment as the teacher drones about the upcoming weekend senior trip to Stratford.

Cabel's back is to her. She has an urge to touch his hair. If she could reach him, she might. But then she shakes her head at herself. She is very confused over her feelings about him. It's more bizarre than flattering to know he dreams about her. Especially when he does it after being that horrid monster-man. She may even admit to being a little afraid of him.

And now she knows where he lives.

Just two blocks from her.

In a tiny house on Waverly Road.

"Your room assignments," Mr. Purcell drones, waving fluorescent yellow papers like sun rays above his head before tossing handfuls at the first person in each row. "No changes allowed, so don't even try."

Janie looks up as titters and groans fill the room. The boy in front of her doesn't turn around to hand her the paper. He tosses it over his shoulder. It floats, hovers, and slides off the slick laminate desk before Janie can grab it, whooshing and sticking under Cabel Strumheller's shoe. He kicks it toward her without acknowledgment. His hair swings lightly around his shoulders.

The list places Janie in a room with three rich snobs from the ritzy Hill section of North Fieldridge: Melinda Jeffers, who hates her, Melinda's friend Shay Wilder, who hates her by default, and the captain of the girls' soccer team, Savannah Jackson, who pretends Janie doesn't exist. She sighs inwardly. She'll have to sleep on the bus on the way.

But she's curious to know if, after all these years, Melinda still dreams about Carrie with ginormous boobs.

OH, CANADA

OCTOBER 14, 2005, 3:30 A.M.

Janie meets Carrie under the black sky in Carrie's driveway. They offer little greeting besides sleepy grins, and Janie climbs into the passenger seat of Carrie's Tracer. They drive in silent darkness to school. Janie's just glad she doesn't have to drive at this hour.

They pass Cabel Strumheller when they get close to school. He's walking. Carrie slows and stops, rolls down the window, and asks if he wants a ride, but he waves her off with a grin. "I'm almost there," he says. Up ahead, the Greyhound bus gleams under the school's parking lot lights.

Janie looks at Cabel. He catches her eye briefly and looks down. She feels like shit.

Cabel and Janie's non-fight in the parking lot began a long series of non-fights. Not only do they not fight, they no longer speak.

But Janie sees him, kisses him, in his library dreams.

She also sees him, a raging maniac. A scarred-faced lunatic with knife-fingers, who repetitively stabs, slices, and beheads one middle-aged man, over and over and over again. She feels only slight relief that he doesn't kill anyone else.

Not yet, anyway.

Not her, so far.

And every time he dreams it, the bell rings before Janie can figure out how to help him. Help him do what? Help him, how?

She has no idea. She has no power. Why do all these people ask her for help? She can't do it.

Just.

Can't.

Do it.

But she sure doesn't get much done in study hall these days.

3:55 A.M.

The oversleepers, latecomers, and don't-give-a-shitters

have either arrived or been written off by the teacher chaperones. Carrie sits with Melinda, near the front.

Janie sits in the last row on the right, next to the window. As far away from everyone as she can get. She stows her overnight bag in the compartment above her seat. She is glad to note that the restroom is at the front of the bus. She twists the overhead TV monitor so its blue glow doesn't blind her, and puts her seat back. It only goes a little way before it hits the back wall.

Before the bus is loaded, Janie is dozing.

4:35 A.M.

She is jarred awake by a splash of water in her face. She's in a lake, fully clothed. She shivers. A boy named Kyle is yelling as he falls from the sky above her, over and over and over, until he finally lands in the water. But he can't swim. Janie feels her fingers growing numb, and she kicks out with her feet, trying to stop it, trying to get out.

And then it's done.

Janie blinks, and sits up, startled. A shadowy face appears above the seat in front of her. "What the fuck?" says Kyle. "Do you mind?"

"Sorry," Janie whispers. Her heart races. The drowning dreams are the worst. Well, almost.

She hears a whisper in her ear as she struggles to see

clearly. "You okay, Hannagan?" Cabel slips his arm around her. He sounds worried. "You're shivering. Did you just have a seizure or something? You want me to stop the bus?"

Janie looks at him. "Oh, hey." Her voice is scratchy. "I didn't know you were there. Um . . ." She closes her eyes. Tries to think. Holds up a weak finger, letting him know she needs a moment. But she feels the next one coming already. She doesn't have much time. And she has to prepare him. She doesn't have a choice.

"Cabel. Do not freak if—when—I do that again, okay? Do NOT stop the bus. Do NOT tell a teacher, oh God, no. No matter what." She grips the armrests and fights to keep her vision. "Can you trust me? Trust me and just let it happen?"

The pain of concentration is excruciating. She is cringing, holding her head. "Oh, fuckity-fuck!" she yells in a whisper. "This was a stupid, stupid idea for me to come on this trip. Please, Cabel. Help me. Don't let . . . anyone . . . gah! . . . see me."

Cabel is gawking at Janie. "Okay," he says. "Okay. Jesus."

But she is gone.

The dreams pelt her, from all directions, without ceasing. Janie is on sensory overload. It's her own physical, mental, emotional, three-hour nightmare.

7:48 A.M.

Janie opens her eyes. Someone is talking on a microphone.

When the fog fades and she can see again, finally, Cabel is staring at her. His eyes, his hair, are wild. His face is white. He is holding her around the shoulders.

Gripping her, is more like it.

She feels like crying, and she does, a little. She closes her eyes and doesn't move. Can't move. The tears leak out. Cabel wipes her cheeks gently with his thumb.

That makes her cry harder.

8:15 A.M.

The bus stops. They are parked in a McDonald's parking lot. Everyone files off the bus. Everyone except Janie and Cabel.

"Go get some food," she urges in a tired whisper. Her voice is still not back.

"No."

"Seriously. I'll be okay, now that everyone's . . . gone."

"Janie."

"Will you go and get me a breakfast sandwich then?" She's still breathing hard. "I need to eat. Something. Anything. There's money in my right-hand coat pocket." The effort to move her arm seems too difficult.

Cabel looks at her. His eyes are weary. Bleary. He

removes his glasses and pinches the bridge of his nose, then rubs his eyes. He sighs deeply. "You sure you'll be okay? I'll be back in five minutes or less." He looks unwilling to leave her.

She smiles a tired half smile. "I'll be fine. Please. I don't think I can stand up if I don't get something to eat soon. That was much, much worse than I expected."

He hesitates, and then removes his arm from behind her shoulders. "I'll be back." He sprints off the bus. She watches him out the window. He runs through the empty drive-through lane and taps on the microphone. Janie smiles. What a dork.

He returns with a bag full of breakfast sandwiches, several orders of hash browns, coffee, orange juice, milk, and a chocolate shake. "I wasn't sure what you'd want," he says.

Janie struggles a little and sits up. She pours the juice down her throat and swallows until it's gone. She does the same with the milk.

"Can you chug beer like that?"

She smiles, grateful he isn't asking questions about her strange behavior. "I've never tried it with beer."

"That's probably wise."

"Have you?" She takes a bite of a sandwich.

"I don't really drink."

"Not even a little, here and there?"

"Nope."

She looks at him. "I thought you were a partier. Drugs?"

He hesitates a split second. "Nada."

"Wow. Well, you sure looked like hell for a couple years."

He is quiet. He smiles politely. "Thank you." He nods at her sandwich.

"Sorry."

He stares at the seat in front of them while she eats. She hands him a sandwich and he takes it, unwraps it, and eats it slowly. They sit in silence.

Janie belches loudly.

He looks at her. Grins. "Jesus, Hannagan. You should enter a contest."

They share the chocolate shake.

8:35 A.M.

The other students board the bus in twos and threes. Some stand outside, sucking on cigarettes.

8:41 A.M.

The bus begins to move again.

"Now what?" asks Cabel. He has a look of concern around his eyes. He combs his hair with his fingers, and it feathers and falls again.

"If it happens again, don't worry." She shrugs helplessly.

"I don't know what to tell you—I promise I'll explain this all when I can. Where are we, by the way?"

"We're getting close."

She rummages around in her pocket and produces a ten-dollar bill. "For breakfast," she says.

He shakes his head and pushes it away. "Let me think of this as our first date, will you?"

She looks at him for a long moment. Feels her stomach flip. "Okay," she whispers.

He touches her cheek. "You look exhausted. Can you sleep?"

"Until somebody else does, I suppose."

His eyes turn weary again. "What does that mean, Janie?" He puts his arm around her shoulders. She rests her head against him and doesn't answer. In minutes, she is sleeping gently. He takes her hand with his free hand and strings his fingers in hers. Looks at her hands, and lays his cheek against her hair. After a while, he is asleep too.

9:16 A.M.

Janie is outside, in the dark. She looks behind her, and the shed is there. She walks around the shed this time, to see him coming.

He looks normal—not a monster—standing at the back door of a house, looking in. Then he slams the door and marches through the dry, yellow grass. The middle-aged man bursts out the door after him, yelling, standing on the step. He carries a rectangular can in one hand, a beer and a cigarette in the other. He screams at Cabel. Cabel turns to face him. The man charges, and Cabel stands there, frozen. Waiting for the man to approach him.

The man punches Cabel in the face and he goes down. He squirms on his back like a scared crab, trying to get away. The man points and squeezes the rectangular can, and liquid hits Cabel's shorts and shirt.

Then.

The man flicks his cigarette at Cabel.

Cabel ignites.

Flops around on the ground in flames.

Screaming, like a poor, tortured baby bunny.

And then Cabel transforms. He becomes a monster, and the fire is gone. His fingers grow knives. His body grows like the Hulk.

Janie watches all this from around the corner of the shed. She doesn't want to see it. No more of it. Feeling so sick, so horrible for witnessing it. She turns around abruptly.

Standing behind her, watching her in horror, is Cabel.

The second.

9:43 A.M.

Janie waits an eternity for her sight to clear. For the feeling to come back. She sits up, frantic. She reaches for him.

Cabel is leaning over, his head in his hands.

He is shaking.

He turns to her, his face enraged.

His voice is raspy. "What the fuck is wrong with you!?"

Janie doesn't know what to say.

His silent anger shakes the seats.

10:05 A.M.

Cabel doesn't speak until they arrive in Stratford. And then all he says is a harsh "good luck." He gets off the bus and heads for his hotel room.

Janie watches him go.

She closes her eyes, then opens them again, and follows the cheerleaders in the other direction to their room.

Once inside, they don't acknowledge one another.

Janie's quite good with that.

2:00 P.M.

The students meet in the lobby. *Camelot* starts in thirty minutes. Janie boards the bus, exhausted, and sits in the back row again.

Cabel doesn't show up.

2:33 P.M.

The play begins. Janie excuses herself from her orchestra seat and finds a spot in the near-empty balcony.

She sleeps soundly up there for three hours, awaking in the closing scene. She slips back down to the orchestra seats and follows the others back to the bus.

6:01 P.M.

The bus stops at Pizza Hut. They have one hour to eat before going back to the evening play.

Janie grabs a Personal Pan to go, eats it on the bus, and sleeps. Sleeps right through the play, in her backseat spot. Nobody seems to notice she didn't get off the bus.

11:33 P.M.

The bus arrives, most kids exhausted, back at the hotel. Janie falls into bed. She is numb, but not from anyone's dream. Not this time. She thinks about Cabel. Cries silently in her pillow in the dark room. The heat register hums loudly. Savannah, the captain of the women's soccer team, collapses on the covers next to her. They don't speak. They hover at the edges of their bed.

OCTOBER 15, 2005, 1:04 A.M.-6:48 A.M.

Janie jumps from one dream to another.

Savannah dreams about making the U.S. women's soccer team, and meeting the legendary Mia Hamm, even though she's retired. Big surprise—this dream could totally be an episode of *Hannah Montana*. Just when Janie wonders if Savannah has even the slightest bit of depth to her, Savannah's dream turns to Kyle, who sat in front of Janie on the bus. Interesting combo, there. Janie's intrigued.

Until the switch to Melinda.

Melinda, no surprise, has a three-way sex party going on with Shay Wilder, who is in bed next to her, and with Carrie. The sex is normal at first, then unbelievably tacky, in Janie's opinion. The bodies of Carrie and Shay are, to use a crass phrase, blown out of proportion. Janie manages for the first time in someone else's dream to turn away.

Janie counts it as a major victory.

And then there's Shay.

Shay dreams about Cabel Strumheller.

A lot.

And in a lot of different ways.

By morning, Janie hates Shay with all her heart. And she has very dark circles under her eyes.

8:08 A.M.

Shay, Melinda, and Savannah head down to breakfast. The matinee is at 10:00.

"See you on the bus," Janie says, even though she is starving. The other girls don't bother to answer. Janie rolls her eyes.

She takes a shower, wraps a towel around her head, and falls back into the bed. She sets the alarm for noon. The bus will be back for the luggage, and the students who didn't elect to take in a third play, at 1 p.m.

8:34 A.M.

Janie dreams for the second time in her life. She dreams that she is alone, drowning in a dark lake, and Cabel is on the shore with a rope, but he won't throw it to her. She waves frantically to him, and he can't see her. She slips under the water slowly. Under the water, she sees others like her. Babies, children, teens, adults. All of them floating just under the surface of the water, no one able to help.

It's because they're all dead.

Their eyes bulge.

She is screaming when the alarm goes off. Her towel has fallen off her head, and her hair is in tangles. She can't see beyond it.

There is an urgent knock on the door.

And it's him.

He's holding a bag of food.

Looking mournful.

He pushes past her into the room, closes the door and locks it, takes her hand, and holds her. He is pleading. "I don't understand," he says. "I just don't understand. Why did you do that to me?" He's broken.

And so is she. "I can explain," Janie says. And she buries her face in his shirt and cries. "Just get me home."

They fall on the bed, and they just hold each other quietly.

That's all they do.

And then, it's time to go home.

2:00 P.M.

Janie and Cabel are in the back seats again. Carrie and Melinda sit in front of them. Across the aisle, Savannah and Kyle are making out. Janie reminds herself to start taking bets on these things.

In front of Savannah and Kyle is Shay, or at least her baggage. Shay appears to be furiously ignoring Janie. She tries to strike up a conversation with Cabel by sitting on the aisle floor, next to him. Cabel is cool and mildly disinterested.

This makes Shay try harder.

Carrie and Melinda turn around in their seats to chat. Cabel makes small talk and jokes, while Janie looks out the window. He slips his hand into hers.

The other girls notice.

Carrie winks.

Melinda looks at Carrie with burning eyes.

Shay shifts in the aisle and leans against Cabel's leg, batting her eyelashes madly. Frighteningly.

At the front of the bus, kids are roaming around and laughing, singing, chattering. Awake and buzzing. Janie slips into a grateful coma, her head propped against the window.

7:31 P.M.

They are back at Fieldridge High School. Cabel shakes Janie awake, gently. She sits up, wondering where she is. Cabel grins at her. "You made it," he whispers. He gathers their bags and follows her off the bus. He walks with her to Carrie's car.

"Come on, Cabel," Carrie says. "Let me give you a ride, at least. Unless you want Shay to—hey, here she comes now." Carrie titters, her eyes dancing.

Cabel's eyes grow wide. He slips into the backseat of Carrie's car without a word. "Get me outa here. Fuckin' creepy cheerleaders."

Carrie laughs. She pulls out of the parking lot and eases onto the road ahead of the pack, and turns to Cabel. "So where do you live?"

"Waverly. Two blocks straight east of your house. But I'll walk from Janie's, if you don't mind. Janie has a superstition about my street."

"What the hell?" Carrie snorts.

Janie laughs. "Nothing! Shut up, Cabe."

Carrie pulls into her driveway. It's cool outside. Crisp. The harvest moon shines orange on Ethel's roof in the Hannagan driveway. Carrie grabs her things and yawns. "I'm turning in. Catch you guys later." She clops to her front door and lets herself in, waving as she closes the screen door.

Janie takes her bag and waves to Carrie. She looks at Cabel. It feels awkward, now that they are in Janie's front yard. They walk to her door. "Can you come in for a bit?" Janie asks, trying not to sound anxious.

"Sure," he says, his voice relieved. "I, uh, figure we have some things to talk about. Are the 'rents home?"

"My mother's probably passed out in her bedroom. That's it, just me and her."

"Cool," he says, but he gives her an understanding look.

They go inside. There is no sign of Janie's mother, except for an empty fifth of vodka on the kitchen counter and a sink full of dishes. Janie throws the bottle in the trash. "Sorry about the mess," she says in a low voice. She is embarrassed. The house was spotless when she left it yesterday morning.

"Forget about it. We can clean it up later, if you want."

Janie waves her hand at the living room. "Well. This is it," she says.

"You sleep out here, huh?" He isn't teasing.

"No, I have a bedroom. Come." She shows him. It's sparse and neat.

"Nice," he says. He glances at the bed, and then abruptly turns around and they walk back to the living room.

"Hungry?"

"My stomach's growling," he says.

"Let me see if we have anything." Janie searches the kitchen cupboards and refrigerator and comes up empty-handed. "Good grief," she says finally. "I'm sorry." She turns around. "We got nothin'."

He's been watching her, she realizes.

"Maybe we could get a pizza."

"Sounds good."

"You want to go out?"

Janie sighs and scratches her head. "Not really."

"Good. Let's order delivery."

Janie finds the number for Fred's Pizza and Grinders and orders. "Thirty minutes."

Cabel tosses a twenty-dollar bill on the coffee table and sits down.

"Cabe."

"Yes."

"What is that?"

"It's twenty dollars, Hannagan."

Janie sighs. "Let's be truthful with each other here, mmmkay?"

"Of course. Our whole relationship is based on it. Right?" He's smiling sardonically, and looks down.

She cringes as the words hang ominously in the room. "Look, I'm sorry," she begins. "I have a lot of explaining to do. But I know you don't have any more money to spare than I do. So how about I pay for this?"

"No. Next question."

Janie sits down next to him. Shakes her head. "Fine," she says, giving up. She draws her legs up under her and turns to face him.

"Okay," she continues. "How did you get in the dream twice?"

He looks away, and then back to Janie.

"Well, let's just jump right into it, then."

"I guess."

"All right . . . uh . . . I guess the answer is, I have No. Fucking. Clue. Oh, and just let me know when it's my turn to ask a few questions. Because I'd like to know how the hell you. Got into. My dream. Hello."

Janie blushes. "Some of your dreams are kind of great."

"Oh, really." Cabel leans forward and catches her chin. Catches her by surprise. He pulls her toward him and traces her cheekbone with his thumb. And then, he puts his lips on hers.

Janie falls into the kiss. She closes her eyes and slips her hand to his shoulder. They explore the kiss for a moment, sweetly. Cabel digs his fingers into her hair and he pulls her closer. But before it grows any stronger, Janie pulls away. She feels like her limbs are rubber.

"Shit," she sputters. "You . . . you . . ."

He smiles lazily, his lips still wet. "Yes?"

"You kiss better than I imagined. Even in—"

He blinks. "No," he says. "No, no, no. Don't even tell me you've been there."

She bites her lip. "Well, maybe if you stopped sleeping during study hall, I wouldn't have a clue."

"Good God!" he says. "Is nothing sacred? Sheesh." He turns away, embarrassed. "Maybe you should start from the beginning."

Janie sighs and leans back against the couch. It was like reliving the dreams. Again.

"The short version? I get sucked into people's dreams. I can't help it. I can't stop it. It's driving me crazy."

He gives her a long look. "Okay, um, how? That's just bizarre."

"I don't know."

"Is this a recent thing?"

"No. The first one I remember, I was eight."

"So, in that dream, *my* dream, where I'm standing behind you, watching myself . . . in . . ." He holds his head. "Okay, so that's how you see the dreams, right? Like I saw mine. While I was dreaming it. Ughh." He rubs his temples.

"That was weird, huh," Janie says softly. "I know this is all really weird. I'm sorry."

There's a knock at the door. Janie jumps up, relieved. She grabs the twenty and goes to answer it.

She sets the pizza and a two-liter of Pepsi on the coffee table and goes to the kitchen for a beer, glasses, napkins, and paper plates. She pours the Pepsi for Cabel and clips open the beer. She takes a sip as Cabel grabs some pizza.

"Now. Tell me what else you've seen in my dreams, before I get really paranoid."

"Okay," she says, suddenly feeling a bit shy. She takes another sip and begins. "We're behind that shed or barn of some sort. Is that your backyard?"

He nods, chewing.

"Up until yesterday, I've seen you as the monster-man-thing"—she cringes, not sure what to name it—"that monster in the house—the kitchen. With the chair. That one was purely coincidental—I didn't even know it was you, dreaming it. Not until later. It was sort of a drive-by thing."

He closes his eyes, cringes, and sets his pizza down on the plate.

"That was you," he says slowly. "I knew I'd seen your car before. I thought you were . . . someone else." He pauses, lost in thought. "The yard—oh, God—your so-called superstition. Damn. So—" He sits up, hands paused in midair, eyes closed. Thinking. Processing.

And then he turns and stares at her. "You could have totally crashed."

"I didn't think anybody saw me."

"The headlights—your headlights. That's what woke me up. They were shining in my window. . . . Jesus Christ, Janie."

"Your bedroom window must have been open. Otherwise, it wouldn't have happened. I think. I had no idea it was your house."

He sits back, shaking his head slightly as he puts the pieces together. "Okay," he says. "Get to the good part before I completely lose my appetite."

"Behind the shed. You walk up to me. Touch my face. Kiss me. I kiss you back."

He's silent.

"That's it," she says.

He regards her carefully. "That's it?"

"Yes. I swear. I mean, it was a good kiss, though."

He nods, lost in thought. "Damn bell always rings then, doesn't it."

She smiles. "Yeah." She pauses, wondering if she should mention the part where he asks her to help him, but he's on to the next thing.

"So when I found you on the desk in the library a few weeks ago, and it took you a while to sit up . . . what was that? You weren't asleep, were you."

"No."

"That was a bad one?"

"Yeah. Real bad."

He puts his head in his hands and takes off his glasses. He rubs his eyes. "Jesus," he says. "I remember that one." He keeps his head down, and Janie waits. "So that's why you said . . . when I asked you if you had a bad dream," he murmurs.

"I . . . I wanted to know if you knew I was there, watching. Even when people talk to me in their dreams, no one seems to remember that part. No one ever mentions it, anyway."

"I don't recall ever seeing you there, or talking to you . . . except when I'm actually dreaming about you," he muses. "Janie," he says abruptly. "What if I don't want you to see it?"

Janie grabs a slice of pizza. "I'm working hard, trying

to bust my way out of them—the dreams. I don't want to be a voyeur—seriously, I can't help it. It's almost impossible. So far, anyway. But I'm making a little progress. Slowly." She pauses. "If you don't want me to see, I guess, don't sleep in the same room as me."

He looks up at her with a sly smile. "But I'm known for sleeping in school. It's my shtick."

"You can change your schedule. Or I can change mine. I'll do whatever you want." She looks at the uneaten pizza and sets her plate down. She is miserable.

"Whatever I want," he says.

"Yes."

"I'm afraid you haven't been privy to that dream yet."

She looks at him. He's looking at her, and she grows warm. "Maybe I'd rather experience that firsthand," she says lightly.

"Mmmm." He takes a sip of his soda. "But before this goes offtrack . . . What the hell is wrong with you?"

She's silent. Not looking at him.

"And," he says, "Jesus. It just occurred to me why you freaked when I pretended I wasn't me. You must be a freaking mess, Hannagan." He tugs her arm, and she falls back on the couch toward him. He kisses the top of her head. "I can't begin to tell you how bad I felt about that."

"It's cool," she says. "Sorry about the flagrant foul," she adds.

"S'all right. I was wearing a cup." He twirls a strand of her hair with his finger. "So, when do you sleep, like, normally?"

Janie smiles ruefully. "Normally, I sleep fine, if I'm alone in a room. When I was thirteen, I finally asked my mother if she would do me the favor of passing out in her bedroom rather than in here. There's something about a closed door that blocks it." She pauses.

"But what happens, exactly?"

She closes her eyes. "My vision goes first. I can't see around me. I'm trapped. If it's a bad dream, a nightmare, I guess I start to shake and my fingers go numb first, then my feet, and the worse the nightmare is, the more paralyzed I become."

He looks at her. "Janie," he says softly.

"Yes."

He strokes her hair. "I thought you were dying. You shake, you spasm, your eyes roll back in your head. I was ready to steal the nearest cell phone, stick a wallet in your mouth, and call 911."

Janie is silent for a long time. "It's not as bad as it looks."

"You're lying."

She looks at him. "Yes," she says. "I suppose I am."

"Who else knows? Your mother?"

She looks at her plate of uneaten pizza. Shakes her head. "Nobody. Not even her."

"You haven't been to a doctor about it or anything?"

"No. Not really. Not for help."

He throws his hands in the air. "Why?" His voice is incredulous. And then, suddenly, he knows why. "Sorry," he says.

She doesn't answer. She's thinking. Thinking hard.

"You know, nobody's ever gone there with me, like you did." Her voice is soft, musing. She gives him a sidelong glance. "I don't understand that part. How did you get there too?"

"I don't know. All of a sudden it was like I had two different angles to watch from: one of them as an observer, the other as a participant. Like virtual reality picture-in-picture or something."

"And don't even tell me you'd believe a word of this if you hadn't come through it with me."

He nods soberly. "You're right, Hannagan."

It's 10:21 p.m. when Cabel says good night at the door. He leans against the frame, and Janie kisses him lightly on the lips.

He hops off the step and starts walking home, but turns back in the driveway. "Hey, can I see you tomorrow night? Sometime around nine or ten?"

She nods, smiling. "I'll be here. Just let yourself in—Carrie always does too. It's cool."

TRUTH OR DARE

OCTOBER 16, 2005, 9:30 P.M.

It's Sunday. The house is clean. Janie had the day off. She ran out for groceries in the morning, vacuumed, dusted, washed, polished, shined, and steam-cleaned.

Now, Janie is asleep on the couch.

Cabel doesn't come.

Or call.

11:47 P.M.

She sighs, clicks off the lamp, and goes to bed, miserable.

OCTOBER 17, 2005 7:35 A.M.

Janie grabs her backpack and heads out the door. She's pissed. And hurt. She thinks she knows why he didn't show up.

On Ethel's windshield is a note, under the wiper. It's wet with dew.

I'm sorry,

it says.

Cabe.

Yeah, well. Not as sorry as I am, she thinks.

She passes him on the way to school.

He looks up.

And eats her dust.

He's late for school.

She doesn't speak to him.

1L:19 P.M.

He's sitting on her front step.

She's pulling up to the house after work.

She gets out of the car, crunches over the gravel, and stands in front of him.

"Yes?" she says.

"I'm sorry," he says.

She stands there, tapping her foot. Searching for words. She blurts them out as they come to her. "So, you got freaked out. I'm a lunatic. An X File. I figured it would happen."

"No—" he stands up.

"It's cool. No, really." She runs up the steps, past him, and fiddles for her key in the dark. "Now you know why I didn't want to tell anybody." The keys rattle in her fingers, and she cusses under her breath. "Least of all, you."

She drops the keys. "Goddamnit," she sniffs, picks them up again, and finds the right one.

"And if you tell anybody," her voice pitches higher as she gets the door open, "you'll learn a new definition of flagrant foul! You big . . . fucking . . . jerk!"

She slams the door.

11:22 P.M.

The phone rings.

"Asshole," she mutters. She picks it up.

"Will you let me explain?"

"No." She hangs up.

Waits.

Pours a glass of milk.

Drinks it.

Cusses.

Turns out the kitchen light, and goes to bed.

She is cursed for life. She will never have a boyfriend. Much less get married. Hell, she'll never be able to sleep with anybody.

She's a freak.
It's not fair.

Sobs shake the bed.

OCTOBER 18, 2005, 7:39 A.M.

Janie calls the school, pretending to be her mother. "She won't be at school today. She has the flu."

She calls the nursing home. "I'm sick," she sniffles. "I can't come in tonight."

Everyone is sorry. The secretary. The nursing home director. "Feel better soon, sweetie," the director says.

But Janie knows there is no "better." This is it. This is her life.

She falls back in bed.

12:10 P.M.

Janie drags her ass out of bed and, sitting on her bedroom floor, does the homework she didn't do the previous night.

She can't stand getting behind in school.

She works ahead, even.

Her mother shuffles around the house, oblivious to Janie's presence. *The sleaze-bitch. It's her fault for giving birth to me*, she thinks. She'd blame her father, too, if she knew who he was. Briefly, she thinks of her mother's kaleidoscope dream. Wonders if the hippie Jesus is her father. Wonders what happened that made her mother give up on absolutely everything. She'll probably never know.

Maybe it's better this way.

2:55 P.M.

The phone rings. Janie's mother answers it.

"She's at school," she slurs.

Janie didn't know her mother ever answered the phone.

4:10 P.M.

Janie sits wrapped in a blanket on the couch, a roll of toilet paper next to her, watching *The Price Is Right*. Carrie lets herself in.

"Hey, bitch," she says cheerfully. "You missed a good one today. You sick?"

"Hey. Yeah." Janie blows her nose loudly in some toilet paper to prove it.

"You look like hell," Carrie says. "Your nose is all red."

"Thank you."

Carrie sits on the couch next to Janie.

"Funny . . . Cabel looks like hell too," she says lightly. "You sure you don't have something you want to tell me?"

"Pretty sure, yeah."

Carrie pouts. Then, she ruffles through her backpack and pulls out a folded piece of paper. She tosses it on the coffee table. "This is from him. You're not preggers or something, are you?"

Janie looks at Carrie. "Ha-ha."

"Well, jeez. Whatever it is, it's got to be a big deal to

keep you home from school. You haven't missed a day since eighth grade. And, sorry to say, you might look like shit, but I don't think you're sick."

"Think what you want," Janie says dully. "I think you have to have sex in order to get pregnant, last I heard."

"Aha, so it's a sex thing!" Carrie shouts triumphantly.

"Go home, Carrie."

Carrie grins. "You know where to find me. Sex tips and advice—just holler out the window."

Janie holds back an urge to strangle her. "Good-bye," she says pointedly.

"Okay, okay. I can take a hint." She heads to the door and turns back to Janie, a curious expression on her face. "This, by chance, doesn't have anything to do with Cabel messing with drugs this weekend, does it?" She blinks rapidly, grinning.

"What?"

"He's sort of a dealer, I guess—or, you know. One of those guys who works as a go-between. Whatever they're called. So Shay danced with him at a party Sunday night. She was really high, though. I heard he got busted. Is that true?"

Janie's stomach twists and shreds.

She's going to be sick.

"No," Janie says slowly, "it doesn't have anything to do

with that." Tears well up in the corners of her eyes and she presses them back with her fingers.

Carrie's face falls. "Oh, shit, Janie. You didn't know."

Janie shakes her head numbly.

She doesn't notice when Carrie leaves.

OCTOBER 19, 2005, 2:45 A.M.

Janie lies awake in bed, staring at the ceiling. Arguing with herself. She knows she shouldn't do it. But she has nothing to lose.

Feeling like a total creep, she gets dressed and slips out of the house. Runs softly through the yards, avoiding the houses with dogs.

Sneaks up to Cabel's house and sits outside his bedroom window, in the bushes. She leans up against the house and waits. The bricks snag her sweatshirt. It's chilly. She puts her mittens on.

Her butt falls asleep.

And her legs.

She gets terribly bored.

5:01 A.M.

She slips away while it's still dark, feeling like a criminal.

A criminal who walks away with nothing.

7:36 A.M.

She gathers her schoolbooks from the coffee table. The note is still there, where Carrie left it. She hesitates, and then opens it.

We really need to talk, Janie. Please. I'm begging. Cabe.

That's all it says.

7:55 A.M.

Janie waits for the bell and slips into school. She gets to English class just before Mr. Purcell closes the door. "Feeling better, I presume, Miss Hannagan," he intones.

Janie *presumes* it's a rhetorical question and ignores him.

She can feel Cabel's eyes on her.

She won't look at him.

It's torture, is what it is.

Every damn class, of every damn day.

Torture.

12:45 P.M.

He gives up.

Janie dreads study hall. But he gives up. He sits in the opposite corner of the library, removes his glasses, and rests his head on his arms.

She notes with satisfaction that he does, indeed, look like shit. Just as Carrie said.

Carrie plops in the chair next to her.

If Cabel dreams, Janie doesn't pick it up. Instead, she lays her head on her arms and tries to take in a nap. But she's sucked into yet another falling dream. This time, it's her own.

And then she's pulled awake and Carrie is there. Or, rather, Janie is with Carrie. And Stu.

Janie watches with curiosity.

Carrie looks like she's enjoying it.

A lot.

Four times.

Once was enough for Janie.

And she really doesn't think Stu's dick could possibly be that large. He could have never fit behind the wheel of ol' Ethel with that thing.

Now Janie knows what else she's missing. She grunts when Carrie nudges her arm.

Gets up.

Two more classes.

Janie is weary. And she has to work a full shift tonight.

Apparently things get worse before they get better.

If they ever get better.

Janie's doubtful.

10:14 P.M.

Miss Stubin is in a coma.

Hospice is in her room all evening.

Janie hovers anxiously.

And then Miss Stubin dies. Right there in front of Janie.

Janie cries. She's not exactly sure why—she's never cried over a resident's death before. There was just something special about this one.

But she's glad Miss Stubin got to make love with that nice young soldier, even if it was just a black-and-white dream.

The head nurse sends Janie home a little early. She says Janie still looks a bit under the weather. Janie is numb. And exhausted. She's been awake since two a.m.

She says good-bye to Miss Stubin. Touches her cold, gnarled hand and gives it a little squeeze.

10:31 P.M.

Janie drives home slowly, windows rolled down, hand ready on the parking brake. She takes Waverly. Past Cabel's house.

Nothing.

She falls into bed when she gets home.

There are no notes, no phone calls, no visits. Not that she was hoping for anything, of course. That bastard.

OCTOBER 22, 2005

Janie works the day shift. It's Saturday. She is assigned to the arts-and-crafts room. This makes her happy. Most of the residents at Heather Home don't sleep through the craft.

At her lunch break, the director is there, even though it's a weekend. She calls Janie into her office and closes the door.

Janie is worried. Has she done something wrong? Has someone caught her in a dream and thought she was slacking off? She sits down tentatively in the chair by the director's desk.

"Is everything okay?" she asks nervously.

The director smiles. She hands Janie an envelope. "This is for you," she says.

"What is it?"

"I don't know. It's something from Miss Stubin. We found it in her belongings after the coroner came. Open it."

Janie's eyes grow wide. Her fingers shake a little. She breaks open the seal and pulls out a folded piece of stationery. When she opens it, a small piece of paper flutters to the ground. She reads. The handwriting is barely legible. Crooked. Written with a blind hand.

Dear Janie,

Thank you for my dreams.

From one catcher to another,

Martha Stubin

P.S. You have more power than you think.

Janie's heart stutters. She draws in a breath. *No*, she thinks. Impossible.

The director picks up the small rectangle of paper from the floor and hands it to Janie. It's a check.

It says, "for college," in the memo line.

It's five thousand dollars.

Janie looks up at the director, whose face is beaming so hard, it looks like it's about to crack. She looks down at the check, and then again at the letter.

The director stands and gives Janie's shoulder a squeeze. "Good job, honey," she sniffles. "I'm so glad for you."

3:33 P.M.

There is a phone call for Janie.

She hurries to the front desk. What a strange day.

It's her mother.

"There's this hippie on the porch, says he ain't leaving until he talks to you. You coming home soon? He wants to know, and I'm going to bed."

Janie sighs. She writes her schedule down every week on the calendar. But she is amused. Maybe because she got a check from Miss Stubin. Maybe because her mother calls Cabel a hippie.

"I'll be home a little after five, Ma."

"Do I need to worry about this character on the porch, or can I go to bed?"

"You can go to bed. He's . . . ah . . . not a rapist." *That I know of, anyway.* They hang up.

5:21 P.M.

Cabel is not on the porch.

Janie goes inside. There's a note on the counter, underneath a dirty glass, in her mother's scrawl.

Hippie said he couldn't stay. Be back tomorrow.
Love, Mom.

It said, Love, Mom.

That was the most notable thing about it.

Janie rips the note into shreds and throws it in the overflowing garbage can.

She changes her clothes, pops a TV dinner in the oven, and pulls out her college applications.

Five thousand. Just a drop in the bucket, she knows. But it's something.

Just like Miss Stubin's note.

That was *really* something.

Janie can't wrap her mind around that one yet.

She looks over everything in her piles of papers. It all looks foreign to her. Financial aid forms, scholarship applications, writing a request essay? Jeez. She needs to get moving on this.

She has no idea what she wants to do with her future.

But science, math . . . maybe research. Maybe dream research.

Or not.

She really wants to forget that part of her shitty, shitty life.

She calls Carrie. "What're you doing?"

"Sitting home. Alone. You?"

"I'm wondering if there's a party somewhere at one of your rich friends' houses."

Carrie is silent for a moment. "Why?" Her voice is suspicious.

"I don't know," Janie lies. "I'm bored. Can't I get in with you? As your date or something?"

"Janie."

"What."

"You don't want to go there."

"What? I'm just bored. I've never been to one of those organized 'Hill' parties. You know, where the parents are gone and leave all the booze and shit for the kids to drink."

Carrie is quiet again. "You're looking for him, aren't you. I'm coming over." She hangs up.

Carrie arrives ten minutes later with her sleeping bag. "Can I stay over?" she asks sweetly. "We haven't had a sleepover in forever."

Janie looks at her skeptically. "What's going on?" she says. "Just tell me."

Carrie throws her stuff on the couch. "You got munchies? I haven't eaten." She sniffs the air and opens the oven. "Eww. Can't we cook something real?"

"Fine," sighs Janie. She rummages around in the kitchen. The refrigerator is surprisingly full today. "Fajitas okay?"

"Perfect," says Carrie gleefully. She mixes two vodka tonics, adds a splash of orange juice, and hands one to Janie.

"Would you stop that, please?"

"Stop what?"

"That whole syrupy sweet-talk thing. It's really grating on me."

Carrie blinks. "I don't know what you're talking about. Anyway, give me some friggin' veggies to chop."

They work up a meal, making guacamole from scratch and everything. Janie takes the TV dinner, wraps it in tinfoil, and puts it in the refrigerator. Her mother will probably eat it. Cold. For breakfast or something.

By the time the fajitas are ready, Janie is buzzing from her second drink and Carrie is doing shots from the bottle.

They move into the living room and flip on music videos.

"So, are you going to tell me what the fuck is going on, or not," Janie says.

Carrie sighs and gives her a sorrowful look. "Oh, Janie. Are you still thumpin' for Cabel or what?"

Janie takes a swallow of her drink, and lies. "I . . . I'm getting over him. I'm not speaking to him."

"I saw him here, on your step this morning. Were you working?"

"Yeah. I guess he was here all day. Ma calls him 'the hippie.'" She laughs.

Carrie takes another shot. "Whooo!" she says when it goes down. "Sheesh. Um . . . oh, yeah. Cabel. Well, he's at Melinda's tonight. With Shay," she adds.

"Well, duh, he wouldn't be with Melinda."

Carrie gives her a curious look. "Why not Melinda?"

Janie's feeling a bit reckless from the effects of the alcohol. "Carrie! Melinda's a lesbian. Didn't you know?"

"What?"

"She's totally in love with you."

"She is not."

"Is."

"How do you know?"

Janie hesitates.

She knows she shouldn't say it.

But she does. "She dreams about you. I've seen her dreams."

Carrie looks at her, confused.

Janie sits, stone-faced.

And then Carrie bursts out laughing. "Holy shit, Janes. You got your funny back."

Janie echoes Carrie's laugh. "Gotcha," she says shakily.

Carrie takes a tentative bite of her fajita. "Hey, it's good, kiddo."

Janie rolls her eyes. Now Stu has Carrie calling her that. "Anyway," prompts Janie.

"Hunh?"

"Cabel?"

"Ohhhh. Right. Well, since you dumped him, he's been going whole hog on the rich girls. He's got Shay wrapped around his little finger."

"Even though he supposedly got busted at her party?"

Carrie giggles. "Who do you think he's working with? Her father! They have a little 'arrangement.' Shay told me. How hilarious is that. Talk about a family business. And we're not talking just pot."

Janie shovels food in her mouth.

Carrie continues. "Shay told Melinda she slept with him." She slaps her hand to her mouth. "Oh, my God. I did not just say that."

Janie is numb. And strangely begging for more. She wants to hate him. "Naw, it's cool," she says smoothly. "I'm so over that guy. He's a big fake. Right?" She eggs Carrie on.

"He IS a big fake," shrieks Carrie, nearly upsetting the vodka bottle. She fills Janie's glass. "No wonder he has all those new clothes, and finally got a cell phone. Sheesh. He's making some bucks. I think it's crack. But that's just a guess."

Janie can't believe it.

He said he doesn't drink. Doesn't do drugs.

She thought he couldn't stand Shay Wilder.

What a liar.

"All the dealers lie, I suppose," Janie says.

Carrie nods, overanimated by the liquor. "They are pretty smooth. I just couldn't believe it when I found out what Cabel was doing. But I knew he was a pothead three years ago, back after he flunked into our grade. I guess it goes on from there."

"Was he really a pothead then?"

"I bought from him," Carrie whispers.

"You did?"

Carrie nods again. "A lot."

Janie stands abruptly and takes the dishes to the sink. She begins washing them as the flurry of information sloshes around in her brain. He had sex with Shay? Janie's whole body stings.

When Janie comes back to the living room, Carrie's eyes are glazed. She stares at the TV.

Janie sits next to her. "So if Cabel is hot for Shay, why did he sit on my step all day, and why does he keep trying to talk to me?"

Carrie looks at Janie. "Maybe he doesn't want to lose you as a future customer. Or a good lay. Face it, baby, you're looking hot these days."

Janie feels her stomach churning.

She excuses herself to the bathroom.

When she returns, Carrie's lying on the couch, passed out.

Janie turns off the TV. She cleans up the mess and gets a drink of water.

OCTOBER 23, 2005 1:34 A.M.

She leaves Carrie on the couch, sprints through the yards to hide in the stand of trees near Cabel's house. There's a light on inside, so she waits. After a while, a car pulls into his driveway. It sits there for five minutes, maybe more. Finally, Cabel gets out and goes inside. When she sees all the lights go out, she deposits herself in the bushes under his window, stepping carefully around the crunchy leaves that insist on falling constantly the past few days.

Luck is on her side when he cracks the window open an inch. She hears him now, and her heart breaks as he sighs and rustles around in the dark. She can hear his bed creak when he lies down, and she can hear him punch his pillow, getting settled for sleep.

She wonders what he wears to bed. She is more than tempted to look.

But she will wait.

She must wait.

She waits.

2:15 A.M.

He doesn't snore.

3:04 A.M.

Janie, asleep in the bushes, is jolted awake. Painfully.

Her body is paralyzed almost immediately, and she is sucked into his mind. Into his fears. His dream.

It lasts two hours.

The same scenes, on an endless loop.

The middle-aged man, spraying lighter fluid, and then flicking a cigarette at Cabel. The monster-man in the kitchen, flinging a knife-pointed chair, hitting the ceiling fan, decapitating the middle-aged man. And a new one. Shay, the rich girl cheerleader, in handcuffs, hooked to a bed. Smiling.

Janie thinks she looks dreadful.

Naked.

As Cabel climbs in bed with her.

And Janie can't pull herself away.

She feels herself become ill, but she cannot move.

She can't pound on the window to wake him.

She's frozen. Paralyzed.

And she thought school was torture.

It's absolutely the worst dream she's ever been stuck in. By far. She passes out. Unconscious. Drained. Right before the scene changes. And ends.

6:31 A.M.

She opens her eyes.

On her belly, facedown, in the stones and branches.

She can hardly move.

But she must.

The sun is coming up.

7:11 A.M.

Janie limps home. Ignores the barking dogs.

7:34 A.M.

Janie crawls in the door, closes it, and falls on the carpet next to Carrie, who is still lying on the couch. She sleeps.

8:03 A.M.

Oh, God. She's in the forest. Again, again, again. So tired.

When they see the boy, bobbing in the water, Stu appears next to Carrie.

The grin.

The struggling.

The plea. Help him.

And Janie can't help him.

She can never help him.

Stu reaches over the water, but he cannot help either. Stu makes love to Carrie as she is crying for the boy, Carson.

The boy is bloody, lost, gone with the shark.

As always.

Janie cries. For Carson, for Carrie. But mostly for herself. She feels like she's about a hundred years old.

9:16 A.M.

Carrie nudges Janie.

"I gotta go," she says.

Janie grunts. Her body aches.

Carrie closes the door softly, and Janie sleeps.

The carpet scratches her face.

11:03 A.M.

There is a soft knock, and a lets-himself-in noise of the door. Janie thinks she's dreaming.

He checks to make sure she is alive, on the floor. Then he sits on the couch and waits.

Janie's mother walks by.

And walks by again, the other way, carrying a tinfoil-covered tray and a glass bottle.

12:20 P.M.

She rolls.

Groans.

Curls up in a ball on her side, clutching her belly.

"Oh, God," she moans, eyes closed. Her head aches. Her muscles scream every time she moves. She is weak and empty. Light-headed. Exhausted.

And he is there, picking her up. Taking her to her bed. Covering her with blankets.

He closes the door.

Sits on the floor, next to her.

12:54 P.M.

He goes to the kitchen. Makes her a cold chicken sandwich. Pours milk. Pours orange juice. Puts it on a plate. Takes it to her room.

Waits.

1:02 P.M.

Until he gets scared because she's sleeping so much. And he wakes her up.

Janie groans and slowly sits up.

She drinks the juice and milk.

Eats the sandwich.

Doesn't look at Cabel.

Or speak to him.

1:27 P.M.

"Why do you keep coming here," she says dully. Her voice is rough.

He measures his words. "Because I care about you."

She chuckles morosely. "Right."

He looks at her helplessly. "Janie, I'm—"

She gives him a sharp look. "You're what? Dealing drugs? Fucking Shay Wilder? Tell me something I don't know."

He puts his head in his hands and groans. "Don't believe everything you hear."

She snorts. "You're denying it?"

"I am not fucking Shay Wilder." He shudders.

"Oh, really. Only in your dreams, then." She turns to the wall.

He stares at the back of her head.

For a painful amount of time.

"You didn't," he finally says.

She doesn't respond.

He stands up. "Jesus, Janie." He spits the words.

Stands there, accusing.

"Maybe you should leave now," Janie says.

He moves to the door, opens it, and turns back to look at her. "Dreams are not memories, Janie. They're hopes and fears. Indications of other life stresses. I thought you of all people would know the difference." He walks out.

NOVEMBER 21, 2005

Janie and Cabel don't speak.

Janie goes about school and her job mechanically, feeling emptier than she's ever felt before in all her life. The one person who knows about the dreams, the one person she really started to care about, feels like her worst enemy. Janie spends a lot of time thinking about being an old maid forever, like Miss Stubin. Preparing herself for a very lonely life.

Working at the nursing home.

Commuting to college.

Living with her mother.

Forever.

At school, the number of sleeping students increases with the waning of daylight hours and the onset of colder weather.

As Thanksgiving approaches, in one especially rough study hall that follows too light a lunch, a science geek girl named Stacey O'Grady takes a rare nap. She's driving an out-of-control car with a rapist in the backseat for almost the entire class period. Fifteen minutes into it, Janie is already fully paralyzed.

Luckily, Carrie is not there to notice when Janie falls off her chair and shakes on the carpet, back in the corner of the library.

Luckily, Cabel notices.

He picks her up, sets her back on the chair.

Rubs her fingers a bit until they move.

Pulls a king-size Snickers bar from his backpack and sets it next to her hand before he leaves for government class.

Distracts the teacher when she slips in late.

Doesn't look at her.

Janie swallows her pride along with the candy bar. Writes something in her spiral notebook in a shaky hand. Rips the paper off the spiral.

Crumbles it into a ball.

Hits him in the back of the head with it.

He picks it up and opens it. Reads it.

Smiles, and puts it in his backpack.

On Ethel's windshield after school is a section of newspaper—the classifieds. Janie looks around suspiciously, wondering if it's some sort of joke. Seeing no one, she pulls it out from under the wiper and gets in the car. She gives it a cursory glance, first one side, and then the other. And then she finds it. Highlighted in yellow.

> Having trouble sleeping? Nightmares? Sleep disorders? Questions answered. Problems solved.

It's a volunteer sleep study. Sponsored by the University of Michigan. For scientific research.

And it's free.

When she gets home, she calls immediately and signs up for Thanksgiving weekend, at the North Fieldridge Sleep Clinic location near school.

NOVEMBER 25, 2005

It's the day after Thanksgiving. Janie worked Thanksgiving Day and today, for double pay. She has tomorrow off, anticipating trouble at the sleep study tonight. Wondering if this is going to be a repeat of the bus ride to Stratford. Wondering if this is going to turn into another big mess.

10:59 P.M.

She grabs an overnight bag from the backseat of her car and walks into the sleep clinic. She removes her coat and registers under a fake name at the desk. Through the tinted glass window, she can see a row of beds with machines all around. There are people already in some of the beds.

This is a very, very bad idea, she thinks.

The door to the sleep room opens, and a woman in a white lab coat stands there, looking at a chart. Janie stumbles. Puts her hands to her face. Grimaces. She reaches blindly for a chair before her body goes numb.

11:01 P.M.

She is on a street in a busy city. It's raining. She stands under an awning, not sure who she's looking for. Not yet. She doesn't feel compelled to follow anyone passing by. Eventually, her stomach lurches. She sighs and rolls her eyes, and looks up.

Here he comes, she thinks.

Through the awning.

It's Mr. Abernethy, the principal of her high school.

11:02 P.M.

Her vision defrosts. The lab-coated woman has moved into the room and is staring at her.

Janie stares back, just to freak her out. She looks around the room at the others who sit there, waiting for their names to be called. They all look at the floor as her gaze passes from one to the next. She knows what they're thinking. *There's no way they want to be in that room with me, the freak.*

Janie sets her jaw.

She's tired of crying.

Refuses to make any further scenes.

When the feeling returns to her fingers and feet, she stands up, grabs her coat and overnight bag, and stumbles to the door.

Her voice is hoarse when she turns to speak to the receptionist. "Sorry. I'm not doing this." She goes outside into the parking lot. The air is crisp, and she sucks it into her lungs.

The woman in the lab coat chases out the door after her. "Miss?"

Janie keeps walking. Tosses her bag back into the car.

Over her shoulder, she yells, "I said, I'm not doing this."

She climbs behind the wheel. Leaves the lab-coated woman standing there as she drives away. "There has to be another way, Ethel," she says. "You understand me, don't you sweetheart."

Ethel purrs mournfully.

11:23 P.M.

Janie pulls into her driveway after the incident in the sleep study waiting room. Wonders if she should have given it a try. But there is no way on earth she wants to know what her principal, Mr. Abernethy, dreams about.

Ew.

Ew, ew, ew.

This is not the right way to fix it, she decides. But what is the right way? Because it's time.

Time to stop crying, time to get her act together and do something. Time to move beyond the pity party.

Before she loses her mind.

Because there's no way on earth she's going to make it through college unless she grows some serious ovaries and turns this train wreck around.

She goes into the house and digs through her papers on her bedside table. She finds it—Miss Stubin's note. Reads it again.

Dear Janie,

Thank you for my dreams.

From one catcher to another,

Martha Stubin

P.S. You have more power than you think.

11:36 P.M.

What does it mean?

11:39 P.M.

She still doesn't know.

11:58 P.M.

Nope.

NOVEMBER 26, 2005, 9:59 A.M.

Janie waits at the door of the public library. When it opens for business, she meanders through the nonfiction section. Self-help. Dreams.

She pulls all six books from the shelf, finds a back corner table, and reads.

When a group of sleepy-looking students comes in and sets up at a nearby table, she moves to a different section of the library.

And she waits patiently for the computer in the corner to open up. Spends an hour there. She can't believe what she finds with Google's help.

Of course, there's no information on people like her. But it's a start.

5:01 P.M.

With four of the six books in tow, Janie drives home. She is fascinated. She makes dinner with a book in her hand. She reads until midnight. And then she takes a deep breath and talks to herself as she gets ready for bed.

"I have a problem," she says quietly, trying not to feel like a dork. "I have a problem, and I need to solve it. I would like to have a dream about how to solve this problem."

She concentrates. Climbs into bed, closes her eyes, and continues in a calm voice. "I would like to dream about what I can do to block out other people's dreams. I want—" she falters. "I mean, I would like to help people, and I also . . . would like . . . to live a normal life. So their dreams don't fuck up my life forever."

Janie breathes deeply. She stops speaking, and instead focuses her mind on her problem. Until she remembers. "And I would like to remember the dream when I wake up," she adds out loud.

Over and over, she repeats the words in her head.

She peeks at the clock quickly and chides herself for messing with the mojo.

12:33 A.M.

She focuses again. Breathes deeply. Lets the thoughts float around and meld together in her mind.

Slowly, she feels the thoughts filling the room. She breathes them in. They caress her skin. She lets her mind be free, allows her muscles to relax.

And she lets the sleep in.

Nothing happens at first.

Which is good, she discovers.

Lucidity comes late.

2:45 A.M.

Janie finds herself in the middle of a dark lake. She treads water for what seems like hours. She grows weary. Panics. Sees Cabel on the shore with a rope. She waves frantically to him, but he doesn't see her. She can't hold on. The water fills her mouth and ears.

She submerges.

There are many people under the surface of the water—men, women, children, babies. She looks at them with panic, her lungs bursting. They stare at her, eyes bulging in death.

She looks around frantically. The pressure in her lungs is overpowering. Everything dims, and goes black. She feels her eyeballs bulging, and hears the haunting inner laughter of the floating bodies around her.

Janie gasps and sits up. It's 3:10 a.m.

She breathes hard. Writes down the dream in a spiral notebook.

Tries not to feel bad that she failed. She expects this.

It's not over, she tells herself, lying back down.

Let me dream it again, she thinks, calmly. *And this time, I won't drown. I will breathe under water, because this is my dream and I can do what I want with it. I will swim like a fish. Because I know how to swim. And . . . and I have gills. Yes, that's it. I have gills.*

She repeats this to herself as she lies down.

3:47 A.M.

She doesn't have gills.

She rolls over and groans, frustrated, into her pillow. Repeats the mantra.

4:55 A.M.

It begins again.

When Janie slips under water, exhausted, her lungs burning, she looks around at the others who are floating under the surface.

She begins to panic.

The bulging eyes.

And then.

Miss Stubin blinks at her from under the water. She smiles encouragingly. She is not one of the dead.

Floating next to Miss Stubin is another Janie, who nods and smiles. "It's your dream," she says.

The drowning Janie looks from Miss Stubin to Janie. Her vision dims.

She grows frantic.

"Concentrate," Janie says. "Change it."

Drowning Janie closes her eyes. Falls farther under the water. She kicks her feet as she loses consciousness, struggling to move, to get back above the water.

"Concentrate!" Janie says again. "Do it!"

Gills pop from the drowning Janie's neck.

She opens her eyes.

Breathes. Long, cleansing breaths, underwater. It tickles. She laughs in bubbles, incredulous.

She looks up, and Miss Stubin and Janie are smiling. Clapping, slow motion and soundless, in the water. They swim over to her.

The formerly drowning Janie grins. "I did it," she says. Bubbles come out of her mouth, and the words appear individually above her head when each bubble pops, like a cartoon.

"You did it," Janie says, nodding, her hair swishing like silk.

"Let's swim now," Miss Stubin says. "Someone's waiting for you on the shore."

Janie and Miss Stubin swim partway with the formerly drowning Janie, and then they stop and wave her on.

She nears the shore, and when she surfaces and can stand, the gills disappear. She walks out of the water, streaming wet in her pajamas—boxer shorts and a T-shirt.

Cabel is there. He's wearing boxer shorts too. His muscles ripple in the sunlight. His body is tan. It glistens.

It looks like they are on a deserted, tropical island.

He doesn't move.

He doesn't have a rope anymore.

He's sitting in the sand.

She waits for him to do something, but he doesn't move.

"Remember, it's your dream," she hears. It's her other Janie speaking, the one who is aware that she is dreaming.

Janie hesitates and approaches Cabel. "Hey, Cabel."

He looks up. "I care about you," he says. His eyes are brown and turning muddy.

Janie wants to believe him. And so she does.

"What about Shay?" she asks.

"Dreams aren't memories," he says. "Please talk to me."

6:29 A.M.

Janie smiles in her sleep. She watches over herself in the dream, and plunges back into it, taking it in different directions, starting over at various spots to make it fun, or sexy, or beautiful, or silly.

NOVEMBER 27, 2005, 8:05 A.M.

The alarm clock rings. Janie keeps her eyes closed and reaches to turn it off. She lies in bed, going over the dream in detail, remembering it. Memorizing it.

When she has it solidly in her mind, she sits up and writes it in her journal.

She can't stop smiling.

It's a small step. But it gives Janie hope.

She studies the books all day, until it's time for work.

9:58 P.M.

It's quiet at the nursing home. The residents are all tucked in their beds, doors closed. Janie fills out charts at the front desk. She is alone.

The call panel is dark, until a white light flashes from the room Miss Stubin once occupied. A new resident is there now. His name is Johnny McVicker.

Janie sets down her pen and goes into the room to see what he needs.

But Mr. McVicker is asleep.

He's dreaming.

Janie grabs hold of the wall as she goes blind.

9:59 P.M.

They are in the basement of a house. It's lit moderately, and it's not very cold down there. Janie sees gray leaves blowing and piling up outside the venting window. Everything is in black and white, she realizes after a moment.

Mr. McVicker is perhaps twenty years younger. He stands at the bottom of the stairs with a young man, whom he calls Edward.

They are yelling.

Hateful things.

Mr. McVicker looks horrified, and Edward storms up the stairs and out of the house, slamming the door.

The old man tries to follow, but he can only move in slow motion. He tries speaking, but no words come out. He is mired by the weight of his feet, sinking through the steps.

He looks at Janie, his face cracked and broken, lined with tears. And then he looks past Janie.

Janie turns around.

Miss Stubin is standing behind her, watching. Waiting. For something. She smiles encouragingly at Mr. McVicker.

His face is anguished.

Fresh tears fall from his eyes.

He is sinking into the steps, and now he can't move at all.

Miss Stubin stands patiently, watching him, compassionate. She closes her eyes, and her brow furrows. She holds deathly still.

"Help me," he finally cries, as if it's forced from his lungs.

Miss Stubin glides over to Mr. McVicker.

Holds her hand out.

Helps him out of the stairs, which magically repair themselves. But instead of guiding him up the stairs, she brings him back to the starting spot of the dream.

Miss Stubin glances at Janie and nods, then turns back to the old man and tells him something that Janie cannot hear.

They stand there, Janie looking on, for several moments. And then the dream begins again.

Mr. McVicker and Edward are yelling.

Hateful things.

Mr. McVicker looks horrified, and Edward turns toward the stairs.

Miss Stubin says something to Mr. McVicker again. The scene pauses.

Mr. McVicker reaches for Edward's sleeve.

"Don't go," he says. "Please. There's something I have to tell you."

Edward turns around slowly.

"Son," the old man says. "You're right. I'm wrong. And I'm so sorry."

Edward's lip quivers.

He opens his arms to his father.

Mr. McVicker embraces the young man. "I love you," he says.

Miss Stubin whispers a third time to Mr. McVicker, and he nods and smiles. He puts his arm around his son, and they walk up the stairs together.

Miss Stubin smiles at Janie and fades away. Janie stands for a moment in the basement. She is surprised that she's not compelled to follow the old man. She looks around and sees bright green grass and petunias growing outside the venting window, and the basement walls have turned a soft yellow.

Strange.

Janie closes her eyes and concentrates, and she pulls herself easily from the dream.

She's still standing. She blinks Mr. McVicker's dark room into view once again. Her fingers are barely tingling.

How bizarre.

But nice to see Miss Stubin. That's for sure.

She turns to leave. Out of the corner of her eye, she notices his call button.

It's on the floor.

Out of reach of the bed.

Janie hesitates, and then picks it up and connects it back to its clip on the wall. She turns the blinking light off.

She looks around the room quickly, hackles raised.

Closes the door behind her.

Shakes her head, mystified.

At the front desk is Carol, the head nurse. "I finished your charts, hon," she says. "Where'd you disappear off to?"

Janie points down the hall. "Mr. McVicker's light was flashing. He's all set now. I just turned it off." Her voice is pure and smooth, and it catches her by surprise.

Carol gives her a curious look. "His light wasn't flashing, Janie." She goes to the light panel, picks it up, and jiggles it. "Hmm," she says. "Maybe it burned out."

"That's odd," Janie says lightly.

She puts the charts away, grabs her coat, and punches out. The stamp says 11:09 p.m. "Welp, gotta go. School tomorrow."

She drives home, a fresh song in her heart.

NOVEMBER 29, 2005, 12:45 P.M.

Janie is obsessed with learning more about dreams. She wills people to sleep in class. And study hall, as always, is full of excitement.

Janie practices on everyone she can.

Most of the time, she fails.

She still hasn't figured everything out.

But she will.

By God, she will.

Because now she has her very good friend Miss Stubin to help her. She suppresses the urge to skip down the hallways.

DECEMBER 5, 2005, 7:35 A.M.

Cabel parks his new car next to Janie's as she arrives at school.

It's not a brand-new car. Just new to him.

But it *is* a Beemer.

People on the south side of Fieldridge do not drive Beemers. Well, maybe the 1976 variety. Definitely not the 2000 variety. Janie's mouth opens, and then she presses her lips shut. Shakes her head and walks toward the building.

He's right behind her. "It's six years old, Janie. Come on."

Janie's eyebrow is permanently raised as he tries to keep up with her on the way in to school.

She loses him when he slips and flips on the icy sidewalk.

Janie finds Carrie by the doorway to English class. "What's the scoop on the pimpster wheels out there?" Janie asks her.

"I don't know, *chica*. He must be makin' some big cake. I can't believe he hasn't been expelled yet."

"Has he actually been arrested?"

"No. Shay's daddy worked it out with the cops. Cabel was at all the parties this weekend with her."

"And now he's driving that."

"It's a friggin' 323Ci convertible. Stu says seventeen grand at least for one of those, used."

Janie's blood boils. "This is just . . . just . . ." The anger swells, and she can't come up with a word. Carrie is giving her the evil eye.

"Unbefuckinglievable?" comes a voice from behind her.

She takes a quick breath, watching Carrie's eyes grow wide. "Shit." She turns around and there's Cabel.

"S'cuse me, please," he says politely, and squeezes past them into the classroom. Janie catches a whiff of the cologne he's wearing. Her stomach flips against her will.

Carrie's eyes sparkle. She giggles. "Oops."

Janie rolls her eyes and laughs reluctantly. "Yeah."

12:45 P.M.

For days, Janie's been in other people's dreams during study hall, with minimal success in helping them change the dreams. She is still puzzled by one thing.

Make that two things.

First, how did Miss Stubin get Mr. McVicker to ask her for help? And second, what was she saying to him to get him to change his dream?

Sorry. Make that three. Three things.

How the hell can Miss Stubin see in the dreams, when she's blind? And how can she be there when she's dead?

Okay, that's four. Janie knows. There are probably more than that, even.

This is so frustrating.

She knows she needs to work harder.

And she's losing weight. Rapidly.

She was already thin enough.

Now her cheeks look caved in, like her mother's. And she has dark circles under her eyes, from getting up so often in the night, working on her own dreams.

She finds Snickers bars in the strangest places.

(She knows they're from him.)

(She wonders if they're laced with pot.)

Cabel has been sitting in his old spot again the past few weeks. But he doesn't sleep.

He reads.

Janie sort of wishes he would fall asleep. But she also worries what she might see.

Exams are coming. She opens her math book and studies it. Every now and then, she glances at Cabel, whose back is to her. From what Carrie said, he was at the Hill parties again all weekend. With Shay. And a lot of drugs. Janie sighs. Pulls herself out of the threatening misery and focuses on the math book again. Refuses to go there.

1:01 P.M.

Cabel's head nods, and jerks back up. He shakes his head swiftly and glances over his shoulder at Janie. Janie looks down. Then he slouches in his chair and puts his chin in his hand. His hair falls softly around his shoulders and over his eyes. Janie reluctantly admires his profile as he turns a page in the book.

His head nods.

The book slips from his fingers.

It doesn't wake him when it thumps on the table.

Janie feels his energy.

She concentrates, and slips into his dream slowly. Another positive step—she's learning to control the speed of her arrivals and departures. It's much easier than —

1:03 P.M.

He's sitting in a dark jail cell. Alone. Above his head is a sign that says, "Drug Pusher."

Janie watches from outside the cell.

His head is down.

The scene changes abruptly.

He's in Janie's room, sitting on the floor, writing something on a pad of paper. Alone. He looks up at her, beckoning her with his eyes. She takes a few steps forward.

He holds up the notepad.

It's not what you think.

That's what it says.

He tears off that sheet of paper. Below it is another sheet in his handwriting.

I think I'm in love with you.

Janie's stomach lurches.

He looks at the tablet for a long moment. Then he turns to Janie and rips off one more sheet. He watches her face as she reads it.

How do you like my new trick?

He grins at her, and fades.

The scene changes again. Back in the jail cell. The sign above his head is gone.

He is alone. She watches from outside. His head is down. Then he looks up at her.

A ring of keys floats in front of her.

"Let me out," he says. "Help me."

Janie is startled. She moves automatically and unlocks the cell. He walks to her, takes her in his arms. He looks into her eyes. He sinks his fingers into her hair and kisses her.

Janie steps out of herself as she's kissing Cabel. She walks away into a dark hallway and eases herself back to awareness in the library.

She blinks.

Sits up.

Looks at him.

He's still asleep at his table.

She rubs her eyes and wonders:

How the hell did he do that?

And.

Now what?

1:30 P.M.

He slides into the seat across the table from Janie. His eyes are moist with sleep and mischief. "Well?"

"Well what," she mutters.

"It worked, right?"

Janie squelches a grin. Poorly. "How the hell did you do that?" she demands.

His face sobers. "It's the only way I could think of to get you to talk to me."

"Okay, I get that. But how did you do it?"

He hesitates. Glances at the clock. Shrugs. "Doesn't

look like I have time to explain right now," he says. "When would you like to go out with me so we can talk about it?" A grin flirts with his lips.

He's got her cornered.

And he knows it.

Janie chuckles, defeated. "You are such a bastard."

"When," he demands. "I promise, all my heart, I'll be your house elf for the rest of my life if I fail to meet you at the appointed date and time." He leans forward. "Promise," he says again. He holds up two fingers.

The bell rings.

They stand up.

She's not answering.

He comes around the table toward her and pushes her gently against the wall. Sinks his lips into hers.

He tastes like spearmint.

She can't stop the flipping in her stomach.

He pulls back and touches her cheek, her hair. "When," he whispers. Urgently.

She clears her throat and blinks. "A-a-after school works for me," she says.

They grab their backpacks and run. As they slip in the doorway of government class, he shoves a PowerBar in her hand.

She sits at her desk and looks at it. She raises her

eyebrow at him, from across the room.

"Protein," he mouths. He gestures like a weight lifter.

She laughs out loud.

Opens it.

Sneaks bites when the teacher isn't looking.

It's not as good as a Snickers.

But it'll do.

In P.E., they're playing badminton.

"I'm watching you," he growls as they change sides. "Don't you dare sneak out of here without me."

She flashes him a wicked grin.

After school, Janie exits the locker room and looks around, then heads for the parking lot. He's standing between their cars. His hair, dripping, has a few tiny icicles attached.

"Aha!" he says when he sees her, as if he's foiled her escape plans.

She rolls her eyes. "Where to, dreamboy?"

Cabel hesitates.

Works his jaw.

"My house," he says. "You lead the way."

She freezes. Her stomach churns. "Is . . . is he . . ." She swallows hard.

He squints in the pale sunlight and reads the question in her voice. "Don't worry, Janie. He's dead."

WHAT BECOMES THE LONGEST DAY

IT'S STILL DECEMBER 5, 2005

Three o'clock.

Janie pulls into Cabel's driveway, tentatively. He pulls in behind her and jumps out of the car, grabbing his backpack and closing his car door gently. It clicks perfectly, solid. "I just love that sound," he says wistfully. "Anyway. Follow me."

He opens the rickety service door to the garage. It creaks and groans. He flips on the garage light and takes Janie by the hand. The garage is tidy. It smells pleasant, like old grass clippings and gasoline. Next to the door that leads into the house hangs Cabel's skateboard. Janie smiles and touches it.

"Remember that?" she says. "That was a sweet thing

for you to do. I hadn't exactly planned on walking home that night."

"How could I forget. You slammed the gymnasium door handle right into my gut."

"That was you?"

He gives her a patronizing smile. "Indeed."

They go inside.

The house is tiny. Clean. Threadbare.

She startles when she sees the kitchen. She's seen this room before, in his dream. The table. And the chairs.

"Jesus," she says under her breath. She looks up. The ceiling fan is there. "Oh, God." She turns and looks where the front door would be, where the middle-aged man came in, and it beckons to her. She drops her backpack on the floor, shuts her eyes, and covers her face with her hands.

And he's touching her shoulders.

Wrapping his arms around her.

Stroking her hair.

Whispering, his lips to her ear. "He's not here. It's just a dream. That never happened. Never happened." And she's soothed by the words. She breathes him in. Her hands leave her face and find his shoulders, his chest. She touches his chest lightly, wondering if scars lie beneath his shirt. Wonders if *that* dream really happened. And then he's kissing her neck and she's falling, turning her head to find his mouth with her lips, and she's tracing his jaw with her fingertips and kissing him hard, their tongues tasting each other madly, and he's pressing into her and she into him, bodies shivering, like they are two scared, lost children, starving, starving to be touched, to be held, by someone, anyone, the first one they can find who seems familiar enough, safe enough, strong enough to rescue them. They breathe, heavy. Hard. Their fingers strain at cotton.

And then they slow down.

Stop. Hold. Rest.

Before one of them, or both, begins to sob.

Before they break another piece that needs to be fixed.

They stand together for a moment, collecting.

And then he finds her fingers and strings them in his, and leads her to the living room.

On the coffee table rests a stack of books.

He looks at Janie. "This is how," he says, his voice catching. "You know these books now, don't you."

"Yes," she says. She kneels next to the table and lays the dream books out.

"I've been practicing," he says. "Hoping."

Dreaming, she adds silently. "Tell me."

He sits beside her with two sodas and an apology. "I don't have anything stronger," he says. "Anyway. I read this book about lucid dreams and taught myself to dream what I wanted to dream about."

She smiles. "Yup. I did it too."

"Good." He sounds businesslike. "What about the sleep clinic?"

"Ugh. Great idea, but not cool, as it turned out. I went in, got stuck in a dream when the lab tech opened the door to the sleep room. Walked out." She pauses. "It was Mr. Abernethy's dream. I just didn't want to know what that country-fried rube was dreaming about."

Cabel chokes on his Pepsi. "Good call." He grows serious a moment, thinking. But then waves the thought away. "Yeah. Really good call."

"Huh?"

"Nothing. Okay, so I first tried to dream me saying specific things to you. But I couldn't get it to happen right. Too much"—he pauses, glancing sidelong at her—"too much came out of my mouth. More than I wanted to say. I couldn't control it." He shifts in his seat. "So I thought I was screwed. But then I thought of writing the words on the page. I practiced it a bunch of times, and the last few nights it worked."

"But you didn't dream me into the dream. At least, not until the end."

"Right. Because I could control it better if I had myself alone, knowing that if—when—I dreamed it around you, you would be there."

Janie closes her eyes, picturing it. "Clever," she murmurs. She opens her eyes. "Really clever, Cabe."

"So you could read the tablet?" he says. His face flushes a little.

"Yes."

"All of it?"

She searches his face. "Yes."

"And?"

She's quiet. "I don't know what to say. I'm really confused."

He takes her hand and leans back on the couch. "I have a lot of explaining to do. Will you hear me out?"

She takes a breath, and lets it out slowly. All the reasons to hate him flood back into her brain. Her self-protective nature percolates. She does not want to ride this roller coaster again. "Well," she says finally, "I can't imagine I'll believe a word of it. You've been lying to me from the beginning, Cabe. Since before, well, anything." Her voice catches.

She looks away.

Withdraws her hand from his.

Stands up abruptly. "Bathroom?" she squeaks.

"Fuck," he mutters. "Through the kitchen, first door on the right."

She finds it, sobs silently over the sink for a moment, blows her nose, and sits on the edge of the tub until she gets it together again. Realizes she's already on this roller coaster, and sitting in the front car.

When she gets to the living room, he's ending a cell-phone call, saying "tomorrow" firmly, elbows on his knees and his head in his hands. He flips the phone off.

"Look," he says in a dull voice, not looking at her. "There's some shit I can't tell you. Not yet. Maybe not for a while. But I'll answer any question—any question I can right now. If I can't, and you don't like that, you are free to hate me forever. I won't bother you."

She is confused. "Okay," she says slowly. Decides to start with an easy one. "Who were you talking to, just now."

He closes his eyes. Groans. "Shay."

Janie stands in the doorway to the living room, tottering. Furious tears spring to her eyes. But when she speaks, her voice is deadly calm. "Jesus Christ, Cabe." She turns and grabs her backpack and walks firmly out the same way they entered the house.

Gets in her car.

She can't get out of the driveway.

She thinks about ramming his pimpmobile.

But that wouldn't be nice for Ethel.

"Goddamnit!" she screams, and puts her head on the steering wheel. She can't even drive through the yard without hurting Ethel, because of the stupid drainage ditch.

And then she hears the front door slam. He's running to move his car. He starts it up and pulls it into the grass next to hers so she can back out.

She doesn't know why she's waiting.

He's coming to her window.

She can still go now.

He taps.

She hesitates, and then rolls down the window an inch.

"I'm so sorry, Janie," he says.

He's bawling.

He goes back inside.

She sits in the driveway, freezing, for thirty-six minutes. Arguing with herself.

Because she thinks she's in love with him too. And there are two ways she can be a fool in love right now.

She chooses the harder one.

And knocks on the door.

He's on the phone again when he opens it. His eyes are rimmed in red. "I'll try," he says, and hangs up the phone. Stands there. Looking like shit.

"Let's try this again," Janie says, angry, hands on her hips. "Who were you talking to on the phone just now, Cabe?" Her words slice through the crisp air.

"My boss."

She's taken aback for a moment. "You mean your dealer? Your pimp?" The sarcasm rings in the dusky house.

He closes his eyes. "No."

She stands there. Uncertain.

He opens his eyes. Takes off his glasses and wipes his face with his sleeve. His voice has lost all hope. "Is there any chance," he says evenly, "that you'll come for a ride with me? My boss is interested in talking to you."

She blinks. She gets nervous. "Why?" she asks.

"I can't tell you. You'll have to trust me."

Janie takes a step back. The words ring familiar in her ears. She asked the same of him once.

She deliberates.

"I'll drive separately," she says quietly.

4:45 P.M.

She follows his car to downtown Fieldridge. He turns into a large parking lot that serves the back entrances to the library, post office, police station, Frank's Bar & Grille, the Fieldridge bakery, and a small fleet of high-rise apartments and condos. He drives into a parking space. She pulls in next to him.

He walks toward the line of buildings and, using a key, enters an unmarked door.

She follows him inside.

They go down a flight of stairs, and a room opens out in front of them, with a dozen partitioned offices and a separate office with a closed door.

Half a dozen people look up as they approach.

"Cabe." They nod, one at a time. He nods in response, and knocks lightly on the door to the office.

On the window, in black lettering, it says, "Captain Fran Komisky."

The door opens. A bronze-haired woman urges them to come in. Her hair is cropped short, and it frames her brown skin. She's wearing a black tailored skirt and jacket with a crisp white blouse. "Sit," she says.

They sit.

She sits behind her desk, which is littered with papers and has three phones and two computers resting on it.

The captain regards the two visitors for a moment. She rests her elbows on the desk, makes a tent with her fingers, and presses them against her mouth. Her eyes crinkle slightly with age.

She lowers her hands.

"So. Ms. Hannagan, is it? I'm Fran Komisky. Everybody calls me Captain." She leans over the desk and reaches for Janie's hand. Janie slips forward in her seat to shake it.

"Pleased to meet you, Captain," Janie says mechanically. She glances at Cabel. He's looking at his lap.

"Likewise," Captain says to Janie. "Cabe, you look

like hell. Shall we get this thing straightened out?"

"Yes, sir," Cabel says.

Janie looks up, wondering if Cabe means to call her that. It doesn't seem to bother the captain.

"Janie," she says in a tough voice. "Cabe here tells me he'd rather quit his job than lose you. Quite a young man he is, I must say. Anyway," she continues, "since that announcement affects me greatly, I've invited you here to discuss this little problem. And you need to know that I'd rather lose my left leg than lose Cabe at this stage of the game."

Janie swallows. Wonders what the hell is going on.

The captain looks at Cabe. "Cabe says you can be trusted with a secret. Is that true?"

Janie starts. "Yes, ma'am . . . sir," she says.

Captain smiles. Breaks the tension a bit.

"So. You're here because this dear boy has been lying to you, and I made him do it, and he's afraid you won't believe a word he says ever again. Ms. Hannagan, do you think you can believe me?"

Janie nods. What else can she do?

"Good. Somewhere I have a list of things I've jotted down, things I'm supposed to tell you, and I'll trust that if you have further questions, Cabel can answer them for you. And you'll believe him."

It sounds like an order.

Captain pages through the pile of papers and slips on half-glasses. Her phone rings, and she reaches automatically for a button, silencing it. "Here we are. First." She glances at Cabe, and then back at the paper. "Cabe is not 'involved' with Shay Wilder." She looks up, peering over her glasses. "I can't really prove that, Ms. Hannagan, but I've seen him nearly hurl after spending a recent evening with her. You good with that one?"

Janie nods. She feels like she's in somebody's weird dream.

"I said, are you good with that one?" Captain's voice booms.

"Yes, sir," Janie says. She sits up straighter in the chair.

"Good. Second. Cabe is not a drug dealer, pusher, liaison, user, and/or other in real life. He just plays one on TV." She pauses, but doesn't wait for a response this time.

"Third." She sits back, sets the paper on the desk, and taps a pen against her teeth. "We're this close"—she holds up her thumb and forefinger an inch apart—"to closing a major drug bust in North Fieldridge, up on the Hill. If this gets messed up because you whisper one word to anybody, and I mean anybody, I will hold you personally responsible, Ms. Hannagan. Besides Cabel and Principal Abernethy, you are the only one who knows about this. Are we clear?"

Janie nods, eyes wide. "Sir, yes, sir."

"Fine." Captain turns to Cabe. Her face softens. Slightly.

"Cabel," she says. "My dear boy. Are you with me or not? I need your head in the game. Now. Or this thing is shot to hell."

Cabel glances at Janie, and waits. She startles. He's leaving it up to her. She nods.

He sits up straight in his chair, looks Captain in the eye. "Yes, sir, I'm in the game."

Captain nods, and flashes an approving grin at both of them. "Good. Are we through here?"

Janie shifts uncomfortably.

And then she gives Cabel a haunting look.

"Fuck," she whispers, and digs her fingernails into the chair's armrests.

5:14 P.M.

Janie tumbles into a bank vault, where a black-haired cop sits on the floor, tied up. He wrestles with the ropes around his wrists and the gag in his mouth—

5:15 P.M.

She's back in the chair, next to Cabel, except Cabel is walking behind her, moving toward his chair again. The door is closed now. He sits down.

"Thanks," she whispers, and clears her throat. "Didn't see that one coming."

Captain is staring at her, eyes narrow. She looks from Janie to Cabel, back to Janie. She clears her throat. Loudly. Waiting.

Janie's face goes white.

Cabel's eyes go wide.

"Do you need medical assistance, Ms. Hannagan?" the captain finally says.

"No, sir. I'm fine, thank you."

"Cabe?"

"She's fine, sir."

Captain taps her pen on the desk, deliberating. She speaks slowly. "Is there anything else you two want to tell me about what just happened here?"

Cabel looks at Janie. "It's your call," he says quietly.

She hesitates.

Looks Captain in the eye.

"No, sir," she says. "Just . . . that . . . one of your officers is asleep at his desk and he's having a nasty dream. Looks like a bank robbery gone bad for the cops. He's tied up in a vault. Sir."

Captain's face doesn't change. She taps her lips with the pen now, and she's holding the wrong end. Blue ink leaves a tiny dotted trail under her nose.

"Which officer, Janie?" the captain asks slowly.

"I . . . I don't know his name. Short black hair. Early forties, maybe? Stocky. He was tied up with rope around his ankles and wrists, and had a white cloth gag around his mouth. Last I saw, anyway. Things change."

"Rabinowitz," Captain and Cabel say together.

"You want to double-check those facts for me, Cabe?"

"Sir, no offense, sir, but I don't need to. I think you might like to go question him yourself."

Captain tilts her head slightly, thinking. She pushes her chair back. "Don't go anywhere, you two," she says. She gives them both a strong, hard look before leaving. A look that says, "You better not fuck with me." When Captain opens the door and strides out, Janie grips the chair in anticipation. "Leave it open, Cabe," she gasps as she goes blind.

And she's back in the vault.

They're running out of air. The cop is struggling to get loose. He's trying to knock his cell phone out of his belt. Janie knows he wants to call his wife. She tries to get his attention. He looks into her eyes, and she concentrates on his pupils. *Ask me to help you,* she thinks as hard as she can think. Though she doesn't know how he will be able say it with the cloth stuffed in his mouth.

She hears a muffled plea and realizes it's good enough.

"Yes! That's it." She unwraps the gag, and realizes she spoke out loud. *Cool.* "Now." She stares into his eyes again. "This is your dream," she says. "You can change it. Get free."

He looks at her, his eyes wild.

"Get free," she encourages again.

He struggles and cries out.

And his arms and legs break free.

He lunges for his phone and calls 911. Closes his eyes, and the vault lock magically appears on the inside of the vault. A piece of paper floats down from nowhere with the information on how to open it.

He does it instantly.

And everything goes black.

5:19 P.M.

Janie's back with Cabel. He's touching her arm. "You okay, Hannagan?" He slips outside and returns, hands her a paper cup full of water, and she drinks it greedily.

She is shaking only slightly, from adrenaline more than anything. "I did it. I helped him," she says. "Oh, God, that was cool! My first time for a tough one like that." She grins.

Cabel is smiling wearily. "You'll have to explain that one later," he says. "If you're still speaking to me."

"Oh, Cabel. I . . ."

Captain comes back into the room and closes the door.

"Tell me what you saw, Ms. Hannagan. If you would, please. Rabinowitz says it's okay."

Janie blinks. She can't believe Captain is taking her seriously. She tells her everything she witnessed in the vault.

There is a long.

Long.

Pause.

"Hot damn," Captain says finally.

She tosses her half-glasses on the desk. "How'd you do that? You're . . . you're . . ."

She hesitates.

Continues, almost as if to herself, in a voice tinged with something. It might even be awe. "You're a regular Martha Stubin."

6:40 P.M.

Cabel and Janie are snarfing down grease-burgers and fries at Frank's Bar & Grille, next door to the police department. They sit at the counter on round red bar swivels, watching the cooks fry burgers five feet away. It's one of those old-fashioned places, where you can get a malted milk shake.

They eat with abandon, minds whirling.

8:04 P.M.

They are back at Cabel's house. Cabel shows her around the two rooms she hasn't seen: his bedroom and the computer room. He has two computers, three printers, a CB radio, and a police scanner.

"Unbelievable," she says looking around. "Wait—wait one second. . . . Do you live here alone?"

"I do now."

"How—"

"I'm nineteen. I was in the class ahead of you until ninth grade. You may remember."

Janie remembers him flunking into their class. "It was before I knew you," she remarks.

"My brother pops in now and then, just to see if I'm staying out of trouble. He and his wife live a few miles away. They moved out, thankfully, when I turned eighteen."

"Thankfully?"

"It's a really small house. Thin walls. Newlyweds."

"Ah. What about your parents?"

Cabel lounges on the couch. Janie sits in a chair

nearby. “My mom lives in Florida. Somewhere. I think.” He shrugs. “Dad raised us. Sort of. I guess my brother actually raised me.”

Janie curls up in her chair and watches him. He’s far away. She waits.

“Dad was in Vietnam, at the tail end. His mind was messed up.” Cabel looks at her. “When Mom left, he got mean. He pretty much beat the shit out of us. . . .” Cabel looks at the table. “He died. A few years ago. It’s cool. Yanno? I’m over it. Done.” Cabel gets up off the couch and stretches.

Janie stands up. “Take me back there,” she says.

“What?”

“Show me. The back of the shed.”

He bites his lip. “Okay . . .” He hesitates. “I haven’t, you know. Been back there in a while. It was—used to be—my hiding place.”

She nods. Gets her coat. Tosses his coat to him. They go out through the back door.

Crunch on the frosty grass.

Taste the air for snow.

When they get close, he slows down.

“You go ahead,” he says. He stops at the edge of a small, dormant garden.

Janie looks at him. She's afraid. "Okay," she says. The grass grows long and squeaks as she walks through it.

Janie slips away into the darkness and disappears from Cabel's view behind the shed. She stops and peers at the shed, getting her eyes accustomed to the darkness. She sees her spot, where she leans against it in the dreams, and stands there.

Looks to the left.

Waits for the monster.

But she knows now that the monster died with his dad.

She crawls to the corner, to view the place where he comes from.

She sees it, vividly.

Cabel, leaving the house. Slamming the door.

The man on the steps, yelling. Following.

The punch to Cabel's face.

The lighter fluid to his belly.

The fire and screaming.

The transformation.

And the monster, running toward her, with knives for fingers. Howling.

She's starting to freak out, in the darkness.

Sucks in a breath.

Needs, desperately needs, to hear it was just a dream.

He's sitting on the back step. Quiet.

She walks to him. Takes his hand. Leads him inside.

The house is dark. She fumbles for a lamp, and in its glow, they cast shadows on the far wall. She closes the curtains. Takes his coat, and hers, and hangs them over the chairs in the kitchen, and he stands there, watching her.

"Show me," she says. Her voice shakes a little.

"Show you what? I think you've seen it all." His laugh is hollow, unsettled. Trying to read her mind.

She reaches up, unbuttons his shirt, slowly. He takes in a sharp breath. Closes his eyes for a minute. Then opens them. "Janie," he says.

His button-down is on the floor.

She pulls the T-shirt up. Just a little. She watches his eyes. He pleads to her with them.

Janie slips her fingers under his T-shirt. Touches the warm skin at the sides of his waist. Feels his shallow breathing quicken. Draws her hands upward.

Feels the scars.

He draws in a staggering breath and turns his head to the side. His lip shadow quivers on the wall. His Adam's apple bobs below it. "Oh, Christ," he says. His voice breaks. And he is shaking.

She lifts the shirt, pulls it over his head.

The burn scars are bumpy like peanut brittle. They pepper his stomach and chest.

She touches them.

Traces them.

Kisses them.

And he's standing there. Weeping. His hair floating up with winter static. His eyelashes, like hopping spiders in the dim light. He can't take it.

He bends forward.

Curls over like a sow bug.

Protecting himself.

Dropping to the floor.

"Stop," he says. "Please. Just stop."

She does. She hands him his shirt.

He mops his face with it.

Slips it back on.

"Do you want me to leave?" she asks.

He shakes his head. "No," he says, and shudders in gripping sobs.

She sits next to him on the floor, leaning against the couch. Pulls him to her. He lays his head in her lap and curls up on the floor while she pets his hair. He grips her leg like a teddy bear.

11:13 P.M.

Janie wakes him gently, fingers through his hair. She walks with him to his bedroom. Lies down beside him in his bed, just for a few minutes. Puts his glasses on his bedside table. Holds him. Kisses his cheek.

And goes home.

BUSTING OUT ALL OVER

DECEMBER 6, 2005, 12:45 P.M.

She waits at his table in the library.

He meets her there.

"I have to work tonight," she whispers.

"After?" he asks.

"Yes. It'll be late."

"I'll leave the front door unlocked," he says.

She goes to her usual table.

And he designs a new dream, just for her.

6:48 P.M.

A man checks in at the front desk of Heather Home. He looks around, unfamiliar. She recognizes him, though he's tinged in gray now. Older. Lined.

"I'll show you," Janie says. She leads him to Mr. McVicker's room.

Knocks lightly on the door. Opens it.

Old Johnny McVicker turns toward the door.

Sees his son.

It's the first time in nearly twenty years.

The old man rises from his chair slowly.

Grabs hold of his walker.

His dinner tray and spoon clatters to the floor. But he doesn't notice. He's staring at his son.

Says, way too fast, "I was wrong, Edward. You were right. I'm sorry. I love you, son."

Edward stops in his tracks.

Takes off his hat. Scratches his head slowly.

Crumples the hat in his hands.

Janie closes the door and goes back to the desk.

11:08 P.M.

She parks her car at her house and sprints through the snow to his.

"I was wild," she says when she slips in the house. "You shoulda seen me with the bedpans."

He waited for her. And now he hugs her. Lifts her up. She laughs.

"Can you stay?" he asks. Begs.

"If I go home in the morning," she says. "Before school."

"Anything," he says.

Janie finishes up her homework, shoves it in her backpack, and finds him. He's sleeping. He's not wearing a shirt. She crawls into his bed and marvels silently at his stomach and chest. He breathes deeply. She settles in.

For now, anyway.

He knows she might have to go away.

Get away from his dreams, so she can sleep.

But when he dreams the fire dream, and meets her behind the shed, kisses and cries, begging for help, she reaches for his fingers in her blind, numb state and takes him with her into it, so he can watch himself.

She shows him how to change it.

It's your dream, she reminds him.

And she shows him how to turn the man on the step, the man who carries the lighter fluid and the cigarette, into the man on the step whose hands are empty, whose head is bowed. Who says, "I'm sorry."

When they both wake, the sun streams in the window.

It's 11:21 a.m. On a Wednesday.

They exclaim and laugh, loud and long. Because there's not one single parent between them who gives a damn.

Instead, they lounge on a giant beanbag in the computer room together, talking, listening to music.

They play truth or dare.

But it's all truth.

For both of them.

Janie: Why did you tell me you wanted to see me that first Sunday after Stratford, and then you didn't show?

Cabel: I knew I had to hit that party—I was going to come back early. I didn't know we were going to hold a fake bust. I got sent to jail overnight, just to make me look real. I was devastated. Captain let me out at six the next morning. That's when I left the note on Ethel.

Janie: Did you ever sell drugs?

Cabel: Yes. Pot. Ninth and tenth grade. I was, uh . . . rather troubled, back then.

Janie: Why did you stop?

Cabel: Got busted, and Captain made me a better deal.

Janie: So you've been a narc since then?

Cabel: I cringe at your terminology. Most narcs are young cops planted in schools to catch students. Captain had a different idea. She's not after the students, she's after the supplier. Who happens to be Shay's father. And she thought this was a good way to go—since he's starting to sell coke to kids at the parties. And implies he's got a gold mine somewhere. I've got to get him to say it on mic.

Janie: So you're a double agent?

Cabel: Sure. That sounds sexy.

Janie: You're sexy. Hey, Cabel?

Cabel: Yeah?

Janie: Did you really flunk ninth grade?

Cabel: No. (pause) I was in the hospital, most of that year.

Janie: (silence) And thus, the drugs.

Cabel: Yes . . . they helped with the pain. But then I got myself into a few, well, uh, situations. And Captain

stepped in my life at exactly the right moment before junior year, before I was too far in trouble. And it sounds weird, but she became sort of this army-type, no-nonsense mother I desperately needed. That was the Goth stage, where I decided I'd never get the girl of my dreams because of my scars. Not to mention the hairstyle.
(pause)
But then she slammed a door handle into my gut. And when a girl does that to a boy, it means she likes him.

Janie: (laughs)

Cabel: So that made me feel better. Because she didn't care what people thought if she spoke to me. Before I changed.
(pause)

Janie: (smiles) Why did you change it? Your look, I mean.

Cabel: Captain's orders. For the job. It's not my car, either, by the way. It's part of the image. I suppose I'll have to give it back after a while.
(pause)
Hey, Janie?

Janie: Yeah?

Cabel: What are you doing after high school?

Janie: (sighs) It's still up in the air, I guess. In two years, I've barely saved enough money for one semester at U of M . . . God, that's just crazy . . . so, unless I get a decent scholarship, it'll be community college.

Cabel: So you're staying around here?

Janie: Yeah . . . I, uh, I need to be close enough so I can keep an eye on my mother, you know? And . . . I think, with my little "problem," I'm going to have to live at home. Or I'll never get any sleep.

Cabel: Janie?

Janie: Yes?

Cabel: I'm going there. To U of M.

Janie: You are NOT.

Cabel: Criminal Justice. So I can keep my job here.

Janie: How do you know? Did you get an acceptance letter already? How can you afford it?

Cabel: Um, Janie?

Janie: Yesss, Cabel?

Cabel: I have another lie to confess.

Janie: Oh, dear. What is it?

Cabel: I do, actually, know what my GPA is.

Janie: And?

Cabel: And. I have a full-ride scholarship.

Cabel is pushed violently from the beanbag chair. And pounced upon. And told, repeatedly, what a bastard he is.

Janie is told that she will most certainly get a scholarship too, with her grades. Unless she plays hooky with drug dealers.

And then there is some kissing.

DECEMBER 10, 2005

The weekend is shot. Cabel is back to courting Shay, and Janie is working Friday night, and Saturday and Sunday first shifts at the nursing home.

But Carrie finds Janie. And Janie, worried that the drug bust will go down over the weekend, really doesn't want Carrie mixed up in it. She asks Carrie if she wants to study for exams sometime. They reluctantly agree on Saturday night at Janie's.

Carrie shows up around six p.m., and she's already loaded. Janie makes her haul out her books and notes, anyway. "Are you gonna go to college or not?" she asks sharply.

"Well, sure," Carrie says. "I guess. Unless Stu wants to get married."

"Does he?"

"I think so. Maybe. Sometime."

"Do you?" Janie asks, after a moment.

"Sure, why not. Get me away from my parents."

"Your parents aren't that bad, really. Are they?"

Carrie grimaces. "You should have seen them before."

"Before what?"

"Before we moved in next door to you."

Janie hesitates. Trying to decide if this is the right time to ask. "Hey, Carrie?"

"What."

"Who's Carson?"

Carrie stares at Janie. "What did you just say?"

"I said, who is Carson?"

Carrie's face grows alarmed. "How do you know about Carson?"

"I don't. Otherwise, I wouldn't need to ask." Janie is walking a thin line here. One she can't see.

Carrie, obviously troubled, paces around the kitchen. "But how did you know to ask me about him?"

"You said his name once," Janie says carefully, "in your sleep. I was just curious."

Carrie sloshes some vodka in a glass. Sits down. Starts to cry.

Oh, *shit*, Janie thinks.

And then Carrie spills the story.

"Carson . . . was four."

Janie's stomach twists.

"He drowned. We were camping by a lake . . . it was . . ." Carrie trails off and takes a swallow of her drink. "He was my little brother. I was ten. I was helping Mom and Dad set up the campsite."

Janie closes her burning eyes. "Oh, shit, Carrie."

"He wandered down to the lake—we didn't notice. And he fell off the dock. We tried . . . we tried . . ." Carrie puts her face in her hands. Takes a long, shuddering breath. "We moved here a year later." Her voice turns quiet. "To start over. We don't talk about him."

Janie puts her arm around Carrie and hugs her. Doesn't know what to say. "I'm so sorry."

Carrie nods, and then whispers in a broken voice, "I should have watched him better."

"Oh, honey," Janie whispers. She holds Carrie close for a moment, until Carrie gently pulls away.

"It's okay." Carrie sniffles.

Janie, feeling completely helpless, fetches a roll of toilet paper from the bathroom. "I don't have any tissues . . . Carrie? Why didn't you ever tell me?"

Carrie wrings her hands. Blows her nose. Sniffles. "I don't know, Janers. I thought it would go away. I was so tired . . . so tired of being sad. I couldn't stand any more silent, pitying looks."

"Does Stu know?"

Carrie shakes her head. "I should probably tell him."

They are quiet for a long time.

"I guess maybe," Janie murmurs after a while, "the bad stuff never goes away. And it's nobody's fault."

Carrie sucks in a shivery breath and lets it out slowly. "Ah, well. We'll see, huh?" She smiles through the tears.

"Thanks, Janers. You're a really good friend." She pauses, and adds in a soft voice, "Just keep being normal now, okay? One sad look and I'm outa here, I swear to God."

Janie grins. "You got it. Kiddo."

DECEMBER 11, 2005, 2:41 A.M.

When Carrie dreams, this time Janie knows what to do.

The forest, the river, the boy, drowning. Grinning.

Carrie, looking at Janie. Only a few minutes before the shark comes.

Carrie, crying out, "Help him! Save him!"

Janie concentrates, staring Carrie in the eyes. "Ask me, Carrie. Ask me."

He's bobbing and sinking, that eerie grin on his face.

"Help him!" she cries again to Janie.

Carrie! thinks Janie with all her might. *I can't help him. Ask me. Ask me to help . . . you.*

In the morning, Carrie remarks at breakfast, "I had the weirdest dream. It was one of these nightmares that I keep getting about Carson, but this time, it all changed and turned into this strange little . . . something. It was surreal."

"Yeah?" munched Janie. "Cool. Must be the feng shui over here or something."

"You think?"

"I dunno. Try rearranging your room, and then at night, tell yourself that you're going to change the nightmares from now on to work with your new harmonious surroundings."

Carrie gives her a suspicious look. "Are you yanking my chain?"

"Of course not."

DECEMBER 12, 2005, 5:16 P.M.

Janie drives home slowly after a long afternoon at Heather Home. With the holidays on the way, the aides try to fit in some decorating in the schedule, along with their regular duties. And Janie managed to help three residents find some peace in their dreams. It was a decent day.

On a whim, she drives past Cabel's house, and is surprised to see his car in the driveway. She slows and pulls into the drive, leaving Ethel running.

She sprints to the front door and knocks briskly.

The door opens, and Cabel gives her a look. "Hey, Janie, what's up?" He's making signals with his eyes when Shay comes up from behind him and peers over his shoulder. She wraps her arms around his waist possessively.

"Hey, Janie," says Shay, a look of triumph in her eyes.

Janie grins, thinking fast. "Oh, hi, Shay. Sorry to disturb. Cabel, I'm wondering if you have those math notes you said I could borrow for tomorrow's exam?"

Cabel's eyes flash a message of gratitude. "Yeah," he says. "Be right back. You want to come in?"

"Nah. My shoes are wet from the snow."

Cabel reappears and hands her a bunch of papers, rolled up and secured in a rubber band. "We're heading out to a party now," he says, "But I kind of need these back tonight, since the exam's in the morning. How late can I stop by to get them?"

Shay bobs over his shoulder, intent on seeing and being seen. Janie notices Cabel has slowly straightened his posture and is standing at full height, and Shay has to jump to see past him. Janie masks a laugh. "I'll be up late, but I can put them in the mailbox for you before I go to bed. Thanks, Cabel. Have fun at the party, you guys! I'm sooo jealous."

Janie trots back to Ethel and heads for home, only a little melancholy over the scene she has just witnessed. She brings the notes in, changes her clothes, and gets out her books.

She pages through the papers Cabel gave her, hoping he didn't give her anything important, since she didn't actually need his stuff. In the middle of the pile, a scribbled note:

I miss you like crazy.
Love, Cabe.

She smiles, missing him. Wanting this mess to be over. She thinks about how he was willing to quit the job, wreck the months of progress the detectives had made, just to get things right with her.

Captain is right. He's a good guy.

Janie studies past midnight, partly hoping Cabe will come over. By one a.m., she's nodding over her work. She calls it a night and gathers Cabe's notes to put them in the mailbox. In case he comes for them. In case Shay is with him, and he has to pretend.

She writes a note and slips it inside the papers, then rolls them up and sets them outside in the mailbox.

She's happy she can sleep in, but checks her alarm clock twice to make sure it's set. The first exam starts at 10:30 a.m. tomorrow.

And she needs to ace it.

So she can get a scholarship.

Because without that, U of M is just an uncatchable dream.

DECEMBER 13, 2005, 2:45 A.M.

When the phone rings, Janie jumps. She thinks it's the alarm clock for one confused moment, but by the fourth ring she's lunging for it.

Hoping it's Cabel.

Hoping he's standing outside, wanting to see her.

"Hello," she croaks, and clears the sleep from her voice.

She hears sniffling. "Janieeee," cries a voice.

"Who is this?"

"Janieee, it's me."

"Carrie? What's wrong? Where are you?"

"Oh fuck, Janie," Carrie mourns, "I'm so messed up."

"Where are you? Do you need a ride? Carrie, get it together, girl. Are you drunk?"

"My parents are gonna kill me."

Janie sighs.

Waits.

Listens to the sniffling.

"Carrie. Where are you."

"I'm in jail," she says finally, and the sobbing starts fresh.

"What? Right here in Fieldridge? What the hell did you do?"

"Can you just come get me?"

Janie sighs. "How much, Carrie?"

"Five hundred bennies," she says. "I'll pay you back.

Every cent. Plus interest. I promise, so much." She pauses. "Oh, and Janie?"

"Yessss?"

"Stu's here too." Janie can feel Carrie cringing through the phone.

Janie closes her eyes and runs her fingers through her hair. She sighs again. "I'll be there in thirty minutes. Stop crying."

Carrie gushes her thanks, and Janie cuts it short by hanging up.

Janie scrambles into her clothes and finds her stash of money that is waiting to be deposited into her college fund. She's twenty bucks short. "Shit," she mutters. She goes out of her room and runs into her mother, of all people.

"Was that the phone?" Her mother is bleary-eyed.

"Yeah . . ." Janie hesitates. "I gotta go get Carrie. She's in jail. Any chance . . . any chance you have twenty bucks to spare, Ma? I'll pay you back tomorrow."

Janie's mother looks at her. "Of course," she says. She goes into her room and comes out with a twenty. "You don't have to pay me back, honey."

If Janie had an extra hour to think about that little exchange, she might have come to the conclusion that there are one or two things more bizarre than falling into people's dreams.

3:28 A.M.

Janie climbs the steps to the front entrance of the police station and gets blown in through the door. It's snowing furiously. She looks around, and an officer waves her into the metal-detector area and through the security checkpoint. She recognizes him. It's Rabinowitz. She smiles, knowing he doesn't have a clue who she is.

"Through the doors. Cash or credit card payments only. No checks," he says, as if he's said it a billion times before.

Janie hears them before she pushes open the doors. There is a short line of sleepy-angry parents in front of her. Some of them are carrying on more pathetically than Carrie did on the phone. She peers around the corner and sees the bars of a holding cell.

She wonders if this is it. The bust. And then she sees Melinda, being escorted by a cop and her father. Her face is smudged in mascara and tears, and she looks terrible. Her father grabs her angrily by the arm and marches her out. Janie looks at the floor as Melinda goes past. She feels sorry for her.

The next three students she knows as well, and she can see their humiliation. Finally Janie is the last person standing at the desk. She sets one thousand dollars cash on the counter.

"Who you here for?" barks the guard.

"Carrie Brandt and Stu, ah . . ." She Googles her memory for his last name. "Gardner."

"I.D., please."

Janie pulls out her driver's license and hands it to the guard, who checks it closely.

He looks up at her for the first time.

"You're not eighteen."

Janie's stomach thuds. "No—not for another month," she says.

"Sorry, kid. Gotta be eighteen."

"But—" *Shit.*

The guard ignores her. She stands there. Thinking of all the things she knows but cannot reveal. She sighs and sits down in the chairs to think. She puts her head in her hands. Does she dare try to approach Rabinowitz, see if he'll vouch for her? But, no . . . Captain said not a word to anyone. That didn't exclude other cops.

"Can I at least go back there so she knows I tried?" Janie pleads.

The guard looks up. "You still here? All right, fine," he says. "Two minutes." Janie smiles gratefully and walks to the holding cell.

And she sees them. Sitting or lying on the benches.

Carrie and Stu. Huddled.

Shay Wilder and her brother. Looking extremely pissed, drunk, high, wasted, whatever.

Mr. Wilder. Looking fucked up in more ways than one.

And Cabe. Who is lounging on the bench like he lives there. And Shay, Janie notices gleefully, is as far away from Cabel as she can get.

She bites her lip.

Carrie rushes to the bars.

Janie looks at Carrie. "Honey," she whispers. "They won't let me. I'm not eighteen till next month. I'm working on it, though, okay? I promise. I'll figure something out, if I have to drag my own mother down here."

Carrie starts bawling. "Oh, it's so horrible being locked up in here," she whines.

Janie, who ran out of sympathy about a minute after the phone rang, just glares at Carrie. "Jeez, Carrie. Shut up already. Or I'm liable to leave you stranded."

"No!" chime the drunken voices of Shay, her brother, and Stu. Stu and Carrie start fighting.

Janie steals a glance at Cabel, who is watching her, the slyest of smiles on his face. He winks, and then nods, ever so slightly, in the direction of Mr. Wilder.

Janie looks.

He's leaning.

Falling.

Asleep.

She feels a rush of adrenaline. "I, uh, I gotta go back

up to the chairs, Carrie, but I'll get you out as soon as I can, okay?" Janie doesn't chance another look at Cabe.

She sits in the chairs nearest the holding cell, out of view of the guy at the front desk. She can just barely see Cabel's feet on the bench. His legs are crossed at the ankles. And she remembers him back when his jeans were too short, standing alone and greasy at the bus stop, less than two years ago.

She can hear Carrie and Stu arguing, and Shay and her brother raising their voices, telling her to get over herself and shut up—

And then she's whirling and blind, gripping the chair, hoping nobody walks by. She doesn't see Cabel stand up in the midst of the Carrie distraction and come to the edge of the cell bars, trying to catch her eye. Trying to tell her something.

She only sees what is in Mr. Wilder's hopes and fears. Or are they memories?

The dream intensifies and turns nightmarish. Janie is whipped around inside it.

Beaten, and blasted.

And she's trying to see everything. Everything. From the eyes and the mind of a criminal.

She doesn't see Cabel at all during that two-hour dream, pacing, burying his head in his hands. She doesn't see him watching her, horrified, as she's falling sideways off the chair, deadweight. Slamming her face on the corner of the coffee cart.

6:01 A.M.

Her head is pounding.

She's clammy. Cold.

Her face slides in blood on a cold tile floor.

She thinks her eyes are open, but her vision is taking a long time to return.

She can't move her body.

In the distance, she hears Cabel, calling her name, calling the guard.

Carrie is screaming.

For Janie, everything is black as night.

6:08 A.M.

Janie is being lifted onto a stretcher. She concentrates. Tries to wake up. Her head pounds.

They wheel her out into the hallway of the police station.

"Stop," she croaks.

Clears her voice, and says it again.

"Stop."

Two paramedics look down at her. She opens her eyes. Only one wants to. But she can see shadows.

"I'm fine," she says, and struggles to sit up. "I get seizures now and then. I'm fine. See?"

She holds her hands out to show them how fine she is.

And sees the blood.

Her eyes grow wide as she strains for her vision to return in full.

She feels her face. The blood is dripping, streaming, from her eyebrow onto her lashes.

"Aw, fuck," she says. "Listen, don't you just have some Steri-Strips? Seriously."

The paramedics look at each other, and back at her.

She tries a different tactic. "I don't have any insurance, guys. I can't afford this. Please."

One of the medics wavers. "It's Janie, right? Listen, you were in a complete spasm on the floor. Rigid. Unconscious. You smacked your head on the corner of a rusty metal coffee cart."

Janie wheedles them. "I'm up-to-date on my tetanus shot. Look, I've got a math exam in—soon, and my college future rides on it. I'm telling you, I'm refusing treatment. Now let me off of here."

Slowly, the paramedics back off so she can get down. She swings her heavy, unfeeling legs over the side of the stretcher just as Captain Komisky breezes through the security check.

"What the hell is going on down here?" she asks brightly. "Why, hello, Ms. Hannagan. Are you coming or going?"

Janie looks around on the stretcher and grabs a hunk of gauze, trying to find the source of the blood. "I'm working my way off this thing any second now," Janie mutters.

She takes a deep breath.

Hops off the edge.

Sticks the landing like ol' what's her name in the Olympics.

Captain is watching her, an amused look on her face. She offers Janie her arm. "Come, dear," she says. "Looks like you've been busy tonight." She waves the paramedics away with a sweeping gesture, and they go like lightning.

Janie smiles gratefully and holds the gauze to her eye. Her sweatshirt is stained with blood. She feels like she's wearing cement shoes, and her head feels like a balloon.

"I called on my way in, got the scoop," she explains when the paramedics are gone. "I wonder if we need to have a chat in my office?"

"I—sure. Um, what time is it?" Janie forgot to put her watch on when she left the house, and she's lost without it.

"Six fifteen, or thereabouts," Captain says. "I imagine Mr. Strumheller has had enough by now, don't you?"

Janie is having trouble concentrating. She knows she needs to eat. She gives a shaky laugh. "I suppose that's up to you, sir," she murmurs.

And then she remembers.

Carrie and Stu.

"Captain," she says nervously. "I came down here a few hours ago trying to spring my friend and her boyfriend. I've got the bail money, but I'm not eighteen until next month. Any chance you can—"

"Of course."

Janie sighs, relieved. "Thank you."

"Before we go in," Captain says, "let's remember that you don't know me. Right?"

"Yes, sir," she says.

"Good girl. Go get your friends."

6:30 A.M.

Carrie rushes out of the holding cell like it's filling up with poison gas. Stu follows. Carrie sees Janie covered with blood and nearly passes out, but both Stu and Janie ignore her dramatics.

"You guys are gonna have to walk. I'm sorry," Janie says firmly. "I have to fill out some dumb paperwork for an incident report or something." She points to her eye and makes like it's the last thing she wants to do. She shakes her head, pretending to be pissed. "Stupid cops."

Stu squeezes Janie's shoulder. "Thank you, Janie." He gives her a grateful look. "You're a good friend. To both of us."

Janie smiles, and Carrie looks abashed. "Thanks, Janers," she says.

"I'm glad you called me, Carrie," Janie says. *Now, go away.*

6:34 A.M.

Janie heads to the restroom, bloodying gauze pressed against her rapidly swelling eyebrow. She checks the mirror. The cut is beautiful in its own right. It lies just below her brow line, from the arch to where the brow tapers, and is straight and clean. One day, she might wish she'd gotten stitches. But as scars go, it's in a perfectly sexy spot.

She turns her sweatshirt inside out to hide the ridiculous amount of blood that oozed from the inch-long gash, and washes her face and hands. She takes a handful of brown paper towels, wets them, and puts the pressure back on it. Then she slurps water from the faucet.

6:47 A.M.

Janie leaves the restroom, and Cabel is there, pulling her into the cloakroom area. He looks tired. And relieved to see her.

"Let me see," he says.

She pulls the paper towels away and shows him her war wound.

"It's very impressive," he says, and then grows serious, his deep brown eyes betraying his concern. "When I saw you about to go down, I—" He stops and sighs. "I watched you. Most of that two hours, whenever I could pull it off without looking suspicious. It made me crazy that I couldn't get to you."

Janie, who is now shivering and getting very light-headed, just leans against him.

He strokes her back, rests his chin on her head. "You sure you're up for a chat with the boss?" he asks.

Janie nods against his chest.

"I'll get you something to eat just as soon as we get out of here, okay?"

She smiles. "Thanks, Cabe."

"Meet me at the back entrance, okay? You remember which door? We need to split up."

"Yeah, okay, good thinking," she murmurs. Cabel walks nonchalantly to a staircase and goes down. Janie heads out the front entrance and walks half a block through the blizzard to get around to the back of the shops and buildings. When she gets to the unmarked door, she's in a cold sweat. She knocks lightly. It opens, and she follows Cabel down the stairs.

The place is buzzing, and Cabel takes a few slaps on the back and swipes upside the head for his overnight work. "We're still not there yet," he says modestly.

He knocks on the captain's door, and she hollers, "Come." Cabel and Janie slip inside.

"You two have exams today, no? Do we have time for this right now?"

"Ten thirty, Captain. We've got plenty of time."

Captain looks at Janie closely. "Jesus, Mary, and Joseph," she says. "You're gonna have a heck of a shiner by the time the day's over. Did you black out?"

"I . . . uh . . ." Janie shrugs. "I really have no idea."

"Yes, I think she did." Cabel cuts in. "I'm going to need to watch her all day. And probably all night, too," he adds. Very, very seriously.

The captain throws a rubber eraser at him and sends him out for coffee. "And get this poor girl some rations, while you're at it, before she breaks in half." She opens her desk drawer and fishes around in it. Pulls out a first-aid kit and tosses a bag of airline peanuts on the desk as well. "Slide in over here, will you?" she says. Janie scoots her chair around the side of the desk.

"Jesus," Captain mutters again, and spreads a liberal amount of antibiotic cream over the cut. She rips open a package of Steri-Strips and neatly and quickly closes the cut. "That's better," she says. "If your mother and/or father have any questions about what happened to you, have them give me a call. I'd appreciate a heads-up if you think they're likely to sue." She slides the bag of peanuts across the desk to Janie. "Eat."

"Yes, sir," she says gratefully, ripping open the package. "You won't hear from anyone."

Cabel returns with three coffees, a small cup of milk,

and a bag full of muffins and doughnuts. He casually sets the milk and bran muffin in front of Janie and pours three creams and three sugars into her coffee.

She drinks the milk, her hand shaking, and feels the ice-cold goodness of it going all the way down. "Excellent," she says, and takes a deep breath.

"So," begins Captain. "You have a report for me, Cabel?"

"Yes, sir. We arrived at the party at nineteen-ten hours, marijuana already in progress, and by twenty-three-thirty, the coke was on the glass. Five minors and several adults snorted lines. Mr. Wilder took me aside, and we discussed our partnership, he being rather pleased at the turnout. He was semicoherent but stoned, and he told me he had a stash he was ready to quote 'put on the market'—his words. Apparently that was enough for Baker and Cobb, though I'm pissed we don't have the actual location of the stash. They arrived within three minutes and broke the place up, taking only those who were too stupid to go peacefully. And, of course, Mr. Wilder and his two children. Mrs. Wilder wasn't present. And I really don't think she's mixed up in it." He glances sideways at Janie and shrugs an apology. "Carrie was really toasted and put up a huge fight. Sorry about that."

Janie smiles. "Maybe the experience will knock some sense into her," she says.

"By two a.m., we were all in what I like to call my

little home away from home," Cabel continues. "Janie here came in to try to bail Carrie and her boyfriend out, and as luck would have it, Mr. Wilder was fucked up enough to fall asleep in the din. Janie settled in for the ride." He sits back, finished with his report.

Captain nods. "Good work, Cabe, as always." She turns to Janie. "Janie. A disclosure. You weren't hired by us, and we didn't ask you to help in this investigation. You have no obligation to share what happened before you creamed your face on our lovely piece of shit coffee cart, which I'm tossing in the Dumpster right after this meeting. But if you wish to, and you feel you have anything pertinent to add, I'd welcome it." She scribbles something on a notepad and puts it in her pocket, and then she continues. "Sounds like Cabe's a little perturbed that we don't have the location of the cake, and I personally would like to have that piece of information so we can go for the maximum sentence. Any chance you picked up something along those lines?" She chuckles quietly at her own pun. "Take your time, dear."

Janie, thinking more clearly now, runs through Mr. Wilder's nightmare in her head. She closes her eyes at one point and shakes her head, puzzled. Then looks up.

"This might sound silly, but do the Wilders own a yacht?"

"Yes," Cabel says slowly. "It's in storage someplace for the winter. Why?"

She is quiet for a long time. She doesn't quite trust her intuition enough to say it, even though she knows she has nothing to lose.

"Orange life jackets?" she says hesitantly.

Captain leans forward, intrigued, and her voice is less harsh than usual. "Don't be afraid to be wrong, Janie. A lead's a lead. Most of them turn out wrong, but no crime gets solved without 'em."

Janie nods. "I'll spare you the endless dream unless you want to hear it all. But the major part that sticks out to me, and kept repeating, is this:

"We're on a yacht, and it's sunny and beautiful on the ocean. What looks like a gorgeous tropical island is in the distance, and Mr. Wilder is heading for it. Mrs. Wilder is sunning herself on the deck of the yacht—at the front end, you know? And then suddenly, the weather turns cloudy and windy, and a storm hits, slamming into the boat, I mean hard, like a hurricane, with the wind . . ."

She pauses, closes her eyes, and she's in it. In a trance. "And Mr. Wilder is getting frantic, because every time he gets close to the shore of this island, one of those backward waves pushes us out farther. Like in that one movie, where Tom Hanks is that castaway dude on that island with his pet volleyball?"

Cabe chuckles. "I think it's called *Cast Away*, Hannagan."

"Yeah. Whatever. Meanwhile, Mrs. Wilder is still sitting on the deck, reading a book, oblivious to the storm. Weird, I know. He calls to her to get inside the cabin and get the life jackets out, but she can't hear him. And then the yacht starts spinning and slams into the reef, and we're all flying out into the water. The yacht is in smithereens, and all the stuff that was inside the cabin is floating around, being carried by waves.

"Mrs. Wilder is flailing and drowning in the water, and Mr. Wilder swims around picking things up out of the water. He sees his wife struggling, and he grabs life jackets—there are at least fifteen of them floating here and there, and he's got maybe eight or nine of them strung on his arms. He starts to swim toward her. . . ."

Janie closes her eyes and swallows. Her voice is shaking. "And I think, he's going to save her. . . ."

Cabel bites his lip.

Captain offers her a break.

She waves her hand, trying not to lose concentration, and continues.

"He starts to swim toward her with life jackets. But instead of saving her, he says . . . um . . . he says, 'You can rot in hell, you old bitch.' And then he swims past her, toward the shore, with all those life jackets." She takes a breath. "Like they are the most important thing in his life. And . . ."

She pauses.

Continues in an odd voice. "And the jackets, they aren't floating anymore—they're dragging in the water. Sinking. Pulling him down. Under. And he won't let go."

Janie opens her eyes and looks solemnly at Captain. "I think the packages you're looking for might just be sewn inside the life jackets, sir."

Captain is already dialing the phone trying to get a search warrant for the yacht.

Cabel's mouth hangs open.

Janie's head throbs. "Do you have any Excedrin?" she whispers.

10:30 A.M.

Janie and Cabel sit down for their math exam.

10:55 A.M.

Janie, parched, salty tears running silently down her cheeks, closes her blank blue book, stands up, turns it in, and walks out of the classroom, every eye in the room staring at her as she goes. Cabel scribbles a few more answers, waits a few minutes, and turns his in too. Initially, he looks in the parking lot for her and, seeing her car being slowly covered in the snowstorm, breathes a sigh of relief she's not out driving in this mess. He goes back inside the school and searches the rooms.

He finds her, finally, passed out on her table in the empty library.

Picks her up.

Takes her to the emergency room.

On the way, he calls Captain. Tells her what's going on. Suggests maybe now's not a good time for Janie to get stuck in the dreams of random hospital visitors.

When they arrive at the ER, they're ushered to a private room. Cabel grins. "I love this job," he murmurs.

Janie is dehydrated. That's all.

They give her an IV, and then Cabel takes her to his house. She sleeps a long time. He sleeps too, on the couch.

She blames it on the salty sea.

GLORY AND HOPE

DECEMBER 16, 2005, 4:30 P.M.

Cabel and Janie sit in Captain's office.

Captain comes in.

Closes the door.

Sits down behind her desk and takes a sip of coffee. Crosses her legs. Leans back in her chair and looks at the two teenagers.

"We got it," she says. She smiles, and then laughs like she won the lottery.

And shoves an envelope toward Janie.

Inside:

a contract

a scholarship offer

a paycheck

"Read it over. Let me know if you're interested," Captain says.

And pauses.

"Good work, Janie."

DECEMBER 25, 2005, 11:19 P.M.

Janie swipes the last bit of frosting from the cake at Heather Home, walks the rounds, says silent good-byes to the sleeping residents, and gives the director a grateful hug. She takes a red helium balloon from the cake table, turns, and walks out the door for the last time, slowly now, through the parking lot to Ethel.

Drives to her house, and sprints through the snow to his.

Opens the door.

Slips in.

He's waiting, in his sleep, for her.

She slides into the dark shadow against his body. She kisses his shoulder. He takes her hand. Strings his fingers through hers. Holds on tightly.

And they are off, through the link of fingers.

Watching themselves, together.

Catching his dreams.

FADE

For Matt, Kilian, and Kennedy

ACKNOWLEDGMENTS

Many thanks to:

My fabulous agent, Michael Bourret.

My incredible editor, Jennifer Klonsky.

Sammy Yuen and Mike Rosamilia, who create the Best. Covers. Ever.

Matt Schwartz for way too many things to mention.

Lila Haber and Kate Smyth for their tireless promotional efforts and for always being available. Also to Victor Iannone and the awesome sales team; to Rick Richter, Paul Crichton, Bethany Buck, Lucille Rettino, Kelly Stocks, Bess Brasswell, Mary McAveney, Matt Pantoliano, Emilia Rhodes, Jeannie Ng, and Molly McLeod.

Cassandra Clare, Chris Crutcher, Ally Carter, Richard Lewis, Lauren Baratz-Logsted, A. S. King, Melissa Walker, FanLib.com, and BookDivas.com.

All the awesome teen and adult reviewers and fans who plaster my books all over their websites and blogs.

My parents, siblings, in-laws, and outlaws for all the support.

Shout-outs to:

Alyssa, Jamie, Hannah, Kevin, Max, Casey, Chloe, Jack, and Lili

Eva Bethel at Primlicious.com.

Scott, Michelle, Danielle, Tyler, and Morgan Bloyer.

Lori Rourke, hairdresser to the stars.

Jade Corn and Cori Ashley at Phoenix Book Company, and to Faith Hochhalter and all of the book club ladies and gents.

Treehouse Books, Anderson's Bookshop, Changing Hands Bookstore, and Kepler's.

My invisible friends who rock: Juliana, Ashlea, Cassie, Nicole, Chelsea, Melissa, and James Booth, and all the peeps at that one place who have given me so much support—you know who you are.

Jill Morgan at Flat Rock High School.

And to Vickie, Sahrie, Tashia, Nikki, and Katherine, the first five MySpace friends I met on book tour. You guys rock!

A NEW YEAR

JANUARY 1, 2006, 1:31 A.M.

Janie sprints through the snowy yards from two streets away and slips quietly through the front door of her house.

And then.

Everything goes black.

She grips her head, cursing her mother under her breath as the whirling kaleidoscope of colors builds and throws her off balance. She bumps against the wall and holds on, and then slowly lowers herself blindly to the floor as her fingers go numb. The last thing she needs is to crack her head open. Again.

She's too tired to fight it right now. Too tired to pull herself out of it. Plants her cheek on the cold tile floor. Gathers her strength so she can try later, in case the dream doesn't end quickly.

Breathes.

Watches.

1:32 A.M.

It's the same old dream Janie's mother always has. The one where a much younger, much happier mother flies through a psychedelic tunnel of flashing, spinning, colored lights, holding hands with the hippie who looks like Jesus Christ. Their sunglasses reflect the dizzying stripes, making it even harder for Janie to stop the vertigo.

This dream always makes Janie sick to her stomach.

What's her stupid mother doing sleeping in the living room, anyway?

But Janie is curious. She tries to focus. She peers at the man in the dream as she floats alongside the oblivious pair. Janie's mother could see Janie, if only she looked. But she never does.

The man can't see her, of course. It's not his dream. Janie wishes she could get him to take off his sunglasses. She wants to see his face. Wonders if his eyes are brown like hers. She can never focus her attention in one place for long, though, with all the spinning colors.

Abruptly the dream changes.

Sours.

The hippie man fades, and Janie's mother stands in a line of people that stretches on for what seems like miles. Her shoulders curl over, worn, like thin pages in a well-read book.

Her face is grim, set. Angry.

She's holding—

jiggling—

a screaming, red-faced baby.

Not this again. Janie doesn't want to watch anymore—she hates this part. Hates it. She gathers all her strength and concentrates. Hard. Groans inwardly. And pulls herself out of her mother's dream.

Exhausted.

1:51 A.M.

Janie's vision slowly returns. She shivers in a cold sweat and flexes her aching fingers, grateful that she never seems to get sucked back into a dream once she's successfully pulled out of it. So far, anyway.

She pushes herself to her feet as her mother snores on the couch, and walks shakily to the bathroom, stomach churning. She gags and retches, then makes a halfhearted attempt at brushing her teeth. Once in her bedroom, Janie closes the door tightly behind her.

Falls to the bed, like a lump of dough.

After last month's ordeal with the drug bust, Janie knows she's got to get her strength back or the dreams will take over her life again.

That night, Janie's own dreams are blasted with churning oceans and hurricanes and life jackets that sink like stones.

11:44 A.M.

Janie wakes to sunlight streaming in. She's ravenous and dreaming about food now. Smelling it.

"Cabe?" she mumbles, eyes closed.

"Hey. I let myself in." He sits on the bed next to her, his fingers drawing her tangled hair away from her face. "Rough night, Hannagan? Or are you still catching up?"

"Mrrff." She rolls over. Sees the plate of eggs and toast, steam rising. Grins wide as the ocean and lunges for it. "You—best secret boyfriend ever."

ASSIGNMENTS AND SECRETS

JANUARY 2, 2006, 11:54 A.M.

It's the last day of winter break.

Janie and Cabel sit in Cabel's spare bedroom—his computer room—checking the school website for their exam grades.

It's a good thing Cabel has two laptops. Or there might be an all-out fight when the grades are posted at noon. But who are they kidding. They might have to roll around on the floor and wrestle, regardless.

Janie's nervous.

She turned in a blank blue book for the math exam after the drug bust went down a few weeks ago. She had a good excuse; there was still blood on her sweatshirt, after all. And the teacher gave her a second shot at it. Too bad it was on the day after a rough night of dream-hopping at Fieldridge High's annual all-night fundraiser danceathon. Also too bad—it was a lock in. No escape.

Janie and Cabe might have skipped the whole dance if they could have, but it wasn't possible. They were on assignment.

Undercover.

Captain's orders.

"We're looking for anybody who dreams about teachers, Janie," Captain had said. "Or any teachers who are dreaming about students."

Janie thought that sounded odd and intriguing. "Anything specific?" she'd asked.

"Not at this time," Captain said. "I'll fill you in more after the New Year, once we've got some things sorted out. For now, just take notes of anything teacher/student related."

For Janie, staying up all night isn't the problem. It's the dream-hopping that sucks the life out of her. And after spending six hours stuck in other people's dreams from her hidden location under the bleachers, she was completely spent.

Of course Cabel was there, at the dance, slipping Janie cartons of milk and PowerBars (she'd reluctantly switched from Snickers). The dreams were on the fertile side, to say the least.

Too bad she didn't pick up anything substantial. Nothing teacher/student related. Only student/student related, to Janie's chagrin.

And when Luke Drake, the Fieldridge High football team's star receiver, fell asleep on the gymnastics mats, already totally plastered when he arrived at the lock in, Janie cried, "Enough."

"Cabe," she gasped between dreams, "wake him the fuck up, and don't let him sleep again. I can't take it."

Luke tends to dream about himself, and it turns out he's a bit overconfident when naked. Cabel's seen Luke in the showers after PE "Luke's definitely overcompensating in his dreams," Cabel says when he hears Janie's description.

Cabe may or may not have had more success in his assignment that night. He's a relationship builder, so his work takes more time than Janie's to see results. He makes connections, builds trust, and has the uncanny ability to get people to admit the most amazing things while bugged. And Janie plays cleanup. At least that's how beautifully it went the first time.

Needless to say, Janie knows she didn't ace the second

math exam either. And today, the last day before going back for their final semester at Fieldridge High, Janie's stressed about her grades.

She doesn't need to be.

She has a terrific scholarship.

But she's funny like that.

At noon exactly, according to Cabel's police scanner, they log on from their respective computers and scan their pages.

Janie sighs. Under different circumstances, it would have been an A. Math's her best subject. Which makes it all the worse.

Cabel's sensitive. He doesn't react to his row of straight As. He feels responsible for Janie's face-first free-fall at the police station that landed her in the hospital during exam week.

They simultaneously close their screens.

Not that they're competitive.

They aren't.

Okay, they are.

Cabel glances sidelong at Janie.

She looks away.

He changes the subject. "Time to go see Captain," he says.

Janie checks her watch and nods. "See you there."

Janie slips out of Cabe's house and runs across the yards of two small residential streets to her house. Janie looks around, sees no one, so she peeks into her mother's bedroom. Her mother is there, passed out but alive, bottles strewn about as usual. She's not dreaming, thank goodness. Janie closes the bedroom door softly, grabs her car keys, and heads back outside in the cold to start up Ethel.

Ethel is Janie's 1977 Nova. She bought the car from Stu Gardner, who has been dating Janie's best friend, Carrie Brandt, for two years. Stu's a mechanic. He babied Ethel from the time he was thirteen years old, and Janie respects the tradition. The car roars to life. Janie pats the dashboard appreciatively. Ethel hums.

Cabel and Janie arrive separately at the police station. They park in different locations. They enter the building using different doors. And they don't meet again until Janie gets to Captain's office. It's important that nobody sees them together until the drug case with Shay Wilder's father is closed, or else their duties with this new assignment could be compromised.

It's because Janie and Cabel work undercover as narcs at Fieldridge High School. Janie's discovering there are a lot of weird things that happen at her school. More than she could have ever imagined.

Cabel's already sitting there with Captain when Janie walks in. He hands out cups of coffee for the three of them. He stirs Janie's with a stir stick after having prepared it just the way she likes it: three creams, three sugars.

She needs the calories.

Because of all the dreams.

She's finally getting some padding and muscle back on her bones, after the last big thing.

Janie sits before she's ordered to sit.

"Nice to see you, Hannagan. You look better than the last time I saw you," remarks Captain in a gruff voice.

"Glad to see you too, sir," Janie says to the woman, Captain Fran Komisky. "You don't look so bad yourself, if I may say so." She hides a smile.

Captain raises an eyebrow. "You two are going to piss me off today, I can just feel it," she says. She runs her fingers through her short bronze hair, and adjusts her skirt. "Anything to report, Strumheller?"

"Not really, sir," Cabel says to her. "Just the usual schmoozing. Making the rounds. Trying to get a better picture of what some of the teachers and students are like outside the classroom."

Captain turns to Janie. "Anything from the dreams, Hannagan?"

"Nothing useful," Janie says. She feels bad.

Captain nods. "As I expected. This is going to be a tough one."

"Sir, if I may ask . . . ," Janie begins.

"You want to know what's going on." Captain rises abruptly, closes the door to her office, and returns to her desk, a serious look on her face.

"Last March, our Crimebusters Underground Quick Cash school program received a phone call on the Fieldridge High School line. You've heard of that program, right? All the schools in the area participate. Each school has its own line, so Crimebusters knows which school the complaint is from."

Cabel nods. "Students can earn a reward—fifty bucks, I think—if they report a crime directly related to schools. That's how we were tipped off about the drug parties on the Hill, Janers."

Janie nods. She's heard of it too. Has the hotline-number magnet on her refrigerator like everybody else in Fieldridge. "Hey, fifty bucks is fifty bucks. It's a smart program."

Captain continues. "Anyway. The caller didn't actually

say much of anything. It's very distant sounding—almost as if she dialed but didn't put the phone to her mouth. It's only about a five-second call before the caller hangs up. Here's the recording of it. Tell me what you hear."

Captain presses a button on a machine behind her. Cabel and Janie strain to make out the garbled words. The voice sounds very far away and music pounds behind it.

Janie furrows her brow and leans forward. Cabel shakes his head, puzzled. "Could you play it again?"

"I'll play it a few more times. Concentrate on the background noise, too. There are other people talking in the distance." Captain plays the short message several times more. She slows the tape and speeds it up, then reduces the background noise. Finally she reduces the voice of the caller until only the background noise remains.

"Anything, either of you?" Captain asks.

"It's impossible to understand a single word the caller's saying," Cabel says. "Nobody's screaming, nobody sounds upset. I heard laughter in the background. The music sounds like Mos Def. Janie?"

"I hear a guy's voice in the background saying 'Mister' something."

Captain nods. "I hear that too, Janie. That's the only word I can make out in the entire call.

"We didn't think much of this call—didn't spend

time on it. There was no information, no complaint, no report of a crime. But then in November, there was another call to Crimebusters Underground. And when I heard this one, I remembered the call you just heard. Listen."

Captain plays the new call. It's a woman's slurred voice, giggling uncontrollably and saying, *"I want my Quick Cash! Fieldridge . . . High. Fucking teachers . . . fucking students. Omigod—this can't—oops!"* More giggles and then the call ends abruptly. Captain plays it for them a few times more.

"Wow," Janie says.

Captain looks from Janie to Cabel. "Anything jump out at you?"

Cabel squints. "Fucking teachers, fucking students? Is that a slam on Fieldridge teachers and students, or is it, you know, literal?"

"The music in the background is similar to the first recording," Janie says.

"Right, Janie. That's what made me think of the first call when this one came in. And yes, Cabe, we're taking it literally until, and unless, we're proven wrong. This call gave us enough information to do something with it. My hunch, from what little we have here, is that Fieldridge High may have a sexual predator hiding in their hallways."

"Can't you find out who made the calls and ask them what's going on?" Janie asks.

"Well, that would be breaking the law, Janie. The whole purpose of Crimebusters Underground is that the calls are anonymous, to protect the person reporting the crime, and they must remain that way. The callers are assigned a code name by which their individual tip is identified. Later, they can use that code name to check on the case and claim their reward if they have managed to give Crimebusters Underground a usable lead."

"That makes sense," Janie says sheepishly.

"What have you done so far, Captain?" Cabel asks. "And," he says more cautiously, "what are you hoping we can do?" His voice, for the first time, sounds edgy. Janie glances sidelong at him with mild surprise. She didn't expect to see him so uncomfortable about an assignment.

"We've done complete background checks on all the teachers. Everyone comes up squeaky clean. And now we're stuck. Cabe, Janie, this is why I had you at the all-nighter. I'm looking for any information you can give me about Fieldridge teachers who might be sexual predators in their spare time. Are you up for the challenge? This one could be a bit dangerous. Hannagan, chances are, the predator is male. If we can determine who we're after, we may need to use you as bait so we can nail him. Think about it and get back to me on how you feel about it.

If you don't want to do this assignment, you're off the hook. No pressure."

Cabel sits up, even more concerned. "Bait? You're going to put her out there for the creep to prey on?"

"Only if she wants to."

"No way," Cabel says. "Janie, no. It's too dangerous."

Janie blinks and glares at Cabel. "Mom? Is that you?" She laughs nervously, not enjoying the confrontation. "What do you mean it's too dangerous?"

Captain interjects. "We'll have your back at all times, Janie. Besides, we don't know what's going on yet. It may be nothing. I'm hoping you can get at least some of the information we need through dreams."

Cabel shakes his head at Janie. "I don't like this."

Janie raises an eyebrow. "Right. Only you are allowed to do something dangerous. Jeez, Cabe. It's really not your decision."

Cabel looks at Captain for help.

Captain pointedly ignores him and looks at Janie.

"I don't need to think about it, sir. Count me in," Janie says.

"Good."

Cabel frowns.

Captain spends the next thirty minutes coaching them on the art of obtaining information. It's a refresher course for Cabel, who's been a narc for a year now (although Janie knows better than to call him that) and was responsible for the most recent Fieldridge drug bust of Shay Wilder's father, who had a gold mine of cocaine hidden on his boat. It was Janie who figured out the location of the cake when Mr. Wilder fell asleep in jail. She and Cabel make a good team.

And Captain knows it.

It's why she puts up with their shit—now and then.

Captain reiterates the assignment and encourages the two seniors to keep plugging away. "If we are dealing with a sexual predator, we need to nail the bastard before he hurts another Fieldridge student."

"Yes, sir," Janie says.

Cabel folds his arms over his chest and shakes his head, defeated. Finally says, "Yes, sir."

Captain nods and rises from her chair. Instinctively Cabel and Janie rise too. The meeting is over. But before they leave the office, Captain says, "Janie? I need to speak with you alone. Cabe, you may go."

Cabe doesn't hesitate. He's gone, without so much as a glance at Janie. Janie can't help puzzling over why Cabel's acting like he is.

Captain walks to a file cabinet and pulls out several thick files.

Janie stands in silence. Watching.

Wondering.

Captain still scares her some.

Because Janie's pretty new at this.

Finally, Captain returns to the desk with the stack of files and loose papers. Puts them in a box. Sits down. Looks at Janie.

"New topic. This is classified," Captain says. "You get what that means?"

Janie nods.

"Not even Cabe, right? You understand?"

Janie nods somberly. "Yes, sir," she adds.

Captain studies Janie for a moment, and then shoves the stack of files and papers toward Janie. "The reports. Twenty-two years worth of reports and notes. Written by Martha Stubin."

Janie's eyes grow wide. Fill with tears, despite her attempt to hold them back.

"You knew her, didn't you," Captain says, almost accusingly. "Why didn't you mention it? You had to know I'd do a full background check on you."

Janie doesn't know the answer Captain wants to hear. She only knows her own reasons. She hesitates, but then speaks. "Miss Stubin is . . . was . . . the only person who understood this—this stupid dream curse, and I didn't even know it until after she died," she says. She looks down at her lap. "I'm so bummed that I didn't have a chance to talk to her about it. And now all I have of her is an occasional cameo when she decides to show up in someone's dream, to show me how to do things." Janie swallows the lump in her throat. "She hasn't been around lately."

Captain Komisky is rarely at a loss for words. But she's showing signs of it now.

Finally she says, "Martha never mentioned you. She was searching. Hard. For her replacement. There were others like her, years ago, but they are gone now too. She must have only discovered you recently."

Janie nods. "I fell into one of her dreams at the nursing home. She talked to me in her dream, but I didn't understand that it was different with her—that she was testing me, teaching me. Not until after she died."

Then Captain says, "I think the only reason she lived as long as she did was because she was determined to find the next catcher. You."

There is a moment of warmth in the room.

And then it is back to business.

Captain clears her throat loudly and says, "Well. I expect there's some interesting stuff in here. Some of it might be tough. Take a month or so to read through it.

And if you find anything you don't understand or are worried about, you'll come talk to me. Is that clear?"

Janie looks at her. She has no idea what to expect from the files. But she does know what Captain expects to hear. "Sir, yes, sir," she says. With a confidence she doesn't feel.

Captain straightens the papers on her desk, indicating that the meeting is over. Janie stands up abruptly and takes the stack of files. "Thank you, sir," Janie says, and heads out the door.

She doesn't see Captain Fran Komisky watching her go, thoughtfully tapping her chin with a pen, after Janie closes the door behind her.

Janie drives home, happy to see the few rays of sunshine forcing their way through the gray clouds on this cold January afternoon. But she's feeling an ominous presence emanating from the pile of materials Captain gave her, and an unsettled feeling about Cabel's strange reaction to the assignment. She stops at her house, makes quick eye contact with her mother, and dumps the literature on her bed.

She'll deal with it later.

But now, she's dying to spend her last vacation day with Cabel.

Before they have to go back to the real world of school.

And pretend they're not in love.

4:11 P.M.

Janie sprints through the yards, taking a different path to Cabel's this time. She can't be seen by anyone connected to her high school. But the good thing is that almost nobody who matters at Fieldridge High lives anywhere near the poor side of town.

Still, Janie doesn't leave her car at Cabel's. Just in case Shay Wilder drives by.

Because Shay's still hot for Cabe.

And Shay has no clue that Cabel busted her dad for drugs.

It's sort of funny.

But not really.

Janie comes in through the back door now, to be safe. She has a key. In case Cabel goes to bed before she can get there. But lately, since she quit her job at Heather Nursing Home, she has more time than ever to spend with Cabel.

They have an unusual relationship.

And when things are good, it's magic.

She closes the door behind her, taking off her shoes. Wonders where he is. Tiptoes around, in case he's grabbing a nap, but he's nowhere on the tiny main floor. Opens the door to the basement and sees the light is flicked on.

She pads down the stairs, and pauses on the bottom step, watching him. Admiring him.

She whips off her sweatshirt and tosses it on the step. Presses up against the metal support beam, stretching her arms, her back, her legs. Wanting to be strong and sexy, too. She lets her hair fall forward over her face as she concentrates on stretching.

He sees her and sets the weight bar in its cradle. Stands up. His muscles ripple under the spread of nubbly burn scars on his stomach and chest. He's narrow and gangly and muscular. Not beefy. Just right. And Janie's really happy that he doesn't seem uncomfortable without a shirt on in her presence anymore.

Janie has an urge to attack him right there on the weight bench. But after all they'd been through together in such a short time, neither of them wants to mess up the relationship on the sex end of things. And Cabel, conscious enough of his many burn scars, isn't quite ready to show off the ones below the belt. So Janie admires him from five feet away instead. And hopes he's gotten over his issues about Janie helping with this case.

"Your eyes are bright again," he says. "It's good to see you rested. And your scar is wicked sexy." He picks up his towel and wipes the sweat off his face, then rubs the towel over his honey-brown hair. A few damp strands travel down his neck. He walks up to her and moves her hair away from her face, getting a good look at the inch-long scar under her eyebrow that is now healing nicely. "God," he murmurs. "You're gorgeous." He plants a gentle kiss on her lips, and then he towels off his chest and back, and slips on his T-shirt.

Janie blinks. "Are you high?" She laughs, self-conscious. She's still not accustomed to attention, much less compliments.

He leans in and runs a finger lightly from her ear, across her jaw line, down her neck. Her heart pounds and she closes her eyes inadvertently, sucking in a breath. He takes advantage of her distraction and begins to nibble on her neck. He smells like Axe and fresh sweat, and it's making her crazy. She reaches for him. Pulls him close. Feels the heat from his skin blasting through his shirt.

It's the touching they both long for.

The holding.

Spent their whole lives, each without any. Figure it's time to make up for it.

Cabel hands her the weight bar.

"So . . . ," Janie says carefully. "You feeling better about me doing this, uh, bait thing?"

"Not really."

"Oh." She lowers the bar to her chest and presses upward.

"I don't want you doing it."

Janie concentrates and presses again. "Why? What's your problem?" she huffs.

"I just . . . don't like it. You could get hurt. Raped. My God . . ." he trails off. His jaw is set. "I can't let you do it. Say no."

Janie sets the bar in the cradle and sits up, her eyes flashing. "It's not your decision, Cabe."

Cabel sighs deeply and rakes his fingers through his hair. "Janie—"

"What? You think I can't handle the job? You can go out and mess with dangerous drug dealers and spend nights in jail, but I can't get involved in anything dangerous? What kind of a double standard is that?" She stands up and faces him.

Looks him in the eye.

His brown silky eyes plead back at hers. "This is different," he says weakly.

"Because you can't control it?"

Cabel sputters. "No—It's just—"

Janie grins. "You are so busted. Better get used to the idea. I'm in for the ride on this one."

Cabel looks at her a minute more. Closes his eyes and slowly hangs his head. Sighs. "I still don't like it. I can't stand the thought of any sicko teacher anywhere near you."

Janie wraps her arms around his neck. Rests her head against his shoulder. "I'll be careful," she whispers.

Cabel is silent.

He presses his lips into her hair and squeezes his eyes shut. "Why can't you just be the one safe thing in my life?" he whispers.

Janie pulls away and looks up at him.

Smiles sympathetically.

"Because safe equals boring, Cabe."

Janie spends almost an hour lifting weights. Three weeks, Cabel says, and she'll start to see the changes. All she knows is that her glutes are killing her.

6:19 P.M.

Janie and Cabel step on each other's feet in the small kitchen as they broil fish in the oven and fix a mountain of veggies. Cabel is a healthy eater. And he insists Janie eats that way too. Now that she's lost so much weight. Now that he realizes what she's in for, for the rest of her life. "It makes me crazy, seeing you so thin like that, you know," he murmurs as he checks the salmon. "And not in a good way."

At night, on the nights she stays over, he massages her aching fingers and toes before she drifts off to sleep. Falling into one nasty nightmare will do that to her—leave her fingers numb and aching for hours after. Cabel, having learned recently to control his dreams to some extent, has made dream control into a religion. He spends an hour a day in meditation, talking himself into calm, sweet dreams, working his way to his ideal—no dreams at all. At least when Janie's over. So he can keep her nearby. He's managed to prevent himself from dreaming one entire night now—with Janie as his witness. She woke up so refreshed, he hardly knew her.

That's another reason why this new assignment is putting him on edge. He knows the dreams will make this harder on her than on him.

Physically, anyway.

Mentally? Emotionally? It'll be harder on him.

Because this love thing is foreign to Cabel. And now that he has found Janie, he's becoming increasingly protective of her. There is no man in the universe he wants to have to share her with. Especially a creep.

Even if it unearths a scandal.

Of greatest proportions.

The biggest scandal Fieldridge High has ever seen.

10:49 P.M.

Janie stays over.

"Are we okay?" she asks softly.

After a silence, Cabel whispers, "We're okay."

He wraps his arms around her in bed, and they talk quietly, like usual.

Janie brings it up first. "So, spill it. All As, right?"

He squeezes her. Closes his eyes. "Yeah."

"I got a B+ in math," she finally says.

He's quiet. Not quite sure what she wants to hear. Maybe she just wants to say it and be done. Get it out there, so it can float away and not be so painful.

He waits a moment. And then murmurs, "I love you, Janie Hannagan. I can't get enough of you. I wake up in the morning and all I want to do is be with you." He props himself up on his elbow. "Do you have any idea how unusual, how important that is to me? Compared to some stupid test you took under extreme duress, twice?"

He said it.

It's the first time he said it out loud.

Janie swallows. Hard.

Understands what he means, completely.

Wants to tell him how she feels about him.

Problem is, Janie can't remember saying "I love you" to anyone. Ever.

She burrows closer into him. How could she have gone so many years without touching people? Hugs? Arms wrapped loosely in slumber, like a tired Christmas package whose ribbon hangs on, even until the last moment.

They confirm their plans for tomorrow under the covers. Opposite schedules unlike last semester, because they need to make a broader canvas through the school. All different teachers, too. This time Cabel set up his schedule with Principal Abernethy after Janie got hers, without Abernethy knowing why he picked the classes, teachers, and times that he chose. Principal Abernethy knows about Cabel's job. But he doesn't know about Janie's, and Captain wants to keep it that way.

Cabel agreed with the schedule setup, except for one thing. His only insistence with Captain was to have study hall at the same time as Janie. So he can cover for her, in case anybody ever sees what happens to her in there. Captain agreed.

Last semester, Janie and Cabel had identical schedules. Which Cabel insists was a fluke.

Janie doesn't believe him.

Or maybe she wants to believe that he found her on purpose. Even Janie can have her dreams.

They drift off to sleep. And when Cabel starts to dream, she startles awake, fights it off, and slides away from him, closes his door, and finishes her night's rest on the couch.

JANUARY 3, 2006, 6:50 A.M.

She wakes up to the smell of bacon and coffee. Her stomach growls, but it's normal hunger, not the famished, about-to-pass-out feeling she sometimes has after a night of falling into others' nightmares.

Janie doesn't want to open her eyes, and then he's there, on top of her and her blankets, kissing her ear. "Next time, kick me out of the bed," he whispers. The weight of him feels amazing on her body.

Maybe it's because she's numb so often.

Or because she was so numb inside, before she let him in.

She opens her eyes slowly. It takes her a moment to adjust to the bright kitchen light, shining in her eyes. "Can we rearrange the furniture this weekend?" she asks sleepily. "So when I sleep out here, you don't shine all of Satan's fiery hell lights in my eyes first thing in the morning?"

"Awww. Don't be grumpy. We're going into the best time of our lives. Be excited!"

He's joking.

Everyone who is heading to college knows that the best semester comes in four more years. Although this one will probably be easier.

Awake now, she shoves him off her, even though she'd rather lie like this all day. "Shower," she mumbles, shuffling off in that direction. Her muscles ache from working out. But it's a good ache.

When she emerges, breakfast is on the table.

She's finally gotten used to eating here, at this table. After Cabel's nightmare about the knives and all.

And then she has to go.

Back to her house to check on her mother and get her car.

She clings to him.

She doesn't understand why.

Except it makes her happy.

He kisses her.

She kisses him.

They kiss.

And then she goes.

Out the door, crunching through the crust on eighteen inches of Michigan snow. Runs into her house. Makes sure her mother has food in the fridge. And grabs money for lunch.

She and Cabel accidentally park near each other at school, which makes Ethel very happy, Janie thinks.

7:53 A.M.

Carrie whaps Janie on the back of the head. "Hey, *chica*," she says, her eyes dancing, as usual. "I've hardly seen you over the holiday break. You all better?"

Janie grins. "I'm good. Check out my cool-ass scar."

Carrie whistles, impressed.

"How's Stu? Did you have a good Christmas?"

"Well, after the whole jail experience, I was pretty bummed out for a few days, but hey, shit happens. We had our court thingy yesterday, and I did what you suggested. I got my charges dropped, but Stu had to pay a fine. No jail time, though. It was a good thing he didn't do any coke." She whispers this last bit.

"Good job." Janie grins. She knew Carrie's drug charges would be dropped. She just couldn't tell her that.

"Oh, that reminds me," Carrie continues. She digs around in her backpack and pulls out an envelope. "Here's your college money back," she says. "Thanks again, Janie. You were awesome to come out in the middle of the night to bail us out. So, what's the deal with your seizures, anyway? That really freaked me out."

Janie blinks. Carrie-speak is almost always at full-speed, and it changes direction often. Which is okay. Because Janie can usually dodge any questions she doesn't want to answer without Carrie noticing.

Carrie is a little self-centered.

And immature at times.

But she's the only girlfriend Janie's got, and they're both loyal as hell.

"Oh, you know." Janie yawns. "The doc's gotta run some tests and stuff. Made me take off work from the nursing home for a while. But if you ever see me do that again—have a seizure, I mean—don't worry. Just make sure I don't fall and crack open my skull on a rusty coffee cart next time, will you?"

Carrie shudders. "Gah, don't talk about it!" she says. "You're giving me the heebs. Hey, I heard Cabel's in some deep shit with the cops over this whole cocaine scandal. Have you seen him? I wonder if he's still in jail."

Janie's eyes widen. "No way! You think? Let me know what you find out from Melinda and Shay."

"Of course." Carrie grins.

Carrie loves a good scandal.

And Janie loves Carrie. Wishes she didn't have to keep secrets from her.

2:25 P.M.

Janie and Cabel have study hall last period in the school library. They don't sit together. Nobody looks sleepy. Things are going smoothly.

Janie, tucked away at her favorite table in the far back corner of the library, finishes a boring English lit assignment and then tackles her Chem. 2 homework. Her first impression of that class is positive. Only a few geeks take it—it's a college-credit course. But Janie, having satisfied all her required courses, is taking whatever she can to help her out in college. Advanced math, Spanish, Chemistry 2, and psychology. Psychology is a Captain requirement. "It's crucial to police work," she'd said. "Especially the kind of work you'll be doing."

A paper wad lands on Janie's page of homework and bounces to the ground. Janie picks it up while still reading her text book, and opens it up, pressing out the wrinkles.

4:00 p.m.?

That's what the note says.

Janie glances casually to the left, between two rows of bookshelves, and nods.

2:44 P.M.

Janie's chemistry book thumps to the table as everything goes dark.

She lays her head on her arms as she gets sucked into a dream.

For crap's sake! thinks Janie. It's Cabel's dream. It figures.

Janie goes along for the ride, although normally she tries to pull out of his dreams now that his nightmares have quieted. But, ever curious, she rides this one out, knowing the bell will ring soon, ending the school day.

Cabel is rummaging through his closet, methodically putting on shirts and sweaters over one another, layering more and more pieces until he can hardly move his blimplike body.

Janie doesn't know what to think. Feeling invasive, she pulls herself out of the dream.

When she can see again, she stacks her books into her backpack and waits, thoughtful, until the bell rings.

4:01 P.M.

Janie slips in the back door of Cabel's house, shakes the snow off her boots, and leaves them inside the heated wooden box next to the door. She folds her coat and sets it next to the boots, and heads to the basement.

"Hey," grunts Cabel from the bench press.

Janie grins. She stretches out her slightly aching muscles, picks up the ten-pound barbells, and begins with squats.

They work out in silence for forty-five minutes.

Both of them are mentally reviewing the day.

They'll talk about it—soon.

5:32 P.M.

Showered and settled at the small, round conference table in the computer room, Cabel pulls out a sheet of paper and a pen while Janie fires up the laptop.

"Here's what your profile sheets should look like," he says, sketching. "I e-mailed you the template."

Cabel points out the various columns, explaining in full as to what sort of information should be written in each one. Janie pulls up the template on her screen, squints and then frowns, and fills in the first one.

"Why are you squinting?"

"I'm not. I'm concentrating."

Cabel shrugs.

"Okay, so first hour is Miss Gardenia, Spanish, room 112, and the list of students. You want their real names or Spanish names?" Janie looks at him, deadpan.

He grins and pulls her hair.

She types quickly.

Like, ninety words a minute.

She uses all of her fingers, not just one from each hand.

Imagine that.

Cabel gawks. "Holy shit. Will you do mine for me?"

"Sure. But you'll have to dictate. Going back and forth between computer screen and handwritten notes gives me a headache. And it makes me very cranky."

"How did you . . . ?" He knows she doesn't own a computer.

"Nursing home," she says. "Files, files, files. Charts,

records, transcribing medical terms, prescriptions, all that."

"Wow."

"Why don't we do yours first. Then I'll have a better understanding of how to do mine."

Cabel flips through a spiral notebook. "Okay," he says. "I already scribbled some notes here, at school—No! Not the evil eyebrow! I'll decipher them and dictate, I promise."

Janie glances at his notes.

"What the . . . ," she says, and grabs the notebook.

Reads the page.

Looks at him.

"Mr. Green, Mrs. White, Miss Scarlet . . . Well, if it isn't Professor Plum. So where the hell is Colonel Mustard?" She bursts out laughing.

"Colonel Mustard is Principal Abernethy," he says with a sniff.

Janie stops laughing.

Sort of.

Actually, she giggles every few minutes as she reads. Especially when she finds out Miss Scarlet is actually Mr. Garcia, the industrial tech teacher.

"It's coded for secrecy, Janie." He's really not sounding amused. "In case I lose the notebook, or somebody looks over my shoulder."

Janie stops mocking him.

But he continues. "It's a smart idea. You should

code your notes too, if you take any. It only takes one stupid mistake to blow your cover. And then we're all screwed."

Janie waits.

Makes sure he's finished.

Then says, "You're right. I'm sorry, Cabe."

He looks mildly redeemed.

"All right then, moving on," he says. "First hour is advanced math. Mr. Stein. Room 134."

She plugs in the info, including the class list. "Anything of note?" she asks.

"In this space here," he says, pointing, "write, 'slight German accent, tendency to trip over words when excited, constantly fidgets with chalk.' The guy's a nervous wreck," Cabel explains.

"Next is Mrs. Pancake." They don't chuckle at the name, because they've known her for years now. "I have nothing of note on her. She's just that sweet, round grandma type—not the profile I expect we'll be after, but we don't rule anybody out, okay? I'll keep watching."

Janie nods and goes to the third page, fills in the appropriate information, and within thirty minutes, Cabel's charts are done for the day. She e-mails them to him.

"I'm going to finish my homework while you're working on your charts, if you don't mind," he says. "Let me know if you have any questions. And be sure to take notes of any intuition, funny feelings, suspicions—anything. There are no wrong things to track."

"Got it," Janie says. She clicks her fingers over the keyboard with finesse, and finishes her charts before Cabel gets his homework done. She goes back and lingers over each entry, trying to think of anything of note, and promises herself to be more discerning tomorrow.

"So," she says lightly when Cabel closes his books, "did you talk to Shay today?" Janie couldn't help noticing Shay was in three of his classes.

Cabel looks at her with a small smile. Knows what she's really asking. "The thought of being with Shay Wilder makes me want to gouge my eyes out with a butter knife," he says. He pulls Janie toward him in a half-hug. She rests her head on his shoulder, and he smoothes her hair. "Are you staying tonight?" He asks after a while. There's hope in his voice.

Janie thinks about the box of files from Captain on her bed.

She hates that they're sitting there, untouched. It's like homework hanging over her head. She can't stand it.

But.

She also hates the thought of leaving Cabel.

The question hangs in the air.

"I can't," she says finally. "I've got some things to do at home."

It's hard, somehow, to say good-bye tonight. They linger near the back door, forehead to forehead and curved like statues as their lips whisper and brush together.

9:17 P.M.

Janie comes home to a mess after getting stuck hiding in a stand of trees for fifteen minutes while Carrie shoveled snow off her car and left, probably off to Stu's apartment. Janie doesn't want any questions about where she was coming from. She knows the day will inevitably come where Carrie discovers Janie's car in the driveway but Janie not home.

Luckily, Stu and Carrie spend most of their time together. Carrie's parents like him all right. Even after Carrie broke down and told them she'd been arrested. They seemed relieved to hear that Stu wasn't into cocaine.

Of course, they still grounded Carrie. For life. As usual.

9:25 P.M.

Janie settles in her bed under the covers, and opens the box of material from Captain. She pulls out the first file, and dives into Miss Stubin's life.

News flash: Miss Stubin never taught school.

And she was married.

Janie's jaw hangs open for two hours. The frail, gnarled, blind, stick-thin, former school teacher who Janie read books to lived a secret life.

11:30 P.M.

Janie holds her aching head. Closes the file. Returns the stack to the cardboard box and hides it in her closet. Then she turns out her light and slips back under the covers.

Thinks about the military man in Miss Stubin's dream.

Miss Stubin, thinks Janie as a grin turns on her lips, *was a player back in the day.*

1:42 A.M.

Janie dreams in black and white.

She's walking down Center Street at dusk. The weather is cool and rainy. Janie's been here before, although she doesn't know what town she's in. She looks around excitedly at the corner by the dry goods store, but there is no young couple there, strolling arm in arm.

"I'm here, Janie," comes a soft voice from behind. "Come, sit with me."

Janie turns around and sees Miss Stubin seated in her wheelchair next to a park bench along the street.

"Miss Stubin?"

The blind old woman smiles. "Ah, good. Fran has given you my notes. I've been hoping for you."

Janie sits on the park bench, her heart thumping. She feels tears spring to her eyes and quickly blinks them away. "It's good to see you again, Miss Stubin." Janie slips her hand into Miss Stubin's gnarled fingers.

"Yes, there you are, indeed." Miss Stubin smiles. "Shall we get on with it, then?"

Janie's puzzled. "Get on with it?"

"If you are here, then you must have agreed to work with Captain Komisky, as I did."

"Does Captain know I'm having this dream?" Janie is confused.

Miss Stubin chuckles. "Of course not. You may tell her if you wish. Give her my fond regards. But I'm here to fulfill a promise to myself. To be available to you, just as the one who taught me remained with me until I was fully prepared, fully knowledgeable about what my purpose was in life. I'm here to help you as best as I can, until you no longer need me."

Janie's eyes grow wide. *No!* she thinks, but she doesn't say it. She hopes it takes a very long time before she no longer needs Miss Stubin.

"We'll meet here from time to time as you go through my case files. When you have questions about my notes, return here. I trust you know how to find me again?"

"You mean, direct myself to dream this again?"

Miss Stubin nods.

"Yes, I think I can do that. I'm sort of out of practice," Janie says sheepishly.

"I know you can, Janie." The old woman's curled fingers tighten slightly around Janie's hand. "Do you have an assignment from Captain?"

"Yes. We think there's a teacher who is a sexual predator at Fieldridge High."

Miss Stubin sighs. "Difficult. Be careful. And be creative—It may be tricky to find the right dreams to fall into. Keep up your strength. Be prepared for every opportunity to search out the truth. Dreams happen in the strangest places. Watch for them."

"I—I will," Janie says softly.

Miss Stubin cocks her head to the side. "I must go now." She smiles and fades away, leaving Janie alone on the bench.

2:27 A.M.

Janie's eyes flutter and open. She stares at the ceiling in the dark, and then flips on her bedside lamp. Scribbles the dream in her notebook. *Wow*, she thinks. *Cool.*

Grins sleepily as she turns out the light and rolls over, back to sleep.

POINTED VIEWS

JANUARY 6, 2006, 2:10 P.M.

Janie codes her notes now, too:

Bashful=Spanish, Miss Gardenia
Doc=Psychology, Mr. Wang
Happy=Chemistry 2, Mr. Durbin
Dopey=English Lit., Mr. Purcell
Dippy=Math, Mrs. Craig
Dumbass=PE, Coach Crater

And, of course, Sleepy=Study hall

There's definitely something sleepy about Michigan in its darkest months of January and February.

Study hall is a disaster. And after relatively few incidents, besides Cabel's dreams, over the past few weeks, Janie's feeling the pull harder than ever.

She needs to practice concentrating at home, in her own dreams again. Stay strong, like Miss Stubin told her in the dream. Or else she's going down.

2:17 P.M.

Janie feels it coming. She sets her book down and glances at Cabel. It's not him. He gives her a pitying half-smile when he sees the look on her face, and she tries to smile back. But it's too late.

It hits her, like a bag of rocks to the gut, and she doubles over in her chair, blinded, her mind whirling into Stacey O'Grady's dream. Janie recognizes it—Stacey was in Janie's study hall last semester too, and had this same nightmare a few months ago.

Janie is in Stacey's car, and Stacey is driving like a maniac down a dark street near the woods. From the backseat, a growl, and then a man appears and grabs Stacey around the neck from behind. Stacey's choking. She loses control of the car, and it careens over a ditch, smashes into a line of bushes, and flips over.

The man is shaken loose of his grasp, and when the car comes to rest in a parking lot, Stacey, bleeding, climbs out of the car through the broken windshield and starts running. He gets out and follows her. It's a mad chase, and Janie is swept into it. She can't concentrate hard enough to get Stacey's attention, and Stacey is screaming at the top of her lungs. Around and around the parking lot, the man chases her, until she runs for the woods . . .

. . . trips

. . . falls

. . . and he is on top of her, pinning her down, growling, like a dog, in her face—

2:50 P.M.

Janie feels her muscles still twitching three minutes after it's over. She didn't hear the bell ring, but Stacey did, apparently, because the dream stopped abruptly.

Janie still can't feel anything. She can't see. But she can hear Cabel next to her. "It's okay, baby," he whispers. "It's gonna be okay."

2:57 P.M.

Cabel's gently rubbing her fingers. He's still whispering, letting her know no one is around, they've all left, and it's all going to be okay.

She sits up slowly.

Squeezes her hands till they ache with pain and pleasure. Wiggles her toes. Her face feels like she's been to the dentist for a filling.

He's rubbing her shoulders, her arms, her temples. She stops shaking. Tries to speak. It comes out like a hiss.

3:01 P.M.

"Cabel," she finally says.

"You ready to try to move?" His voice is concerned.

She shakes her head slowly. Turns toward him. Reaches out. "I can't see yet," she says quietly. "How long has it been?"

Cabel moves his hands over her shoulders and back down to her fingers. "Not that long," he says softly. "A few minutes." *More like twelve.*

"That was a bad one."

"Yeah. Did you try to pull out of it?"

Janie rests her forehead on the heel of her hand and rolls her head slowly, side to side. Her voice is weak. "I didn't try to get out. I tried to help her change it. Couldn't get her to pay any attention to me."

Cabel paces.

They wait.

Slowly Janie can make out shapes. The world fades back in. "Phew," she says. Smiles shakily.

"I'm driving you home," Cabel says as the janitor

comes into the library, eyeing them suspiciously. Cabel shoves Janie's books into her backpack, a grim look on his face. He searches around in the pack and comes up empty-handed. "Don't you carry anything with you? I'm out of PowerBars."

"Um . . ." Janie bites her lip. "I'm okay now. I'll be fine. I can drive."

He scowls. Doesn't respond. Helps her stand up, slings her backpack over his shoulder, and they walk out to the parking lot. It's lightly snowing.

He opens the passenger-side door of his car and looks at her, his jaw set.

Patient.

Waiting.

Until she gets in.

He drives in silence through the snow to a nearby mini-mart, goes in, and returns with pint of milk and a plastic bag. "Open your backpack," he says.

She does it.

He pours half a dozen PowerBars into it. Opens a bar and hands it to her with the milk. "I'll get your car later," he says, holding his hand out for her keys. She looks down. Then hands them over.

He drives her to her house.

Stares at the steering wheel, his jaw set.

Waits for her to get out.

She glances at him, a puzzled expression on her face. "Oh," she says finally. She swallows the lump in her throat. Takes her backpack and the milk and gets out of the car. Closes the door. Goes up the steps and kicks the snow off her shoes. Not looking back.

He pulls out of the driveway slowly, making sure Janie gets inside okay. And drives away.

Janie goes to bed, confused and sad, and takes a nap.

8:36 P.M.

She's awake. Starving. Looks around the house for something healthy and finds a tomato, growing soft in the refrigerator. There's a tuft of mold on the stem. She sighs. There's nothing else. She shrugs on her coat and slips on her boots, grabs fifty dollars from the grocery envelope, and starts walking.

The snow is beautiful. Flakes so tiny they sparkle, sequins in the oncoming headlights and under street lamps. It's cold, maybe twenty degrees out. Janie slips on her mittens and secures her coat at her throat. Glad she wore boots.

When she reaches the grocery store a mile away, it's quiet inside. A few shoppers stroll to the Muzak piping from the speakers. The store is bright with yellowy light, and Janie squints as she enters. She grabs a cart and heads to the produce section, shaking the snowflakes from her hair as she walks. She loosens her coat and tucks her mittens in her pockets.

Shopping, once Janie actually gets there, is relaxing to her. She takes her time, reading labels, thinking about things that seem like they might taste good together, picking out the best vegetables, mentally calculating the total cost as she goes along. It's like therapy. By the time she's spent her approximate allotment, she slips through the baking aisle to get to the checkout. As she meanders, looking at the different kinds of oils and spices, she slows her cart.

Glances to the left.

Recalculates what's in her cart.

And hesitantly picks out a red box and a small round container. Puts them in the cart next to the eggs and milk.

She wheels to the front of the store and stands in a short line at the one lonely check-out counter. Janie glances at the periodicals while she waits. Rides through a wave of hunger nausea. Loads her things onto the belt and watches the scanner anxiously as the number creeps upward.

"Your total comes to fifty-two twelve."

Janie closes her eyes for a moment. "I'm sorry," she says. "I have exactly fifty dollars. I need to put something back."

The checker sighs. The line behind Janie grows. She flushes and doesn't look at any of them. Decides what's necessary.

Hesitantly picks out the cake mix and the frosting.

Hands them to the checker. "Take these off, please," she says quietly. *It figures*, she thinks.

The checker makes like this is huge deal. Stomps on the buttons with her fingers.

People thaw, drip, and shift on their feet behind Janie.

She ignores them.

Sweating profusely.

"48.01," the checker finally announces. She counts out the $1.99 in change like it's breaking her back to lift so many coins at once.

Janie strings the pregnant bags over her arms, three on each side, and flees. Sucks in the cold fresh air. Pumps her arms once she reaches the road to get in her workout for the day, trying not to crush the eggs and bread. Her arms ache pleasantly at first. Then they just plain ache.

After a quarter mile a car slows and comes to a stop in front of Janie. A man gets out. "Ms. Hannagan, isn't it?" he says. It's Happy. Also known as Mr. Durbin, her Chem. 2 teacher. "You need a ride? I was a few customers behind you in line."

"I'm . . . I'm okay. I like the walk," she says.

"You sure?" He flashes a skeptical smile. "How far are you going?"

"Just, you know. Up the hill a ways." Janie gestures with a nod of her head up the snowy road that disappears into the darkness beyond Mr. Durbin's headlights. "It's not that far."

"It's really no trouble. Get in." Mr. Durbin stands there, waiting, arm draped over the top of the open car door, like he won't take no for an answer. Which makes Janie's skin prickle. But . . . maybe she should take the chance to get to know Mr. Durbin a little better, for investigation purposes.

"Well . . ." Janie's starting to get shaky with hunger. "Thanks," she says, opening the passenger-side door. He slips back inside the car and moves four or five plastic grocery bags to the backseat, and she gets in. "Straight ahead, right on Butternut. Sorry," she adds. She's not sure why. For the inconvenience, maybe.

"Seriously, no problem. I live just across the viaduct on Sinclair," he says. "It's right on my way." The blast of the car heater fills the silence. "So, how do you like the class? I was happy to see so many students. Ten is big for this one."

"I like it," she says. It's Janie's favorite class, actually. But there's no need for him to know that. "I like the small size," she adds, after more silence, "because we each get our own lab station. In Chem. 1, we were always doubled up."

"Yep," he says. "Did you have Mrs. Beecher for Chem. 1?"

Janie nods. "Yeah."

Mr. Durbin pulls into the driveway when she points it out, and looks puzzled to see Janie's car standing there, looking like it's just been driven. There's no snow built up on it, and steam rises off the hood. "So, you prefer to walk on a frigid night like this and lug all that junk home through the snow?" He laughs.

She grins. "I wasn't sure I'd have ol' Ethel back tonight. Looks like she's here now." She doesn't explain further. He puts the car in park and opens his door. "Can I give you a hand?"

The bags, once she got into the car, had slipped every which way, and are now a tangled mess. "You don't need to do that, Mr. Durbin."

He hops out and hurries to her side of the car. "Please," he says. He gathers three bags and scoots out of her way, then follows her to the door.

Janie hesitates, knocking the snow off her boots, adjusting her bags, so she can open the door. Notices things about her house that she overlooks most days. Screen door with a rip in it and hanging a little bit loose on its hinges. Wood exterior rotting at the base, paint peeling from it.

Awkward, Janie thinks, going inside, Durbin at her heels. She flips on the entrance light and is momentarily blinded by the brightness. She stops in her tracks until she can see again, and Mr. Durbin bumps into her.

"Excuse me," he says, sounding embarrassed.

"My fault," she says, feeling a little creeped out by having him in the house. She's on her guard. Who knows? It could be him they're after.

They turn the corner into the shadowy kitchen. She puts her bags on the counter, and he sets his next to hers.

"Thank you."

He smiles. "No problem. See you Monday." He waves and heads back outside.

Monday. Janie's eighteenth birthday.

She rummages through the bags on a mission. Grabs a handful of grapes, rinses them off quickly, and shoves them in her mouth, craving the fructose rush. She starts to put things away when she hears a step behind her.

She whirls around. "Jesus, Cabe. You scared the crap out of me."

He dangles her car keys. "I let myself in. Thought you'd be here. Heard an extra voice, so I hid in your room. So, who was that?" he asks. He's trying to sound nonchalant. Failing miserably.

"Are you jealous?" Janie teases.

"Who. Was. It." He's enunciating.

She raises her eyebrow. "Mr. Durbin. He saw me walking home and asked if I wanted a ride. He was in line behind me at the store."

"That's Durbin?"

"Yes. It was very nice of him, I thought." Janie's gut thinks otherwise, but she's not feeling like having a work discussion with Cabel right now.

"He's . . . young. What's he doing, picking up students? That's odd."

Janie waits to see what his point is. But there doesn't seem to be one. Still, she makes a mental note to record this incident in her case notebook—can't be too cautious. Janie turns and continues to put things away. She's still confused over how quiet Cabel was earlier. Doesn't say anything.

"I didn't know where you were," he says finally.

"Well, if I knew you were coming, I would have left a note. However," she continues coolly, "I was under the impression that you were pissed at me. So I didn't expect I'd see you." She's visibly shaking by now, and grabs the milk, rips open the cap, and chugs from the bottle. She sets it down and looks for something that won't take long to prepare. She grabs a few more grapes and snarfs them.

He's watching her. There's a look in his eye, and she doesn't understand it.

"Thanks for bringing my car. I really appreciate it. Did you walk all the way back to school?"

"No. *My* brother Charlie gave me a lift."

"Well, thank him for me."

She's got the peanut butter open now, and globs it on to a piece of bread. She pours some of the milk into a tall glass, grabs the sandwich, and slips past Cabel into the living room. Flips on the TV and squints at it. "You want a sandwich or something?" she asks. "Would you like to stay?" She doesn't know what else to say. He's just looking at her.

Finally he pulls a piece of paper from his jacket pocket. Unfolds it. Turns off the TV. "Humor me for a minute," he says.

He stands directly in front of her, then turns and walks fifteen paces in the opposite direction. Stops and turns to face her again.

"What the hell are you doing?"

"Read this. Out loud, please."

It's an eye chart.

"Dude, I'm totally trying to eat, here."

"Read. Please."

She sighs and looks at the chart.

"*E*," she says. And smirks.

He's not laughing.

She reads the next line.

And the one after that. Squinting. And guessing.

"Cover your right eye and do it again," he says.

She does it.

"Now cover your left."

"Grrr," she says. But does it.

By memory.

All she can make out with her right eye is the *E*. She doesn't say anything. Just says the letters she remembers from before.

And then he takes a second, different chart out.

"Do that eye again," he says.

"What is the deal with you?" she almost yells. "Jeez, Cabel. I'm not your little kid or something."

"Can you read it or not?"

"*N*," she says.

"Is that as much as you can read?"

"Yeah."

"Okay." He bites his lip. "Excuse me for a minute, will you?"

"Whatever," she says. So she needs glasses—maybe. Big deal. Cabel disappears into her bedroom, and she hears him pacing over the creak in the floor and talking to himself.

Janie eats her sandwich and downs the glass of milk. Goes into the kitchen and makes another. Grabs a carrot and peels it over the garbage can. Pours another glass of milk.

Takes her feast to the living room again and sits down. Turns the TV back on. She's feeling much better. Her hands have stopped shaking. She swallows the last drops of milk and feels it sloshing around in her belly. She smiles, contented. Thinks she ought to be the poster girl for the Got Milk? ads.

10:59 P.M.

Janie pulls herself out of her post-dinner stupor and wonders what Cabel's doing in her room all this time. She gets up and heads down the short hallway, pushes the door open, and gets sucked into darkness immediately.

She staggers.

Drops to the floor.

Cabel's frantic, trying to lock a door. Each time he locks it, another lock appears. As he secures each new one, the others spring open. He can't keep up.

Janie reaches for the door, blindly.

Backs out of her room on her hands and knees, pulling the door shut with her.

And the connection is broken.

She blinks, seeing stars, and gets back to her feet. Pulls a ratty old blanket from the closet and settles on the couch, sighing. She can't even sleep in her own bed these days.

JANUARY 7, 2006, 6:54 A.M.

Janie is startled awake. She looks around as a cold blast of air washes over the living room. She sits up and goes to the kitchen, looking out the window. Fresh footprints in the snow lead down the drive, across the street, and into the yard on the other side.

She checks her bedroom.

He's gone.

She shakes her head. *What a jerk*, she thinks.

Then she finds his note.

J.,
Shit, I'm such a jerk. I'm sorry-you should have smacked me awake. I've got some things to do today, but will you call me? Please?
Love,
Cabe

There's something about a guy who admits he's a jerk that makes him forgivable.

Janie climbs into her bed. Her pillow smells like him. She smiles. Hugs it.

Talks to herself.

"I would like to dream about Center Street and I

would like to talk to Miss Stubin again," she says over and over as she drifts off to sleep.

7:20 A.M.

Janie rolls over and rouses herself. Looks at the clock. Sighs. She's rusty at it. Repeats her mantra. Pictures the scene in her head.

8:04 A.M.

She's standing on Center Street. It's dark, cool, and rainy again.

Looks around.

No one is there.

Janie wanders up and down the street, looking for Miss Stubin, but the street is vacant. Janie sits on the bench where she sat before.

Waits.

Wonders.

Recalls the previous conversation.

"When you have questions about my notes, return here," Miss Stubin had said.

Janie slaps her hand to her forehead and the dream fades.

When Janie wakes, she vows to practice directing and controlling her dreams every night. It will help. She knows it will.

She also vows to keep reading Miss Stubin's notes, so she can come up with some questions.

10:36 A.M.

Janie munches on toast as she pulls out the box of files from Captain. She begins where she left off, and reads the reports, fascinated.

4:14 P.M.

She finishes the second file. Still sitting on her bed in her pajamas. Remains of snacks everywhere. The phone rings, and with a gasp she remembers Cabel's note from this morning. "Hello?"

"Hey."

"Shit."

He laughs. "Can I come over?"

"I'm totally still sitting here in my pajamas. Give me thirty minutes."

"You got it."

"Hey, Cabe?"

"Yes?"

"Why are you mad at me?"

He sighs. "I'm not mad at you. I promise. I just . . . I worry about you. Can we talk about this when I come over?"

"Sure."

"See you soon."

4:59 P.M.

Janie hears a light knock and the door opening. She peeks her head around the corner, and to her great surprise, it's Carrie.

"Hi, it's me, your fair-weather friend!" Carrie grins sheepishly.

Shit, Janie thinks.

She grabs her coat and puts on a smile. "Hey, girl," she says. "I was just going out to shovel. Care to join me?"

"Uh . . . I guess."

"What's up?"

"Nothin'. Just bored."

"Where's Stu?"

"Poker night."

"Ahhh. Does he do that regularly?"

"Not really. Just whenever the guys call him."

"Mmmm." Janie grabs the shovel and starts clearing the steps first, then the sidewalk. She keeps her face turned toward the direction she thinks Cabel will come from. It's growing dark, and she hopes he notices her.

"So, what are you doing tonight?"

"Me?" Janie laughs. "Homework, of course."

"You want company?" Carrie's looking wistful.

"Do you have homework to do?"

"Of course. Whether I do it or not is the real question."

Janie sees him out of the corner of her eye. He's stopped

still in the side yard of the neighbors across the street. She laughs with Carrie and says, "Well, that's enough of that." She bangs the shovel and climbs the steps. "Go on in," she says.

Carrie steps inside, and Janie gives Cabel a fleeting glance over her shoulder. He shrugs and flashes the okay sign. Janie follows Carrie in.

Carrie stays until midnight, when she's good and drunk on Janie's mother's liquor.

Janie thinks about going to Cabel's after Carrie leaves, but decides she'll get a good night's sleep here and see him in the morning.

JANUARY 8, 2006, 10:06 A.M.

Janie calls Cabel. Gets his voice mail.

11:22 A.M.

Cabel returns Janie's call. Leaves a message on the answering machine.

12:14 P.M.

Janie calls Cabel. Gets his voice mail.

2:42 P.M.

The phone rings.

"Hello?" Janie says.

"I miss you like hell," he says, laughing.

"Where are you?"

"At U of M. I had a thing to go to."

"Fuck."

"I know."

There is silence.

"When will you be home?"

"Late," he says. "I'm sorry, sweets."

"Okay," she says with a sigh. "See you tomorrow, maybe."

"Yeah. Okay," he says softly.

BIRTHDAY UNDERCOVER

JANUARY 9, 2006, 7:05 A.M.

Janie wakes up on her birthday feeling terribly sorry for herself.

She should know better.
This happens every year.
It seems worse this year, somehow.

She greets her mother in the kitchen. Her mother gives her a half-grunt, fixes her morning drink, and disappears into her bedroom. Just like any ordinary day.

Janie fixes frozen waffles for breakfast. Sticks a goddamn candle in them. Lights it. Blows it out.

Happy birthday to me, she thinks.

Back when her grandma was alive, she at least got a present.

She gets to school late. Bashful gives her a tardy, and won't reconsider.

Janie always hated Bashful.

Stupidest. Dwarf. Ever.

Psychology is interesting.

Not.

Mr. Wang is the most incompetent psych teacher in the history of the subject. So far, Janie knows more than he does. She's pretty sure he's just teaching until he makes his big break in showbiz. Apparently he likes to dance. Carrie told Janie that Melinda saw him in Lansing at a club, and he was tearing it up.

Funny, that. Because he seems very, very shy. Janie makes a note, and then spills her red POWERade over her notebook. It spatters on her shoe and soaks in.

And then, in chemistry, her beaker explodes.

Sends a shard of glass, like a throwing star, into her gut.

Rips her shirt.

She excuses herself from class to stop the bleeding. The school nurse tells her to be more careful. Janie rolls her eyes.

Back in class, Mr. Durbin asks if she'll stop by the room after school to discuss what went wrong.

Lunch is barfaritos.

Dopey, Dippy, and Dumbass are all on their toes today. Somebody falls asleep in each of those classes, even PE, because they're doing classroom studies on health today. Janie finally resorts to throwing paper clips at their heads to wake them up.

By the time she gets to study hall, she feels like crying. Carrie doesn't remember her birthday, as usual. And then, Janie realizes with that keen, womanly sense of dread that she has her period.

She gets a hall pass and spends most of the hour in the bathroom, just getting away from everybody. She doesn't have a tampon or a quarter to get one from the machine. So back to the school nurse for the second time that day.

The nurse is not very sympathetic.

Finally, with five minutes left of school, she heads back to the library. Cabel gives her a questioning look.

She shakes her head to say everything's cool.

He glances around. Slides into the seat across from her. "Are you okay?"

"Yeah, just having a shitty day."

"Can I see you tonight?"

"I guess."

"When can you come?"

She thinks. "I dunno. I've got some shit to take care of. Like five, maybe?"

"Feel like working out?"

Janie smiles. "Yeah."

"I'll wait for you."

The bell rings. Janie finishes up her English homework, gathers up her backpack and coat, and heads over to Mr. Durbin's room. She already knows why her beaker exploded, and she doesn't feel like telling him what happened.

She opens the door. Mr. Durbin's feet are propped up on the desk. His tie hangs loose around his neck, and the top button of his shirt is undone. His hair is standing up a bit, like he's run his fingers through it. He's grading papers on a clipboard in his lap. He looks up. "Hi, Janie. I'll be just a second here." He scribbles something.

She stands waiting, shifting her weight from one

foot to the other. She has cramps. And a headache.

Mr. Durbin scribbles a few more notes, then sets his pen down and looks at Janie. "So. Rough day?"

She grins, despite herself. "How can you tell?"

"Just a hunch," he says. He looks like he's trying to decide what to say next, and finally he says, "Why the cake and frosting?"

"I'm sorry?"

"Why did you put back the cake and frosting, out of all the other things you had in your cart?"

"I didn't have enough cash on me."

"I understand that. Hate when that happens. But why didn't you put back the grapes or carrots or something?"

Janie narrows her eyes. "Why?"

"Is it your birthday? Don't lie, because I checked your records."

Janie shrugs and looks away. "Who needs a cake, anyway," she says. Her voice is thin, and she fights off the tears.

He regards her thoughtfully. She can't read his expression. And then he changes the subject. "So. Tell me about your little explosion."

She cringes.

Sighs.

Points at the chalkboard.

"I'm having some trouble reading the board," she says.

Mr. Durbin taps his chin. "Well, that'll do it." He

smiles and slides his chair back. "Have you been to the eye doctor yet?"

She hesitates. "Not yet." She looks down.

"When's your appointment?" he asks pointedly. He stands up, gathers a beaker and the components for the formula, and sets them at her lab table. Waves her over.

"I don't have one yet."

"Do you need some financial help, Janie?" His voice is kind.

"No . . . ," she says. "I have some money." She blushes. She's not a charity case.

Mr. Durbin looks down at the formula. "Sorry, Janie. I'm just trying to help. You're a terrific student. I want you to be able to see."

She is silent.

"Shall we try this experiment again?" He pushes the beaker toward her.

Janie puts on her safety glasses, and lights the burner.

Squints at the instructions and measures carefully.

"That's one quarter, not one half," he says, pointing.

"Thanks," she mutters, concentrating.

She's not going to fuck this up again.

Mixes it up. Stirs evenly for two minutes.

Lets it come to a boil.

Times it perfectly.

Cuts the heat.

Waits.

It turns a glorious purple.

Smells like cough syrup.

It's perfect.

Mr. Durbin pats her on the shoulder. "Nicely done, Janie."

She grins. Takes off her safety glasses.

And his hand is still on her shoulder.

Caressing it now.

Janie's stomach churns. *Oh god*, she thinks. She wants to get away.

He's smiling proudly at her. His hand slides down her back just a little, so lightly she can hardly feel it, and then to the small of her back. She's uncomfortable.

"Happy birthday, Janie," he says in a low voice, too close to her ear.

Janie fights back a shudder. Tries to breathe normally. *Handle it, Hannagan*, she tells herself.

He steps away and begins to help her clean up the lab table.

Janie wants to run. Knows she needs to keep her cool, but instead she escapes at the first reasonable opportunity. It was one thing talking about what might happen, and it was an entirely different thing to actually experience it. Janie shudders and forces herself to walk calmly. Get her thoughts together.

She heads outside for the parking lot. And then she remembers she left her goddamned backpack on the goddamned lab table.

Her keys are in that bag.

The office is closed by now.

And she doesn't have a fucking cell phone. *Hi, this is 2006, calling to tell you you're a loser.*

She goes back anyway, feeling like a dork, and meets Mr. Durbin halfway. He's carrying it. "Thought I might find you on your way back for this," he says.

Janie thinks fast. Knows what she needs to do. She struggles to get over the creep factor. "Thanks, Mr. Durbin," she says. "You're the best." She gives his arm a quick squeeze, and flashes a coy smile. And then she turns and heads down the hallway, taking long, loose strides. She knows what he's looking at.

When she rounds the corner, she glances over her shoulder at him. He's standing there, watching her, arms folded across his chest. She waves and disappears.

And now she doesn't want to tell Cabel.

He's going to be upset.

She drives home and looks up Captain's number. Calls her cell phone.

Tells her about her hunch.

"Good job, Janie. You're a natural," she says. "You okay?"

"I think so."

"Can you keep it going for a while?"

"I—I'm pretty sure I can, yes."

"I know you can. Now I want you to research. Isn't there a chemistry fair or something? A high-school statewide competition that Fieldridge sends a team to? Something like that?"

"I don't know. Yeah, I think so. There must be. There's one for math, anyway."

"Check into it. If there is one, and this Durbin goes to it, I want you to sign up. We'll pay for it, don't worry about that. I've been racking my brain, and I can't think of any other way you're going to land in his or some of the other students' dreams. Can you?"

"No, sir. I mean, okay, I'll sign up." Janie sighs, remembering the bus trip to Stratford.

"Have you taken a look at Martha's reports yet?"

"Some," Janie says.

"Any questions?"

Janie hesitates, thinking about what Miss Stubin said in the dream. "Nope. Not yet."

"Good. Oh, and Janie?"

"Yes, sir?"

"You're calling from home. Haven't I given you a goddamned cell phone yet?"

"No, sir."

"Well, I don't want you to go anywhere without one from now on. You hear me? I'll have one for you tomorrow. Stop by after school. And you need to tell Cabel about this guy if you haven't already. I don't want you in this project alone. It already makes me ill, knowing that creep is hitting on other high-school girls, much less you."

"Yes, sir."

"One more thing," Captain says.

"Yes?"

There's a pause.

"Happy birthday. There's a gift on my desk for you. The cell phone will be next to it by tomorrow after school, if you come while I'm not here."

Janie can't speak.

She swallows.

"Is that clear?" Captain says.

Janie blinks her tears away. "Sir, yes, sir."

"Good." There's a smile in her voice.

It's well after six before Janie makes it to Cabel's house. She jiggles her keys, trying to find the right one, and he opens the door. She looks up at him. Smiles. "Hi."

"Where've you been?"

"Sorry. Stuff happened." She enters the house. Takes off her coat and boots.

"What stuff?"

She sniffs the air. "What are you cooking?"

"Chicken. What stuff?"

"Oh, you know. Got to school late, and everything fell apart after that. You ever have one of those days?"

He goes to the stove and flips the chicken. "Yeah. Practically every day last semester, when you wouldn't talk to me. So what happened?"

She sighs. "My beaker exploded. Third hour. Durbin. I had to go in after school to redo the experiment."

He looks at her, tongs in hand. "The guy with the groceries?"

She nods.

"And?"

"And . . . I think he's the guy we're after. I called Captain."

He sets the tongs down loudly on the counter. "What makes you think that?"

"He touched me. It was . . . weird." She says it quickly, and then turns and goes into the bathroom.

But he's right behind her, and she can't get the door closed because his foot is in the way. "Where?" he shouts.

She cringes. Squeaks. She takes a breath, gathers her nerve, and gives him a furious look. "Stop it, Cabe! If you can't handle this without getting in my face about it, I'm not going to tell you anything."

He hears her.

His eyes grow wide.

"Oh baby," he whispers. Steps back. Out of the doorway. His face is ashen. He walks slowly back to the kitchen. Leans over the counter. Puts his head in his hands. His hair falls over his fingers.

The bathroom door clicks shut.

She stays in there for a long time.

He's pulling his hair out.

Finally, frustrated, he calls Captain. "What's going on, sir?"

There is a pause, and then he says, "She said he touched her. That's all I've gotten out of her so far."

He nods.

Yanks his hair.

"Yes, sir."

He listens intently.

His face changes.

"It's what?"

Then.

"Bloody fucking fuck," he mutters. "You're kidding." He closes his eyes. "Shoot me now. I didn't know."

He turns off the phone.

Sets it on the table.

Walks to the bathroom door.

Leans his forehead against the molding.

"Janie," he says. "I'm sorry I yelled. I can't stand the thought of that creep touching you. I'll get a handle on it. I promise."

He waits. Listens.

"Janie," he says again.

Then gets worried.

"Janie, please let me know you're okay in there. I'm worried. Just say something, anything, so I—"

"I'm okay in here," she says.

"Will you come out?"

"Will you stop yelling at me?"

"Yes," he says. "I'm sorry."

"You're driving me crazy," she says, coming out. "And you scared me."

He nods.

"Don't do that."

"Okay."

7:45 P.M.

Cabel turns the burner on low under the chicken, hoping to salvage it. Janie's in the computer room, writing up her notes.

He comes in and sits opposite her, at the other computer. Does some surfing. Some typing. Hits Send. Janie's computer binks. When she finishes her notes, she checks her Gmail. Clicks on the link. Watches the screen.

It's a Flash e-card.

Simple and beautiful.

I love you, and I'm sorry I'm an asshole.

Happy birthday.

Love,

Cabe

She looks down at the keys. Composes her thoughts. Hits Reply.

Dear Cabe,

Thank you for the card.

It means a lot to me.

I haven't received a birthday card since I turned nine. I just realized that was half my life ago.

I'm sorry I'm an asshole too. I know it frustrates you when I don't take care of myself—that's why you were mad the other day, isn't it? I'll try harder to work on the dreams, so they don't mess me up so badly. And I'll keep supplies in my backpack from now on. I should have been doing that all along, so you don't have to worry so much.

Thing is, I like it when you are there to help me. It makes me feel like somebody cares, you know? So maybe I've neglected some things on purpose, just so you notice. It's stupid. I'll stop with that.

Why are you so upset about this case?

All I know is that I really miss you.

Love,

J.

She reads it over and hits Send.

Cabel's computer binks.

He reads the e-mail.

Hits Reply.

Dear J.,

I want to explain something.

After my dad set me on fire . . . Well . . . He died in jail while I was still in the hospital getting skin grafts. And I never got to tell him how much he hurt me. Not just physically, but inside, you know? So I took it out on other things for a while.

I'm better now. I got counseling for it, and I'm really better. But I'm not perfect. And I'm still fighting it.

See . . . You're, like, the only person I have in my life that I really care about. I'm selfish about that. I don't want anybody to touch you. I want to keep you safe. That's why I hate this assignment so much. Now that I have you, I'm afraid to see you get hurt or messed up, like I was. I'm afraid I'll lose you, I guess.

*I wish you could always be safe. I worry a lot. If you weren't so damned independent . . . Ah, well. *smile**

As much as we have been through in the past few months, we still don't know each other very well, do we? I want to change that about us. Do you? I want to know you better. Know what makes you happy and what scares you. And I want you to know that about me, too.

I love you.

I will try to never hurt you again.

I know I'll screw up. But I'll keep trying, as long as you let me.

Love,

Cabe

Send.

Janie reads.

Swallows hard.

Turns toward him. "I want that too," she says. She stands up and scoots over onto his lap. Holds him around the neck. His arms circle her waist, and he closes his eyes.

JANUARY 10, 2006, 4:00 P.M.

Janie slips into the police station, goes through the metal detector, and heads downstairs.

"Hey, new girl," says a thirtysomething man when she gets to Captain Komisky's door and knocks. "Hannagan, right? Captain said to tell you to go on in. She left you some stuff. I'm Jason Baker. Worked with Cabel on the drug bust."

Janie smiles. "Pleased to meet you." She shakes his hand. "Thanks," she adds, and opens the office door. On the corner of the desk is the tiniest cell phone she's ever seen, and next to it is a medium-size box and an envelope. The box has a bow on it. She grins and takes the items, then slips back out. When she gets to the car, she examines the gift box and the envelope, savoring it.

Decides to wait.

4:35 P.M.

Sitting on her bed, she opens the envelope first. It's a traditional birthday card with a simple signature on the bottom—"Fran Komisky." Inside the card is a gift certificate to Mario's Martial Arts for a self-defense class. Cool.

And inside the box is every kind of pampering item that Janie would never buy for herself. Relaxation votives, stress massage oils, aromatherapy bath salts, and a plethora of scented lotions in tiny adorable bottles. Janie squeals. Best present ever.

She calls Mario's and signs up for a class that starts the next day. And then, she goes to the phone book and looks up optometrists. Finds a vision shop that's open evenings and calls for an appointment. The receptionist says there's a cancellation for a five thirty p.m. appointment today, and can she make it?

She can.

And does.

She raids her college fund.

Walks out an hour later, four hundred bucks poorer but wearing new, funky, sexy glasses. She loves them, actually.

And she can see.

She had no idea how poorly she was seeing before.

Can't believe the difference.

She drives straight to Cabel's, knowing she can't stay long. She knocks on the front door. He opens it, towel drying his hair. She grins brightly.

He stands there, gaping. "Holy shit," he says. "Get in here." He pulls her in the house and slams the door. "You look fantastic," he says.

"Thank you," she says. She bounces on the balls of her feet. "And an added bonus," she says.

"Let me guess. You can see?"

"How'd you know?"

"Just a hunch."

"Hey, let's trade!"

He grins slyly. Takes his off and hands them to her. She whips hers off and puts his on while he watches, amused.

"Holy Moses, your eyes are terrible."

"No," he says. "Yours are. My glasses are clear."

She takes his off and playfully pummels him in the chest. "You are *such* a dork! You don't even need to wear glasses?"

He clasps his hands around her back and holds her tight against him. "It was all part of the image," he says, laughing. "I kind of got used to them. I like the look, so I kept them. Makes me look sexy, don't you think?" he teases, and then kisses her on the top of the head.

"You smell great," Janie says. She wraps her arms around him and looks up. "Oh! Check this out." She reaches into her pocket and pulls out the cell phone. "I have no idea how it works, but isn't it the cutest little thing you've ever seen?"

Cabel takes the phone and examines it. Thoroughly. "This phone," he says finally. "I want this phone."

She laughs. "No. S'mine."

"Janie, I don't think you understand. I want it."

"Sorry."

"It's got photo Caller ID; Internet; video, camera, and digital recorder?! Holy Hannah . . . It's making me warm all over."

"Oh, yeah?" Janie says in a sexy voice. "Wanna play with my phone, baby?"

He looks at her, his eyes smoldering. "Hell yes, I do." He runs his fingers through her hair, slips his hands in the back pockets of her jeans, and leans down to kiss her.

Their glasses clink.

"Fuck," they whisper together, laughing.

"I can't stay, anyway," she says. "Plus, I'm parked in your driveway."

"Wait one second, 'kay?" Cabel slips away and comes back a moment later. "Here," he says, handing her a small box. "For you. For your birthday."

Janie's lips part in surprise. She takes it. Feels really strange about opening it in front of him. She wets her lips as she examines the box and the ribbon that surrounds it. "Thank you," she says softly.

"Um . . ." He clears his throat. "The gift, see, is actually inside the box. The box is like an extra bonus gift. It's how we do things here on planet Earth."

She smiles. "I'm still enjoying the box and the fact that you bought me a gift. You didn't have to do that, Cabe."

"I just wish you'd told me it was your birthday, so I could have had it on the right day."

"Yeah," she says with a sigh, "that was me, having a little pity party for myself. I should have said something. When's yours?" She says suddenly.

"November 25."

She looks up at him. Her eyes remember. "Thanksgiving weekend."

"Yeah. You were at the sleep study. And we weren't exactly on speaking terms."

"That must have been a shitty weekend," she says.

He's silent for a moment. "Open it, J."

She slides the ribbon off.

Opens the box. It's a tiny diamond pendant on a silvery chain. It sparkles in the box.

Janie gasps.

And bursts into tears.

THE GREEN AND THE BLUES

JANUARY 26, 2006, 9:55 A.M.

Mr. Wang stops Janie after second hour. "Do you have a moment, Janie?"

"Sure," she says. Mr. Wang is dressed in Polo.

The room clears out.

"I just wanted to compliment you on your work so far. You seem to have a real understanding of psychology. Your essay answers on the first test were brilliant."

Janie grins. "Thanks."

"Have you ever thought of a career in psych?"

"Oh . . . you know. I've toyed with the idea a bit. I'm not sure yet what I'll go for in college."

"So you *do* have college plans?" His voice has a hint of incredulity to it. "Franklin Community, maybe?"

Janie blinks, feeling the snub.

Feeling poor.

As if living on the wrong side of town means less is expected of her.

"Well, I would," she says, her voice taking on an innocent twang, "if'n I didn't have Earl Junior on the way, and you know mamaw can't stay alone in the trailer so good no more. I got to go find Earl Senior, so I can git me some money, know whut I mean?"

Mr. Wang stares at her.

She turns away when the bell rings and walks in late to chemistry.

"Sorry," she mouths to Mr. Durbin as she slides into place at her lab table at the back of the room. The others are working already. Janie copies down the equations from the board. She is still amazed at how well she can now see.

She hunches over her desk and scratches the figures on a piece of notebook paper, working out the formula, checking and double-checking her work. Mr. Durbin strolls around the room, giving hints and joking occasionally with the students as usual. She joins in like the others.

Every now and then, she glances up to see where he is, watching his body language as he interacts with the students. He hasn't said or done anything inappropriate that Janie's seen since their little incident a few weeks before, and now Janie's starting to question her judgment. Did it really happen? Or was she feeling so badly about herself that day that she imagined it?

He really is a terrific teacher.

And then he's next to her at her table, checking out her work. "Looking good, Hannagan," he says quietly. But he's not looking at her formula, bubbling merrily over the burner.

He's looking down her shirt as she's leaning over.

After class he stops her on the way out the door. "Do you have a slip for me?"

Janie is stumped. "A what?"

"A note?"

"For what?"

"You were late."

Janie thumps her forehead. "Oh! Um . . . No, I don't, but Mr. Wang kept me after class last period. He'll vouch for me."

"Mr. Wang, hm?"

"Yes."

"Hang out here a moment while I call him."

"But . . ."

"I'll write you a note for your next class, don't worry." He picks up the phone and dials Mr. Wang's room.

Mr. Wang apparently confirms that he held Janie after class. The bell rings. Mr. Wang says something else, and Mr. Durbin chuckles. "Is that so." He listens again. "I'll say," he says. He gives Janie a sidelong glance. His eyes come to rest on her chest as he hangs up.

"Okay, you're off the hook," he says, smiling. "So, who's your baby daddy?"

She grins, embarrassed. "That was a little joke," she says, and wets her lips. "Thanks. Can you write me a note now?"

"Sure," he says lazily. He reaches for his pen and scribbles on a square sheet of recycled paper. He holds the note out in front of him, so she has to approach to get it. "How's that sound?" He's grinning.

She takes the paper. "You want me to read this?" she says.

He nods and scribbles on a second square of paper now. "And this is for your next teacher."

She reaches for it. "Oh, okay," she says. "Uh . . ."

"The first one is some information about a little chemistry party I have every semester at my house, just for the Chem. 2 students. Any chance you can whip up a flyer for me to hand out to everybody?"

Janie looks at the paper. "Of course, I'd love to."

"You look like the type who would be good with computer graphics," he says. "You know what I mean." He wiggles his fingers. "Savvy . . . with electronics."

"It must be my geeky glasses that gives me away," she says smoothly.

"The glasses are nice, Janie. Are they working out for you okay?"

"Yeah, great. Thanks for asking." She smiles. "I should . . . probably get to my next class now. Don't you have a class this period?"

"Nope. This is my free hour."

"Oh, cool. I've been meaning to ask you—Is there a chemistry fair or a competition that you take students to?"

Mr. Durbin taps his chin thoughtfully. "I wasn't planning to do it this year, because it's all the way up in the UP at Michigan Tech, but you're the third person to ask me about it. Are you interested in me getting a team together? We'd have to do it quickly. The fair's next month."

Janie's eyes light up. "Oh, yes," she says. "I'd love to go!"

"It's a heck of a drive all the way up there. We'd have to book a hotel. Is that . . . um . . . feasible? I don't think there are any scholarships available."

Janie smiles. "I could handle a couple hundred bucks, yeah."

Mr. Durbin eyes her. "I think it could be a great experience," he says, his voice low and slow.

She nods. "Well, cool! Let me know. And I'll get that flyer to you soon. You want ten copies?"

"No hurry. The party's not until the first week of March. Ten copies would be perfect. Actually, make it twelve, in case Finch loses his, like he loses everything else. Thanks, Janie."

"Anything for you," Janie says, and blushes. "I mean . . . you know." She laughs and shakes her head, like she's embarrassed. "Never mind."

He's smiling at her chest. "See you tomorrow."

2:05 P.M.

Janie sits at her table and sneaks her cell phone out of her backpack. She fires it up. Sends Cabel a text message to his phone. "Can you get Durbin's past Chem. 2 class lists?"

A few moments later she gets the reply. "Sure. CU@4?"

Janie leans forward and sees him. He winks. She smiles and nods.

3:15 P.M.

Janie calls Captain.

"I may have talked Durbin into taking a group to the chemistry fair. It's next month. Way the heck up in Houghton."

"Excellent job, Janie. He'll have to take a female chaperone with him. You should be perfectly safe."

"He's hosting a party for the Chem. 2 students too. I guess he does it every year in March and in November."

Captain pauses. Grabs her notes. "Bingo. Call number one was March 5. Call number two was early November. I think we've got something here, Janie. Good work."

Janie hangs up to a rush of nervous excitement. *This is too weird*, she thinks.

4:00 P.M.

At Cabel's house Janie recounts the conversation with Durbin from memory, even though she took notes once she got to her next class. Cabel refrains from getting upset, like he promised.

He has the previous semester's list, as well as the one from last spring.

"Smart thinking, Cabe."

"Tomorrow I'll track the girls from these previous classes to see what they're taking now."

"Great," she says.

Janie whips up a flyer for the Chem. 2 party. It's

set for Saturday night, March 4. She prints out fifteen copies. Hands two to Cabel. "One for you, one for Captain."

"You don't know how much I wish I could be there."

"You'll be nearby, won't you?"

"Hell yes."

She stands and gives Cabel a hug. "I've gotta go."

He looks at her longingly. "Should I be feeling badly about the fact that you haven't stayed overnight in three weeks?"

"How's tomorrow night sound?"

He smiles. "Saturday too?"

"Yeah. You don't have any 'things' to go to?"

"Not this weekend."

"It's a date."

"Sweet," he says. "See you." He pulls her toward him for a kiss, and then she's gone, sprinting across the snow.

6:37 P.M.

Janie tackles the Stubin files. She knows Captain wants her to get through them. And Janie's had them for nearly a month. But everything is so interesting, and she's learning like crazy. How to get information from a dream. How to know what to look for in one. Miss Stubin could occasionally pause and pan dreams, as if she were a camera, and see the things behind her as well as in front of her. A few times Miss Stubin mentioned rewinding to see something twice. Janie hasn't been able to do any of that yet. She's trying, every study hall. Maybe she'll try it with Cabel this weekend.

10:06 P.M.

Janie's nearing the end of the last file. She rubs her temples as she reads. Her head aches. She grabs an Excedrin and a glass of water from the kitchen, and returns to her reading.

She's fascinated. Enthralled. Building up a list of questions for Miss Stubin and planning a dream visit soon.

Finally she closes the last file and sets it aside. All that's left are a few stray papers and a thin, green spiral notebook.

Janie glances at the papers. They appear to be notes, scrawled in illegible handwriting that doesn't stay between the lines. All the other files were typed. Janie's glad she didn't have to try to read them all like this. They must have been written late in Miss Stubin's career, after she retired and lost her eyesight.

Janie sets the papers aside and opens the spiral notebook.

Reads the first line. It's written in a controlled, sprawling hand—it's infinitely more legible than the notes on the bed next to Janie. It looks like a book title.

A Journey Into the Light
by Martha Stubin

There is a dedication below the title.

This journal is dedicated to dream catchers. It's written expressly for those who follow in my footsteps once I am gone.

The information I have to share is made up of two things: delight and dread. If you do not want to know what waits for you, please close this journal now. Don't turn the page.

But if you have the stomach for it and the desire to fight against the worst of it, you may be better off knowing. Then again, it may haunt you for the rest of your life. Please consider this in all seriousness. What you are about to read contains much more dread than delight.

I'm sorry to say I can't make the decision for you. Nor can anyone else. You must do it alone. Please don't put the responsibility on others' shoulders. It will ruin them.

Whatever you decide, you are in for a long, hard ride. I bid you no regrets. Think about it. Have confidence in your decision, whatever you choose.

Good luck, friend.

Martha Stubin, Dream Catcher

Janie feels her stomach churning.

She slides the notebook off her lap.

Closes it.

Stares at the wall, barely able to breathe.

Buries her head in her hands.

And then.

Slowly.

She picks up the notebook.

Puts it in the box.

Stacks the files on top of it.

And hides it deep in her closet.

3:33 A.M.

Janie's falling at top speed. She looks down dizzily and Mr. Durbin is there, waiting for her to land. He's laughing evilly, arms outstretched to catch her.

Before he can grab her, Janie swoops sideways and is sucked into Center Street, pulled through the air to the park bench and deposited there. Mr. Durbin is gone.

Next to the bench, in her wheelchair, sits Martha Stubin.

"You have questions," Miss Stubin barks.

Janie tries to catch her breath, alarmed. She grips the bench's armrest. "What's going on?" she cries.

Miss Stubin's gaze is vacant. A blood tear drips from the corner of her eye and slides slowly down her wrinkled cheek.

But all she says is, "Let's talk about your assignment."

"But what about the green notebook?" Janie grows frantic.

"There is no green notebook."

"But . . . Miss Stubin!"

Miss Stubin turns her face toward Janie and cackles.

Janie looks at the woman.

And then.

Miss Stubin transforms into Mr. Durbin. Slowly his face melts until all that remains is a hollow skull.

Janie gasps.

She breaks out into a cold sweat.

And wakes up, sitting straight up in bed and screaming.

Janie whips off her blankets and hops to her feet, turns on her light, and paces between the door and the bed, trying to calm down.

"That wasn't real," Janie tries to convince herself. "That wasn't Miss Stubin. It was a nightmare. It was just a nightmare. I didn't try to go there."

But now she is afraid to go to sleep.

Afraid to go back to Center Street again.

JANUARY 27, 2006

Janie's mind is far away, inside the front cover of a green spiral notebook and dwelling on her nightmare. She walks down the school hallways in a daze, nearly bumping into Carrie between classes with Bashful and Doc.

"Hey, Janers, wanna hang out tonight?"

"Sure." Janie thinks. "Um, I mean, I can't. Sorry."

Carrie gives her an odd look. "You okay? You're not gonna keel over, are you?"

Janie shakes the cobwebs from her head and grins. "Sorry. No, I'm fine. I've just got my mind on other shit. Colleges and stuff. I've got a bunch of junk to fill out, the house is a mess, and I'm working on a nasty headache already today."

"Okay," Carrie says. "I just thought you might like the latest gossip." She looks crestfallen. Of course, lately, Carrie only wants to hang out with Janie if Stu is playing poker. Janie doesn't mind being called upon only when Carrie's first choice is busy, though. She keeps busy enough without Carrie hanging around all the time.

"What about Melinda?"

"Thanks," Carrie says sarcastically, "but you don't need to set up a playdate for me. I can find my own things to do. I'll catch you later."

Janie blinks. "Whatever," she says under her breath. And walks into Mr. Wang's room. He's watching her walk in as he pretends to look at a paper in his hands. She smiles automatically. When he doesn't smile or look away, she winks.

That does it.

He flushes and sits down abruptly.

Third hour. Mr. Durbin's class. Janie waits until after class to present the flyers for the March 4 party. She takes her time packing up her table. Soon she is the last one there. From the corner of her eye, she sees Mr. Durbin watching her.

She pulls the flyers out and hurries up to his desk, like she doesn't want to be late for her next class. "Does this look all right?"

He takes them and gives an approving whistle. "Great," he says. He turns to her and raises his eyebrows. "I like," he says, staring at her now.

She leans forward on his desk, just slightly. "There's more where that came from," she says. "If you ever need any."

He swallows. "I'll have to take you up on that sometime."

She smiles. "Gotta go."

"Before you go," Mr. Durbin says, "I've got the okay on the chem. fair and a team of seven students, if you're game. It's February 20. We'll leave Sunday the nineteenth at noon, set up our display, stay overnight, do the fair, and start home around six p.m. on Monday, so we only miss one day of class. Here's the info and permission slip for your parents to sign. Cost is two hundred and twenty bucks, plus money for meals. You in?"

Janie grins. "I'm in." She takes the slip of paper from Mr. Durbin and darts out the door before she's late to her next class, glancing as she runs at the list of students who will be on the Fieldridge team. Janie's the only one from her class who is going.

Excellent, she thinks.

Dopey, Dippy, and Dumbass are the same as always. Janie actually likes PE now, since Cabel got her into working out. Although she could do without Dumbass. She also adores her self-defense class she's taking twice a week. Sometimes Cabel lets her practice on him.

Not really very often, though.

Not after she landed his ass on the floor.

PE is coed again, and Dumbass Coach Crater likes to use her as an example for why they no longer play guys versus girls with contact sports. It's because she cracked Cabel's 'nads in a basketball game last semester. On purpose.

Today, Dumbass makes them do the state-required strength tests, and Janie takes the class record for the girls in the flexed-arm hang. Dumbass notices her muscular arms and shoulders, and calls her Buffy as she's hanging there. She rolls her eyes and wishes he'd stand right in front of her. If she ever sees him on a dark street, she'll teach him to sing, she decides.

Study hall is quiet. Janie only gets sucked into one dream, and it's a weak one. Not a nightmare. When she realizes it's a sex fantasy between two fellow seniors who she really doesn't want to see naked, she doesn't stick around. She pulls herself out of it.

Smiles triumphantly.

Cabel's watching her, and she gives him the thumbs up and flashes a smile. He grins back.

Janie finishes all her homework for the weekend, so she jots down a few notes about Durbin and Wang.

Correction: make that Happy and Doc.

And then she sits there. Staring into space.

Thinking about Miss Stubin and the green spiral notebook. Feeling a sense of . . . well . . . dread.

On the way home from school Janie makes a quick dash into the grocery store to pick up some things for her house, so her mother doesn't starve to death, and a few personal items for the weekend. She packs an overnight bag. Toothbrush, shampoo, and the massage oil and candles that she got from Captain. She shoves it all in her backpack and heads over to Cabel's, leaving her mother a note on where to find her if she needs anything.

They work out, shower, and then lounge side by side in the giant beanbag chair and talk about the day. But Janie's having trouble keeping her mind on topic. She grows quiet, thinking about the green notebook and the assignment from Captain.

Cabel notices.

"Where are you?" he says after a while.

Janie startles. Smiles at Cabel. "I'm sorry, sweets—I'm here." But she's not really there. She's going over the Durbin/Stubin dream in her head, now more convinced it was a nightmare and not really a visit from Miss Stubin.

Cabel sits up quietly. Watches her face. Clears his throat.

Janie sees him suddenly, the one guy she wants to be with—and is with for the whole weekend—hovering over her. She shakes the thoughts of creepy nightmare Durbin from her brain and tilts her head to the side, grinning. "Oops. I did it again."

Cabel gives her a quizzical look. "I am totally not getting enough attention here."

Janie thumbs his cheek. Pulls his face to hers and kisses him, her tongue darting across his teeth playfully until she coaxes him to play along.

A surge of something—love?—makes Janie's skin tingle. But it scares her, too, when she thinks of her future, always with this dream curse hanging over her. She never thought she'd be with someone. Never imagined someone would sacrifice so much to deal with her strange problems. Wonders when Cabel will get tired of it all and give up on her.

Desperately she pushes that thought aside. Her lips are hot against his neck.

She tugs at his T-shirt and slips her quivering fingers under it, re-exploring Cabel's nubbly skin. Touching the scars on his belly, his chest. She knows that Cabel feels the same way she does, sometimes—like no one would want to be with him because of his issues. *Maybe the two of us really could last*, Janie thinks. *Misfits, united.*

Cabel's fingers trace a slow path from Janie's shoulder to her hip as they kiss. Then he slips his shirt over his head and tosses it aside. Presses against her. "That's a little better," he whispers in her ear.

"Only a little?"

The winter dusk of late afternoon falls into the room. Janie reaches for her blouse and slowly unbuttons it. Lets it fall open.

Cabel pauses and stares, not sure what to do. He closes his eyes for a moment and swallows hard.

She reaches between her breasts and unhooks her bra.

And then she turns her face slowly toward him. "Cabel?" She looks into his eyes.

"Yes," he whispers. He can barely get the word out.

"I want you to touch me," she says, taking his hand and guiding it. "Okay?"

"Oh god."

She pulls a newly purchased condom from her pocket.

Sets the package on the skin of her belly.

Reaches for his jeans.

Cabel, momentarily rendered speechless, helpless, and thoughtless except for wanting her, sighs in shudders as he touches her skin, her breasts, her thighs, and then, as the light fades from the window, they are kissing as if their lives depend on their shared breath, and urgently making love for the first time, with their eyes and bodies, like it's the only chance they'll ever have.

In the evening, as they lie together in Cabel's bed, she knows it's time. Before she reads the green notebook, before what happens, happens, she needs to say what she feels. Because he is the only one who matters.

She practices in her mind.

Forms the words with her mouth.

Then tries them, softly, out loud.

"I love you, Cabe."

He's quiet, and she wonders if he's sleeping.

But then he buries his face in her neck.

FEBRUARY 1, 2006

Janie spends the school week swapping sexual innuendos with Mr. Durbin, trading confusing glances with Mr. Wang, and bantering spiteful barbs with Coach Crater.

Cabel tracks down the whereabouts of last semester's Chem. 2 class. He's working madly behind the scenes, not saying much about it. Controlling his feelings about the creep being near the woman he loves. Knowing if he says what he's really thinking, the tension grows between them.

"So," he says carefully, "it's you and six other students on this trip, plus Durbin. And who's your female chaperone?"

Janie glances up from her chemistry book. "Mrs. Pancake."

Cabel scribbles in his notebook.

"Four girls. You have a room together?"

"No, I thought I'd sleep in Durbin's room," Janie says.

"Har, har." Cabel scowls at Janie, and then tosses her chemistry book aside and tackles her. He buries his fingers into her hair and kisses her. "You're asking for trouble, Hannagan," he growls.

"And you would be . . . ?" Janie asks. She giggles.

"Trouble."

ON HER OWN

FEBRUARY 5, 2006, 5:15 A.M.

Janie, sprawled out on Cabel's couch, finally finds Miss Stubin on Janie's own terms.

She's on the bench. Miss Stubin is there, next to her. It's dusk. Perpetual rain.

"I'm going on an overnight trip with the teacher who we think is the sexual predator. Some of his former students are going too—they may be victims," Janie says.

"What season is it?" Miss Stubin asks.

Janie looks at her, puzzled. "Winter. It's February."

"Wear a bulky coat to disguise the shaking in case you

get sucked into a nightmare. Drape it over you. You're taking a school van?"

"Yes."

"Grab the backseat. And if you get sucked into a dream that's unimportant to the case, pull out of it. Don't waste your strength. You can pull out of them now, can't you?"

"Most of the time—the regular dreams, anyway. Not always with nightmares."

"Keep working at that. It's very important."

"I want to try pausing the dreams. Panning the scene. How did you do that?"

"It's all about focus, just as you focus to pull out of dreams, Janie. Just as you focus to help people change their dreams. Stare hard at the subject and talk to them with your mind. Tell them to stop. Focus on panning first—that comes most easily. Then pausing the scene. Who knows, perhaps you'll be able to zoom and rewind someday—that really comes in handy when solving crimes. And keep studying the meanings of dreams too. You've read books on the subject, haven't you?"

"Yes."

"Your work will be easier the more you can interpret some of the strange aspects that naturally occur in dreams. This, too, will help you immensely. Study my notes, see how I've interpreted dreams over the years."

Janie nods, then blushes, remembering Miss Stubin can't see her. "I will. Miss Stubin?"

"Yes, Janie?"

"About the green notebook . . ."

"Ah, you've found it, then."

"Yes."

"Go on."

"Does Captain know about it? About what's in it?"

"No. Not the notebook."

"Does she know anything about how dream catching works?"

"Some," Miss Stubin says guardedly. "We talked a little over the years. She's certainly someone you can talk to when you need to."

"Does anyone else understand this besides you and me?"

Miss Stubin hesitates. "Not that I know of."

Janie fidgets. "Should I read it? Do you want me to? Is it horrible?"

Miss Stubin is silent for a very long time. "I can't answer those questions for you. In good conscience, I can neither encourage you to read it nor discourage you from reading it. You must decide without my words swaying you either way."

Janie sighs and reaches for the old woman's hand, stroking the cool, paper-thin skin. "That's what I thought you'd say."

Miss Stubin pats her gnarled hand on top of Janie's soft one. She smiles wistfully and slowly disappears into the misty evening.

7:54 A.M.

It's Sunday morning. And it's time. It's been ten days since Janie found the green spiral notebook.

She slips back into bed with Cabel for a few minutes. He's just dozing now, not dreaming, and she holds him tightly, taking in whatever she can from him before she goes.

"I love you, Cabe," she whispers.

And goes.

Back to her room two streets away.

8:15 A.M.

With the notebook resting ominously on Janie's bed, Janie procrastinates.

Does her homework first.

And pours herself a bowl of cereal. Breakfast—one of the five most important meals of the day. Not to be skipped.

10:01 A.M.

She can't stall any longer.

Janie stares at the green notebook.

Opens it.

Reads the first page again.

Takes a deep breath.

10:02 A.M.

Takes another deep breath.

10:06 A.M.

Picks up her cell phone and hits memory #2.

"Komisky," she hears.

Janie's voice squeaks. She clears her throat. "Hi, Captain. I'm sorry to call on a—"

"It's okay. What's up?"

"Um, yeah. The dreams . . . Did Miss Stubin ever show you what was in the files?"

"I've read the police reports she's made, yes."

"What about her other notes on handling dreams and stuff?"

"I glanced at the first few loose pages in the file, but I felt like I was invading her privacy, so I put everything away as she requested."

"Did you two ever . . . you know, talk about her ability?"

There is silence.

Plenty of it.

"What do you mean?"

Janie cringes silently. "I don't know. Nothing."

Captain hesitates. "All right."

"Okay."

There is a nervous sigh.

"Captain?"

"Janie, is everything okay?"

Janie pauses.

"Yeah."

Captain is quiet.

Janie waits. And Captain doesn't press it.

"Okay," Janie says finally.

"Janie?"

"Yes, sir." It's a whisper.

"Are you worried about Durbin? Do you want out of this?"

"No, sir. Not at all."

"If something else is bothering you, you may say it, you know."

"I know. I'm . . . I'm fine. Thanks."

"May I give you some advice, Janie?"

"Sure," Janie says.

"It's your senior year. You're too serious. Try to have some fun. Go bowling or to a movie or something once in a while, okay?"

Janie grins shakily. "Yes, sir."

"Call me anytime, Janie," Captain says.

Janie's throat is closed. "Bye," she finally says.

Hangs up.

10:59 A.M.

Janie takes a deep breath.

Turns the page.

It's blank.

11:01 A.M.

Turns the blank page.

Sees the familiar scrawl.

Smoothes out the page.

And then her stomach lurches, and she slams the notebook shut.

Puts it back in the box.

Into the closet.

11:59 A.M.

Janie calls Carrie. "Do you feel like going bowling?"

She imagines Carrie shaking her head and laughing, telling Stu, coming back to the phone. "You are such a dork, Hannagan. Hell yeah, why not. Let's go bowling."

NITTY-GRTITTY

FEBRUARY 13, 2006

The names and schedules of Chem. 2 students are burned in Janie's brain. But the problem is, most science nerds don't sleep in school. And even if they did, the issue remains of how Janie can be in the same room with them when—if—it happens. It appears impossible.

And seeing how it's winter, it's futile to creep around outside their bedroom windows at night. She has high hopes for the chemistry fair. It's all she has to bank on.

Cabel tries making a connection with each student on the list. He has more of them in his classes than Janie does. But they remain aloof, associating him with the popular Hill crowd, because of his past ties to Shay Wilder. He's frustrated.

There are eighteen Chem. 2 students in all this year. There were thirteen Chem. 2 students last year. All thirteen graduated and went to college, Cabel discovers, some of them as far away as southern California. Doggedly, Cabel tracks them, in case their lives changed somehow in the nine months since graduation. He spends hours each evening on the computer, checking their blogs, their Facebook and Myspace pages, looking for any wild tales they may have thought they were keeping semiprivate.

And together, they have a whole lot of nothing.

The one and only lead Janie has at the moment is Stacey O'Grady from first semester of Chem. 2. She's in Janie's study hall. Stacey has horrible nightmares, if she sleeps at all. Which is rare.

But lots of people have horrible dreams, and it doesn't mean anything, as far as Janie can tell. Even if the dream is about a rapist. Janie knows that a dream about being chased by a rapist could possibly be literal, but more likely it's a hint of an underlying fear in some other part of your life. The fear that something's catching up to you, or that you can't run fast enough, or that you've lost your voice and can't scream—all could simply indicate being overwhelmed with school or home pressures or feeling helpless to change things. Being a senior could do that to many people.

Still, Janie wills Stacey to fall asleep in study hall again, so she can get a better look.

Six of the ten students in Janie's Chem. 2 class are female. She doesn't know any of them well, although they're friendly enough with one another. None of them are going to the chem fair.

When Desiree Jackson suggests a study group night at her house before an upcoming test, Janie jumps at it. Maybe she can get some information that way. Several others like the study group idea too. They agree to meet Thursday night at seven at Desiree's.

Mr. Durbin hands out the flyers for the March 4 party, and Janie raises a question. "What do you think about inviting the first semester group to join us? More people, more fun, I'm thinking. Or maybe you don't have room for so many in your house, Mr. Durbin."

Janie has driven by Mr. Durbin's house. Cabel managed to snag the floor plan from the township office. She's got it memorized. It's a three-bedroom home with a large kitchen that overlooks the spacious great room. With its finished basement, the house is easily large enough for twenty or more.

Mr. Durbin scratches his chin. "I like that idea. Class, what do you think? You guys good with that?"

The class wants to know who those people would be. Mr. Durbin flips through the eight names by memory, and the consensus is affirmative.

"Cool," Janie says. "I'll make some more flyers. We should get a head count on how many are planning on coming."

"Good idea. Sheesh, eighteen kids. You guys are gonna break my bank account," Mr. Durbin jokes.

Several girls offer to bring appetizers, and Mr. Durbin gratefully accepts the offer. Janie's puzzled now. She thought he might balk at the idea. But he's giving no indication of this being anything other than a cool party for science geeks.

"Don't let me see you bringing any alcohol," Mr. Durbin says lightly, and grins like he's young enough to be hip with the thoughts of seniors and wants to nip it in the bud. But the mere acknowledgment sets several students exchanging mischievous glances.

He said that on purpose, Janie thinks. *To get the students thinking about it.*

After class Mr. Durbin stops Janie. "Good idea for the party, Janie. Maybe a few of you girls could come early to help set it up?" He's giving her a helpless bachelor look.

The back of Janie's neck is prickling, but she smiles

excitedly. "Awesome. This is going to be a blast! You are such a cool teacher. You're just like one of us, you know?"

Mr. Durbin grins. "I try. It's only been eight years since I was a senior in high school. I'm not some old geezer, you know." He's languid, leaning against the side of his desk, arms crossed in front of him.

And then he's reaching out his hand. "Hold still," he says. "You've got an eyelash." He brushes lightly across Janie's cheek with his thumb, and his fingers linger at her hairline just a second longer than necessary.

Janie lowers her eyes demurely, then looks back up into his. "Thanks," she says softly.

He gives her a smoldering look that is unmistakable. Janie hesitates a moment, then waves her fingers lightly as she turns and hurries out the door to her next class.

In study hall, Janie finds Stacey and slides into the chair across from her. Janie wants to be the first to announce the invitation to the party at Mr. Durbin's, so she can gauge Stacey's reaction. "Hi," she says with a grin.

Stacey looks up from her book with surprise. "Oh, hey, Janie. What's up?" Janie notes with a creepy shudder that she's reading Margaret Atwood's *The Handmaid's Tale*.

"You were in Durbin's Chem. 2 class last term, right?"

"Yesss . . ." Stacey looks suspicious.

"And you're going to the chemistry fair, right?"

"Oh, that. Yeah—you are too?"

"Yep. Sounds like fun. I'll be at the meeting next week to create our display."

"Cool. It should be easy enough."

"Anyway, I'm actually here to ask you about Durbin."

Stacey's eyes narrow. "What about him?"

"Well, he's having his Chem. 2 party at his house, and our class decided to invite your class to come too."

Stacey gets a goofy smile on her lips. "Oh cool! He didn't, by chance, tell you guys what happened last semester, did he?"

Janie cocks her head. "No, not really. Just said everybody had a great time."

Stacey's grin grows wider. She leans forward across the table, and whispers, "Everybody got completely plastered. Even Durbin and Wang."

Janie's heart jumps. She controls her surprise, and speaks softly. "Wang was there too?"

"Yeah. Durbin and Wang are buddies. I think they play a lot of rec basketball together or something. Durbin said something about Wang being there for entertainment and crowd control." She laughs, and then grows serious. "Don't tell anybody about the alcohol, 'kay? Durbin and Wang could both get canned for it. But we chem geeks are a loyal bunch. And we know how to keep our mouths closed," she adds. She's chuckling to herself.

"Of course," Janie says seriously. "I'd never rat on him—He's the best."

"Yeah." Stacey sighs. "He's sooo hot. Wang's not bad either, for a snooty guy who lives up on the Hill." The girls giggle softly, and Janie pulls out an extra copy of the party flyer. "Here's the info. Do you think you can make it? We're getting a head count so we know how much food to make."

"Hell yes, I'll be there. I could use a break from this crazy pace. You want me to spread the word? Most of the others are in my physics class."

"Sure. I'll get you some more flyers tomorrow."

"Sweet. And that was real cool of your class to invite us," she adds with a grin.

Janie grins back. "So, you think most of them will want to be there?"

Stacey thinks a moment. "I can't think of anyone who wouldn't jump at the chance."

7:02 P.M.

Janie wraps up her notes at Cabel's house, and muses, "This is getting curiouser and curiouser."

Cabel reads over her shoulder. He growls lightly. "He did that lame eyelash trick on you? God, what a loser." He begins pacing.

"Easy, big fella," murmurs Janie distractedly as she types in the info she got from Stacey that day. When she finishes, she flips screens to the party flyer and prints out ten copies.

Cabel's on the phone.

"It's Cabe," he says. "I think we need to watch Durbin's house in the evenings up until—" He pauses. "Oh. Well, that's why you're in charge." He grins sheepishly into the phone. "Thank you, sir."

He hangs up. "Did you know Captain's been surveilling Durbin's house for two weeks already?"

"Nope. But it's a good idea. How's your progress going, Cabe? I think it's strange that I can't find a single student who doesn't like Durbin. Have you been able to approach that question yet with your new contacts?"

"Some. He seems to be gunning for teacher of the year, though, the way things are going."

"If a student was the one who made the call, what would make them *not* follow through and get their reward? I don't understand that. Not everybody drinks. And if they showed up there last year not knowing it was that kind of a party, wouldn't they back out slowly, or at least talk to somebody about it? I've never heard of this happening before. You'd think Carrie'd know."

Cabe begins pacing again. After a while he says, "Carrie wouldn't know. She and Melinda and Shay and people into high-end Hill parties aren't science geeks. There's not one person on the list who I've ever seen at a Hill party. It's two different worlds."

"So, what is Durbin's hold over the geeks that makes them want to protect him?"

Cabel's in the zone. Janie can almost see the wheels turning in his head. She glances at the flyers, and on a whim, goes to her Gmail account and types up an e-mail to the address Mr. Durbin gave her.

Hey Mr. Durbin,
I talked to Stacey O'Grady today, and she's stoked about being invited to your party. She told me you guys had a terrific party last semester. If it's okay with you, she's going to distribute the flyers to the other kids from that class. Would it be cool if she and I came about an hour early to help you set it up?
And I know you said no alcohol, but I've got this great dessert recipe I wanted to bring . . . It has crème de menthe in it. Just a little. Not enough to get anybody even a buzz from eating a huge piece. Would that be okay with you? If not, I could always bring Rice Krispies treats instead.
Janie Hannagan
P.S. I'm a little worried about Friday's big test—trying to study and get ready for the chem fair is taking up a lot of time. Can I set up a meeting to talk over some formulas with you?
Thanks. J.

She presses Send and keeps the computer booted, turning up the volume a notch, just in case he's online and gets back to her quickly.

"What are you doing?" Cabel says suddenly.

"Flirting with Durbin."

"Oh." He turns back to his pacing, and then stops again. "You know, I think I finally understand how it felt for you. Remember when you stopped by my house and Shay was over?"

"Ah . . . yeah. It's burned like a cross into my brain."

"I didn't want you to see that. Not because I wanted to hide it from you. But because it would hurt."

Janie smiles at him. "I know. Sucks, doesn't it."

"It's driving me nuts," Cabel admits. "If that bastard hurts you, I'll kill him. I'm still not sure about you putting yourself in a position like that."

"Good thing I don't work for you, then." She knows it's harsh.

He stops pacing. Looks at her. "Damn. You're right." Starts pacing again. "So, do you think Durbin is hot?"

"I can see why girls are attracted to him."

"Are you attracted to him?"

Janie sighs. "Oh Cabe. Shay is hot, rich, sexy, popular. A cheerleader. Were you attracted to her?"

"No. She was a facet of my job."

"Exactly."

"You didn't answer my question."

Janie hesitates, wanting to be truthful. "Durbin is attractive. I can't deny that. But when he did the eyelash thing, it made the hair stand up on the back of my neck. He creeps me out, Cabe."

Cabel nods absentmindedly as he walks. "Okay. That makes me feel better."

She smiles. Gets it—it was the same with Cabel and Shay. And is proud of him for the new way he's approaching it now. "I love you, you know," she says. It's getting easier to say.

He comes over to where she's sitting and massages her shoulders lightly. But his voice is grim. "I love you too, Janie."

"And I'm getting really good at protecting myself," she adds. "My self-defense class kicks ass."

He tugs her hair. "I'm glad you're taking that class. You're really getting buff, you know that? It's very sexy. As long as you're not beating me up."

"Don't make me hurt you," she murmurs. "Hey, can I stay tonight?"

"Wow, I don't know, jeez, I'm, like, really busy and shit. . . ."

She grins.

And then she hears the binking sound of an e-mail arriving.

Janie,

LOL! Bring the dessert. And the bottle.

And a resounding yes to everything else you asked me, and more.

I could do tomorrow (Tues.) after school, for us to go over the formulas in question. The rest of my afternoons are tied up until around 7 p.m., but if you don't need much equipment, you could always stop by my house after 7 either tomorrow or Wednesday.

Dave Durbin

"He is so freaking smooth," remarks Cabel. "He knows tomorrow is Valentine's Day, and there's not only a big basketball game, but also the pep rally after school and the Valentine's dance from seven to ten. He's not expecting you to make it then." Cabel thinks for a moment. "When you write him back, call him Dave. He's begging for it."

With that, Cabel walks away.

Janie purses her lips, and hits Reply.

Dave,

How's Wednesday around 8? I know right where you live. Thanks!

J.

She hits Send, and waits less than a minute before she has a reply.

Looking forward to it.

Dave

Janie shuts down the computer and finds Cabel in the living room, watching some old western on the movie channel. She slides in next to him.

"I'm going to his house Wednesday at eight," she says. "Will you spot me?"

He snakes his arm around her neck and tugs gently. "Of course," he says. "I'm going to alert Captain to it, too."

"'Kay," Janie says, snuggling close.

After a while of watching TV, the volume on too low to actually hear the story line, Cabe says, "I wish we could go out tomorrow night. I'm so tired of this routine, hiding out all the time. Our biggest excitement is lifting weights or deciding between green beans and broccoli."

Janie sighs. "Me too. Do you think we'll ever be able to go out on a date?"

"Yeah. Maybe this summer. For sure in the fall. Once we rid ourselves of the web of lies we leave behind at Fieldridge High."

It's a sober moment.

Janie nods.

Rests her head on his shoulder.

He tousles her hair.

"Hey Cabe?" she asks as they climb into bed.

"Yeah, baby?"

"Do you mind if I practice on your dreams tonight?"

"Of course not. You don't have to ask me."

"I feel weird about not asking you if I'm planning it in advance," she says.

"It's cool. You working on something in particular?"

"Yeah . . . I'm trying to TiVo."

He laughs. "What, you mean pause, rewind—that sort of thing?"

"Exactly."

"That'll be interesting. I hope you pull it off. You don't want to take me with you, do you?"

"Not this time. I need all the concentration I can muster. Once I get it, I'll gladly show you, though."

He turns off the light and lets his arm rest around her midsection. He strokes her belly with his thumb, like he's strumming guitar. "You know," he says, "you could really have fun with a good dream once you learn how to do that."

"Guess why I want to practice on you," she says with a smile in the darkness.

"Be careful or you might go to school tomorrow flushed with sex."

She chuckles softly. "All part of the plan, babycakes."

"Well, that oughta turn Durbin on." Cabel's voice turns bitter.

Janie turns toward Cabel. "Have you figured out yet why nobody narcs on Durbin?"

"I think so," Cabel says. "It's because he's only a few years older and good-looking and athletic, and he really acts as if he likes the science-type kids. He accepts their geek minds and praises them for it. He's the epitome of a cool, popular kid, whose groupies have never been popular in their lives. They lap it up."

Janie clears her throat.

Waits.

Clears it again.

"I—I mean," stutters Cabel, "ah, I mean, some of them are like that, and some, you know, some others, like you, for example, see right through the facade and . . . uh . . . shit like that."

"Mmm hmm," Janie says.

"And . . . I love you so much? And now I'm going to shut up and go to sleep, so you can manipulate my mind in a dozen ways and more?"

"Weak," she says. "But it'll do."

Cabel dreams.

Janie slides into the darkness, and then into the computer room.

It's a dream that's loosely based on the night they made love there. She's watching him, she's watching herself, curiously, surprised to see how quickly they find their rhythm together for the first time.

She concentrates with all her might. Stares at Cabel. *Pause*, she thinks, over and over again.

A minute goes by, but nothing changes.

Another minute.

And then the scene slows.

Ten seconds later it's paused. In a very interesting spot, Janie notes.

Janie looks around the room, trying to notice everything. The office items on the desk; the clock on the wall stopped as well; the color of everything. It's incredibly difficult to hold the scene there. And then she begins to lose it. She can feel her body shaking, weakening, and the dream slips into regular speed again.

Her head pounds. Her fingers are numb. She bumps Cabel with her behind, trying to wake him just enough so she doesn't have to use her waning energy to pull out of the dream too. She knows she can't do it after that. She can barely feel her arms and legs as it is, already.

Cabel takes in a sharp breath, and she can feel him against her backside, aroused in his sleep. He begins to stroke her numbing body while he's still in the dream. She can feel his touch, fading in and out on her skin, as she's seeing it in his mind. And she's stuck. And falling. And very aroused and blind and numb and watching it in her mind while feeling it on her body, all at the same time, and she wants it. Wants to make love right now. But she is completely paralyzed.

She can't move.

She can't feel anything.

She can't speak.

It can't happen. Not like this.

She needs to wake him up, before something happens. So they can do it right.

She takes all her strength, all her concentration, all her will. She bites blindly. Feels hair in her teeth. Pulls back with her neck.

And everything goes black.

She's shuddering.

Shaking.

Trying to catch a breath as she aches to see something. Anything. His face. She wants to see his face.

He's talking to her.

His hand is on her cheek, sliding through tears.

And she realizes it now.

Realizes that there will scarcely be a time when they roll together, unawares, and make love sleepily in the dead of a winter night, lingering on their dreams.

She's broken.

Her muscles are like water.

And he's there, lifting her shoulders, holding a glass to her lips, telling her to drink and swallow.

She can feel his fingers pushing the hair out of her eyes. Hear his voice in her ear. Smell his skin nearby. Taste the milk on her tongue, in her throat. And then slowly she sees shadows. Black and white, at first, and then his face, looking wild. His hair, flipping every which way. His cheeks flushed.

And she speaks roughly. "It's okay," she says.

But it's not okay.

Because she wants him, and now he's afraid to touch her like that.

He makes her eat.

Sits by the bed.

Waits for her sleep to come.

She finds him, awake, on the couch in the morning.

Sits in the crook of his body.

And they look at each other, both so very sorry and neither one needing to be.

Cabel, feeling helpless. Janie, trapped by her own ability. Despairing in their own minds for a while, until they can come to terms with the life that lies ahead. And each, in their private thoughts on this Valentine's Day, wonders briefly if it should go on.

If they should go on.

Torturing each other unexpectedly, indefinitely.

"Cabe," she says.

"Yes?"

"You know what always makes me feel better?"

He thinks a moment. "Milk?"

"Besides milk."

"What?"

"When you hold me. Tightly. Squeeze my body like you can't let go. Or lie on top of me."

He's quiet. "Serious?"

"I wouldn't joke about that. There's something about the pressure on my body that helps the numbness go away." She waits. Hopes she doesn't have to ask him point-blank.

She doesn't.

DURBIN DAZE

FEBRUARY 15, 2006, 8:04 P.M.

Janie pulls into Mr. Durbin's driveway.

Cabel's parked half a block away with a pair of binoculars and a view through the side window of the great room.

Baker and Cobb are stationed.

Janie's not wired.

No one expects anything to happen.

Not quite yet.

Mr. Durbin's too smart to ruin it.

She grabs her books and walks to the front door. Rings the bell.

He opens the door. Not too quickly. Not slowly, either. Invites her inside.

She takes off her coat and hands it to him. She's wearing jeans and a low-cut, see-through shirt with a camisole underneath—an ensemble that wouldn't be allowed in school.

He's wearing sweatpants and a U of M T-shirt.

Sweating.

"Just got done working out," he says, draping a towel around his shoulders. He shows her to the kitchen table.

"Great house," she says. "Perfect for a party."

"Which is why I bought it," he says. "I like having a place for the students to kick back and crash now and then." He grabs a bottle of water, offers her one, and says, "You get organized. I'm going to take a three-minute shower. Be right back."

Janie rolls her eyes as he walks out, and then suddenly realizes.

He's gone.

She glides through the main floor, checking things out. She hears the shower running.

Two bedrooms and a bath down the hallway off the great room. An office beyond the kitchen area, with all sorts of science-type chemical charts and books and bottles. And a master suite, which is where he's showering. She peeks in quickly. It's a large room with a king-size bed and a few items of clothing strewn around. On the bedside table, a porn magazine.

She moves quickly back to the kitchen table when she hears the water shut off, and she's sitting there, looking engrossed in her notes, when he returns. Now he's wearing jeans and a white T-shirt, à la James Dean. All he needs is a cigarette.

He moves through the great room, closing blinds. Janie cringes internally, knowing that Cabel must be bristling right now. But Cabe promised Captain he'd be under control, and he knows he's not allowed to be on the case if he's not this way—he's too close to it. Janie thinks he'll stay put.

"Okay, kid, what seems to be the problem?" Durbin asks as he walks back toward the table. He sits in the chair next to her, running his fingers through his wet hair.

"Kid?" She laughs. "I'm eighteen."

"S'cuse me. What was I thinking. Ahhh," he says, leaning in to see her notes. "Poisonous gases." He rubs his hands together gleefully. "How exciting, eh?"

She turns and gives him a look. "Well, it's interesting. But I don't understand how this"—she points with her pencil—"leads to this. It doesn't make sense."

"Hrm," he says, and draws the pencil from her fingers slowly. "Let's start from the beginning."

He flips the paper over and scribbles equations expertly on the back side. Whistles lightly under his breath as he goes. Janie leans in, as if to see better, an inch at a time, until he's slowing his pencil.

Making a mistake or two.

Erasing.

Shifting in his seat.

She stops moving, and she's nodding slightly. Fully, completely, overwhelmingly enthralled by the scratching of his pencil.

She takes a sip of water from the bottle he offered, and her swallow is the only sound in the room.

She watches his Adam's apple bob reflexively.

"Okay," he says finally. He explains the half-page-long equation from start to finish, and she's turned toward him, her elbow on the table and fingers in her hair, nodding, thinking, waiting.

"I think I've got it," she says when he's finished.

"Now, you give it a try," he says, looking at her. He takes the paper and slips it under her notebook, brushing her breast with his forearm. Both pretend not to notice.

Janie pulls out a fresh piece of paper and begins from the initial equation. She leans over the paper, so her hair falls in front of her shoulder, and scribbles away. After a moment he draws her hair back over her shoulder. His fingers linger an extra moment on her neck. "I can't see," he explains.

"Sorry about that." She flips her hair to the other side of her neck, and she can feel him looking at her. She hesitates in the middle of the process. Mulls it over. "Hang on," she murmurs, "don't tell me."

"It's okay," he says quietly. He's leaning over her, his breath on her shoulder. "Take your time."

"I'm never going to get this," she says.

His fingers touch her back lightly.

She pretends not to notice.

She calculates her moves, trying to get into the mind of someone who would welcome such advances. She decides that the someone would do absolutely nothing now, not wanting to risk a problem, and so she lets out a shallow breath and moves her pencil again, and then after a moment, dares a quick glance at him that tells him everything he wants to know.

"How's that?" she asks, pointing to her work.

"It's good, Janie. Perfect." He lets his hand rest centrally on her back.

She smiles and looks at the paper a moment, and packs up her books slowly. "Well. Thanks, Mr. Durbin, for, uh, you know. Letting me barge in on your evening like this."

He walks her to the door and leans against it, his hand on the handle. "My pleasure," he says. "I hope you come by again sometime. Just shoot me an e-mail. I'll make it work."

She steps toward him, goes to open the door so she can leave, but he's still holding on to the door handle. Trapping her. "Janie," he says.

She turns. "Yes?"

"We both know, don't we," he says, "why you wanted to come here this evening."

Janie gulps. "We do?"

"Yes. And don't feel badly about it. Because I'm attracted to you, too."

Janie blinks. Blushes.

"But," he continues, "I can't have a relationship with you while you're my student. It's not right. Even though you're eighteen."

Janie is silent, looking at the floor.

He tips her chin up. His fingers linger on her face. "But once you graduate," he says with a look in his eye, "well, that's a different story."

She can't believe this.

And then she can.

It's how he keeps them quiet.

Blames them.

She knows what to say.

It's the *saying it* that makes her want to puke on his shoes.

"I'm sorry," she says. "I'm so embarrassed."

"Don't be," he says, and she knows he wants her to be.

She waits for it. Waits for the line she knows is coming next from this egocentric bastard. She resists the urge to say it first.

"It happens all the time," he says.

She manages to turn her cringe into a sad smile, and

leaves without another word, although she's tempted to follow the movie ending by crying out, "I'm such a fool!"

About four seconds after she pulls out of the driveway, her cell phone rings. She waits until she's out of view of the house before she picks it up.

"I'm fine, Cabe."

"'Kay. Love you."

She laughs. "Is that it?"

"I'm trying to behave like a good cop."

"He's tricky. I'm heading home. You wanna stop by for the details?"

"Yeah."

"I'm calling Baker now, and then Captain. I'll see you at my place."

Janie makes the calls and reports the events, and Captain makes sure she knows this is a classic case of "fucked-up authoritative egomaniac syndrome."

She made up the term herself.

And then Captain says, "I'm not too worried about the chem fair trip since you'll be with Mrs. Pancake all the time, but be very careful at that party, Janie. I'm guessing he gets off on getting the girls drunk, maybe taking advantage of them then, while the party's going on. Keep your wits about you."

"I will, Captain."

"And do some research on date-rape drugs. I've got some pamphlets on it that I want you to read."

"Yes, sir."

9:36 P.M.

Janie arrives home, steaming with a new hatred for Mr. Durbin. What a manipulator. She'd like to get inside his dream sometime. Turn it into a nightmare.

Ten minutes later Cabel slips in and looks at her all over. Gives her a hug. "Your shirt smells like his after-shave," he says, eyes narrow. "What happened?"

"I did my job," she says.

"And what did he do?"

"Here. Sit here. Pretend you're working on chemistry formulas." She acts it out for him.

"Fucker."

"And then he tried to tell me I was a bad girl to think he'd ever want to touch me. Even though he just did."

Cabel closes his eyes. "Sure," he says, nodding. "That's how he keeps them quiet."

"That's exactly what I thought as he patronized all over me while leaning against the door so I couldn't get out."

Cabel paces.

Janie grins. "I'm going to bed. You can let yourself out when you're through with that."

FEBRUARY 17, 2006, 7:05 P.M.

Janie sits on the living-room floor of Desiree Jackson's house for the study date. A handful of Chem. 2 classmates surround her. They get right down to work on formulas.

Whenever anyone brings up Mr. Durbin's name, the other girls gush over him. Janie fakes it, easing questions about Mr. Durbin into the conversation as carefully as she can. But nobody has anything bad to say about him.

10:12 P.M.

Janie packs up her books and notes, sighs, and goes home with nothing new besides rave reviews of Mr. Durbin. Everybody loves the guy.

A night of studying, wasted. She knows this stuff by heart.

ROAD TRIP

FEBRUARY 19, 2006, 12:05 P.M.

It's snowing.

Hard.

The chemistry students pack their project and their overnight bags into the fifteen-passenger van in the school parking lot while Mr. Durbin paces outside, his gloved hand holding a cell phone loosely to his ear. His hair is thick with snow. He talks in spurts, his words dying in the blustery wind.

Everybody tumbles inside the van, excited and nervous. The students congregate on the front three bench seats.

Except Janie.

Janie takes the fourth bench seat.

Alone.

Shivering.

Mrs. Pancake, shrouded in a full-length, lilac, puffball, goose-down winter coat, peers anxiously out the front passenger window at Mr. Durbin and the blowing, drifting snow.

"We should cancel," she mutters to no one in particular. "It's only going to get worse the farther north and west we go. Lake effect."

The students speak in hushed voices.

Janie pleads with the weather to lighten up. As much as she hates these class trips, she knows she needs this one.

Finally Mr. Durbin blows into the driver's seat with a gust of snow and freezing cold wind. He starts up the van.

"The fair's secretary says it's clear and sunny up north," he says. "And the latest weather reports show this band of snow is isolated to the bottom half of lower Michigan. Once we get past Grayling we should have clear skies."

"So we're going?" Mrs. Pancake asks nervously.

Mr. Durbin winks at her. "Oh yes, my dear. We're going. Put on your seat belt." He puts the van into drive and plows through the snowy parking lot. "Here we go!"

The students cheer. Janie smiles and checks her backpack for supplies. She has everything she needs to get her through the next thirty-six hours. She pulls out *Harry Potter and the Order of the Phoenix*, along with her book light, and dives in.

5:38 P.M.

It takes more than five hours to get to Grayling when it should have taken three. But at least the snow has stopped. The school van limps into a Wendy's parking lot.

"Eat quickly and get back in here," Mr. Durbin hollers. "We have six hours to go. We'll have to set up early in the morning—they're closing the gymnasium at midnight, reopening at six a.m. I suggest you try to get some sleep in, people."

Janie perks up.

Stays far away from Mr. Durbin. She's still pissed about the other night at his house, although she knows she has to get past her contempt. Funnily enough, Mr. Durbin seems to hover around Janie even more when she tries to avoid him.

He slips in step with her as they enter the restaurant, but she ignores him and heads for the bathroom.

Everyone else heads for the bathroom too.

Janie calls Cabel.

"Hi, uh, Mom," she says.

Cabel snorts. "Hello, dear. Did you make it through the blizzard?"

"Yeah. Barely." Janie grins into the phone.

"Anything yet?"

"Nope, not yet. We still have six hours to drive. It's going to be a long night."

"Hang in there, sweets. I miss you."

"I—I love you, Mom."

"Call me when you get a chance. If anything happens."

"I will."

"Love you, Janie. Be safe."

"I will. Talk to you soon."

Fifteen minutes later they are back on the road.

Nobody sleeps.

Figures, Janie thinks.

She takes a nap while she can.

12:10 A.M.

In the hotel room with Janie are three other girls. Stacey O'Grady, Lauren Bastille, and Lupita Hernandez. The four of them chat and giggle softly for a few minutes, but growing tired, they fall into bed, the alarm set for 5:30 a.m.

1:55 A.M.

Janie is sucked into the first dream. It's Lupita, her bed mate. Janie can feel Lupita, twitching in the bed next to her.

They are in a classroom. Papers fly around everywhere.

Lupita frantically scoops them up, but for each paper she picks up, fifty more fall from the ceiling.

Lupita is frantic.

She looks at Janie. Janie stares back, concentrating.

"Help me!" Lupita cries.

Janie smiles encouragingly. "Change it, Lupita," she says. "Order the papers to come to a rest in a pile. It's your dream. You can change it."

Janie concentrates on delivering the message to Lupita. Slowly, Lupita's eyes grow wide. She reaches out her hands to the papers, and they float gently down into a neat stack on Lupita's desk. Lupita sighs, relieved.

Janie pulls herself out of the dream.

Lupita is no longer twitching. She is breathing steadily, deep, calm breaths.

Janie grins and rolls over.

Waits patiently for the one she needs.

2:47 A.M.

It's Lauren Bastille this time.

They are in a room of a house that looks vaguely familiar to Janie. Folding chairs are set up in a circle. People are sitting and standing all around. Some are laughing and falling over. Everyone is drinking some sort of pink punch; some dip their hands into the punch bowl and slurp.

All the people, except Lauren, look fuzzy. Janie can't see any faces, no matter how hard she tries to focus.

Lauren dances in the center of a circle. Her shirt is off and she twirls it as she stumbles around, laughing, wearing just a black bra and jeans.

Someone joins her.

He strips his shirt off and grabs Lauren.

Everyone claps and cheers as the guy pulls Lauren to him. They kiss and grind as the music pounds in the background.

Hip-hop music.

Janie watches in horror as the guy removes Lauren's clothing and shoves his jeans down to his knees. The guy pushes Lauren to the floor, falling on top of her, their drinks spilling everywhere, and the rest of the group begins making out and tearing off one another's clothes. Then they pile up on top of Lauren until people are stacked to the ceiling. Lauren is screaming, muffled. She's being crushed to death.

Janie's numb. Her body shakes. She's had enough, but it's too horrible. She can't escape. She tries to pull herself away, but the nightmare is too strong.

Janie tries to scream, but she knows she can't.

Look at me! she cries mentally to Lauren. *Ask me to help you!*

But this nightmare is out of control. Janie can't get Lauren's attention. She can't pull out of it. She watches in horror as

Lauren fights, tearing uselessly at the people on top of her, shouting, "No! Stop! No!"

Janie summons all her strength and tries to pause it. Tries to scan the room again. It's not working.

Until.

With a final, heroic effort, Janie manages to pry her eyes off of Lauren. Looks around the room.

There.

In the kitchen.

Laughing and drinking, watching the craziness, like it's a football game or something.

Someone has a cell phone out.

A strange expression on her blurry, laughing face.

When Lauren screams, everything goes black. Janie is paralyzed, blind. She hears Stacey mumble, "What the heck?" and feels Lupita groan and shove her head under her pillow. And Janie waits for three things:

Lauren to stop breathing so hard.

Her own sight to return.

And to feel something.

Anything.

It takes a very long time for all three things to happen.

Morning comes too quickly.

FEBRUARY 20, 2006, 8:30 A.M.

The chem team finalizes their display. It's a DNA helix, with posters theorizing how cloning could safely be done with humans.

Janie doesn't care much about it. She lets the real chem geeks do all the work.

Which they probably preferred anyway.

Mrs. Pancake arrives with doughnuts, and they sit and wait for the observers and judges to come by. Everyone looks exhausted, including Mr. Durbin.

Janie excuses herself and goes into the restroom.

Calls Cabel.

Tells him everything about Lauren's dream.

They hover together in grim silence over the phone.

"Be careful," Cabel says for the hundredth time.

"I just can't understand how no one seriously reported it or followed up on it, unless they were all too wasted to remember," Janie murmurs. "There must have been something in that punch. Captain told me to study up on date-rape drugs. I think she nailed it."

"Sounds like it, J."

The door to the restroom opens and Lupita walks in, waving cheerily at Janie.

"I've got to go," Janie says quietly as she returns Lupita's wave, and hangs up.

4:59 P.M.

The team packs up the display. They walk away with white third-place ribbons. Not bad for a stupid theory and a hundred brazillion Popsicle sticks.

By nine p.m. everyone is dozing in the van. Everyone but Janie and Mr. Durbin, that is. Janie struggles and pulls herself out of a variety of ridiculous dreams. Thankfully the silly ones are the easiest to pull out of.

She snacks and tries to sleep between dreams.

Finally Mr. Durbin pulls over along the highway. The sleeping troupe rouses to see what's going on.

"My dear Rebekkah," Mr. Durbin says to Mrs. Pancake, "can you drive for a bit? I'm falling asleep."

Mrs. Pancake glances nervously at Mr. Durbin.

"Just for an hour or so," he says. Pleads.

"Fine," she says.

Mr. Durbin climbs out of the van and enters the rear sliding door. "Somebody, go sit up there with Pancake, will you, please? I need to stretch out."

He drops into the backseat with Janie. "Hey," he says. His eyes travel up and down her cloaked body.

"Hey," Janie says, trying to appear interested, but then gives it up and looks out the window into the night. Watches the snow beginning to fall lightly around them. Wonders if something terrible is about to happen.

That she'll be discovered shaking and blind because of Mr. Durbin's dreams, or that he'll try something creepy in the dark nether regions of the van.

Neither one sounds especially good right now.

Mr. Durbin stretches and yawns. By the time they've gone ten miles, he's snoring lightly next to Janie, his legs splayed out into the aisle, his upper body tilting and sliding an inch at a time toward Janie.

She's trapped.

She wills herself to stay awake and keep her wits about her. Manages to last an hour, maybe.

11:48 P.M.

Janie startles awake.

The van is humming. Everyone else is asleep except Mrs. Pancake up front. Everyone too exhausted to dream.

Janie looks at Mr. Durbin.

His shoulder is against hers. His hand on her thigh.

Janie blanches. Shoves his hand away. Shrinks farther into her little corner and turns her back to him.

He doesn't wake up.

He doesn't dream.

Useless piece of shit, thinks Janie.

3:09 A.M.

The van pulls into Fieldridge High's parking lot. All the students' cars are blanketed in nearly two feet of snow.

Janie shoves Mr. Durbin awake.

"We're here," she says gruffly. She just wants to go home to bed.

The group stumbles out of the van.

"See you in the morning, bright and early for school," Mrs. Pancake calls out into the crisp night as the students wearily shove the snow from their windshields.

Janie calls Cabel.

"Hey. I've been waiting up for you," he says, sounding worried. "Are you safe to drive?"

"I can't imagine any people will have their windows open on a night like tonight," she says.

"Come to me."

"I'm five minutes away."

Janie falls into Cabel's arms, exhausted. Tells him about Mr. Durbin in the backseat of the van.

He leads her to the bedroom, helps her into one of his T-shirts, and whispers in her ear as she falls asleep, "You did great work."

Closes his bedroom door.

Makes his bed on the couch.

Lies awake, pounding his pillow in silence.

FEBRUARY 21, 2006, 3:35 P.M.

Janie, dark circles under her eyes, and Cabel, concerned look on his face, sit in Captain's office. Janie snacks on almonds and milk as she relays the events of the chemistry fair adventure.

"It looked sort of like Durbin's house," she says. "His living room."

"But you couldn't see anyone's face?" Captain presses her.

"No," Janie says. "Just Lauren's. She's the one who was dreaming." She wrings her hands.

"It's okay, Janie. Really. You've given us a lot of information."

"I just wish I had more."

Cabel reaches over and squeezes her hand. A little too tightly.

Afterward, Janie heads home, checks on her mother, grabs dinner, and hits the sack. Sleeps twelve hours straight.

FEBRUARY 27, 2006

Cabel calls Janie on the way to school.

"I'm right behind you," he says.

"I see you," she says, and smiles into the rearview mirror.

"Hey Janie?"

"Yeah?"

"I've got a huge, terrible problem."

"Oh no! Not that horrible toenail fungus that takes six months to cure?"

"No, no, no. Much worse. This is shocking news. Are you sure I should tell you while you're driving?"

"I've got my headset on. Both hands on the wheel. Windows rolled up. Go for it."

"Okay, here goes . . . Principal Abernethy called me this morning to let me know I'm in the running for valedictorian."

There is silence.

A rather loudish snort.

And guffaws.

"Congratulations," she finally says, laughing. "What ever are you going to do?"

"Fail every assignment from today onward."

"You won't be able to."

"Watch me."

"I am so looking forward to this. Oh, and also? You suck."

"I know."

"I love you."

"Love you too. Bye."

Janie hangs up and laughs all over again.

Second-hour psych is a sleeper. Janie stumps Mr. Wang with a question on dreams, just for the hell of it. Leaves him stuttering, so she isn't late to Mr. Durbin's.

For the week leading up to the party, Janie continues to play the woman scorned in front of Mr. Durbin, and he appears to eat it up. In fact, the more she avoids him, the more he comes up with excuses to call her to his desk after class or requests she stop by after school.

She remains aloof, and he goes out of his way to compliment her—on the test, her experiments, her sweater. . . .

MARCH 1, 2006, 10:50 A.M.

"You still coming an hour early on Saturday?" Mr. Durbin asks Janie after class.

"Of course. I promised I would. Stacey and I will be there at six."

"Excellent. Hey, I couldn't do this big party without you, you know."

Janie smiles frostily and walks to the door. "Of course you could. You're Dave Durbin." She slips out and heads to English lit, with boring old Mr. Purcell. He is the epitome of moral character.

Study hall outright sucks. By the time it's over, Janie has too much information about nothing important. And when she lifts her head, she sees the shadows of feet and legs next to the table.

"Are you okay, Janie?" It's Stacey's voice.

Janie clears her throat, and a crashing noise comes from the section of the library to the left. Stacey whirls around and gawks. Janie can't see what's happening, but once she can feel her lips, she smiles. *Cabel's up to something*, she thinks.

She sits up as if she can see, and, indeed, her vision is returning somewhat now. She coughs and clears her throat again, and Stacey turns back to her.

"Sheesh. What a klutz. Anyway, I came over to make sure Saturday at six was right."

"Yep," Janie says. "That's just you and me heading over to Durbin's house to set up. Are you comfortable with that?"

Stacey gives her a quizzical look. "Why wouldn't I be?"

"I have no idea, but you can't be too careful these days, can you?"

Stacey laughs. "I guess. Well, we've got the appetizers all figured out. I hope he has enough electrical outlets, 'cause there's going to be a shitload of Crock-Pots. Of course, we could always use Bunsen burners."

"Good one! Hey, I've got a list of desserts and snacks. Phil Klegg is bringing something called 'dump cake,' and I just don't even want to know what's in there."

They chitchat a little about the party and about the chem. fair, and when the bell rings, Stacey hustles off. Janie peers between the bookshelves and, after the library empties out, sneaks over to where Cabel's sitting.

"Are you okay?" she whispers, giggling.

"Me? Oh sure. You might have to carry me out of here, though."

"What happened?"

"I created a distraction."

"I gathered that."

"Step stool, encyclopedias, floor."

"I see. Well, I can't thank you enough."

"Sure you can. Help me flunk enough tests, so I drop out of the 'torian range."

"Can't you just tell Abernethy that you have a reputation as a dumbshit to keep up, and you don't want the attention?"

"Flunking is more fun."

Janie shakes her head and laughs. "Maybe the first few times. But I bet you won't be able to handle it after that."

"I'll take that bet."

Janie puts her hands on her hips. "All right. After the fourth flunk of something quizlike or weightier, you will struggle and fail to flunk number five. That's my prediction. Loser pays for our first real date."

"You're on. Start saving your money."

SHOWTIME

MARCH 3, 2006, 10:04 A.M.

Chem. 2 is buzzing with excitement, and the students goof around more than anything else. Mr. Durbin lets them. They all did relatively well on the most recent test, the chemistry fair garnered them higher-than-expected results, and everyone is jazzed for tomorrow's party. Mr. Durbin is practically giddy himself, and when Coach Crater stops at the door, because of the ruckus, he pokes his head in.

"Must be a Chem. 2 party coming up," he remarks, eyeing the students one at a time.

"Tomorrow night, Jim," Mr. Durbin says. "Stop by, if the wife will let you out." They chuckle.

Janie's eyes narrow at the comment, but she goes back to her text book. She's looking for a formula—the formula for date-rape drugs. Not that she'd find it in a high-school text book. There's a recipe for disaster. Yet maybe a clue lies within.

But when Mr. Durbin starts walking around to the various stations, she flips her book to the current lesson page and pretends to read. Mr. Durbin pauses for a moment behind her, but she ignores him. He moves on.

In PE, they're in the weight room for four weeks, learning the machines and proper free-weight stance. Dumbass calls Janie up to the front to help demonstrate.

"How much weight do you want, Buffy?"

Janie looks at him. "Well, sir, I guess that depends on the exercise you'd like me to demonstrate."

"Right!" he says, like it was a teaching question. Janie's expression doesn't change. "How about the bench press," he says.

"Free weights or machine?"

"Oooh, aren't you smart? Let's start with free weights."

She gives him a long look. "Are you spotting me or not?"

He chuckles for the audience, like he's doing a magic trick. "Of course I'll spot you."

Janie nods. "All right, then. One-twenty's good."

He laughs. "How about we start at, say, fifty or something."

"One-twenty is fine for a single lift." She bends down and starts adding the weights herself. The students are highly amused, at the encouragement of Coach Crater.

Janie tightens the caps and lies down on the bench, the bar above her chest. "Ready?"

She waits for him to get into spotter position, and grips the bar. Closes her eyes. Concentrates, breathes, until she no longer hears the distraction around her. She pushes up on the bar, holds it a moment, then lowers it evenly to just above her chest and presses upward with all her might. She holds it for a few seconds, and then lets it down slowly in the cradle. "Eighty-five for reps," she says, making the proper adjustments. She presses eight reps, replaces the bar when she's finished, and only then does she tune back in to the room. It's pretty quiet.

Coach Crater is standing, looking down at her, amazed, stupid grin on his face. Janie turns to her side and sits up on the bench, and then walks to the back of the room. Later in the class, she's getting in half her workout for the day. Bonus.

"Asshole," she mutters to Coach Crater as she leaves at the end of class.

"What?"

She keeps walking.

Five minutes into study hall, a paper wad from Cabel hits her in the ear. She rolls her eyes. Opens it up.

Stacey, it says.

Janie looks up. Stacey's head is on her books. Her eyes are closed. Janie bites her lip and nods at Cabel. He gives her an encouraging smile.

Her blood is still pumping from PE. She feels strong. She slept well, ate well . . . has everything going for her. Now all she needs is for Stacey to—

She grips the table, and they are in Stacey's car. Stacey's driving furiously, as before. From the backseat, the growl, the man, his hands gripping Stacey's neck.

Janie wonders if this is the best shot she'll have or if she should wait. She decides to take it, in case Stacey wakes up before they get to the woods.

Stacey's driving erratically. Janie concentrates and squeezes her hands into fists, pumping them before they become numb, focusing on pausing the dream. It's slowing, and Janie tries to turn to look at the man. But the dream speeds up again.

She can't do both things at once. Janie concentrates again on pausing the scene, and she knows her power is limited. One broad push of energy, and the scene slows and stops. She stays perfectly focused, turns slowly, evenly. Sees the look of horror on Stacey's face, sees the man's hands around her neck, his arms, and then slowly, slowly, turns to see the face of the man.

He's wearing a ski mask.

Janie loses concentration, and the dream goes to regular speed again. Damn it. They hit the ditch, the bushes; the car rolls, comes to a stop. Bloody Stacey climbs out through the broken windshield and runs, the rapist follows, into the woods, and Janie tries again to pause the dream, when he grabs Stacey. Janie tries with all her might. But she can't do it. The rapist has Stacey, she trips, he falls on top of her, and then it ends abruptly, just where it always does.

She wishes now she'd tried to help Stacey change it. Next time, maybe.

She actually hopes there isn't a next time.

Fifteen minutes later, when she can see and move again and the library has emptied out for the day, Cabel spends a moment squeezing her tightly, and she can't explain how amazing that feels. He walks with her to the parking lot, takes her home, and goes back for her car, like last time.

Janie eats and drinks, checks on her mom, and falls asleep on the couch.

He's there when she wakes up. Reading a book, his feet on the coffee table.

"Hey," she says. "Time?"

"A little after eight p.m. How you doin'?"

"Good," she says.

"Your mom here?"

"In the bedroom, like always."

Cabel nods. "Captain wants to meet with us in the morning to go over tomorrow night."

"Yep, I figured."

"I'm worried about you, Janie."

"About the dream? It was only worse because I paused it."

"You did it? Cool!"

"Yeah. But I didn't see anything."

"Oh well. What I'm actually worried about is tomorrow night."

"Please don't be. It'll be fine. Eighteen students there, Cabe. I'm not going to get drunk. I'll have a beer or something in my hand, so Durbin doesn't get suspicious, but I'll just fake like I'm drinking it. I'll eat a lot before I go too."

"I hope Captain has an escape plan. You'll have your phone?"

"Yep. And all I need to do to call you is push one button."

"I'll be close by."

"Not too close, Cabe, okay?"

Cabel tosses his book on the table. "You can still back out of this, you know, Janie."

Janie sighs. "Cabe, hear me: I. Don't. Want. To. I want to do this. I want to stop this guy! Why can't you understand that?"

Cabel cringes. "I can't help it. I can't stand the thought of that creep touching you, Janie. What if something awful happens to you? God, I just hate this."

"I know." Janie pushes up on her elbows and sits up. The last thing she wants right now is a fight. Changes the subject. "Is Ethel back home?"

"Yes, she's in the driveway."

"Thank you. I don't know what I'd do without you."

"I wouldn't worry about it if I were you."

Janie leans against him. Strokes his thigh with her fingertips. "Why do you put up with this?"

Cabel relaxes and twirls a string of Janie's hair. "Well, duh. Because one day you'll be really rich and famous, I bet. Your own TV show, people throwing money at you just to get you to change their dreams. I'm holding out for the money. After that I'm outta here."

She laughs. "Did I tell you I benched one-twenty in

PE today? And then I called Coach Crater an asshole."

Cabel roars in laughter. "He *is* an asshole. And one-twenty is probably a national record or something. That's almost more than you weigh."

"The national record is more than two hundred for my age and size category. But I'll take it."

They talk for an hour, and then Cabel heads home. Tomorrow they'll meet again in Captain's office.

After Cabel leaves, Janie pulls out her chemistry book; curiously searches through a chapter; uses her cell phone to peruse the Internet for an hour or so, until she finds the information she's looking for on date-rape drugs; and goes to bed.

MARCH 4, 2006, 9:00 A.M.

Baker and Cobb join Cabel and Janie in Captain's office. Janie meets Cobb and says hello again to Baker.

Captain goes through the schedule for the evening. Janie will arrive at six p.m. along with another girl. The rest of the guests will come at seven.

Captain gives Janie a thin, sexy cigarette lighter, one of the newly popular, old-fashioned flip-top kinds. "It's not a real lighter, Janie. If you flip the lid open, it sends a distress signal to Baker and Cobb outside the house. They'll call your cell phone first, just in case it's an accident, and don't panic if that happens. Answer if it happened by mistake. But just try to keep the lighter in your pocket, and it'll be fine. If you don't answer your phone, they'll move in and call you once again. If you do not pick up, they will come in for you.

"In other words, if you're in trouble, flip open the lighter lid. Put your cell phone on vibrate and wear it in your underwear if you have to, but you must answer that phone if nothing's wrong. If you do not answer, they will assume trouble is afoot. Is that perfectly clear?"

"Yes, sir," Janie says.

"Good. Let's talk about drinking. Believe me, Durbin's going to be watching that everybody has a drink in hand."

Janie looks at her suspiciously. "You're not going to arrest me or anything if I have a drink in my hand, right?"

Captain raises an eyebrow. "Not unless you do something stupid. But I think you should carry around a beverage, yes, so nobody gets suspicious. I don't encourage drinking on the job, though."

"Okay . . . and no setting my beverage down at any time, right? No keg, no punch bowl, no mixed drinks."

Captain nods, impressed. "You've done your homework on date-rape drugs, I see. Good job." She pulls a small package of date-rape drug testers from her desk drawer and hands them to Janie. "Are you familiar with these?"

Janie smiles, reaches inside her bag, and pulls out an identical package.

"Excellent." Captain nods. "Cabel. What's your job?"

"Watching in agony, sir."

Captain suppresses a smile. "I'd make you stay home if I didn't know you'd sneak out, anyway. While you are watching in agony, feel free to take note of anyone who comes or goes that's not on the list."

"Thank you," Cabel says meekly.

"Baker and Cobb, you clear on procedure?"

"Yes, sir," they say together.

"Great. You two may go."

Baker and Cobb slap Janie on the back, like she's one of the guys, give her the thumbs-up, and head out. Janie grins.

Captain turns to Janie.

"Tonight is not the night to get sucked into any drunk

person's dream. Try and steer clear if you can. If you can't, we'll deal with that later. I do understand you can't control the actions of other people, so don't panic if it happens and you get stuck."

Janie nods.

"And be safe. Follow your gut. You're smart. You have a terrific sense of intuition. Use it like you have in the past, and we'll all walk away just fine. All right?"

"Yes, sir."

"Any questions?"

"No."

"Good. Call me if you think of any," Captain says. "And, Janie, I have never been more serious. Use that panic lighter if you need it. Don't be a martyr and don't think you can handle this job alone. We work as a team. Got it?"

"Got it. I'm ready, sir."

"And a reminder. This could be nothing more than just an ordinary party. Our goal is to find and arrest a sexual predator. Not to bust the guy for serving a few drinks to minors. We can always get him next time for that. Like I said, use your intuition and judgment."

"I will."

"Cabel. Any questions?"

"No, sir."

"Get on out of here, then. I'll see you sometime in the next twenty-four hours, I expect. Damn, I hate this job."

10:09 A.M.

Janie makes her crème-de-menthe bars and puts them in the refrigerator, and then makes lunch. Cabel stops by and mopes around uselessly, unable to talk about anything. Janie finally sends him away.

"Be careful, baby," he says, kissing the top of her head.

Janie's quiet.

And he's gone.

2:32 P.M.

Janie lights her relaxation votive candle and sits still on her bed, clearing her mind, meditating. Preparing herself. She mentally runs through her profile sheets. All the events that led up to today. And then her mind strays to Stacey's car dream. She goes through it, step by step. She knows there's a connection between the dream and Mr. Durbin, but how? Did Mr. Durbin actually rape her? Janie thinks about Lauren. Wishes she could have focused on the faces in her party dream, but they were blurred beyond recognition. And if Lauren has nightmares about the party, why doesn't she have qualms or reservations or downright contempt for the host? Why didn't the anonymous caller follow up with another call to Crimebusters Underground?

She dozes for an hour, asking herself to figure out

the connection between the dreams and this party tonight.

Herself says no.

When she wakes up, Janie takes a shower and puts on tight jeans and a low-cut V-neck sweater. She adds a hint of makeup and ties her hair back, low, in a ribbon, leaving a few wisps out to frame her face. She grabs a snack and a glass of milk, making quick work of them, and brushes her teeth. Puts on some lip gloss.

It's showtime.

5:57 P.M.

"I'm pulling up to the house. I'll see you after," Janie says.

"If you get a chance to call me . . . safely . . . you know . . ." Cabel's voice is anxious.

"I will if I can. Love you, Cabe."

"Love you, Janie. Be safe."

They hang up. It's a warm night for early March, and the snow is gone, leaving muddy yards, puddles, and potholes everywhere. Janie parks on the street, double-checks her pockets, grabs her dessert, and takes a deep breath, then strips off her coat and tosses it on the passenger seat next to her. Never hurts to have an excuse to get out of the house. She bought a pack of cigarettes earlier and leaves them in the coat pocket.

Janie closes her eyes momentarily, gets into her character, and gets out of her car. She sees the tail end of Baker's "soccer-mom" minivan down the street, and he flashes the brake lights at her. For some reason that makes her feel tremendously more confident, and she smiles in his direction, knowing he can see her with his high-powered binoculars. Cobb is stationed on the next street, with a partial view of the back of the house. She doesn't look for Cabel, but she knows where he is—around the corner.

She slams her car door and walks up the driveway to Mr. Durbin's front steps, hoping Stacey shows up soon. She knocks and hears footsteps. Mr. Durbin opens the door and ushers her in.

"Hey, Janie," he says, letting her in and closing the door behind her.

"Looking good, Mr. Durbin," Janie says with a grin, glancing around. He's rearranged the furniture, set up extra folding chairs, and added two card tables to the great-room area.

"You too, Janie," he says, looking her up and down. "You can call me Dave outside of school, you know."

She turns and gives him her full attention, and watches his eyes move to her chest. "Dave," she repeats. "I should probably keep this refrigerated," she says, indicating her dessert. "Mind if I poke around your kitchen so I know where to find things? I figure I can help you out with the food and drink distribution once everybody gets here."

"Be my guest," he says. Not a hint of apprehension.

Strike one, Janie thinks. He follows her and shows Janie where he keeps extra dishes, glasses, silverware, and napkins.

"The fridge is packed pretty tightly," he says, "but there's room on the bottom shelf, if you move a few beer bottles around." He stands behind her while she bends over and shoves her dessert inside. "You want a beer or something? I'm making punch, too."

"Are you having one?" she asks.

"Sure."

On the fridge, holding—what else?—two snapshots of Mr. Durbin himself, is a magnet. *The* magnet, with the Fieldridge Crimebusters hotline number. Janie's heart pounds. *He screwed himself*, she realizes, thinking of the blurred, anonymous person in the kitchen, making the call.

Swiftly, Janie pulls out two bottles of beer and Durbin shows her where the bottle opener is, when from the hallway comes none other than Mr. Wang. He's barefooted and his hair is wet.

"Mr. Wang," Janie says, controlling her surprise. "I didn't know you were here."

"Ms. Hannagan," he says with a nod.

Mr. Durbin grins. "So formal, you two. Chris, Janie," he says. "Janie, you want to grab a beer for Chris? I've got to get this punch going. Chris came early to help me with the tables and chairs, and then we ended up in a rather competitive game of one-on-one. Basketball," he adds.

"I see. Well it's very nice to see you, uh, Chris." She winks and he looks nervous.

"Likewise, Janie."

Janie hands Mr. Wang a beer. He looks around the room to see what needs to be done, and finally, rather helplessly, he goes to the stereo and starts rummaging through the CDs. "I'll take my usual spot as the DJ," he says.

The doorbell rings, and Stacey lets herself in with a shriek of "Woo hoo!" Janie raises her eyebrow.

"Hey, Stacey," Janie says when Stacey brings her Crock-Pot to the kitchen's island.

"Janie!" Stacey smells like beer already. "Are you ready to party?"

Mr. Wang has Coldplay on now, and he cranks the volume. "Now I am," Janie says, holding up her beer. Wonders how wild the party has to get before Mr. Wang moves to hip-hop.

She takes the paper cups and beverage napkins to the great room, where Mr. Durbin is pouring a bottle of cranberry juice into a punch bowl that already has a clear liquid in it. He adds a bottle of Ruby Red Squirt to the mixture as Janie sets up the table display, and then he goes to the sink to get an ice ring, and plops that in as well.

Janie opens the package of napkins and lays them out in a spiral design. "What goes on the other table?" she asks.

Mr. Durbin stirs the punch with a ladle. "I figured we'd put some munchies out there. You want to be in charge of keeping that going?" He takes a cup and pours a little of the punch in it, tasting it, nodding approval.

"Sure. I saw some stuff on the counter. I'll get serving bowls and put those things out here."

"I have a little apron you can wear if you'd like," he says under the noise of the music, so only she hears it.

Janie raises her eyebrow and glances at him. He's grinning.

Stacey comes over to the punch table. "Is this the same stuff you made at the last party, Dave? And if it is, I should probably test it, don't you think?" She gives him an innocent look.

"Absolutely," he says, pouring a glass for her.

Janie goes to the kitchen and begins to distribute the munchie items into various-size bowls. When she takes them to the table, Mr. Wang is downing some punch too. "How about it, Janie?" Mr. Durbin offers her a glass.

"After my beer," she says with a grin. "What's in that stuff, anyway?"

"Just a little vodka. You can't even taste it," he says.

"But you can feel it." Stacey giggles.

Mr. Wang is beginning to loosen up now, and by seven p.m., Mr. Durbin, Mr. Wang, and Stacey are bantering comfortably.

Janie takes advantage of the moment to pour some of her beer into the sink before the doorbell starts ringing. It doesn't stop for the next hour. She plays hostess.

8:17 P.M.

Everyone has arrived, and the party is beginning to pick up speed. Janie works the kitchen, arranging the dishes as people bring them in. She spreads the dining table with the appetizers, and at one point, uses the excuse of looking for an extension cord to scout around the other rooms in the house.

She's in his office/den off the kitchen when Mr. Durbin finds her. "Whatcha doin', hot stuff?"

She turns and grins, hiding her guilt from snooping. "I'm looking for an extension cord, so we can keep all the appetizers warm. Do you have one handy?"

He's standing very close. "Downstairs," he says. "Come on, I'll show you," he says. His voice is sexy.

She licks her lips, looking into his eyes. "Show me

the way," she says, pointing with her beer. Her heart thuds heavily at the thought of going downstairs with Mr. Durbin.

The door to the basement is through the kitchen. It's a finished basement, with a full bar, big-screen TV, and two giant fluffy-looking couches. Janie follows Mr. Durbin through a door into a workshop with a small worktable. On it sits a Bunsen burner and several flasks and beakers. On the shelves above it are a variety of chemicals. Janie strolls over to it and rapidly checks them out. "Oh cool! I want a lab table in my house," she whines.

He comes up behind her and puts his hand lightly on her waist. His thumb rolls gently, back and forth on her side. She leans into him slightly as her eyes scan the shelves.

And then he's taking her arm and pulling her with him. "I gotta go mingle," he says. They climb the stairs, to where the music is loud again. "Here's the extension cord," he says, handing it to her. "Come on, you need to have some fun now. Get out of work mode and enjoy yourself. It's a party, for Chrissake." He grins and pinches her ass. "Get some of this punch, Janie," he says, holding up his empty cup. "I promise you, you'll lighten up and have a great time."

He sets his cup on the kitchen counter, and after Janie has the network of plugs configured, so that nobody could possibly trip over all the cords, she glances around, grabs the cup, and makes a beeline to the bathroom.

There's a line. She doesn't want to wait.

She slips down the hall, peers into a dark bedroom, and sneaks inside, locking the door. Turns on the lamp on the dresser, and pulls a package out of her pocket. She rips open the package, takes out a round paper circle, and tips the near-empty cup, so a single drop pauses on the rim of it and splashes on the paper.

She rubs it in and waits.

Thirty seconds, and it's dry.

And nothing happens.

She takes a second paper circle and tries again.

Still nothing.

"Hm," she says. She crumples up the papers and shoves them into her pocket, replaces the package to the other pocket, grabs the cup and her beer, and goes back out to the party.

Janie tosses the cup in the trash and peeks inside quickly. Two empty fifths of Absolut lay at the bottom of the trash bag. She closes the wastebasket and washes her hands. She can hear the students, louder now, laughing and dancing.

9:45 P.M.

Janie's bored. And dying of thirst. All the soda is in open two-liter bottles left unattended, and maybe she's paranoid, but Janie doesn't trust the tap water because it has one of those filter things on it. She looks at the warm, half-full bottle of beer in her hands. Knows it's probably the only safe thing in the house, since it hasn't left her hands from the moment she opened it.

Many of the guys have gone downstairs to watch basketball, and a few girls too. But most of the girls are swaying and laughing in the great room, and Mr. Wang is entertaining them with his dance moves. Four girls sit on the floor playing Texas hold 'em. The food has hardly been touched. Everybody has a beer or a cup of something in hand. Janie stabs a meatball with a toothpick and nibbles at it. It's delicious, but only succeeds in making her even more thirsty.

And then Mr. Durbin emerges from the kitchen with a fresh bowl of punch. He makes a general announcement, and half the girls gather around, holding out cups. He generously ladles punch, and he pours one for himself, and Mr. Wang too. Mr. Wang, sweating from dancing, downs his punch and lifts his cup to Janie, who sits on the couch making small-talk with Desiree. Desiree is nicely half-drunk, not too slobbery, and Janie has really learned to like her. She's smart and funny.

Mr. Wang pours a second cup of punch and brings it over to Janie. "For you," he says. His black eyes are shiny. He sits next to Janie and leans back, closing his eyes.

"Long day, Chris?" Janie says when Desiree slips away to refill her glass.

He opens a lazy eye. "Long and hard," he says wickedly.

Janie nods. "Thanks for sharing." She holds the cup in her hand. Listening to the music. It's the Black Eyed Peas. "Got any Mos Def?" Janie asks.

"Mos' definitely," Mr. Wang says, laughing at his own stupid joke. He lunges unsteadily toward her. "Whoa," he whispers, catching himself on her thigh. "I'll just get that on later. Hey, you know, lighten up already, princess," he says, tilting his head quizzically. "Your type is supposed to get plastered at these kinds of parties. You know, free booze." He leans in and sniffs her neck. "You smell terrific," he says. He rests his sweaty head on her shoulder.

My type? Janie burns. She can't help it. She wants to kick Mr. Wang's ass. "Jesus Christ," she mutters. "You wanna know what the trailer trash like, huh, Chris?"

"Not all the trailer trash. Just you." He's slurring his words.

"Wait right here for me, then," she says, shrugging Mr. Wang's head off her shoulder and trying to hold in her disgust. "I'll be back."

"Oh yeah," he says, grinning happily.

Janie mingles her way to the bathroom with her untouched punch and stands in line. By the time she gets in there, she hears the clumping of a dozen feet coming up the stairs. Mr. Durbin's explaining boisterously that somebody's gotta be the one to start eating, because the girls aren't doing it. She locks herself in the bathroom and does the drink test again.

Spreads the drop of punch on the paper.

Waits thirty seconds.

Watches it change to bright blue.

Her stomach lurches.

Rooffies.

She dumps the punch into the toilet, and flushes.

Searches through the drawers and cupboards for bottles of liquid, powder, or pills. Finds nothing. Janie could call in the cops now, she knows. But she doesn't have proof that it was Mr. Durbin who did it. What if one of the other students brought it in? If Janie can find the drugs, it'll help even more in prosecuting the bastard. She remembers the last case, how frustrated Cabel and Captain were when Baker and Cobb busted the drug scene before Cabel could get the location of the cocaine. Janie wants proof. Wants to get this done right. *It's still early*, she thinks as she rifles through Mr. Durbin's things. *I can find it.*

Heads across the hall and searches the bedroom. Slips into the other bedroom and searches it, too. Nothing, nothing. *Back downstairs*, she thinks.

It's hot, and Janie's really thirsty now. She takes a sip from the beer in her hand. It's flat and warm. But it'll have to do. Captain won't blame her for trying to stay hydrated, will she? After all, Janie's just being smart. She knows from experience that she can easily handle two beers without it affecting her.

Janie eases past a few guys standing in the kitchen and heads to the basement. The TV and lights are all on. But everyone is upstairs now. She hopes they stay that way. She slips into the dark room with the lab table, and peers at the labels, moving the big items to search for smaller containers. She doesn't see what she's looking for. Frustrated, she turns and goes back upstairs. Dumps out the rest of her stale beer. Grabs a fresh one from the refrigerator and a paper plate from the food table.

She loads up her plate, taking a long, thirsty swig of her beer between the meatballs and the veggie tray. *It's gotta be here somewhere*, she thinks. *Maybe Durbin's bedroom? But the door's closed, and it's right off the great room. I'd be seen. And what if he's in there?*

Janie shoves half a meatball in her mouth, and chews. Delicious. She noshes on a carrot stick, and moves toward the great room. Finds a place in the crowd to stand and eat. Thinking. Thinking hard.

People are out of control.

She munches, eyes like slits, looking for Mr. Durbin and Mr. Wang. The roar of voices is growing stronger every minute. The music grows steadily louder.

She concentrates on her watch. Makes her eyes focus. 11:08 p.m.

11:09 P.M.

Squeezes between two guys with her plate of food and her beer, and discovers what they are so engrossed in watching.

Janie stares at the scene. She's feeling the effects of the beer, even though she only sipped a little from the first and drank half of the second. Still, she's dying of thirst and doesn't dare to drink anything else. She chugs down the rest of this beer, and then eats quickly, knowing she still has work to do. Knowing things are getting a little crazy.

She glances at the punch bowl. Nearly empty. Students are sprawled around the room, sitting on one anothers' laps, making out. A few are sitting alone, a vacant, dazed look on their faces. And in the middle of the room, where everyone else's eyes are riveted, Mr. Wang and Stacey O'Grady are dirty dancing. Very dirty. Mr. Wang's shirt is off, and his muscles bulge and shine with sweat. Janie's eyes wander over his body, and she is surprised to find him suddenly, strangely, attractive.

Stacey is completely toasted. She can hardly stand up. Janie reminds herself to keep an eye on her. People are slurping the dregs of the punch, like it's a desert oasis. Mr. Durbin comes from the kitchen with more.

Janie lets her eyes wander lazily as she eats. She's feeling tired. Mellow. The guys who aren't otherwise occupied head back downstairs, tripping and shoving their way to the TV. Janie's head is buzzing now, and she's surprised—she's only really had one beer. She should eat more, she tells herself, to stop the buzz.

Back in the kitchen, she loads up her plate a second time, head starting to spin. She leans against the counter, hoping it will pass.

And then she stops.

A distant thought—a nudge. Something she was about to do. She pictures it.

Looks up on top of the refrigerator.

A can of paint stripper.

A bottle of Red Devil Lye.

That's . . . something, she thinks, screwing her eyes shut, trying to concentrate. But her brain isn't working right. *That's . . . that's it.* She knows she needs to remember it, but now she can't imagine why.

Janie's buzzing hard now, and she's not sure she likes it. She sits down on the floor and digs into the food, trying to stop spinning, finish the food on her plate, feeling sleepy. *Gotta call . . .* The thought pops into her head, but leaves again just as quickly. Someone trips over her leg, and Janie drags her body up off the floor and stands, and then tries to remember why she stood up at all. She shakes her head, attempting to clear her mind, and gets dizzy, nearly falls, bumping into somebody else who looks vaguely familiar. She laughs at herself and remembers what she has to do. She picks up her plate and throws it in the garbage can. Two points.

Her skin is tingling as she wanders around, checking out the students on the couches who are in various stages of pre-sex. Janie watches them curiously. And then she thinks maybe she's in somebody's dream. She stumbles around the great room, knowing that if she really is in somebody else's dream, no one else can see her. Stacey and Mr. Wang are gone. Too bad, because Janie wanted to watch them dance some more.

Twelve something in the morning. Janie's eyes linger on the clock, not quite comprehending the position of the hands.

There's a sudden ruckus in the room, and Janie rouses herself, trying to remember where she is and why she is there. She stands up from the floor, wondering how she got there in the first place. Mr. Durbin is standing by the door, handing Coach Crater a drink. Crater drinks it down in one shot, and Janie is impressed. He's cute, too, she thinks. And she is still so thirsty. She wanders to the kitchen, looks in the refrigerator, and sees her dessert. "Hey," she says, her tongue feeling strangely thick. "I should set that out." She reaches for it, misses on the first try, but gets it on the next one—after serious concentration. And someone is touching her bum.

She stands up and sets the dessert on the counter, so she doesn't drop it. "Whoa," she says, laughing.

"Mm," says Mr. Durbin. "Here, I brought you something to drink. You look thirsty." *He's slurring his words too*, thinks Janie. It must be his dream. Janie remembers that she should be glad to be in Mr. Durbin's dream, but she can't remember why.

She smiles gratefully. "Thank you so much," she gushes, and holds up the cup, feeling like there might be something she's supposed to know about it, but her thirst overwhelms her. "Is everything tipping just a little bit in here?" she asks, laughing like it's the funniest thing she's thought of all day, and then puts the cup to her lips. The punch slides down her throat, cooling it. "I thought all the punch was gone. Mm, oh god. That's so yummy," she says.

And then Mr. Durbin's pushing her back against the counter and kissing her, and she's feeling his hot tongue on hers. She starts kissing him back, because that's what feels right. The fuzziness in her brain grows.

"I gotta go . . . ," she says suddenly, pulling away.

"No, you don't have to go."

"I mean, to the bathroom," she says seriously.

"There's one in my bedroom," he says, his eyes hungry.

"Oh, cool. Do you still have that porn magazine in there?" Janie hesitates too late, wondering if she was supposed to say that, but she can't remember why she shouldn't.

"Lots of them," he says. "Not that I need them with you here."

"Huh." She follows him through the dazed and half-naked crowd. He stops to grab another glass of punch, and gives her another one too. On the way to Mr. Durbin's bedroom, Janie waves at Coach Crater. "Hey," she says, turning back to Mr. Durbin. "Wasn't Stacey here? Before?"

"She's still here, Janie." His words are deliberate, like he's concentrating. "She's fucking Chris in the other bedroom, so we can fuck in here." His words sound like slow-motion, matter of fact, and Janie is certain she's in his dream now.

He shows her to the bathroom, and she decides maybe she should close the door, even though she doesn't feel like it. It's so much work. But that's weird, because if it's Mr. Durbin's dream, why would she be in a room where she can't see him?

She sits down on the toilet, her head heavy. Something seems wrong, but she doesn't know what it is. She sits there for a long time, in a half-dream. She almost falls asleep, she's feeling so warm and mellow. And in her mind, she's whirling through memories that pop in and out of her brain.

She hears a knocking sound, far away.

"Just go home, Carrie," she mumbles.

She can't seem to open her eyes.

She leans to the right, and there's a cool, comfortable wall to rest her cheek on.

There is another knocking sound. But this one turns into a car's-engine knock, and Stacey's driving. There's going to be a man coming any second from the backseat, Janie remembers, and then he's there, gripping Stacey around the neck. *His hands are sexy*, she thinks.

"Come on, Janie, don't be shy," she hears from far away, and Janie rouses herself.

"What?" she says.

"Come on out, sweetheart. We're all waiting for you."

It must be Cabel. He sleeps a lot. And then she remembers she's sitting on the toilet, and she chuckles silently to herself and finishes up.

She drinks a long drink from the bathroom tap. She's so thirsty. She wants milk. Milk always makes her feel stronger. She turns to leave, but the door is gone. It's just a wall now.

She scratches her head.

Looks around.

Laughs.

It's on the other wall.

Stumbling, Janie bumps against the door, trying to push it, and finally tries pulling it. It opens, and Mr. Durbin is on the bed. There are three girls from class with him, and he's taking their clothes off as they lie there.

Janie finds this fascinating.

But now she remembers that she wants milk, so she walks carefully out of the bedroom, trying not to bang into anything.

Mr. Wang is standing by the slider door in his underwear, letting the cool air inside the house. "That feels great," Janie says. She breathes it in.

It smells like cigarette smoke.

She stands there, spinning. There it is again. That thing that feels funny.

Coach Crater comes down the hallway toward them, as Janie tries to remember why she came to the kitchen.

"Hey, there you are, Buffy," he says.

Surprisingly he's wearing jeans and a shirt, although his shirt is open and his chest hair shows.

Janie looks around. Walks back to look in the great room. Everyone is practically naked. *How bizarre*, she thinks, and goes back to feel the cold air again.

And then Coach Crater grabs her by the shoulders and turns her toward him. He plants a big wet kiss on her mouth. And moves on.

He's tripping as he walks to get more punch.

She remembers that she doesn't think she likes him. But maybe that's not really true.

It's so hard to decide what is true.

She smells more cigarette smoke, and she has an urge to go outside to have a cigarette. So she goes to the door.

Outside on the deck, it's dark. Mr. Wang follows her out there, in his Calvin Klein briefs. Janie breathes in the cold air. She holds on tightly to the railing when Mr. Wang starts touching her. "I smelled smoke," she explains, but she doesn't see anyone smoking.

And then Coach Crater comes out too. Mr. Wang is kissing her neck, and Coach is telling her how hot she is and feeling her up, and he says something about bench pressing.

Finally she remembers why she hates him.

And she remembers that she smelled smoke, but no one is smoking.

Then, in her mind, while the two men kiss and touch her, is Miss Stubin.

Telling her something.

Janie struggles to listen. She remembers liking that old lady for some reason.

Cigarette, Miss Stubin says in Janie's mind.

"I need a cigarette," Janie whispers.

Use your lighter, Miss Stubin says. *In your pocket.*

"I need a cigarette," Janie says louder. "Now."

Coach Crater goes inside and comes back with a joint. "How's this, Buffy?"

"Okay." Janie takes the joint with a shrug and reaches into her pocket. She didn't know she had a lighter. Maybe the old maid put it there.

And then the words register, from what Coach Crater just said.

Janie.

Does not like.

To be called.

Buffy.

Janie reels back against the deck's handrail, stumbling, grabs Coach's arm off her breast, wrenches his elbow around so he twirls and faces the other way, and she kicks him, hard, in the kidneys. "Don't call me 'Buffy,'" she says mildly. "Ever again."

His feet splay sideways and he lands with a thud on the wet deck, moaning.

Janie pulls the lighter from her pocket as Mr. Wang stares. She examines it, puts the joint in her mouth, and pulls back the lid.

She tries lighting it.

No fire comes out.

She tries it again.

Mr. Wang is confused, looking at Coach Crater, who is groaning and barely moving on the deck.

"Get me a fucking lighter that works, or I'll beat the shit out of you, too," she says to Mr. Wang, and sinks to the deck, exhausted. When her hip starts buzzing, she just figures it's one of those weird things that have been happening all night.

She looks at Coach Crater. He's sprawled every which way. His hands are reaching. Reaching for her leg. She watches them, like it's not happening to her. She focuses on his fingers, thinking how weird fingers are. Like little animals, all their own.

He's wearing a strange, square ring. She wants it, sort of. It looks cool, like he belongs to something.

Mr. Wang returns with a lighter just as Janie's hip buzzes again. Maybe she'll have to have her whole leg amputated, she thinks sadly. That would really suck.

She lights the joint and inhales the smoke. Holds it in. Lets it out slowly. Mr. Wang falls to the deck next to her and starts kissing her cleavage.

She doesn't like that, she decides. He's in her way. She's trying to smoke a joint here.

She makes a peace sign with her fingers, marveling over them. Then, when Mr. Wang grabs her nipple in his mouth, she stabs him in the eyeballs.

She learned that somewhere.

She doesn't know where.

Mr. Wang swings his fist wildly, crying out in pain. He catches her on the jaw, her head flies back and hits the deck's rail, and she blacks out. The joint burns down between her fingers.

NOT ALL RIGHT

MARCH 5, 2006, 6:13 A.M.

Janie is dreaming. She's dreaming Stacey's dream, over and over again, and she's dreaming that she can't pull out of it. She tries. Hard. But she's stuck on the rapist in the backseat.

Over and over again, the dream pauses on the rapist's hands. And then she sees it.

She gasps awake and sits up wildly, even though she's numb. "Oh god," she croaks, her voice gone. She can't see. But someone is talking, rubbing her hands, her arms. Soothing her with his voice. She's breathing hard, in and out, and she cries hot tears, because all she wants is to open her eyes. But they feel open.

"I need my glasses," she cries out in a broken voice. "I can't see."

"Janie, it's me, Cabel. I'm right here. I have your glasses, and you'll be able to see in a few minutes. You're safe." His voice breaks and he pauses. "You're safe. Just sit back and rest. Wait for it. You'll see shadows in a minute, and then everything else will come back, okay?"

Janie slumps back.

She shudders, but she can't remember why.

She tries to breathe, in and out.

"What time is it?" she whispers.

"Six fifteen."

She hesitates. "Morning?" she guesses.

"Yes, morning."

She breathes again. "What day?"

There is a short silence. "It's Sunday morning, sweetheart. March 5."

"Is Stacey O'Grady in this room?"

"No, baby. She's down the hall."

"Is the door closed?"

"Yes."

Janie doesn't understand, but her brain is still fuzzy, like her eyes. And then slowly, bits of things return.

And she knows there are two very important things she told herself to remember, even when everything was out of control. She speaks slowly.

"Cabel?"

"Yes?"

"GHB. Mr. Durbin cooked it up himself out of paint stripper and lye. That's my guess. I looked it up before. I didn't see him do it. But he has the stuff. And, obviously, the ability."

She breathes, exhausted. "Only twelve hours before it's out of the body. Urine tests. Everyone. Every fucking one."

She doesn't see him blink.

"Good job," he murmurs, and he's on the cell phone. Talking gibberish.

She's trying hard to focus. There's something else. What is it? She can't remember.

He stops talking on the phone, and he's rubbing her arm.

And then she remembers. "Meatballs," she says. "The drug was in the punch, but I swear to god I didn't drink the punch. Not that I can remember. I tested it. The tests are in my jeans pocket. Right side." She pauses. Sobs a little. "He must have put the GHB in the meatball sauce, when I was in the bathroom, testing the punch. God, I'm so stupid."

She drifts off, still blind, and sleeps fitfully for a few hours.

9:01 A.M.

Janie blinks awake. The light above her on the ceiling is blinding.

"Where the hell am I?" she asks.

"Fieldridge General," Cabe says.

She sits up slowly. Her head aches. She holds her hands to her face. "What the fuck," she says.

"Janie, can you see?"

"Of course I can see, you asshole."

He does a double take, looks at the woman next to him, who chuckles, and he closes his eyes briefly. "You feel like talking?" he asks carefully.

She blinks a few more times. Sits up. "Where the fuck am I?" she asks again.

Cabel plants his forehead in his hands. Captain steps to the plate.

"Janie, do you know who I am?"

Janie peers at her. "Yes, sir."

"Good. And who is this?"

"Cabel Strumheller, sir. You remember him, don't you?"

Captain buries a grin. "I do, now that you mention it." She pauses. "What do you remember?"

Janie closes her eyes. Her head aches. She thinks for a long time.

They wait.

She finally speaks. "I went to the party at Durbin's house."

"Yes," Captain says.

Cabel slips out of his chair and begins to pace the floor.

"I remember setting up the food." She strains against the fuzziness.

"That's good, Janie. Take your time. We've got all day."

Janie pauses again. "Oh god," she says. Her voice shivers and falls.

"It's okay, Janie. You were drugged."

A tear slips down Janie's cheek. "That wasn't supposed to happen," she whispers.

Captain takes her hand. "You did everything right. No worries. Just take your time."

Janie sobs quietly for a moment. "Cabe's gonna be mad," she whispers to Captain.

"No, Janie. He's fine. Right, Cabe?"

Cabel looks at Captain and Janie. His face is ashen. "I'm fine, Janie," he manages to croak.

Captain captures Janie's eyes. "You know this, Hannagan, goddamnit. Anything that happened as a result of you being drugged against your will is not your fault. Right? You know your stuff. And you know that. And whoever did anything to you will go to jail, okay? Not your fault. Don't turn soft on me, Janie," she adds. "You're a strong woman. The world needs more like you."

Janie swallows hard and turns her head away. She wants to bury herself under the covers and disappear. "Yes, sir."

"Would it help you remember if I mention some of the names?" Captain asks.

"Maybe," Janie says. "I don't remember much. Just wisps of things."

"Okay. Let's start with Durbin. What happened with him."

Janie sighs. Then she opens her eyes wide. "GHB," she says, and sits up. "GHB."

Cabel gives Captain a frightened look. "Settle," she says to him, under her breath. "She doesn't remember talking earlier. It's normal." She turns back to Janie. "What about GHB, Janie?"

Janie thinks. "I tested the first punch," she says. "I thought for sure there'd be rooffies in it. But it was clean. Just vodka. That's what he told me."

"Good job. You are a professional."

"And then people started getting weird. Durbin brought out a new bowl." The wisps are a little stronger.

Captain sits quietly, letting her think.

"He made all the guys come upstairs from the basement. They were watching TV. He said they should start eating, because the girls wouldn't do it."

Captain scowls, but holds in her disgust.

"And then . . ." She thinks. "Wang gave me some punch and gave me shit about being trailer trash. What a fucker," she says, her eyes stinging. She cries for a minute, and then pulls it together.

"He was messed up by then," she continues. "I thought something was going on. So I took the punch he gave me and tested that—I didn't drink any. The paper turned blue, and I flushed it all down the toilet." She closes her eyes again.

"I went downstairs," she says slowly. "I checked the chemicals on his lab table, and I didn't see the ones I was looking for—GBL and NaOH. Those two chemicals combined make GHB, a drug-facilitated, sexual-assault weapon. I studied about it, like you told me to."

Captain nods.

"But when I got upstairs, I remembered seeing some bottles on top of his refrigerator. Paint stripper and lye. The same chemicals that create GHB."

"By then I was paranoid and worried. All the soda was in open two-liter bottles, and I didn't even want to get a glass of water, because he had one of those water-filter things on the tap, and I thought he maybe put the drug in it. So I grabbed a beer—I'm so sorry, Captain—and drank it sort of fast, but I had food by then too. And a beer, honestly, is not too much for me. I don't know what happened," she says, crying again, covering her face. "I screwed up, didn't I?"

Captain closes her eyes. "No, Janie. You did fine. We should have thought to send you with some individual water bottles or something."

Cabel stops pacing and rests his forehead against the window. Bounces it against the glass a few times. Mutters unintelligibly.

Captain carefully continues. "You told us a few hours ago, something about the meatballs. Do you remember that?"

Janie is silent. Confused. "I don't remember meatballs."

Captain nods at Cabel. He looks quizzically at her, then he nods. He dials his phone. Talks to someone. Eventually hangs up.

"GHB, confirmed in the meatballs and in the veggie dip," he says. "Jesus Christ." He takes off his rugby, leaving his T-shirt on. Begins pacing some more. "I didn't know you could put it in food."

"Apparently Durbin wanted to cover his bases," Captain says quietly, eyeing Cabel carefully. She turns back to Janie. "Is there anything else you remember? Don't worry if you can't. I expect that's probably about it."

Janie remains quiet for a long time. Finally she says, "This is weird, but I know Coach Crater raped Stacey. Not this time. Last semester."

The room rings in silence.

"How do you know, Janie?" Captain asks.

Janie hesitates. "I can't prove it."

"That's okay. Give me your hunch. Remember? We can't solve crimes without leads."

Janie nods. Tells her the car dream Stacy's had since last fall. And then tells her about pausing the dream and not being able to see the face. "But I saw his hand," she says. "In the dream he's wearing a square fraternity ring. I remember seeing the same ring on Crater's right hand last night."

Silence.

And more silence. Cabel makes another phone call.

Captain ventures another question with an almost-smile on her face. "Do you remember when you activated the panic button?"

Janie looks at her. Shakes her head no.

"So you don't remember beating the shit out of Crater and Wang?"

Janie stares. "What?"

Captain smiles. "You were amazing, Janie. I hope someday you remember it. Because you should be very proud of yourself, like I am of you."

Janie closes her eyes.

Finally she says, "Cabe, can you step out for a minute?"

He gives her a fleeting look, then goes.

"Captain," Janie says, "did anything happen? You know. With me?"

Captain holds her hand. "Nothing below the belt, kiddo. When Baker and Cobb found you, your sweater was off your shoulder. That's it. The doctors did an exam. You stopped them, Janie."

Janie sighs in relief. "Thanks, sir."

6:23 P.M.

Cabel drives Janie to his house.

"Twenty-one positives on the GHB, Janie." Cabel's voice is harsh. "Everyone at the party was drugged. Durbin even drugged himself. Rumor has it, the drug is known to enhance stamina." He pauses. "Ewww." They both shudder. "When Baker and Cobb and the backup crew arrived, Durbin had three female students in his bed with him."

Janie is quiet.

"He's going to jail for a long time, Janie."

"What about Wang?"

"Him too. Sadly, he raped Stacey before Baker and Cobb got there. They found his DNA. She asked for the morning-after pill. She doesn't remember anything that happened last night." Cabel's hands grip the steering wheel. His knuckles are white.

Janie's quiet. "Fuck," she says.

She should have done better.

Done better for Stacey.

Janie's headache dulls by evening. She eats everything Cabel gives her, and then declares herself fit. "Stop babying me already," she says with a cautious grin. She knows Cabel hasn't slept.

Cabel gives her an exhausted, lost look. Sucks in a breath as his face crumbles. He nods. "I'm done," he says. "Excuse me." He walks out of the room, and Janie hears him in his bedroom. Yelling into his pillow.

Janie cringes.

Realizes now she was in way over her head. And, maybe, so was Cabel.

After a while he is quiet. Janie ventures a peek into his bedroom, and he's asleep on his stomach, fully clothed, glasses flung on the nightstand, his arm and leg hanging off the edge of the bed, tears still clumping his eyelashes, cheeks flushed. Not dreaming.

Janie kneels next to the bed, smoothes his hair from his cheek, and watches him for a very long time.

MARCH 9, 2006, 3:40 P.M.

The uproar at Fieldridge High School has settled, some. Janie's three substitute teachers are less than exciting. Which is okay, because Janie's having trouble concentrating, anyway. Not because of Mr. Durbin's party. But because of what happened after, with Cabel.

After school Janie's at home, lying on the couch, staring at the ceiling, when Carrie pops her head inside Janie's front door.

Janie sits up and forces a smile. "Hey. Happy, happy. Did you do anything fun for your birthday?" She hands Carrie a small gift bag that's been sitting on the coffee table for days.

"The usual. Nothing fancy. Stu thinks I should go register to vote, of all things. I hope he's joking."

Janie attempts a laugh, even though she feels numb. "You should register to vote. It's your right as an American."

"Did you?"

"Yes."

"Oh my *god*!" Carrie exclaims, slapping her hand to her mouth. "Did I miss your birthday?"

Janie shrugs. "When have you ever remembered it?"

"Hey! That's not fair," Carrie says, grinning sheepishly. But Janie knows it's true. So does Carrie.

Not that it matters.

That's just the way things are with them.

Carrie ooohs over the CD Janie bought her. And they are okay. But Janie knows that things are changing rapidly.

Carrie doesn't stick around long.

Janie has no plans for the evening.

Or for the rest of her life, it seems.

She calls Cabel.

"I miss you," she says to his voice mail. "Just . . . had to tell you that. Um, yeah. Sorry. Bye."

But Cabel doesn't call back.

She knew he wouldn't.

"I need a break." That's what he said that Monday after the hospital, when he tried to touch her but couldn't.

NOTHING LEFT TO LOSE

MARCH 24, 2006, 3:00 P.M.

Janie is in a daze now. It's been nearly three weeks. She goes through her classes like a zombie. Goes home after school. Every day, alone.

Alone.

It's fierce. There's so much more to miss now. Being alone before Cabel was much easier than being alone after Cabel.

He doesn't sit nearby in study hall anymore, either. Doesn't call. Doesn't check on her when she gets sucked into dreams.

He can't even seem to look at her. And when it happens

by accident—in the hallways, the parking lot—his face gets a stricken look, and he hurries on, without a word.

Away from her.

Even at the follow-up meeting with Captain, she was alone. Cabel met with Captain separately.

Janie drives home, windows open on this fresh spring day, with nothing to lose.

3:04 P.M.

She stops for an elementary-school bus whose red lights are blinking. She looks at the children, crossing the street in front of her. Wonders if any of them are like her.

Knows they probably aren't.

And then.

She's taken by surprise. Blind, sucked into a little kid's dream.

Falling, falling off a mountain.

Janie gasps silently.

Her foot slips from the brake pedal.

The bus horn wails and screams.

She grips the steering wheel frantically and struggles with her mind to focus. Pulls herself out of the dream as Ethel strays dangerously close to the street-crossing children.

Slams a numb, heavy foot on the brake and blindly reaches for the keys in the ignition.

Ethel conks out and dies as Janie's sight returns.

The bus driver gives Janie a hateful look.

The children scurry to the side of the road, staring at Janie, eyes wide in fear.

Janie, horrified, shakes her head to clear it. "I'm so sorry," she mouths. She feels sick to her stomach.

The bus roars away.

While the drivers who are lined up behind Janie begin honking impatiently, Janie struggles to start Ethel.

Bawling her eyes out.

Hating her life.

Wondering what the fuck is going to happen to her, wondering how she's going to get through life without killing somebody.

She makes it home.

Wipes her face with her sleeve.

Walks determinedly into the house. Goes directly to her bedroom, tossing her coat and backpack on the couch without stopping.

Until she gets to her closet.

Janie pulls out the box and sits on her bed. Dumps

it all out in a pile and picks up the green notebook. Recklessly opens it up. Reads the dedication again.

A Journey Into the Light
by Martha Stubin

This journal is dedicated to dream catchers. It's written expressly for those who follow in my footsteps once I am gone.

The information I have to share is made up of two things: delight and dread. If you do not want to know what waits for you, please close this journal now. Don't turn the page.

But if you have the stomach for it and the desire to fight against the worst of it, you may be better off knowing. Then again, it may haunt you for the rest of your life. Please consider this in all seriousness. What you are about to read contains much more dread than delight.

I'm sorry to say I can't make the decision for you. Nor can anyone else. You must do it alone. Please don't put the responsibility on others' shoulders. It will ruin them.

Whatever you decide, you are in for a long, hard ride. I bid you no regrets. Think about it. Have confidence in your decision, whatever you choose.

Good luck, friend.

Martha Stubin, Dream Catcher

Janie ignores the rush of fear and turns the page. And then turns the blank page. And she reads.

> You've read the first page by now, at least once. I imagine you spent some time on it, perhaps days, deciding if you wanted to continue. And now here you are.
>
> In case your heart is thumping, I'll tell you that I'm starting with "Delight." So you can change your mind if you wish to go no farther. There will be a blank page in this notebook before you reach the information I've titled "Dread." So you'll know and not turn the pages with fear.
>
> I am sorry to have to place this fear in your heart. But I do so for my own reasons. Perhaps you'll understand when you are through reading.
>
> But for now, there is still time to go back and close this notebook. If you choose to go on, please turn the page.

3:57 P.M.

Janie turns the page.

> Delight
>
> You have experienced a bit of this already, I imagine. If not, it will come.
>
> With time comes both success and failure. Some of your best successes as a dream catcher will not be realized for many years.

By now you've discovered that you have more power than you once knew. You have the ability to help someone change a dream to make it better. Less frightening, perhaps. Or even a complete change, such as turning a monster into a cartoon.

What you need to know before you assist in altering someone's dream is that not all dreams can be altered. Your power is strong, but there are a few dreams stronger than you. Please don't expect you can change the course of the world.

That said, I, Martha Stubin, have been in the dreams of many successful individuals. They arrived at success only after their dreams changed. Can I take credit for these things? Of course not. But I was a factor in the future of many a businessperson. While I will not reveal names, as the individuals are still alive at the time I write this, I might ask you to think about the computer industry, and that will give you a clue.

You have the ability to influence the unconscious mind, my dear dream catcher.

Marriages have been saved.

Relationships rekindled.

Sports events won.

Lives lived in confidence rather than fear.

Because our power is motivating, and gives momentum and ownership of changes to those who dream of failure.

This is a most redeeming job when things go right.

And you can change a community.

You are a rarely gifted individual.

You can use your power to help create or restore peace in a troubled community—whether it's a school, a church, a place of business, or a government entity. You have more power to solve crime than anyone with a badge.

Do not forget this.

As you hone your skill—your gift—you will be able to assist the law in ways the keepers of them cannot imagine. And in ways that are impossible, in their minds. You have tremendous power to do good.

Use it if you dare.

You will never be without a job. Think big. The country's many law enforcement agencies will get wind of your existence. Travel the country—maybe even the world. Seek out others with various gifts, who work underground, like you.

Let me take it a step deeper. Into your own heart.

With practice, you will master your own dreams.

Some of you might not dream.

That will come with time.

You can dream to work out the problems you face, and you will dream to find the refreshing love you long for in an isolated world.

And the loved ones you lose along the path of life will live forever, if you use your power. You'll never say good-bye for long. Just until you sleep again. You can bring them back to you.

This has been the most redemptive factor for me. It's what has kept me alive beyond my years. I will die happy, even after a life of distress.

Do not overlook the positives of this factor, once you view the rest.

And now, when you turn the page, you will find the next one blank. Following it are the things I wish I didn't have to tell you. Use your judgment right now to decide if you wish to go on.

4:19 P.M.

Janie buries her head in her hands, and goes on.

Dread

My eyes water as I write this section.

There are things about yourself you may not want to hear or know.

Will they help you?

The answer is yes.

Will they hurt you?

Absolutely, yes.

Rights and Obligations

First of all, let us revisit how you change people's dreams.

Because you have the power does not always mean you have the right or the obligation.

And because you have the power of manipulation, some of you will use that to hurt people.

I can't stop you from doing that.

I can only implore you to resist the temptation to hurt others in this fashion.

It's been done.

And it's been ugly.

People die.

Here are some facts you should know:

- There is no "cure," should you see this as a disease. Until the reason for the dream catcher's gift is discovered, there will be no cure.

- I've spent fifty years trying to change it. And all I can do is control it—sometimes.

Driving

You might already be aware of the hazards of driving. Perhaps you've had a rare incident. And you're still alive. But because of the stray possibilities—even with the windows closed, I must add—you are a time bomb.

It's happened before.

You've seen it in the papers, haven't you?

Somebody blacks out on the highway. Crosses the line. Kills a family of three in the oncoming lane.

Dream catchers. Catching, by accident, the dreams of the sleeper in the car next door.

Right through the glass windows of both cars.

It happens.

It has happened.

And I've never forgiven myself.

Don't drive.

You risk not only your life, but the lives of innocent others.

You can ignore me.

I'm asking you not to.

If you wish to continue, please turn the page.

4:53 P.M.

Janie—shaking, crying, remembering the school children—continues.

Side Effects

This is the hardest section. If you make it through this, you are done.

And maybe you won't think it's as bad as I made it out to be. I hope for that.

There are several side effects of being a dream catcher. You've experienced the caloric drain by now. It gets worse as you age.

The stronger you are, the more prepared you are, the better you'll fare. Have nourishment with you at all times. Dreams are where you least expect them.

The more dreams you enter, the more you can help people. This is true; it's the law of averages.

But for a dream catcher, the more dreams you enter, the worse the side effects.

The faster you decline.

You must work at controlling which dreams you enter.

Practice pulling out of them, as I explained in the many files of cases I've participated in.

Study them.

Practice the moves, the thought processes, the relaxation exercises.

However, you must realize by now that it's a catch-22. Because the more practice you get, the harder it is on your body.

You must choose your dreams carefully, if you choose to use your gift to help others.

Or there is the alternative.

Isolation.

If you isolate yourself, you might live a normal life. . . . As normal as isolation allows, of course.

And now.

You can still stop reading here.

Your last chance.

5:39 P.M.

Janie looks away. Reads that part over again. Her head is pounding. And she continues to the bitter end.

Quality of Life

I knew, personally, three dream catchers in my life, besides myself. I am the last one alive. At the time of this writing, I know of no others. But I am convinced you are out there.

I'll tell you first that the handwriting in this journal is not from my hand. My assistant writes to you in this book, because my hands are gnarled beyond use.

I lost the function of my hands and fingers at age thirty-four.

My three dream-catcher friends were thirty-five, thirty-one, and thirty-three, respectively, when they could no longer hold a pen.

That is what these dreams are doing to you.

6:00 P.M.

Tears stream down Janie's face. She holds her sodden sleeve to her mouth. And continues.

And finally.

What I see as the worst.

I was eleven at the time of my first dream catch. Or at least, that's as far back as I can recall.

The dreams came few and far between at first, as I expect they did for you, unless you shared a room with someone.

By high school the number of dreams grew.

College. In class, the library, walking across campus on a spring day . . . not to mention having a roommate. In college dreams are everywhere. Some of the worst experiences you'll ever see.

And then, one day, you won't.

You won't see.

Because you'll be completely, irreversibly, heartlessly blind.

My dream catcher acquaintances: Twenty-three. Twenty-six. Twenty-one.

I was twenty-two.

The more dreams you enter, the sooner you'll be blind.

You suspected already, didn't you.

Perhaps you've already lost some of your vision.

I'm so sorry, dear friend.

Choose your profession wisely.

All the hope I can add is this:

Once you are blind, each dream journey you take will bring you back into the light, and you will see things in the dreams as if you are seeing them in life.

These dreams of others are your windows. They are all the light you'll see. You will be encased in darkness except for the dreams.

And since that is the case, I ask you, who would

not live for one more dream? One more chance to see your loved one as he ages, one more chance to see yourself if he dreams of you.

You don't have a choice.

You are stuck with this gift, this curse.

Now you know what lies ahead.

I leave you with a note of hope, and it is this: I don't regret my decisions to help others through catching dreams.

Not a single instance would I take back.

Now is a good time to sit and think. To mourn. And then to get back up.

Find your confidant. Since you are reading this, you have one. Tell him or her what to expect.

You can get to work. Or you can hide forever and delay the effects. It's your decision.

No regrets,

Martha Stubin, Dream Catcher

Janie stares at the book. Turns that page, knowing there's nothing more. Knowing it's not a joke.

She looks at her hands. Flexes her fingers. Sees them, their wrinkly knuckles and short fingernails. The way they bend and straighten. And then she looks around the room.

Takes off her glasses.

Thinks hard and knows the answer already. The dreams, the headaches, Miss Stubin's gnarled hands and blind eyes. Janie's own failing eyesight. Janie knew.

Knew it for a while now.

She just didn't want to think about it. Didn't want to believe it.

Maybe Cabel knows already, she thinks. His stupid eye charts. Maybe that's really why he needs a break. He knows she's falling apart. And he can't handle one more problem with Janie.

Janie is so stunned she cannot cry anymore.

She grabs her car keys and rushes to the door before she remembers.

Miss Stubin killed three people in a car crash because of a dream.

Janie looks at Ethel through the window, and then slowly she falls down to the floor, sobbing as her world comes to an end.

She doesn't get up.

No.

Not that night.

MARCH 25, 2006, 8:37 A.M.

Janie is still on the floor in the living room, near the front door. Her mother steps over her once, twice, unalarmed, disappearing again into the dark recesses of her bedroom. She's seen Janie asleep on the floor before.

Janie doesn't move when there is a knock on the door. A second knock, more urgent, does nothing to her.

And then words.

"Don't make me break open the door, Hannagan."

Janie lifts her head. Squints at the door handle. "It's not locked," she says dully, although she tries to be respectful.

And Captain is there, in Janie's living room, and somehow, in the small house, she looks so much bigger to Janie.

"What's going on, Janie?" Captain asks, alarm growing on her face as she sees Janie on the floor.

Janie shakes her head and says in a thin, bewildered voice, "I think I'm dying, sir."

Janie sits up. She can feel the carpet pattern indented deep in her cheek. It feels like Cabel's nubbly burns. "I was going to go see you yesterday," she says, looking at the keys on the floor next to her. "I was going out the door, and then it all hit me. The driving. And the everything. And I just . . ." She shakes her head. "I'm going blind, sir. Just like Miss Stubin."

Captain stands, quiet. Waits patiently for Janie to explain. Holds her hand out to Janie. Pulls her up, and embraces her. "Talk to me," Captain says gently.

And Janie, who ran out of tears hours ago, makes new ones and cries on Captain's shoulder, telling her everything about the contents of the green notebook. Letting Captain read it herself. Captain squeezes Janie tightly when the sobs come again.

After a while Janie is quiet. She looks around for something to use to wipe Captain's coat, and there is nothing. There is always nothing at Janie's house.

"Did you call into school for your absence yet?"

"Shit."

"No problem. I'll do it now. Does your mother go by Mrs. Hannagan? I don't want the office staff to know that I know you."

Janie shakes her head. "No, not 'Mrs.,'" she says. "Just go with Dorothea Hannagan." When Captain hangs up the phone, Janie says, "How did you know to come?"

She scowls. "Cabel called me. Said you didn't show up at school, wondered if I'd heard from you. I guess he tried calling your cell phone."

So I have to disappear in order to get him to call me. Janie doesn't say anything. She wants, with all her heart, to ask Captain why Cabel won't speak to her. But Janie knows better than to do that. So all she says is, "That was thoughtful."

And then she thinks for a moment. "Did you suspect this? Did Miss Stubin tell you any of this?"

"I knew something was bothering you after you called me a few weeks ago, but I didn't know what. Miss Stubin was a very private person, Janie. She didn't speak much about herself, and I didn't ask. It wasn't my place."

"Do you think Cabel knows?"

"Have you thought about asking him?"

Janie glances up to read her face. Bites her quivering lip to still it. "We're not exactly on speaking terms right now."

Captain sighs. "I gathered that." Carefully she says, "Cabel has his own demons, and if he doesn't get on with killing them soon, I'm going to kick his ass. He's having trouble dealing with some things right now."

Janie shakes her head. "I don't understand."

Captain is silent. "Maybe you should ask him. Tell him what you're going through too."

"Why? So that when I tell him I'm going to be a blind cripple, he'll never want to come near me again?"

Captain smiles ruefully. "I can't predict the future, Janie. But I doubt a few physical ailments would turn him off, if you know what I mean. But nobody says you *have* to tell him, either." She pauses. "You look like you could use some breakfast. Let's go for a ride, Janie," she says.

Janie looks down at herself, rumpled in her clothes from yesterday. "Sure, why not," she says. She takes a few minutes to brush through her hair, and she looks in the mirror. Looks at her eyes.

Captain takes Janie to Ann Arbor. They stop for breakfast at Angelo's, where Captain apparently knows everybody in the place, including Victor, the short-order cook. Victor himself delivers a feast to their table. Janie, not having eaten since lunch the day before, wolfs down the meal gratefully.

After breakfast, Captain drives around the campus of the University of Michigan. "Some of the finest research and medical facilities are here, Janie. Maybe there's something . . ." Captain shrugs. "Keep in mind, Martha Stubin lost her eyesight fifty years ago. A lot has changed in the medical world since then. Don't doom yourself before you know what doctors can do now. And not just your eyes—your hands too. And, perhaps, your dreams. See that building?" Captain points. "That's the sleep study. Perhaps something can be arranged to accommodate you properly sometime. I have a couple friends on campus I trust. They knew about Martha. They'll help us."

Janie looks around at everything. Feels a tiny surge of hope. She and Cabel had planned to come out here a few times over the upcoming summer, once they could be seen together. Now Janie doesn't know what to think. Maybe Cabel would be back.

And maybe he would be scared away again.

Janie doesn't know how many more breakups and fixes she can handle in their relationship. "Why does everything have to be so hard?" she asks out loud. And then she blushes. "Rhetorical question. Sorry, Captain."

Captain smiles. "What made you read it, finally?"

Janie swallows hard. "Now that Cabel won't come near me, I figured I didn't have much else to lose. Joke's on me, huh."

Captain purses her lips as she drives and mutters something under her breath. "Okay," she says, "and how do you feel about being a dream catcher now?"

Janie thinks. "I guess I don't know any different."

Captain gets a curious look on her face. "How does your mother play into this picture?"

"She doesn't."

"And your father . . . ?"

"Doesn't exist, as far as I know."

"I see." Captain pauses. "Are you sorry you read it?"

Janie is quiet for a moment. "No, sir."

They sit in silence, and then Captain points out a few more buildings on the U of M campus. "Do you want to quit your job with me, Janie? Isolate yourself?"

Janie looks at Captain. "Do you want me to quit?"

"Of course not. You're brilliant at it."

"I'd like to stay on if you have more assignments for me, sir."

Captain smiles, and then she turns serious again. "Do you think you can still work with Cabel, even if you don't resume your romantic relationship with him?"

Janie sighs. "If he can handle it without being an ass, I can." And then her voice catches. "I just . . ." She shakes her head and collects her wits, not wanting to cry.

Captain glares through the windshield. Bites her lip. Shakes her head. "I swear to god I'm going to smack that boy," she mutters. "Listen, Janie. Cabel doesn't have much—he has a mother who abandoned him, a father who nearly killed him . . . And now, when he's with you, he desperately wants to keep you safe in his pocket all the time. But he knows he can't. He's got to learn how to handle that."

Janie takes this in. "But, Captain, he couldn't even bear to touch me after the Durbin bust." She starts crying. "It's like he was so disgusted that they had touched me or something. . . ." She reaches for a tissue from between the car seats.

"Jesus Christ," Captain says. "Janie, listen to me. You're a good detective already. You know that in our work, we have hunches and we seek out the answers. You do this so well in your work. Why don't you follow that same line of logic in your personal life? You'll need to talk to Cabel if you want answers. Endless speculation only leads to dead ends."

Janie closes her eyes. Rests her head on the headrest. "I'm sorry, Captain. You're right. I swear I won't let this mess affect my work. Working for you is the best thing in my life. I feel like I can actually make a difference, you know?"

Captain gives Janie's arm a quick squeeze. "I know, kiddo. And I've got big plans for you, if you're game."

"Captain?"

"Yes."

"How am I going to get anywhere if I'm not supposed to drive?"

Captain sighs. "I haven't figured that one out yet."

"Did you know Miss Stubin had a car crash because of a dream? She killed three innocent people."

Captain slows the car and glances at Janie. "I knew from her background check that she was in a terrible car accident once. I didn't know it happened because of a dream." Captain pauses. "She was sixteen when it happened."

Janie sits in stunned silence.

Captain continues. "She was convicted of vehicular manslaughter, Janie. She lost her license and did three years in a women's correctional facility. It would have been more if she hadn't been a minor at the time. This is serious stuff."

Janie's stomach churns. "I almost hit some school kids yesterday," she says softly. "Some little kid on the bus was dreaming."

Captain shakes her head resolutely. "Well. That

settles it. If I catch you driving again, Janie, I'll write you a ticket myself, I swear to god. Meanwhile, if I need you somewhere, I'll drive you or send a car. I don't want you wasting dreams on some damn city bus."

Janie feels like she just got put in a cage. "What about school?" she asks. "I'll have to take the school bus. What am I going to tell people? Cabel will figure it out. This is such shit."

Captain gives her a hard look. "You know what shit is? Killing three innocent people. Think your life is bad now, try living with that." Her voice is harsh.

Janie's quiet.

They head back to Fieldridge.

When Captain's cell phone rings, she glances at it and answers. "Komisky." She pauses. "Yes, I've got her." Another pause. "Yes, she's just fine." She nods, glances sidelong at Janie with a grim smile, and then hangs up the phone.

"Juuust fine," Captain repeats, her lips pressed tightly together in a thin line.

12:36 P.M.

Captain drops Janie off at home and gives her a swift hug. "You call me if you need to talk more about this stuff," she says.

"Thanks, Captain."

"And it's your call, what you want to tell Cabel, if

anything. Be assured it's not my place to tell him unless it directly affects your work as partners, and even then, I'd ask you to do it. As for you not driving, I think Cabel will take that very well. He worries enough about it. Blame me."

Janie waves weakly as Captain pulls away. She looks sadly at Ethel, quiet and alone in the driveway. Turns and enters the house.

Not quite sure what to do now.

She goes into her room. The green notebook gleams menacingly from the place on the bed where she left it open.

Carefully Janie closes it and puts it in the box in the closet.

Drops to the bed and lies there, staring at the ceiling.

2:23 P.M.

The cool, damp wind blows briskly through Miss Stubin's dusky Center Street purgatory.

"Now you know as much as I know, Janie."

Janie sits silently next to Miss Stubin. Tears trickle from the old woman's blind eyes.

There are no more words to say. Only an understanding, a resolution, a small strength, passes and grows between them. And a release. Miss Stubin's work is done.

This is good-bye.

Slowly Miss Stubin squeezes Janie's hand with her own gnarled fingers. "I must go see my soldier now." And then she begins to fade away.

"Will I ever see you again?" Janie calls out anxiously.

"Not here, Janie."

"Somewhere else, then?" Her voice is hopeful.

But the old woman is already gone.

Janie looks around. Bites her lip. In front of the dry goods store strolls a young man in uniform and a bright-eyed young woman who turns to look over her shoulder. She blows a kiss at Janie as they turn the corner into the alley and disappear from sight.

Janie remains seated on the cold, wet park bench.

Alone.

MARCH 31, 2006, 2:25 P.M.

Cabel dreams of layering clothes and more clothes on his body. Janie pulls herself out of it. She can't stand to watch him. She knows what the dream means. He's trying desperately to protect himself. His heart.

When the bell rings, Cabel startles awake. Janie watches him. He glances at her, looking worried. She pleads with him with her eyes across the vast library.

He drops his.

Turns.

Goes.

APRIL 6, 2006, 8:53 A.M.

It's spring break. Janie awakes to a late spring snowfall, five fresh inches on the ground. Vows, one of these years, to go to Florida for spring break. Even if it means falling into dreams on the plane the entire way there. Even if it means spending the whole week alone, watching other people having fun.

She gets dressed and waits for the car Captain is sending. Brushes off Ethel so that the "For Sale" sign shows from the window again. Shovels the sidewalk and begins on the driveway. The snow is heavy and wet with the late-morning sun shining on it.

When Carrie bursts from her house next door and sprints through the yard, Janie grins.

"Hey," she says.

"Janie Hannagan!" Carrie says. "How dare you sell Ethel! Poor girl. Stu's a wreck over it."

Janie has been ready for this question. "I can't afford the insurance and the gas anymore, Carrie. Tell Stu I'm really sorry."

Carrie grins impishly. Whips out a wad of cash from her coat pocket. "How much?" she asks. "I'm selling my piece of junk. Ethel told me she wants to stay in the 'hood."

Janie's eyes light up. "No way!"

"*So* way!" Carrie giggles. "How much?"

Janie hops up and down in the snow. "For you? Twelve hundred bucks. It's a bargain!"

Carrie whips out twelve one-hundred-dollar bills and shoves them at Janie. "Sold!"

"Oh my gosh. I can't believe you're really buying Ethel!"

"Stu lent me the moolah until my car sells. He's probably happier than anyone. Now, take that sign out of the poor girl's window before she gets a complex! I gotta go call Stu and tell him we've got a deal. We'll figure out the paperwork later, cool?" Carrie lopes back to her house without waiting for an answer, while Janie, grinning, removes the sign from Ethel's window and lovingly pats the snowy hood.

It's Detective Jason Baker who picks her up, in his soccer-mom van. "Hey, little dreamer," he says with a grin. "I saw what you did to those bastards out on Durbin's deck. Remind me not to get in your way."

"I wish I remembered it," Janie says. She likes both Baker and Cobb.

"Still no memory of any of it, huh? Yeah, that's the way it is with those date-rape drugs. That's also why so many rapes go unnoticed or unreported. The memory loss allows sickos, like Durbin and his ilk, to get away with that shit time after time. You really saved the day, Janie."

Janie blushes and looks at her hands. She doesn't feel like much of a hero.

Inside the police station, Janie knocks on Captain's door.

"Come!" Captain yells, as usual.

Janie grins and enters.

Stops short.

Cabel is there too.

His smile is formal and strained as Janie gathers her composure and sits down next to him.

Captain gets down to business immediately.

"Stacey O'Grady will be returning to Fieldridge High, after all. Her parents are now satisfied that all the perps have been arrested, and Stacey really wants to put everything behind her and come back to graduate with her classmates."

Both Janie and Cabel nod. Janie's glad to hear it.

"There are several lawsuits in the works from various angry parents—and I don't blame them. But I'm afraid we're likely going to need you to testify, Janie. The hearings are set for June. You'll meet beforehand with the DA to go over your testimony. It could be difficult. So be prepared for some horrible questions to be asked of you by the defense attorneys. And you'll have to do it while Durbin, Wang, and Crater are sitting there, staring you down. You understand?"

Janie presses her lips together to stop them from quivering. "Yes, sir."

"Atta girl. We'll do everything within the law to keep your dream-catching ability a secret. However, it'll likely come out that you were at that party on assignment and working undercover for me. We'll need your story and your drug-tester sheets as evidence. If the perps are too stupid to plead guilty once they see the pile of evidence we have, we'll go to trial and your cover for Fieldridge assignments will probably be blown. But you need to tell the truth if asked, and we'll deal with it."

Janie's eyes widen. "So, um, if my cover is blown . . . will I . . . will you . . ."

Captain smiles. "You'll still have a job. No worries. Martha had a few close calls too, but her secret was never revealed on the stand. Defense attorneys don't know about dream catchers—They never think to ask the right questions. So, let's not fret about that right now, okay? I want you to take a little time off to relax and rejuvenate until school's out." Captain swivels in her chair and continues seamlessly, "And, Cabe, I've got some minor assignments for you starting Monday after school. Alone. Is that clear?" She looks at both of them.

"Yes, sir," Janie and Cabel say in unison.

"Will you two be able to work together again in the

future, or do I have to reconfigure my plans?" Captain asks bluntly.

Janie looks at Cabel. Cabel looks at his shoes.

"Yes, sir," Janie says finally. Daring Cabel to answer.

"Of course," Cabel says. He doesn't look at Janie.

Captain nods and shuffles the papers on her desk. "Good. Janie, see if Cobb or Baker or Rabinowitz is out there to give you a lift home. I'll talk with you soon."

"Yes, sir." Janie stands up, her face burning. Feeling like a baby in front of Cabe. She flees out the door, leaving Cabel and Captain standing there, and decides to walk home rather than beg for a ride.

She doesn't get far before Cabel's car whizzes past her, snow flying in his wake.

He slows.

Stops.

Backs up.

Janie glances longingly at the bushes, wishing for a place to hide.

Cabel lowers the passenger window and peers out at Janie. Smiles grimly. Bites his lip. "How about a ride, Hannagan?"

Janie nods coolly and gets in. Knows they're going to have to talk sometime if they're going to keep working together. "I can walk from your house so it's not too much trouble for you," she says civilly.

They ride in silence the entire way.

Cabel pulls into his driveway.

They get out.

Stare at each other for a minute, until Janie looks away, emotions welling up. She's angry. Still doesn't understand why he broke up with her so suddenly. Feels like it was because the teachers touched her. Wants to know the truth. But doesn't want to get shot down again. "Thanks for the ride," she finally says.

When he doesn't speak, doesn't move, she turns slowly and starts walking home.

GLIMMERS

"Wait," Cabel says.

Janie's been waiting. Waiting for answers. Waiting for him to admit that he can't touch her because she'd been violated by the creeps. Janie doesn't want to wait anymore. She walks faster.

He hesitates, and then runs after her. Stops her in the middle of the road. "Come inside with me," Cabel says. He looks tired. "Please. We need to talk."

Janie's eyes flash, but she follows him inside. Maybe at least she'll get some answers.

Janie sits on the edge of the living-room chair, leaving her coat on. She takes a deep breath and decides to get it over with. "You have three minutes to tell me that it's not because those bastards touched me."

Cabel reels. "What?"

Janie looks at her watch.

Cabel begins to pace.

"I can put up with the pacing," Janie says after a minute goes by. "I can put up with you having some issues you need to work out. I can even put up with you saying you just don't love me. I mean, I thought this weird dream curse would probably keep me from ever having a relationship, so I guess I'm lucky it lasted as long as it did. But when you suddenly decide you can't touch me anymore immediately after a bunch of jerks try to rape me, well, I just need to know if you are really that horrible. And if you are, it'll be a hell of a lot easier for me to walk out of here in"—she checks her watch—"one minute and twenty-four seconds."

He stares. His face is fraught with emotion. He walks over to Janie, kneels in front of her. His hands quiver as he touches her face.

She watches him solemnly. Gives him a chance.

"Janie," he finally says. "Is this the way it's going to be with you?"

Her eyes flash angrily as she squints at her watch.

"What? Stop changing the subject. You have one minute to say it's not because they touched me. Is it? Is that really it, Cabe? They touched me, and now I'm violated, and you can't stand to think of being with me again?"

"Oh god. You're serious?"

Janie's voice pitches higher. "Thirty seconds."

"Would you even believe me if I said it?" He's breathing hard. Stands abruptly and turns his back to her. His fingers rake through his hair.

"Fifteen seconds." Janie's voice is even, now. She stands up to leave.

He whirls around and grabs her arm. Pulls her to him. Kisses her hard, tangling his fingers in her hair. His tongue darts into her mouth and finds hers, tasting her, an oasis in the desert, his body urgently pressing against hers as his hands caress her neck.

Janie stands frozen for a moment, and then she moans and reaches for him. Cabel slips her coat off her shoulders, and it falls to the floor, and he lifts her up, holds her until she wraps her legs around his waist. His lips move to her neck and strain at the buttons of her shirt.

"Time's up," she says, gasping.

He lifts his lips from her skin. Runs his hand over her body. A button falls to the floor, bounces, and rolls under the chair. He walks, with her still attached, to the couch and sits with her on his lap. "Janie. Oh god, I can't do it," he whispers, and holds her tightly. Squeezes her. Just like she loves. "Janie," he says again. "I'm so messed up. Such an idiot. I'm sorry. No. I mean, the answer is no, it's not because they touched you. I just didn't know if I could handle this. You're too . . . I don't know. You're dangerous! I couldn't handle it. Couldn't handle loving you."

"What the heck does that mean? You didn't seem to have a problem being in love before. What happened?"

He gives her a miserable look. "What if I love you, give you everything I have inside me, open my heart up, and something horrible happens? What if you *did* get raped? It would change you so much, Janie. Change you forever. What if you get sucked into a dream while you're driving again? Have you thought through the consequences? To you? To others? To me, for god's sake. Janie, my father—He lit me. On. Fire. In that instant everything changed. I became a different person. Crap like that changes you. It scarred me, fucked up my life," he says. "In a bunch of ways." Cabel fingers the scars through his shirt as he talks. "I haven't let anybody inside since then, except for you. It's hard, Janie. It feels impossible. And then you go off being all reckless and shit. . . ." He takes a breath. "I needed safe, but I fell in love with you. Now I'm having a really shitty time dealing with the thought that something could happen to you. That you could change too. And I'd lose you."

Janie, jaw dropped, blinks. "You have a really funny way of showing it."

"I know. I . . . I'm fucked up. I thought it would be easier this way, you know? To take a break. It's just . . . It isn't . . ." He struggles for words. "This is intense, Janie. It scares the hell out of me. I wanted you to be my safe thing. No serious risks; just some simple dream stuff for Captain. Nothing like what you went through with Durbin! I mean, who the hell thought *that* would be your next assignment? God, wonder what comes next . . ."

"So you broke up with me because you couldn't handle it if I changed or got hurt or left you. Is that what you're saying? Doesn't everyone have to take that risk? Do you still love me or don't you?" Janie's lip quivers. She thinks about all the changes that will be happening to her in the next years, and feels Cabel slipping away again.

"I'm saying I love you and I'm still learning. . . . I want to learn how to deal with that. All I know is that I thought this break would help, but all it's doing is making me batshit crazy." Cabel pauses. Smiles weakly. "So, um, can you please just not do anything dangerous? Isn't life bad enough when you can't control what the nightmares do to you? Do you really have to take even more risks?"

Janie smiles ruefully. She wraps her arms around his neck and rests her head on his shoulder. Thinking. "What if I do get hurt? Or if something . . . happens to me. Will you stop loving me?" she asks quietly.

"How could I?" Cabel strokes her hair. "But I have to learn how to handle the feelings that come with that. I'm just not used to caring about something, about someone, so much that it hurts. Not like this."

Janie is quiet, thoughtful. "Did you know that you were the first person I ever remember saying 'I love you' to? I don't even remember saying it to my mother. Which is really sad."

"I didn't know," he says. He lets his head fall back on the couch and takes a deep breath. Lets it out. "Do you still love me, Janie?"

Janie stares at him, incredulous. "Yes, of course! I don't say it lightly."

"Say it lightly in my ear," he demands.

She smiles, rests her soft cheek on his scratchy one, and whispers it. "I love you, Cabe."

They sit, holding each other. And then Cabel asks her, "Truth or dare?"

Janie blinks. "Do I really have an option here?"

"No," Cabel says. "Okay, um . . ." Takes a deep breath. "What's happening to you, Janie? I just . . . I need to know. Please." He shifts her, so he can see her eyes.

They fill with tears.

He straightens her glasses and takes a deep breath. "Tell me," he says.

Janie bites her lip. "Nothing, Cabe. I'm fine." She can't look at him.

Cabel rips his fingers through his hair. "Just . . . just say it. Get it out there, so we can deal with it. You're going blind from all the dreams, aren't you."

Janie blinks. Her lips part in surprise.

He touches her cheek, stroking it with his thumb.

"What . . . how . . . ?" she begins.

"You squint, even with your glasses on. You get headaches all the time. Bright light bothers you. It takes you longer to get your sight back after each dream you get sucked into." He pauses. Anxious. "And then, in the hospital, when you weren't sucked into anyone's dream, but you were having your own nightmare, you couldn't see when you woke up. That was the first time for that, wasn't it?"

She sinks back into his shoulder. Doesn't remember that dream in the hospital. Also doesn't want to cry anymore. "Damn," she says. "You're a good detective."

"How soon?" he whispers.

She presses her lips to his cheek, and then she sighs. "A few years."

He takes in a sharp breath and slowly lets it out again. "Okay. What else, Janie."

She closes her eyes, resigned. “My hands,” she says. “They’ll be gnarled and ugly and useless in fifteen years.”

He waits, stroking her back. “Anything else?” His voice is anxious.

“Not really,” she whispers. “Just . . . I can’t drive anymore. Ever again.” She loses her fight with the tears. “Poor Ethel. At least she’s got a good home now.”

He holds her, rocking, stroking her hair. “Janie,” he says after a while. “How old was Miss Stubin when she died?”

“In her seventies.”

He breathes a sigh. “Oh. Thank god.”

“Can you deal with this, Cabel? Because if you can’t . . .” She chokes. “If you can’t, tell me now.”

He looks into her eyes.

Touches her cheek.

4:22 P.M.

Cabel calls Captain.

“Komisky.”

“Sir, any chance Janie and I can be seen together now?”

“Under the circumstances, that would pretty damn much make my day, yes. Besides, the Wilder cocaine case got settled on Monday. He pleaded guilty.”

“You rock, sir.”

“Yes, yes, I know. Go out to a movie or something, will you?”

"Right away. Thank you."

"And stop bothering me."

"Good-bye, sir."

"Take care. Both of you."

Cabel smiles and hangs up. "Guess what."

"What," Janie says.

"We can go out on our first date."

"Woo hoo!"

"And guess what else—You're buying."

"Me? Why?"

"Because you lost the bet."

Janie thinks a moment. Punches Cabel in the arm. "You did not fail five quizzes or tests!"

"I did. I have proof."

"Shit!"

"Yep."

DON'T LOOK BACK

MAY 24, 2006, 7:06 P.M.

Janie strides into the Fieldridge High School auditorium, where hundreds of parents, grandparents, brothers, and sisters are seated in bleachers, folding chairs, and balcony seats, and waving programs near their soppy necks in ninety-five-degree heat and humidity. It seems the old building's air-conditioning can't take the pressure of another graduation ceremony.

She glances around and spots Cabel several rows behind her. He blows an impish kiss, and she grins. Her cap's band threatens to squeeze her brain into mush, and she feels the sweat soaking into it.

Janie looks in the other direction, scanning the

audience. Some familiar faces. Carrie's parents sit off to the side on the wooden bleachers, and Janie offers a small smile, even though they aren't looking at her.

Even with her newly updated prescription glasses, it's difficult to see far away. Colors bleed from one dress to the next. But finally Janie spots her. It's the bronze hair contrasted with her dark skin that helps. Sitting next to Captain is a large man who looks like Denzel Washington, twenty years from now. His arm is spread lazily across the back of Captain's chair. Janie can see Captain poke her husband and point. Janie squints and smiles, and then lowers her eyes. She's not sure why.

The valedictorian takes the stage, and the crowd quiets, leaving only the rush of flapping programs.

It's not Cabel.

Thankfully.

He managed to pull his grades down successfully to a mere 3.93. Third place. Enough to keep him out of the limelight. Which is all he wants, really. Janie's not far behind with a 3.85. She's thrilled.

There are three faculty chairs empty in the auditorium this year. Doc, Happy, and Dumbass. Suspended without pay. Awaiting the hearing. Janie feels a pang of sadness for those chairs.

Not for the men who sat there.

Just so we're clear.

Even so.

They are reminders of pain and embarrassment, horror wrapped up like a gift. Janie's glad that box exploded.

Up at the microphone, Stacey O'Grady begins speaking. She has a different air about her now. New, in the past few months. Reserved. Solemn. A maturity, perhaps, or a sense of understanding that not all things turn out the way you'd wish them to.

Janie's mother isn't there.

Neither is Cabel's, but no one expected her. Although Cabel's older brother, Charlie, and Charlie's wife, Megan, are somewhere in the crowd.

Expectations. It's what they always talk about at these things. Making a difference in the future. Striving for excellence. Blah, blah, blah.

Janie wipes a drop of sweat from her forehead. Looks around as Stacey says from the podium, "The best years are yet to come," and Janie watches the room explode in applause.

Janie doesn't join them.

The ominous words ring in her ears.

The crowd of seniors stands and, one by one, over the course of an hour, their names are called. Janie steps carefully across the stage, prays that the little sleeping baby nearby doesn't dream yet, and takes her diploma. Shakes hands with Abernethy. Moves her tassel over to the other side. Walks lightly down the stage stairs and back to her folding chair to wait.

When the stage is silent and Principal Abernethy gives one last word of congratulations, the hats fly and the voices around Janie rise to fill the auditorium. Janie takes her hat off her head and tucks it under her arm, waiting, waiting. Waiting to be done. So she can say good-bye to this place, once and for all.

When the madhouse clears, she's still standing there. Only a few lingerers remain in the building that now feels like a rain forest after a downpour. She walks slowly down the aisle toward the exit steps, where she'll meet Cabel and whoever else he's schmoozing with. But for now, she is alone.

The custodian comes by with a broom, and he smiles at her. Janie nods and smiles in return, and he begins sweeping the wood-floored aisles that most often serve as a basketball court. And then the lights fade a bit.

Janie blinks and leans against the wall, just in case.

But it's no one's dream.

It's just the end of some things.

And the beginning of others.

GONE

For all those who have trouble at home.
You are not alone.

ACKNOWLEDGMENTS

Many thanks to all my invisible friends who shared their painful stories about what it's like to live with an alcoholic parent, and to Carl Loerwald at the Washtenaw Alano Club in Ann Arbor, Michigan, for all his help.

Thanks also to:

Jennifer Klonsky, whose tough suggestions made ~~me cry~~ *Gone* so much better. And, of course, to my agent, Michael Bourret, my favorite person on earth, for everything and more.

Diane Blake Harper, for being wonderful and for having the tackiest snow-globe collection ever. To Marcia and Dan Levy for all the early help—it was an honor to learn things from you. And to Joanne Levy for the priceless feedback. Go, NDP!

Matt and Kilian, for being awesome guys; Rachel Heitkamp and Kennedy, for letting me use their cool buzzword; and to Trevor Bowler, because I promised.

And to all the fans of the Wake trilogy: Thank you from the bottom of my heart for spreading the word about Janie and Cabe. You are amazing. I am grateful.

To anyone whose life is impacted by someone else's drinking problem, please check out Alateen or Al-Anon at www.al-anon.alateen.org.

JUNE 2006

24/7/365

It's like she can't breathe anymore, no matter what she does.

Like everything is closing in on her, crowding her. Threatening her.

The hearing. The truth coming out. Reliving Durbin's party in front of a judge and the three bastards themselves, staring her down. Cameras following her around the second she steps outside the courtroom. Exposed as a narc, all of Fieldridge talking about it.

Talking about her.

For weeks, it's on the local news. Gossip in the grocery store. Downtown. People point, murmur with heads close together, those looks on their faces. Randomly coming up to her and asking invasive questions. Strangers, former classmates, leaning into her space, whispering, like they're her closest confidantes: *So, what did they really do to you?*

Janie's not cut out for this—she's a loner. She is underground. It's like she hasn't even had time to let all the other stuff sink in—the real, the important. The Janie life-changing stuff. The stuff from the green notebook.

Going blind. Losing the use of her hands.

The pressure is breathtaking.

She's suffocating.

Just wants to run.

Hide.

So she can just be.

JULY 2006

FIVE MINUTES THAT MATTER.

Across the desk. The spot beside her, empty.

"I don't know anymore," she says. "I just don't know." Presses her palms into her temples, hoping her head doesn't explode.

"Whatever you decide," the woman says.

It is their secret.

AND THEN

TUESDAY, AUGUST 1, 2006, 7:25 A.M.

"I can't breathe," she whispers.

His hot fingers lace her ribs, sear through her skin to her frozen lungs. He holds her. Kisses her. Breathes for her. Through her.

Makes her forget.

Afterward, he says, "We're going. Right now. Come."

She does it.

On the three-hour drive, she looks through eyelashes at her blurred fingers, curled in her lap. Pretends to be asleep. Not sure why. Just soaking in the quiet. And knowing, deep down.

Knowing that he,

and this,

are not answers to her problems.

She's beginning to realize what is.

THE FIRST THURSDAY

AUGUST 3, 2006, 1:15 A.M.

The inquisitors are nowhere to be found on this side of the state. Here, at Charlie and Megan's rental cabin on Fremont Lake, no one knows her. The days are peaceful but the nights . . . in a tiny cabin, the nights are bad. Dreams don't take vacations when people do.

It's always something, isn't it? Always something and never nothing for Janie. Never, ever nothing.

Like the car a doctor once told her never to drive, she craves it. Craves the rebellious never, the elusive nothing. And when the next nightmare begins, she thinks about it for real.

1:23 A.M.

Janie shakes on a lumpy sofa. Beside her, stretched out in a reclining lawn chair, is Cabe. Asleep.

He's dreaming about her.

Janie watches, as she sometimes does when his dreams are sweet. Storing up memories. For later. But this . . .

They're playing paintball in an outdoor field with a dozen faceless people. It looks like a video game. Cabe and Janie move through the obstacles and shoot at each other, laughing, ducking, hiding. Cabel sneaks up and takes two shots at Janie, two red paintballs.

They nail her right in the eyeballs.

Red paint drips down her cheeks, her eye sockets hollow.

He keeps shooting and takes out one limb at a time, until Janie is just a body and a paint-striped face.

He sobs, remorseful, kneels next to her on the ground, and then picks her up and carries her, puts her in a wheelchair. Rolls her away to an empty part of the field and dumps her out onto the yellow grass.

Janie pulls out of it. Knows she shouldn't be wasting dreams. But she can't help it. She can't look away.

When she can see, she stares in the dark at the ceiling while Cabe tosses and turns. She slides her arm over her eyes, trying to forget. Trying to pretend like this hasn't been happening for two months straight, on top of everything else. "Please stop," she whispers. "Please."

4:23 A.M.

He dreams and she is forced awake again.

She holds her head.

Janie and Cabel are in the backyard of Cabe's house, sitting in the green grass. Janie's arms end at the elbows. Her eyes are sewn shut, needles still connected and hanging from the thread, down her cheeks. Black tears.

Cabel is frantic. He pulls an ear of corn from a paper grocery bag and strips the silk away. Attaches it to one of Janie's elbows. He plucks two marbles from the paper bag. Big brown Tiger's Eye shooters. He pushes them into Janie's sewn-up eyelids, pushes hard, but they won't stick. Janie falls over backward like a rag doll, unable to catch herself without hands. The ear of corn breaks off her elbow and rolls away. Cabe cradles the Tiger's Eye marbles in his hands.

Janie, numb, can't watch anymore. And she won't try to change it. Not a dream like that. Because it's about her, and how Cabe is dealing with things. It feels completely wrong to manipulate that. She just hopes he never asks her to help.

Still, she doesn't want him dreaming it, period. Not

any of it. She kicks out her leg. Connects. Everything goes black.

"Sorry," he mumbles. Goes back to sleep.

It's been like this.

It's like everything he can't say comes out in his dreams.

9:20 A.M.

Familiar stirrings put an end to dreams. A welcome relief. Janie rests on her couch half-asleep. Talking herself back up. Back to normalcy. She puts on her facade.

Until she can figure out what to do about it.

About life.

About him.

9:33 A.M.

She hears the lawn chair creak, and then feels Cabel snuggling up behind her on the sofa. She stiffens, just a little. Just for a second. Then takes a deep breath. He slips his warm fingers under her cami and slides them across her belly. She smiles and relaxes, eyes still closed. "You're going to get us in trouble," she says. "You know your brother's rules."

"I'm on top of the blanket. You're under it. They'll be okay with that. Besides, I'm not doing anything." He strokes her skin, kisses her shoulder. Slips his fingers under the waistband of her jammie pants.

"Dude." Janie links her fingers in his. "Nope," she calls out, in case Charlie and Megan are paying attention. "Nothing happening over here." She murmurs to Cabel, "You're making breakfast. Right?"

"Right. I'm starting the fire with my mind, frying bacon with my darkest, crispiest thoughts. And you thought you had a special ability. Think again, missypants."

Janie laughs, but it comes out strained. "Did you sleep okay?"

"Yeah." His chin scratches her shoulder. "Well, as good as anybody can sleep on weaved strips of fibrous plastic and a metal rod riding his ass." He nips her earlobe and adds, "Why? Did I have a nightmare? You always make me nervous when you ask that."

"Shh," Janie says. "Go make me some bacon."

He's quiet for a moment, and then he gets up. Slips into his jeans. "Okay, then."

9:58 A.M.

They do vacationy things. Sitting around with Charlie and Megan, drinking coffee, making breakfast over the campfire. Relaxing. Getting to know one another better.

Janie's distracted.

She stares at everything, afraid she'll miss something

that needs to be seen before it's too late.

She really doesn't know how to do vacations.

Besides, some stuff you just can't get away from.

But she's brave. Everything appears normal. Even though inside, she's wrecked.

It's been a tough few months.

Facing them—Doc, Happy, and Dumbass—was way more difficult than she thought it would be. Reliving all the lies. The setup. The assaults. All the things those teachers did. It was horrible.

Now it's over, the buzz has died down, but things are still hard. Getting on track again, and facing the reality of a blind and crippled future—it's hard. Having a mother who's a drunk is hard too. Thinking about college, where sleeping people are everywhere . . . and a boyfriend, whose doubts and fears only come out in his dreams. Life in general . . . yeah. All of it.

Really.

Fucking.

Hard.

Janie and Cabe do the dishes together. Cabel washes, Janie dries. It feels so homey. She grips a plate tightly, wiping it with the towel. Thinking.

Wants to know if he'll voice his dream fears.

And so she blurts it out. "Do you ever think about what it'll be like? You know, if we stick together, and me all blind and hobbling around, dropping and breaking dishes 'cause I can't hold on to them. . . ." She puts the plate in the cupboard.

Cabel flicks his fingers at her, spraying her with water. Grinning. "Sure. I think I'm pretty lucky. I bet blind people have great sex. I'll even wear a blindfold so it's fair." He bumps his hips lightly against hers. She doesn't laugh. She steadies herself and then grabs a stainless steel skillet by the handle and starts drying it. Stares at her contorted reflection in it.

"Hey," Cabe says. He dries his hand on his shorts and then strokes Janie's cheek. "I was just joking around."

"I know." She sighs and puts the pan away. Throws the towel on the counter. "Come on. Let's go do something fun."

1:12 P.M.

She focuses her mind.

It's cold in the water, but the afternoon sun is warm on her face, her hair.

Janie bobs in place, knees bent, arms straight but not locked, trying to balance. The life vest knocks about her ears. Her well-toned arms are like sticks shooting from the vest's enormous sockets. Janie's glasses are safely stowed inside the boat, so everything is blurry. It's like looking through a wall of rain.

She takes a deep breath. "Hit it!" she yells, and then she is yanked forward, knees knocking, arms shaking. She grips the rope handle, knuckles white, palms and muscles already sore from two previous days' efforts. *Lean back*, she remembers, and does it. *Let the boat pull you up.*

She straightens, sort of.

Wobbles and catches herself.

Her bum sticks out, she knows. But she can't help it. Doesn't care, anyway. All she can do is grin blindly as spray slaps and stings her face.

She's up. "Woo hoo!" she yells.

Megan is a gentle driver at the wheel of the little pea-green speedboat. She watches Janie in the rearview mirror like the good mothers watch their children, her brow furrowed in concern but nodding her head. Smiling.

Cabel faces Janie, in the spotter position at the back of the boat, grinning like he does. His teeth gleam white next to his tan skin, and his brown hair, streaked with gold from the sunshine, flips wildly in the wind. His nubbly burn scars on his belly and chest shine silvery brown.

But they are both just blobs to Janie from seventy-five feet away. Cabe yells something that sounds enthusiastic but it's lost in the noise of the motor and the splash.

Janie's legs and arms shiver as they air-dry and then get

slapped with spray again. Her skin buzzes.

Megan keeps them close to the willow-treed shore. As they approach the town's beach and campground, Megan eases the boat into a wide semicircle, turning them around. Janie tenses into the turn, but it's only a mild bump over the wake. Once they straighten out again, Janie moistens her lips, and then, determined, she gives Megan the thumbs-up.

Faster.

Megan complies, and speeds toward the dock near the little red-brown shellacked cabin, one of six dotting the shore at the Rustic Logs Resort, and then she continues past it. Exploring new territory.

I am such a badass, Janie thinks. She squints and makes a daring and ultimately successful attempt to cross the wake again as the two in the boat cheer her on.

By the time Janie senses it, it's already too late.

A woman lies sunning herself on a water trampoline, skin gleaming from tanning oil and sweat. Janie can't make out the scene, but she's all too familiar with the warning signs. Her stomach twists.

Janie flies past the woman and becomes engulfed in darkness. There's a three-second-flash of a dream before it's all over and she's out of range again. But it's enough to throw Janie off-kilter. Her knees buckle, skis tangle underneath her, and she flips forward wildly, water forcing its way into her throat and nostrils. Into her brain, it seems, by the way it burns. A ski slams into her head and she's forced back under the water. She's not slowing down.

If you fall, let go of the rope.

Der.

Janie surfaces, coughing and sputtering, her head on fire. Amazed that the oversize life vest is still attached, though she's all twisted up in it. Feels queasy after swallowing half the lake. She wipes the water from her stinging eyes and peers through the blur, disoriented, wishing for her glasses. Ears plugged. When weeds suddenly tickle her dangling feet, she *eeps* and her body does a little freak-out spasm of oogy-ness, after which she tries not to think about being surrounded by big yellow-orange carp . . . and their excrement.

Blurg. Not fond of this, hello.

Boats whine in the distance.

None of them sounds like it is coming to rescue her.

Finally she hears a muffled chugging. When the motor cuts, Janie calls out. "Cabe?"

It's still the only name that feels safe on her tongue.

1:29 P.M.

In the boat, Cabel wraps a towel around her. Hands Janie her glasses. "You sure you're okay?" His eyes crinkle and he's trying not to grin.

"Fine," Janie growls, peeved, teeth chattering. Megan checks out the bump on Janie's head, and then hauls in the tow rope.

Cabel coughs lightly and then presses his lips together. "That was quite, uh, quite the display, Hannagan."

"Are you actually laughing at me? Seriously?" Janie rubs her hair with a towel. "I almost died out there. Plus my brain is now infested with plankton and carp shit. You'd better watch it, or I'll blow a snot rocket at you."

"I'm . . . eww. That's disgusting." Cabe laughs. "But seriously, you really should have seen yourself. Right, Megan? I wish we had a video camera."

"Dude, I am so Switzerland," Megan says. Rope stowed, she revs up the engine and swings the boat around, back to the dock.

For the second time today, Janie's not laughing.

Cabel continues over the noise. "I mean, the flip was one thing, but the drag, that was something entirely out of control. Your legs were flying. Remember rule number one of water skiing?"

"I know. Sheesh. When you fall, let go of the rope, I

know. There's just a lot of shit to remember when you're out there."

Cabel snorts. "A lot . . . yeah, a whole lot of shit to remember." He laughs long and hard, wipes his eyes and tries to get control of himself. "Shouldn't 'let go of the rope if it's drowning you' be sort of an automatic response, though? Basic survival technique?"

She glares at him.

He stops laughing and gives her a helpless, innocent look. "Okay, okay, I'm sorry," he says.

"Go suck a mean one," Janie says. She turns away and squints through her glasses, locating the sleeping woman on the trampoline, now a tiny island in the distance. *You still don't catch it all, do you, Cabe?*

He probably never will.

"Get over yourself, Hannagan," she mutters. "You're on vacation, damn it. You're relaxing and having fun." It sounds wooden.

"What's that, sweets?" He slides over to her on the bench seat.

"I said, it *was* kinda funny, wasn't it?" Janie looks into Cabel's eyes. Smiles sheepishly.

With his finger, he catches a drip of water from her chin. Smiles. He brings his finger to his lips and licks the water. "Mmm," he says, nuzzling her neck. "Carp shit."

1:53 P.M.

Cabel nods off on a blanket under a shady oak.

Janie sits, chin on her knees, staring at her toes. Listening to the rhythm of the soft waves washing up on shore. After a while, she gets up. "I'm going for a walk," she whispers. Cabel doesn't move.

She slips a long T-shirt over her swimsuit, shoves her toes in her flips, grabs her cell phone, and walks behind the cabin and through the little parking lot, up the steep driveway to the main road. Across the road there's a field and a railroad track. The rails glint in the late afternoon sunshine. Janie walks along the track and thinks, glad to have a quiet place where she can let her dream guard down.

After a while, she stops walking. Sits on the track, feeling the hot metal against the backs of her thighs through the thin cover-up. Opens her phone and dials memory #2.

"Janie—what's going on? Everything all right?"

Janie gently waves a bumblebee away. "Hi. Yeah. I'm just doing a lot of thinking. About what we talked about . . . you know? Lots of time to think on vacation," she says, and laughs nervously.

"And?"

"And . . . you're sure you are okay with whatever I decide?"

"Of course. You know that. Did you make up your mind, then?

"Not really. I'm—I'm still deciding."

"Have you talked to Cabel about it?"

Janie winces. "No. Not yet."

"Well, I don't blame you for wanting—and needing—to consider all of your options."

Janie's throat grows tight. "Thank you, sir."

"You know the drill. Call me anytime. Let me know what you choose."

"I will." Janie closes the phone and stares at it.

There's nothing more to say.

On the way back, she picks up a train-flattened penny from the track and wonders if one of the vacationers down the hill placed it there. Wonders if some excited little kid will come back for it. She sets it on the railroad tie so whoever it is will be sure to see it. Walks slowly back to the cabin to drop off her stuff. And then it's back outside, under the tree.

She watches Cabe sleep. Later, she dozes too, whenever she can get a chance while she wearily dodges Cabel's dreams, and the dreams of a sleeping child somewhere, probably in the cabin next door.

There is no getting away from it all here. Or anywhere.

No escape for her.

5:49 P.M.

A whistle blasts and the train rushes past up at the top of the hill. Everyone who was sleeping awakes.

"Another busy day at the lake," Cabel murmurs. "My stomach's growling." He rolls over on the blanket. Janie can't resist. She snuggles up to his warm body.

"I can hear it," she says. "And I smell the charcoal grill."

"We should really get up now."

"I know."

They remain still, Janie's head on Cabel's chest, a nice breeze coming off the lake. She squinches her eyes shut and holds him, takes in the scent of him, feels the warmth of his chest on her cheek. Loves him.

Breaks a little more inside.

6:25 P.M.

Janie hears the click of the cabin's screen door and sits up guiltily as Megan walks over to them. "I'm sorry, Megan—we should be helping you get dinner."

"Nah," Megan grins. "You needed a nap after all that skiing and drowning. But your cell phone is beeping inside the cabin. I don't know what to do with it."

"Thanks. I'll check it."

Cabel sits up too. "Everything okay? Where's Charlie, anyway?"

"In town picking up some groceries. It's all good.

Relax," Megan says. "Seriously. It's been a tough time for you guys—you need the rest."

Obediently, Cabel sinks back down on the blanket as Janie gets to her feet. "Be right back," she says. "It better not be Captain with an assignment or I'm quitting."

Cabel laughs. "You wouldn't."

6:29 P.M.

Voice mails.

From Carrie. Five of them.

And they're bad.

Janie listens, incredulous. Listens again, stunned.

"Hey, Janers, dammit, where are you? Call me." *Click.*

"Janie, seriously. There's something wrong with your mom. Call me." *Click.*

"Janie, seriously! Your mom is stumbling around your front yard yelling for you. Didn't you tell her you were going to Fremont? She's totally drunk, Janie—she's wailing and—oh, shit. She's in the road." *Click.*

"Hey. I'm taking your mom to County Hospital. If she blows in Ethel, you are so dead. Call me. Jesus. Also? Shit. My phone battery is dying, so maybe try the hospital or something . . . don't know what to tell you. I'll try you *again* when I have a chance." *Click.*

"Oh, my God." Janie stares at her phone, not really seeing it. Then she calls Carrie.

Gets Carrie's voice mail. "Carrie! What happened? Call me. I've got my phone now. I'm so sorry. I was—taking a nap." It sounds hollow. Careless. Frivolous, even, when Janie says it aloud. *What was I thinking, leaving my mother alone for a week?* "God. Just call me."

Janie stands there, all the breath being sucked out of her, replaced by fear. *What if something's really wrong?*

And then anger.

I will never have a life as long as that woman is alive, she thinks.

Squeezes her eyes shut and takes it back, immediately.

Can't believe she would be such a horrible person, think such a horrible thing.

Charlie walks into the tiny cabin kitchen with a brown bag of groceries and stops short when he sees the look on Janie's face. "Are you okay?" he asks.

Janie blinks, unsure. "No, I don't think so," she says quietly. "I think . . . I think I have to go."

Charlie sets the groceries down hard on the counter. "Cabe!" he shouts through the screen door. "Come 'ere."

Janie sets her phone down and pulls her suitcase from the wardrobe. Starts throwing her clothes in her suitcase. She looks at her disheveled self in the mirror and rakes her fingers through her dark blond tangles. "Oh, my God," she says to herself. "What the hell is wrong with my mother?"

And then it hits.

What if her mother really is dying? Or dead?

It's both fascinating and horrifying. Janie imagines the scene.

"What is it?" Cabel says, coming into the cabin. "What's going on?"

"Here," she says. She dials voice mail and hands the phone to Cabel. "Listen to all the messages."

As Cabel listens, Janie, in a daze, continues to pack.

After all her things are crammed inside, she realizes that she needs something to change into—she can't drive all the way to Fieldridge in her swimsuit.

She can't drive at all.

Cue major detail.

"Fuck," Janie mutters. She watches as Cabel listens to the messages. Watches his expression intensify.

"Holy shit," he says. He looks at Janie. Takes her hand. "Holy shit, Janie. What can I do?"

Janie just buries her face in his neck. Trying not to think.

Endless.

7:03 P.M.

It's a three-hour drive home. Cabel's at the wheel of the Beemer that Captain Komisky lets him drive. A Grand Rapids radio station deejay cracks a lame joke and then plays Danny Reyes's "Bleecker Street" in his all-request hour, and Janie stares at her phone, willing Carrie to call. But it's silent.

Janie calls the hospital. They have no record of a Dorothea Hannagan being admitted.

"Maybe she's fine and they didn't have to admit her," Cabel says.

"Or maybe she's in the morgue."

"They'd have called you by now."

Janie's silent, trying to think of reasons why the hospital hasn't called, much less Carrie with an update.

"We can call Captain," Cabel says.

"What good will that do?"

"The police chief? She can get info from anybody she wants."

"True. But . . ." Janie sighs. "I don't . . . my mother . . . never mind. No. I don't want to call Captain."

"Why? It would put your mind at ease."

"Cabe . . ."

"Janie, seriously. You should call her—get the scoop. She'd totally do it for you if you're worried about imposing."

"No thanks."

"You want me to call her?"

"No. Okay? I don't want her to know."

Cabel sighs, exasperated. "I don't get it."

Janie clenches her jaw. Looks out the window. Feels the heat in her cheeks, the tears stinging. The shame. Says softly, "It's embarrassing, all right? My mom's a freaking drunk. Stumbling around in the front yard, yelling? My God. I just don't need Captain seeing that. Or knowing about that—that part of my life. It's personal. There are things I talk about with Captain, and things that are private. Just drop it."

Cabel is silent. After a few minutes of radio deejay babble, he plugs his iPod into the car stereo. Josh Schicker's "Feels Like Rain" washes through the car. When the song ends and the first notes of the next song begin, he stiffens and then hastily flips it off. Knows what's next. Knows it's "Good Mothers, Don't Leave!"

An hour passes as they travel eastward across Michigan, leaving the sun setting orange and bright in their wake. Traffic is light. Janie leans her head against the window, watching the blur of deep green trees and yellow fields pass by. There's a deer in a grassy area as darkness approaches—or maybe it's just that burned-out tree stump that fools her every time.

She wonders how many more times she'll witness

scenes like this. Trying to remember everything she sees now, for later. When all she has is darkness and dreams.

She tries the hospital again. Still no record of Dorothea Hannagan. It's a good sign, Janie thinks . . . except that Carrie still isn't calling. "Where is she?" Janie bounces her head against the headrest.

Cabel glances sidelong at Janie. "Carrie? Didn't she say her phone's dead?"

"She said her battery was low. But there are other phones. . . ."

Cabel taps his chin thoughtfully. "Does she actually know your cell number or are you on her speed dial?"

"Ahh. Good point. Speed dial."

"So that's why she hasn't called. She doesn't know your number, it's in her dead phone and she can't get to it."

Janie smiles. Lets go of a worried breath. "Yeah . . . you're probably right."

"Did you try calling your house to see if your mom is there?"

"Yeah, I did that, too. No answer."

"Do you have Stu's number? Or Carrie's home phone?"

"I tried her home. No answer. And I don't have Stu's. I should. I've always meant to. . . ."

"What about Melinda?"

"Yeah, right." Janie snorts. "Just what I need—the knobs from the Hill spreading this story around." She turns back to the window. "I'm sorry I was snippy. You know—earlier."

Cabel smiles in the darkness. "S'okay." He reaches for Janie's hand. Snakes his fingers between hers. "I wasn't thinking. My bad." He pauses. "You know nobody thinks badly of you for things you can't control, like what your mother does."

"Nobody?" Janie scowls. "Right. They all have their opinion on the Durbin mess."

"Nobody who matters."

Janie tilts her head. "Yanno, Cabe, maybe neighbors, the entire town of Fieldridge . . . maybe what they think actually does matter to me. I mean, God. Forget it. I'm just so tired of all of this. Sheesh, what next?"

After a pause, Cabel says, "Straight to the hospital, then, right?"

"Yeah, I figure that's the best thing we can do. She could just be sitting, waiting in the ER. We'll try that first . . . you think?"

"Yeah."

9:57 P.M.

Janie and Cabel stand in the ER, unsure of what to do. No sign of Carrie or Janie's mother anywhere among the assortment of ill and injured. No one at the desk has any record of her either.

Cabel taps his fingers against his lips, thinking. "Is Hannagan your mom's married name?"

Janie squinches her eyes shut and sighs. "No." She's never told Cabel much about her mother, and he's never asked. Which was just the way Janie liked it. Until now.

"Um . . . ?" Cabel prompts. "How do I put this PC. Let's see. Okay, has your mom ever gone by any other name besides Hannagan?"

"No. Her name's Dorothea Hannagan, and that's the only name she's ever had. I'm a bastard. Okay?"

"Janie, seriously. Nobody cares about that."

"Yeah, well, I care. At least you know who both your parents are."

Cabel stares at Janie. "Fat lot of good that did me."

"Oh, jeez, Cabe." Janie grimaces. "I'm sorry. Major verbal typo. I'm stressed—I don't know what I'm saying."

Cabel looks like he's about to say something, but he holds back. Looks around again, futilely. "Come on," he says, grabbing Janie's hand. "Elevator. We'll walk around, check waiting rooms. Ten minutes, tops, and if we don't find Carrie, we head back to your house and wait. I don't know what else to do."

A shiver crawls over Janie's skin. Her mother, the drunk, is missing.

10:02 P.M.

There, in the third-floor waiting room.

ICU.

Elbows on her knees and face in her hands, fingers threaded through her long dark curls. Leaning forward. Like she's ready to jump to her feet at any second and run like hell.

"Carrie!" Janie says.

Carrie pops up. "Oh, good, you got my note."

"Where's . . . Is my mother . . . ?"

"She's in the room with him."

"What? Who?"

"Didn't you get my note?"

"What note? All I know is what you left on my voice mail."

"I left a note on Ethel—in the parking lot. Figured you're a detective now, or whatever. You oughta think to look for my car. Anyways, how the hell did you find me, then? Never mind. Your mom—she's fine. I mean, she's still drunk but I think she's coming down now . . . like way down. She's all weepy and shaky. But—"

"Carrie," Janie says firmly. "Focus. Tell me what's wrong with my mother and where I can find her."

Carrie sighs. She looks tired. "Your mom is fine. Just drunk."

Janie glances nervously through the open door to the

hallway as a nurse walks by. Her voice is low and urgent. "Okay, okay, I get that she's drunk. She's always drunk. Can we stop shouting that please? And if she's fine, why the fuck are we all in Intensive Care?"

"Oh, man," Carrie says. She shakes her head. "Where to start?"

Cabel nudges Janie and Carrie toward the chairs and sits down with them. "Who's 'him', Carrie? Who is she with?" he says gently.

Janie nods, echoing the question.

But she already knows.

There's only one "him" it could possibly be. There is no one else in the world. No one else that would make Janie's mother react this way. No one else Janie's mother dreams about.

Carrie, whose normally dancing eyes are dulled from the weariness of the unusual day, looks at Janie. "Apparently, it's your father, Janers. He's, like, really sick."

Janie just looks at Carrie. "My father?"

"They don't think he's going to make it."

10:06 P.M.

Janie falls back into the chair. Numb. No idea how she's supposed to feel about this news. No. Freaking. Clue.

Cabel lifts his hand to pause the conversation. The three sit in the waiting room in silence for a moment, Janie looking blank, Carrie working a piece of gum, Cabel closing his eyes and shaking his head ever so slightly. "Start from the beginning," he says.

Carrie nods. Thinks. "Yeah, so, this afternoon, probably around three o'clock, I heard somebody hollering outside. I ignored it 'cause there's always somebody yelling around our neighborhood, right? And I'm folding laundry on the bed and then through my window I see Janie's mom, which is so weird, because she, like, never goes outside unless she's walking to the gas station or the bus stop to get booze, right? But today she's in her nightgown wandering around the yard—"

Janie flushes and puts her hands to her face. "Oh, God," she says.

"—and, uh, she's calling 'Janie! Janie!' and then she sort of stumbles and I go running outside to see what's wrong with her. And Dorothea, she's crying and says, 'The phone! I gotta go to the hospital,' over and over about twenty times, and I'm calling you and leaving you messages and finally I just drive her here 'cause I don't know what else to do. And it takes us like an hour of sitting in the ER and talking to the receptionist before she's . . . um . . . calmed down and able to explain that she's not sick—that she got a phone call and she needs to see Henry."

Janie looks up. "Henry?"

"Yeah, Henry Feingold. That's the guy's name."

"Henry Feingold," Janie says. The name sounds empty. It has no meaning to her. It doesn't sound like what she imagined her father's name would be. "How would I even know if that's him? Dorothea," she says, emphasizing each syllable, "never bothered to share any information with me about him."

Carrie nods solemnly. She knows.

And then.

Janie blinks back the tears as she realizes the truth. "He must live nearby if they brought him here. Guess he didn't ever bother to know me, either."

"I'm sorry, hon." Carrie looks at the floor.

Janie stands abruptly and turns to Cabel and Carrie. "I can't believe she ruined our vacation. And I'm so sorry, Carrie, that you wasted your whole day and evening here. You are such a good friend—please, go on home or to Stu's or whatever."

She turns to Cabel. "Cabe, I'll handle this from here. I'll take the bus home once I collect my mother. Please, guys. Go get some rest." She walks toward the door, hoping Carrie and Cabe will follow so she can usher them out and suffer the embarrassment of all of this in private. Her bottom lip quivers. *God, this is so fucked up.*

Cabel stands up, and then Carrie stands too. "So," Cabel says to Carrie as they follow Janie to the door. "What's wrong with him? Do you know?"

"Some brain injury or something. I don't know much—I heard the doc tell Dorothea that he called 911 and was still conscious until after he got here, but now he won't wake up. They finally let Dorothea in to see him about thirty minutes ago. And Janers," Carrie says, "it was no problem, okay? You'd do the same if my mom needed help. Right?"

Janie's throat tightens and she blinks back the tears. All she can do is nod. When Carrie hugs her, Janie chokes back a sob. "Thanks," Janie whispers in Carrie's hair.

Carrie turns to go. "Call me."

Janie nods again, watching Carrie walk to the elevators. And then she looks at Cabel. "Go," she says.

"No."

He's not going anywhere.

Janie sighs uneasily. Because it's great he's so supportive, but this situation is totally weird. And Janie's not quite sure what to expect.

Some things are really just easier done alone.

It's quiet and the lights are low as Janie and Cabel push through the double doors into the ICU patients' hallway. Janie feels the faint pull of a dream from a distance and she combats it immediately, impatiently. Spies the culprit's room whose door stands ajar and silently curses him. Frustrated she can't ever get away from people's dreams, even when her mind is extremely busy doing other things.

They check in at the nurses' station. Janie clears her throat. "Henry, uh, Fein . . . stei—"

"Feingold," Cabel says smoothly.

"Are you family?" the nurse asks. She looks at them suspiciously.

"I, uh," Janie says. "Yeah. He's my . . . father . . . I guess."

The nurse cocks her head to the side. "The trick to getting into someone's room is to lie *convincingly*," she says. "Nice try."

"I—I don't want to go into his room. Just tell my mother I'm here, will you? She's in there with him. I'll be in the waiting room." Janie turns around abruptly and Cabel shrugs at the nurse and follows. They march back through the double doors to the waiting room, leaving a puzzled nurse watching them go.

Janie mutters under her breath as she flings herself in a chair. "Feingold. Harvey Feingold."

Cabe glances at her. "Henry."

"Right. Jeez. You'd never guess I work for the cops."

"Which is probably why you're so convincing undercover," Cabel says, grinning.

Janie elbows him automatically. "Well, not anymore. Don't forget you're talking to narc girl." She turns to him.

Grabs his hand. Implores. "Cabe, really, you should go. Get some sleep. Go back to Fremont and enjoy the rest of the week. I'm fine here. I can handle this."

Cabel regards Janie and sighs. "I know you can handle it, Janie. You're such a damn martyr. It's tiring, really, having this same argument with you every time you've got shit happening. Just let it go. I'm not leaving." He smiles faux-diplomatically.

Janie's jaw drops. "A martyr!"

"Ahh, yeah. Slightly."

"Please. You can't be *slightly* a martyr. You either are, or you aren't. It's like *unique*."

Cabel laughs softly, the corners of his eyes crinkling. And then he just gazes at her, smiling the crooked smile that Janie remembers from the awkward skateboard days.

But right now, Janie can't seem to smile back.

"Um, about this little adventure," she begins. "This is really mortifying, Cabe. I'm . . . I'm so embarrassed about it, and I have a lot on my mind, and I can hardly stand how nice you are being. I hate that I'm ruining your time too, instead of just my own. So, really, please. It would make me feel better if you'd just, you know . . ." Janie gives him a helpless look.

Cabel blinks.

His forehead crinkles and he looks earnestly at her.

"Ahh," he says. "You really do want me to go home.

When you say this is embarrassing, you mean it's embarrassing to you for *me* to know this stuff too?"

Janie looks at the floor, giving him the answer.

"Oh." Cabel measures his words, stung. "I'm sorry, Janers. I didn't pick up on that." He gets up quickly. Walks to the door. Janie follows him to the hallway by the elevators. "I'll . . . I'll see you around, I guess," he says. "Call me when—whenever."

"I will," Janie says, staring at the big CELL PHONES MUST BE TURNED OFF sign on the wall. "I'll text you later. This is just really something I'd rather handle alone at the moment, okay? I love you."

"Yeah. Okay. Love you, too." Cabel swivels on his flips and waves an uncertain hand at her. He looks over his shoulder. "Hey? Bus doesn't run between two and five a.m., you know that, right?"

Janie smiles. "I know."

"Don't get sucked into any dreams, okay?"

"Okay. Shh." Janie says, hoping no one else heard that.

Before he can think of anything else, Janie slips back inside the waiting room to sit and think.

Alone.

1:12 A.M.

She dozes in the waiting room chair.

Suddenly feels someone watching her. Startles and sits up, awake.

At least her mother is wearing clothes and not the nightgown Carrie mentioned.

"Hey," Janie says. She stands. Walks over to her mother and stops, feeling awkward. Not sure what to do. Hug? That's what they do on TV. Weirdness.

Dorothea Hannagan is sweating profusely. Shaking. Janie doesn't want to touch her. This whole scene is so foreign it's almost otherworldly.

And then.

Madness.

"Where were you?" Janie's mother crumples and she starts crying. Yelling too loud. "You don't tell me nothing about where you are, you just disappear. That strange girl from next door has to drive me here—" Her hands are shaking and her shifty eyes dart from the floor back up to Janie's, accusing, angry. "You don't care about your mother now, is that it? You just running around wild with that boy?"

Janie steps back, stunned, not just at the sheer record number of words uttered by her mother in one day, but even more by the tone. "Oh, my God."

"Don't you talk back to me." Dorothea's shaking hands rip open her ragged vinyl purse and she rifles through it, dumping wrappers and papers onto the waiting room chairs. It becomes painfully obvious that what she's looking for is not there. Dorothea gives up and slumps in a chair.

Janie, standing, watches.

She's shaking a little bit too.

Wondering how to handle this. And why she has to. *Haven't you given me enough shit to deal with already?* she says to no one. Or maybe to God. She doesn't know. But she does know one thing. She'll be glad to be away from this mess.

Janie picks up the scattered objects from the waiting room, shoves them into the purse, and takes her mother by the arm. "Come on. You've got some at the house, right?"

Janie tugs Dorothea to her feet. "I said, come on. We have to catch the bus."

"What about your car?" Dorothea asks. "That girl was driving it."

Janie blinks and looks at her mother, dragging her along to the elevator. "Yeah, Ma. I sold it to her months ago, remember?"

"You never tell me—"

"Just . . ." Janie burns. *I don't tell you anything? Or you're too drunk to remember?* She takes a breath, lets it out slowly. "Just come on. And don't embarrass me."

"Yeah, well don't you embarrass me, either."

"Whatever."

Janie gives a fleeting glance over her shoulder down the hallway where presumably her father lies, dead or alive, Janie doesn't know.

Doesn't really care.

Hopes he hurries up and dies so she doesn't ever have to deal with him. Because from all Janie knows, parents are nothing but trouble.

2:10 A.M.

Dorothea fidgets like a junkie the entire way home on the bus. Janie, frustrated, wards off the dream of a homeless passenger and is just glad it's a short ride.

When they get home, there on the front step is Janie's suitcase. "Damn, Cabe," she mutters. "Why do you always have to be so fucking thoughtful?"

Janie's mother makes a beeline to the kitchen, grabs a bottle of vodka from under the sink, and retreats to her bedroom without a word. Janie lets her go. There will be time tomorrow to figure out what's going on with this Henry person once Dorothea is good and sloshed and halfway reasonable again.

Janie texts Cabel.

Home.

Cabe responds without delay, despite the hour.

Thx baby. Love. See you tomorrow?

Turns off her phone. "Yeah, about that," Janie whispers. She sighs and sets the phone on her bedside table and her suitcase next to it, and falls into bed.

4:24 A.M.

Janie dreams.

There are rocks covering her bedroom floor and a suitcase on her bed. Each rock has something scribbled on it, but Janie can only read the rocks when she picks them up.

She picks one. "HELP ME," it reads. "CABE," reads another.

"DOROTHEA. CRIPPLED. SECRET. BLIND."

When she puts them back on the floor, they grow bigger, heavier. Soon, she knows, she will run out of room on the floor to put the rocks, but she can't stop picking them up, reading them. The floor is crowded, and Janie's having trouble breathing. The rocks are sucking the air from the room.

Finally, Janie sets a rock in the suitcase. It shrinks to the size of a pebble.

Janie slowly, methodically, picks up all the rocks and puts them in the suitcase. The task seems endless. Finally, she picks up the last one, "ISOLATE." Sets it down with the others. It becomes a pebble, and all the other pebbles disappear.

Janie stares at the suitcase. Knows what she has to do.

She closes it.

Picks it up.

And walks out.

FRIDAY

AUGUST 4, 2006, 9:15 A.M.

Janie lies awake, staring at the ceiling. Thinking about everything. About this one more thing. The green notebook, the hearing, the gossip, college, her mother, and now this guy Henry. What's next? It's too much already. A familiar wave of panic washes over her, captures her chest and squeezes it. Hard. Harder. Janie gulps for air and she can't get enough. She rolls to her side in a ball.

"Chill," she says, gasping. "Just chill the fuck out."

It's all too much.

She covers her mouth and nose with her hands, breathes into them, in and out, until she can get a good breath. She makes her mind go blank.

Focuses.

Breathes.

Just breathes.

9:29 A.M.

The door to Janie's mother's room remains closed.

Janie wanders aimlessly around the little house, wondering what the hell she's supposed to do about Henry. She nibbles on a granola bar, sweating. It's a scorcher already. She flips on the oscillating fan in the living room and props open the front door, begging for a breeze, and then she plops down on the couch.

Through the ripped screen door Janie sees Cabel pulling into the driveway, and her heart sinks. He hops out of the car and takes long, smooth strides to the front door. Lets himself in, as usual. He stops and lets his eyes adjust.

Smiles a crooked smile. "Hey," he says.

She pats the worn couch cushion next to her. "I haven't brushed my teeth yet," she says as Cabel leans in. "Your nose is peeling."

"Don't care, and don't care." Cabel leans in and kisses her. Then he plops down on the couch. "You okay that I'm here . . . and stuff?" he asks.

"Yeah." Janie slides her hand on his thigh and squeezes.

"Last night . . . I just didn't know what to expect. I wasn't sure about my mom, you know? Wasn't sure what she'd do."

"What *did* she do?" He looks around nervously.

"Not much. She was a little obnoxious. Not impossible. But she didn't say a word about Henry and I didn't dare ask. God, she can't even go twelve hours without a drink. And if she doesn't have one, she gets mean." Janie drops her chin. "It's embarrassing, you know?"

"My dad was like that too. Only he was mean with or without. At least he was consistent." Cabel grins wryly.

Janie snorts. "I guess I'm lucky." She glances sidelong at Cabel.

Considers.

Finally says, "Did you ever wish your dad was dead? I mean, before he hurt you? Just so you could, like, not have to deal with him anymore?"

Cabel narrows his eyes. "Every. Damn. Day."

Janie bites her lip. "So, are you glad he died in jail?"

Cabel is quiet for a long time. Then he shrugs. When he speaks, his voice is measured, almost clinical, as if he is talking to a shrink. "It was the best possible outcome, under the circumstances."

The fan blows a knee-level path from the TV to the coffee table, catching the two pairs of bare legs on the couch in the middle of its run. Janie shivers slightly when the air hits her sweat-dampened skin. She thinks of Henry

Feingold, the stranger, presumably her father. Dying. And for the third time in twenty-four hours, Janie wishes it were someone else.

She leans her head against Cabel's shoulder and slips her arm behind his. He turns, slides her onto his lap, and they hold on tightly to each other.

Because there's no one else.

She's so conflicted.

Janie imagines life without people. Without him. Broken heart, loneliness, but able to see, to feel. To live. To be, in peace. Not always looking over her shoulder for the next dream attack.

And she imagines life with him. Blind, gnarled, but loved . . . at least while things are still good. And always knowing what struggles he's dealing with through his dreams. Does she really want to see that, as years go by? Does she really want to be this incredible burden to such an awesome guy?

She still doesn't know which scenario wins.

But she's thinking.

Maybe broken hearts can mend more easily than broken hands and eyes.

9:41 A.M.

It's too hot to sit like that for long.

Cabe stretches. "You going to wake her up? Head down to the hospital again?"

"God, I hope not."

"Janie."

"Yeah, I know."

"At least it's air-conditioned there."

"So's your car. Wanna go make out in the driveway instead?"

Cabel laughs. "Maybe after dark. In fact, hell yes, after dark. But seriously, Janie. I think you need to talk to your mom."

Janie sighs and rolls her eyes. "I suppose."

9:49 A.M.

She taps softly on her mother's bedroom door.

Glances at Cabel.

To Janie, this room doesn't feel like a part of the house. It's more just a door to another world, a portal to sorrow, from which Dorothea appears and disappears at random. Rarely does she even catch a glimpse inside unless her mother is coming or going.

She waits. Enters, bracing herself against a possible dream. But Janie's mother isn't dreaming at the moment. Janie lets out a breath and looks around.

Filtered sunlight squeezes into the room through the worn patches of the window drape. The furnishings are spare but what's there is messy. Paper plates, bottles, and glasses are on the floor next to the bed. It's hot and stuffy. Stale.

In the bed, Janie's mother sleeps on her back, the thin nightgown gripping her bony figure.

"Mom," Janie whispers.

There's no response.

Janie feels self-conscious. She shifts on the balls of her feet. The floor creaks. "Mother," she says, louder this time.

Janie's mother grunts and looks up, squinting. Hoists herself with effort on her elbow. "Issit the phone?" she mumbles.

"No, I . . . it's almost ten o'clock and I was just wondering—"

"Don't you got school?"

Janie's jaw drops. *You've got to be kidding me.* She takes a deep breath, considers blowing up at her mother, reminding her of the graduation she didn't attend, and the fact that it's summer, but decides now is not the time. The words rush out before Dorothea can interrupt again. "No, ah, no school today. I'm wondering what the deal is with Henry and if you have to go to the hospital again or what. I don't want to—"

At the mention of Henry, Janie's mother sucks in a loud breath. "Oh, my God," she says, moaning, as if she just remembered what happened. She rolls over and shakily gets to her feet. Shuffles past Janie, out of the bedroom. Janie follows.

"Mom?" Janie doesn't know what to do. As they turn toward the kitchen, Janie gives Cabel a helpless look and he shrugs. "Mother."

Dorothea pulls orange juice from the fridge, ice and vodka from the freezer, and pours herself some breakfast. "What?" she asks, sniffling.

"Is this Henry guy my father?"

"Of course he's your father. I'm no whore."

Cabel makes a muffled noise from the other room.

"Okay, so he's dying?"

Janie's mother takes a long drink from the glass. "That's what they say."

"Well, was he in an accident or is it a disease or what?"

Dorothea shrugs and waves her hand loosely. "His brain exploded. Or a tumor. Something."

Janie sighs. "Do you need me to go with you to the hospital again today?"

For the first time in the conversation, Janie's mother looks Janie in the eye. "Again? You didn't go with me yesterday."

"I got there as soon as I could, Ma."

Janie's mother drains the glass and shudders. She

stands at the counter, one hand holding the empty glass, the other holding the bottle of cheap vodka, and she stares at it. She sets both glass and bottle down hard and closes her eyes. A tear escapes and runs down her cheek.

Janie rolls her eyes. "You going to the hospital or not? I'm"—she grows bold—"I'm not sitting around all day waiting."

"Go do whatever you want, like you always do, you little tramp," Dorothea says. "I'm not going back there anyways." She shuffles unsteadily past Janie, down the hall and into her room, closing the door once more behind her.

Janie lets out a breath and moves back into the living room where Cabel sits, a witness to it all. "Okay," she says. "Now what?"

Cabel looks peeved. He shakes his head. "Well, what do you think you should do?"

"I'm not going back to see him, if that's what you're asking."

"Me? Of course not. It's totally up to you if you want to see the guy."

"Right. Good."

"I mean, he's a deadbeat dad. Never done a thing for you. Who knows, maybe he has another family. Think of how awkward that would be if you just showed up and they were all there. . . ." Cabel trails off.

"Yeah, God, I never thought of that."

"I'm trying to think if there were any Feingolds at Fieldridge High. Maybe you have half-siblings, you know?"

"There's that one guy, Josh, that freshman who played varsity basketball," Janie says.

"That's Feinstein."

"Oh."

And then there is a moment, a pause, as Cabel waits for Janie.

"So, Feingold, that's Jewish, right?" she asks.

"Does that change anything if it is?"

"No. I mean, wow. It's interesting, anyway. I never really thought about my roots, you know? History. Ancestors. Wow." Janie's lost in thought.

Cabel nods. "Ah, well. You'll never know, I guess."

Janie freezes and then looks at Cabel.

Winds up and slugs him in the arm.

Hard.

"Ugh!" she says. "You loser."

Cabel laughs, rubbing his arm. "Dang! What'd I do this time?"

Janie seethes, half-jokingly. She shakes her head. "You made me give a shit."

"Come on," he says. "You cared before. Didn't you ever wonder who your father was?"

Janie thinks about the recurring dream her mother has—the kaleidoscope one where Dorothea and the hippie guy hold hands, floating. She'd wondered more than once who her father was. Wonders now if that was Henry in the dream.

"He's probably some suit with two-point-two kids and a dog and a house by U of M." Janie looks around her crap-hole of a house. Her crap-hole life, playing mom to an alcoholic twice her age. Knowing that without Dorothea's welfare check and Janie's income to supplement it, they are just one step away from being homeless. But Janie doesn't want to think about that.

Janie takes a deep breath and lets it out slowly. "All right. I'm grabbing a shower now, and later I'll head over to the hospital. I suppose you're coming with me then?"

Cabel smiles. "'Course. I'm your driver, remember?"

11:29 A.M.

Cabel and Janie take the stairs up to the third floor. By the time they reach the double doors that lead to the ward, Janie's moving more and more slowly until she stops. She turns abruptly and goes into the waiting room instead.

"I can't do this," she says.

"You don't have to. But if you don't, I think you'll be pissed at yourself later."

"If he has any other visitors, I'm leaving."

"That's fair."

"What if . . . what if he's awake? What if he sees me?"

Cabel presses his lips together. "Well, after what your mother said about his brain exploding, I highly doubt that will happen."

Janie sighs deeply and again walks toward the double doors with Cabel following. "Okay." She pushes through and does an automatic cursory glance, like she used to do at Heather Home, to see if any of the patients' doors are open. Luckily, most are closed, and Janie's not picking up any dreams today.

Janie approaches the desk, this time with confidence. "Henry Feingold, please."

"Family only," the nurse says automatically. His name tag says "Miguel."

"I'm his daughter."

"Hey," he says, looking at her more carefully. "Aren't you that narc girl?"

"Yeah." Janie tries not to fidget visibly.

"I saw you on the news. You did a good job."

Janie smiles. "Thank you. So . . . what room?"

"Room three-twelve. End of the hall on the right." Miguel points at Cabel. "You?"

"He's—" Janie says. "He and I. We're together."

The nurse eyes Janie. "I see. So. He's your . . . brother?"

Janie lets out a small breath and smiles gratefully. "Yes."

Cabel nods and remains quiet, almost as if to prove to Miguel that he will behave despite being completely unrelated to anyone in the vicinity.

"Can you tell me what his condition is?"

"He's not conscious, hon. Doctor Ming will have to give you an update." Miguel gives Janie a look of sympathy. A look that says, "Things are not good."

"Thank you," Janie murmurs. She sets off down the hallway with Cabel close behind. And when she opens the door . . .

Static. The noise is like top-volume radio static. Janie drops to her knees and holds her ears, even though she knows that won't help. Bright colors fly around her, giant slabs of red and purple; a wave of yellow so shocking it feels like it burns her eyeballs. She tries to speak but she can't.

There's no one there. Just wretched static and blinding lights. It's so painful, so void of feeling or emotion, it's like nothing Janie's ever witnessed before.

With a huge effort, Janie concentrates and pulls hard. Just as she feels herself pulling away, the scene blinks and clears. For a split second, there's a woman standing in a huge, dark room, and a man sitting in a chair in the corner, fading as Janie closes the door on that nightmare.

Janie catches her breath and when she can see again and feel her extremities, finds herself on her hands and knees just inside the doorway of the room. Cabel's right there beside her, muttering something, but she's not paying attention. She stares at the tiles on the floor and wonders briefly if that dream, that chaos, is what hell might be like.

"I'm okay," she says to Cabel, slowly getting to her feet, dusting invisible floor-dirt particles from her bare knees.

And then she straightens. Turns.

Looks at the source of the nightmare, and sees him for the first time.

The man who is her father. Whose DNA she carries.

Janie sucks in a breath. Slowly, her hand goes to her mouth and she takes a step backward. Her eyes grow wide in horror.

"Oh, my God," she whispers. "What the hell is that?"

WHAT THE HELL IT IS

STILL FRIDAY, AUGUST 4, 2006, 11:40 A.M.

Cabel puts his arm around Janie's shoulders, whether to show support or to keep her from bolting from the room, Janie doesn't know. Doesn't care. She's too horrified to move.

"He looks like a cross between Captain Caveman and the Unabomber," she whispers.

Cabel nods slowly. "Whoa. That's some funky Alice Cooper frizz." He turns to look at Janie. Says, in a soft voice, "What was the dream like?"

Janie can't take her eyes off the thin, very hairy man in the bed. He's surrounded by machines, but none of them are attached, none turned on. He wears no casts, no bandages. No gauze or white tape.

Just a look of incredible agony on his face.

She glances at Cabel, answers his question. "It was a strange dream," Janie says. "I'm not even sure it was a dream. It was more like a nondream. Like . . . when you're watching TV and the cable goes out. You get that loud, static, fuzzy noise at full blast."

"Weird. Was it black-and-white dots, too?"

"No—colors. Like giant beams of incredibly bright colors—purple, red, yellow. Three-dimensional colored walls turning and coming at me, coming together to make a box and closing in on me, so bright I could hardly stand it. It was awful."

"I'm glad you got out of it."

Janie nods. "Then for a split second, the walls disappeared and there was a woman there, way at the end, but it was too late for me to see. I was already pulling out of it. It felt like I was about to glimpse a piece of a real dream, maybe."

"Can you go back in?"

"I don't know. I've never tried that," she says. "Maybe if I go out of the room, shut the door, and come back in. But I don't really think I want to, you know?"

Cabel nods. He takes a step closer to the man. Picks up the chart that dangles from the foot of the bed. Stares at it intently for a moment and flips the top page over to look at the next page. Hands it to Janie. "I don't really understand this stuff. You want to know what's going on?"

Janie takes the clipboard uncertainly, feeling like she's intruding on a stranger. Still, she looks at it. Tries to decipher the terminology. But even with her experience working at Heather Home, there's not much Janie can understand.

"Huh. Looks like they detected sporadic, mild brain activity."

"Mild? Is that good?" Cabel sounds worried.

"I don't think so," Janie says. She puts the chart back.

"Can he hear us?" Cabel whispers.

Janie's quiet for a moment. Then she whispers too. "It's possible. At Heather Home, we always talked to the Hospice coma patients as if they could hear us, and told the families to do it too. Just in case."

Cabel swallows hard and looks at Janie, suddenly tongue-tied. He nudges her and nods toward the bed.

Janie frowns. "Don't rush me," she whispers.

She peers at the man. Steps closer. A shiver overtakes her and she stops when she's just a step away from her grizzly father. *What if he's faking and he jumps up at me?* Janie shivers again.

She takes a deep breath, and for a moment, she's Janie Hannagan, undercover. Looks more closely at Henry's distressed expression. Under all the long, black facial hair his skin is rough. Pockmarked. Janie wonders if he's the one she has to thank for her occasional zitbreaks. The hair on his head is patchy and thin in spots—as if great bunches of it had been pulled out. In places, she can see Henry's scalp. It's covered in red scratches.

She looks at his hands. His fingernails are clean but chewed down to the quick. Little scabs dot his cuticles. The hair on his chest that protrudes from his hospital gown is also patchy and decidedly grayer than the hair on his head. His complexion is grayish-white, as if he hadn't seen much sun all summer, but his arms have a light farmer's tan line.

"What happened to you?" She whispers it, more to herself than to him.

He doesn't stir. Still, the look of agony on his face is more than a bit unsettling. She wonders if the static is still going on in his mind. "That must be very painful," she murmurs.

Abruptly she looks at Cabel. "This is too weird," she mouths. Points at the door. Cabel nods and they step out. Closing the door again. "Too weird," Janie says aloud. It's more than she can deal with. "Let's go. Let's just . . . go work out or mess around or get lunch or something. I gotta get this guy out of my head."

12:30 P.M.

They stop at Frank's Bar and Grille and run into half a dozen cops who are on their way out.

"Come back from vacation early just because you missed us?" Jason Baker teases.

Janie likes him. "You wish. Little family emergency brought us home early. It's all fine now," she says lightly.

Cabel and Janie sit up at the counter for a quick lunch. Janie gets a free milkshake for being narc girl.

It's not all bad.

1:41 P.M.

Janie slings her smooth leg over Cabel's hairy one.

Their toes play together quietly while they work in Cabe's basement.

Janie searches WebMD for brain illnesses and injuries and gets nowhere—there are way too many to narrow down.

Cabel Googles "Henry Feingold." "Well," he says. "There's no information on a Henry Feingold in Fieldridge, Michigan. There's a pretty prolific author with that name, but he doesn't appear to be the same guy. Whatever your dad does—er, did—for a living, it's not out there on the Internet. At least not under his real name."

Janie closes the lid of her laptop. Sighs. "This is impossible, trying to figure him out. I wonder why they're not doing anything for him, you know?"

"Maybe he doesn't have insurance," Cabel says in a low voice. "Not trying to judge him by the way he looks, but he's no corporate exec, obviously."

"That's probably it." Janie closes her eyes. Rests her

head on Cabel's shoulder. Thinks about the two people that are related to her. Her mother—alcoholic-thin, greasy, stringy hair, old and brittle-looking in her mid-thirties; her father some sort of weird cross between Rupert from *Survivor* and Hagrid. "How can you even stand to think about what I'll look like in fifteen years when I'm all blind and gnarled, Cabe? Good fucking grief, what a familial circus of deformity."

"Why do you care so much about how you'll look?" He strokes her thigh. "You'll always be beautiful to me." He says it casually, but Janie can hear the strain in his voice.

"Still, they're both such freaks."

Cabel smiles. He sets his laptop on the floor, takes Janie's from her and does the same, and then slowly pushes against her until she's lying on her back. She giggles. He lies on top of her, pressing against her, squeezing her just like she likes. She wraps her arms around his neck, pulling his nose to hers. "I lurve you, circus freak," Cabel says.

It almost hurts to hear him say that.

"I lurve you, too, you big lumpy monster man," Janie says.

That hurts even more to say.

And then they kiss.

Slowly, gently.

Because with the right person, sometimes kissing feels like healing.

Still, something edges to the front of Janie's mind. Wonders if it's worth it—worth going blind, when there's another option.

Besides, what if Cabel won't own up to his fears about being with her?

It's fucking scary, is what it is.

It's like Cabe's the one who's blind.

The kissing slows and Cabel rests his face in crook of Janie's neck, nibbling her flushed skin. "What are you thinking about?"

"Uh . . . besides you?"

"Clever," Cabel says, a grin spreading, his moving lips tickling Janie's neck. He nips at her. "Yes, besides me. If it's possible for you to think about anything else, that is."

"Oh," she says. "If there were anything else, it would probably be how I need to get some cajones and go confront my mother." Absently, she smooths his hair away from his eyes. "Try and figure out what happened with them, and with me, and what we're supposed to do now with hermit dude."

Cabel sits back and nods. And then he hoists himself up with a grunt. Pulls Janie to her feet too. "You want me to come with you?"

"I think it'll be better if I do it alone. But thanks."

"I figured. Call me, 'kay?"

Freakishly, Janie's phone rings as he says it.

"It's Carrie—I gotta take this." Janie blows a kiss to Cabel as she ascends the stairs and she answers it. "Carrie!"

"Yo, bitch, my phone's charged up again. How's the whole family soap opera going today? You okay?"

"It's weird, and it's a mess, but it's okay. Thank you again for taking care of my mother. You're the best."

"No problem. Somebody's gotta clean up the neighborhood, right?"

"Ouch. Jeez, Carrie!" But Janie chuckles anyway.

"Well, you know where to find me if you need me," Carrie says. "Hey?"

"Hey what?"

"I'm engaged."

"What?"

"Stu asked me last night."

"Oh Em Gee what the Ef barbecue!" Janie says. "And you said yes?"

"Obviously, since I just said I was engaged."

"Wow, Carrie. Are you . . . are you sure? Are you happy about it?"

"Yeah. I mean yes, totally! I know Stu's the guy I want to be with."

"But?"

"But I wasn't quite expecting it yet."

Janie, having walked from Cabel's to her own house, walks to Carrie's instead. "Are you home?"

"Yeah."

"Can I come in?"

"Sweet," Carrie says, sounding relieved. "Yeah, come on in. My room, of course."

"Okay, bye." Janie hangs up her phone and lets herself in. She barges into Carrie's room and flops down on the bed. Carrie sits at a little dressing table, working her hair with a straightening wand in front of the mirror.

"So," Janie says. "You got a ring or what?"

Carrie grins and holds out her hand. "It feels weird. It's sort of embarrassing, you know?"

"What did your mom say?"

"She said I better not be pregnant."

Janie snorts. "What the hell is wrong with our parents, anyway? Wait—you're not, are you?"

"Of course not! Sheesh, Janers! I may not have gotten the best grades in school, but I'm not stupid. You know I'm on the Pill. And his Jimmy doesn't get near me without a raincoat, yadamean? Ain't nothin' getting through my little fortress!"

"Okay, good. Sheesh." Janie laughs again. "So . . . but you sounded a little like you're not sure about this."

Carrie sets the straightening wand on her dressing table and sighs. "I want to marry Stu. I do. There's nobody else and he's not pressuring me or anything. But he talked about setting a date, like next summer so I can get in my year of beauty school first but I'm just . . . I don't know. It's such a huge thing. I don't want to screw it up."

Janie remains quiet and lets Carrie get it all out. It feels weird to be normal again, sitting and hanging out with Carrie.

Janie wouldn't mind trading problems with her.

"Anyway, that's my junk of the day. What are you up to?" Carrie smoothes her straightened hair with some gooey, shiny product.

"I gotta go home, try and figure out what the deal is with my mother and this guy Henry. I don't have a clue what's going on. I need to get my mother to talk to me."

Carrie looks at Janie in the mirror and shakes her head. "Good luck with that. Talking to your mom is like talking to that Godot guy."

Janie laughs. Loves Carrie. Says, "Maybe I'll just get drunk with her and we'll fight it out, barroom style."

"Heh. Call me if you do that. I'd like to watch."

Janie grins and gives Carrie a quick hug. "Will do."

As Janie walks home, she thinks maybe that's not such a bad idea.

SHE SPEAKS

4:01 P.M.

Janie takes a few deep breaths, filling herself with confidence that's not quite there. But she'll take what she can get. She grabs a can of beer from the fridge stash and pops it open, taking a bitter sip. She hasn't had any alcohol since the night at Durbin's, so this feels a little creepy.

She waits on the couch, hoping her mother will come out on her own.

4:46 P.M.

Still waiting. Beer gone.

Grabs another beer. Turns on the TV and watches *Judge Judy*.

Switches the channel to a game show—judges conjure up too many bad memories.

5:39 P.M.

Where the hell is she? Figures she's got to go after her. Right after she pees.

5:43 P.M.

Janie opens her mother's door, two cans of beer in hand. One as an offering. Or maybe a bribe. But then Janie falls to the floor unceremoniously, dropping the cans, sucked into a dream. She hears a pop and a fizzing sound and knows at least one can broke open.

The noise isn't even enough to rouse Dorothea Hannagan from her drunken stupor. *Damn it,* Janie thinks. *Dreams plus booze equals not cool.*

Janie's head spins as she tries and fails to pull out of the dream.

They are in a line outside a building, Dorothea jiggling a crying baby. Janie knows she is the baby—who else would it be? They move slowly but the building moves too, farther away, making the wait endless. It's a shelter, or maybe a food bank. Janie stands in the road, watching her mother, trying to get her attention. Maybe this time, Janie can help change it. *Look at me,* Janie thinks, trying to concentrate. *Look at me.*

But Janie's sensibilities are off, not strong enough at the moment, and Dorothea merely glances at Janie and then looks away. She grows more impatient as she waits in line. Finally, Janie pulls her gaze away from her mother and looks to the front of the line, to the building. There are two windows.

Above the windows, a giant sign.

BABIES FOR FOOD.

That's what the sign says.

Janie watches people deposit their babies in one window and take a box of food from the other.

With all her might, Janie wants to scream, but she can't. She pulls her strength together and crawls blindly across the floor to the bed, butting her head up against it, flailing her numb arms on top of the mattress, not even sure if she's hitting her mother, trying to wake her. Trying to get out of this nightmare.

Finally, everything goes black.

At the same time, from both yelling mouths:

"What is wrong with you?"

Janie still can't see. She's feeling wet, soaked by the beer can that exploded. Dorothea shoves Janie. "What the hell are you doing?"

Janie pretends she can see. Her eyes are open, after all. "I—I tripped."

"Get outa here, you good for nothing—"

"Stop it!" Janie is half-drunk, confused, and blind. But she's done with this. "Stop talking to me like that! Don't give me that 'good for nothing' bullshit. Without me, you'd be on the street and you know it, so just shut your damn mouth!"

Janie's mother is stunned.

Janie is shocked by her own words.

Thus, the silence.

As the world comes back into view for Janie and she can move once again, she gets unsteadily to her feet and picks up the cans. "What a freaking mess," she mutters. "I'll be right back."

Janie returns with dishcloths and starts wiping it up. "You know, Mother, it wouldn't kill you to help me."

After a minute, Janie's mother eases her way to the floor and helps. "You been drinking?" Dorothea grunts.

"So what? Why should you care?" Janie's still pissed off and a little freaked out by the nightmare. "Why do you hate me so much?"

Janie's mother leans over to reach a wet spot on the floor. When she speaks, her voice is softer. "I don't hate you."

Janie's frustrated. "What's going on? What's the deal

with this Henry guy? I think I deserve to know what happened."

Dorothea looks away. Shrugs. "He's your father."

"Yeah, you mentioned that. What, do I have to ask specific questions here or can you just tell me about him? Sheesh!"

Dorothea frowns. "His name's Henry Feingold. We met in Chicago when I was sixteen. He was a student at U of M, but home for the summer. Working over at Lou Malnati's Pizzeria in Lincolnwood. I worked there too, waitressing."

Janie tries to imagine her mother actually working. "And then what? He got you pregnant and took off? He's an asshole? How did you end up here in Fieldridge?"

"Forget it. I'm not talking about this."

"Come on, Mother. Where does he live?"

"No idea. Around here somewheres. I quit school. Followed him here. We lived together for a while and then he took off and I never saw him again. There. Happy?"

"Did he know you were pregnant?"

"No. None of his business."

"But—but—how did you know he was in the hospital?"

Janie's mother has a vacant look in her eyes, now. "He had one of them legal papers—gave it to the paramedics. He had me down as the person to contact. It says he don't want any heroic measures. That's what the nurse told me."

Janie is silent.

Dorothea continues, softer. "I think maybe I oughta have one of them papers too. So you don't have to keep me hanging on when my liver rots out."

Janie looks away and sighs.

Feels like she's supposed to protest.

But who is she kidding? "Yeah," she says. "Maybe."

Dorothea lies down on the bed again. Turns away. "I mean it. I don't want to talk no more about this. I'm done with it."

After a moment of quiet, Janie gets up, unsteadily walks to the bathroom, throws up a few cans worth of cheap beer, and then some. "Never again," she echoes.

Then she crawls into her room, closes the door, climbs into bed and sleeps.

2:12 A.M.

Janie's running.

And running.

All night long.

She never gets there.

SATURDAY

AUGUST 5, 2006, 8:32 A.M.

"Yes," croaks Janie into her cell phone. "What." She's still half-asleep.

"Janie, is everything all right?"

Janie's silent. She should know this voice, but she doesn't.

"Janie? It's Captain. Are you there?"

"Oh!" Janie says. "God, I'm sorry, I—"

"Sorry I woke you. I normally wouldn't call but I heard from Baker that you had a family emergency and you're back in town. I'm calling to ask if everything is all right. And to find out more, if you're willing to tell me. Which you'd better be."

"I—ugh, it's complicated," Janie says. She rolls onto her back. Her mouth feels like it's stuffed with toilet paper. "Everything's fine, though. Well, I mean . . . it's a long story." *Ugh.*

"I have time."

"Can I get back to you? Somebody's buzzing me on the other line."

"I'll hold."

Janie smiles through the dull pain in her head and switches over to the other call.

It's Cabe. "Hey, baby, everything okay? What happened last night?"

"Yeah, let me call you back in a few."

"Done." He hangs up.

Janie switches back to Captain. "I'm back," she says.

"Fine."

"And, uh, I'd rather not go into all the details. So." Janie's feeling bold.

Captain pauses a split second. "Fair enough. You know where to find me, right?"

"Of course. Thank you, sir."

"I'll see you Monday for our meeting if not before. Take care, Janie." Captain hangs up.

Janie flips her phone shut and groans. "What is with everybody calling me at eight-thirty in the freaking morning?"

9:24 A.M.

Showered, fed, brushed. Janie feels a tiny bit better after taking an ibuprofen and drinking three glasses of water. "Never again," she mutters to the mirror. She calls Cabel back. "Sorry it took me so long." Janie explains what happened last night as she walks across the yards, up his driveway, and into his house.

"Hey," she says, hanging up.

Cabel grins and hangs up too. "Did you get breakfast?"

"Yeah."

"Wanna go for a drive?"

"I—sure. I was actually thinking about going to the hospital."

Cabel nods. "Cool."

"Not that I feel obligated, because I don't."

"Nor should you."

Janie is lost in thought. Going over what her mother said last night, although much of it is fuzzy after all that beer. "I think," she says slowly, "he's probably not a good person."

"What?"

"Just a feeling. Never mind. Let's go."

"Are you sure you want to go if he's a bad person?"

"Yeah. I mean, I want to find out for sure. I just want to know, I guess. If he's bad. Or not."

Cabel shrugs, but he understands. They take off.

9:39 A.M.

At the hospital, Janie moves carefully through the hallways as usual, watching for open doors. She gets caught in a weak dream but only for a few seconds—she barely even has to pause in step. They stand outside Henry's room, Janie's hand tense on the handle.

Static and shockingly bright colors. Again, Janie nearly crumples to her knees, but this time she is more prepared. She steps blindly toward the bed and Cabel helps her safely to the floor as her head pounds with noise. It's more intense than ever.

Just when Janie thinks her eardrums are going to burst, the static dulls and the scene flickers to a woman in the dark once again. It's the same woman as the day before, Janie's certain, though she can't make out any distinguishing features. And then Janie sees that the man is there too. It's Henry, of course. It's his dream. He's in the shadows, sitting on a chair, watching the woman. Henry turns, looks at Janie and blinks. His eyes widen and he sits up straighter in his chair. "Help me!" he pleads.

And then, like a broken filmstrip, the picture cuts out and the static is back, louder than ever, constant screamo in her ears. Janie struggles, head pounding. Tries pulling out of the dream, but she can't focus—the static is messing up her ability to concentrate.

She's flopping around on the floor now. Straining.

Thinks Cabel is there, holding her, but she can't feel anything now.

The bright colors slam into her eyes, into her brain, into her body. The static is like pinpricks in every pore of her skin.

She's trapped.

Trapped in the nightmare of a man who can't wake up.

Janie struggles again, feeling like she's suffocating now. Feeling like if she doesn't get out of this mess, she might die here. *Cabe!* she screams in her head. *Get me out of here!*

But of course he can't hear her.

She gathers up all her strength and pulls, groaning inwardly with such force that it hurts all the way through. When the nightmare flickers to the picture of the woman again, Janie is just barely able to burst from her confines.

She gasps for breath.

"Janie?" Cabel's voice is soft, urgent.

His finger paints her skin from forehead to cheek, his hand captures the back of her neck, and then he lifts her, carries her to the chair. "Are you okay?"

Janie can't speak. She can't see. Her body is numb. All she can do is nod.

And then, there's a sound from across the room.

It's certainly not Henry.

Janie hears Cabel swear under his breath.

"Good morning," says a man. "I'm Doctor Ming."

Janie sits up as straight as she can in the chair, hoping Cabel's standing in front of her.

"Hi," Cabe says. "We—I—how's he doing today? We just got here."

Dr. Ming doesn't answer immediately and Janie breaks out into a sweat. *Oh, God, he's staring at me.*

"Are you . . . ?"

"We're his kids."

"And is the young woman all right?"

"She's fine. This is really . . ." Cabel sighs and his voice catches. "Ah . . . really an emotional time for us, you know." Janie knows he's stalling for her sake.

"Of course," says the doctor. "Well."

Janie's sight is beginning to return and she sees that Dr. Ming is glancing over the chart. He continues. "It could be any day or he might hang on for a few. It's hard to say."

Janie clears her throat and leans carefully to the side of the chair so she can see past Cabel's bum. "Is he . . . brain-dead?"

"Hm? No, there appears to be some minor brain activity still."

"What's wrong with him, exactly?"

"We don't actually know. Could be a tumor, maybe a

series of strokes. And without surgery, we might not ever know. But he made it clear in his DNR that he didn't want life-saving measures and his next of kin—your mother, I believe?—she refused to sign off on surgery or any procedures." He says this in a pitying voice that makes Janie hate him.

"Well," she says, "does he even have insurance?"

The doctor checks the paperwork again. "Apparently not."

"What are the chances that surgery will help? I mean, could he be normal again?"

Dr. Ming glances at Henry, as if he can determine his chances by looking at him. "I don't know. He might never be able to live on his own. That is, if he even survived the surgery." He looks at the chart again.

Janie nods slowly. That's why. That's why he's just lying here. That, and the DNR. That's why they aren't fixing him—he's too broken. She tries to sound simply curious but it comes out nervous. "So, uh, how much does it cost for him to just be here, waiting to die . . . and stuff?"

The doctor shakes his head. "I don't know—that's really a question for the accounting office." He glances at his watch. Puts the chart back. "Okay, then." He walks briskly out of the room, pulling the door closed behind him.

When Dr. Ming is gone, Janie glares at Cabel. "Don't ever let that happen again! Couldn't you tell I was trapped in the nightmare? I couldn't get out, Cabe. I thought I was going to die."

Cabel's mouth opens, surprised and hurt. "I could tell you were struggling, but if I did break it, how was I supposed to know you wouldn't be mad at me for that? And what did you want me to do, drag you out in the hallway? We're in a freaking hospital, Hannagan. If anybody saw you like that you'd be strapped to a gurney in thirty seconds and we'd be stuck here all day, not to mention the bill for that."

"Better that than sucked into full frontal static-land. No wonder the guy's crazy. I'm half-crazy just spending a few minutes listening to that. Besides," Janie adds coolly, pointing to the private bathroom, "hello."

Cabel rolls his eyes. "I didn't think of it, okay? You know, it's not like I spend every waking moment planning my life around your stupid problems. There's more—"

He slams his lips together.

Janie's jaw drops.

"Oh, crap." He steps toward her, sorry-eyed. And she steps back.

Shakes her head and looks away, fingers to her mouth, eyes filling.

"Don't, Janie. I didn't mean it."

Janie closes her eyes and swallows hard. "No," she says slowly. Doesn't want to say it, but knows it's true. "You're right. I'm sorry." She gives a morose laugh. "It's good for you to say it like it is, you know? Healthy. And shit."

"Come on," he says. "Come 'ere." He steps toward her again and this time she goes to him. He runs his fingers through her hair and holds her to his chest. Kisses her forehead. "I'm sorry too. And that's not like it is. I just . . . it just came out wrong."

"Did it? Are you really saying that you aren't concerned about what's going to happen to me? About how that will affect you?"

"Janie—" Cabel gives her a helpless look.

"Well?"

"Well what? What do you want me to say?"

"I want you to tell the truth. Aren't you worried? Not even a little bit?"

"Janie," he says again. "Don't. Why are you doing this?"

But he doesn't answer the question.

To Janie, that says it all. She closes her eyes. "I think I'm a little stressed out," she whispers after a moment, and then shakes her head. At least now she knows. "Got a lot on my mind."

"Oh, really?" Cabe laughs softly.

"Some great vacation week, huh?"

Cabel snorts. "Yeah. Seems like forever since we were lazing around in the sun."

Janie's quiet, thinking about her mother, her father, and everything else. Cabel, and her own stupid problems, as Cabel calls them. And now, she wonders, *Who's going to pay this hospital bill?* She hopes like hell Henry has money, but by the looks of him, he's homeless. "No insurance," she groans aloud. Bangs her head against Cabel's chest. "Ay yi yi."

"It's not your problem."

Janie sighs deeply. "Why do I feel so responsible for it then?"

Cabel's quiet.

Janie looks up at him. "What?"

"You want me to analyze you?"

She laughs. "Sure."

"I'll probably regret saying anything. But it's like this. You're so used to playing the responsible one with your mother. Now you see this dysfunctional guy, somebody tells you he's your father and boom, your instinct is to be responsible for him, too, since he appears to be even more fucked-up than your mother. God knows we never thought that was possible."

Janie sighs. "I'm just trying to get through it all, you know? Get through the messes one by one, hoping each time it's the last one, and then I look beyond it and realize, crap, there's one more. Just hoping that someday, finally, I'll be free." Janie looks over at Henry and walks over to the side of the bed. "But it never happens," she says. Looks at her father for a long moment.

Thinking.

Thinking.

Maybe it's time to change.

Time to be responsible for just one person.

"Come on," she finally says to Cabel. "I don't think there's anything we can do for him. Let's just go. Wait for them to call my mother when he's . . . when it's over."

"Okay, sweets." Cabel follows Janie out of the room. He nods to Miguel at the desk and Miguel offers a sympathetic smile.

"Now what?" Cabel says, grabbing Janie's hand as they walk out to his car. "Food?"

"I think I'd rather you just drive me home, will you? I need some process time. Better check on my mother, too."

"Ah. Okay." Cabel doesn't sound thrilled. "Tonight?"

"Yeah . . ." Janie says, distracted. "That would be good."

1:15 P.M.

Janie flops onto her bed. Sinks her face into her pillow.

Her fan full blast and blowing on her, window and shade closed to keep the heat out. It's hot in the house, but Janie doesn't care. She's still recuperating from last night. She falls hard into an afternoon sleep. Her dreams are jumbled and random, flitting from a creepy, hairy homeless man chasing her to her mother stumbling around drunk in the front yard naked, to Mr. Durbin threatening to kill her, to a parade with all the people from the Hill lined up along the street, watching. Pointing and laughing at Janie the narc girl.

Then she dreams a horrible dream about Miss Stubin dying, and even though she's already dead, it still hurts. In the dream, Janie cries. When she wakes, her eyes are wet.

So is the rest of her. She's sweating so hard her sheets are damp.

And she feels like somebody beat the crap out of her.

Janie hates naps like that.

4:22 P.M.

She slips on her running shoes, stretches, and heads out the door, water bottle in hand. Thinks maybe this is what she needs. She hasn't worked out all week.

She walks down the driveway, feet crunching the gravel, and eases into a jog. Pounds the tar-patched pavement, her shoes making dents in the black blobs that are made even softer by the sun. Sweat pours down her back, between her breasts. Her legs are tired but she keeps going, waiting for that rush to hit. She runs all the way to Heather Home without realizing where she's going. The rhythmic step, the measured breathing, both slamming bad thoughts and memories through her head, trying to pound them out.

Not really succeeding.

Up the drive and into the cement parking lot she runs and then she stops. Stands in a parking space whose lines look tired from years of wear and lack of paint. Looks up to the sky, above the enormous maples, picturing that night a few summers ago when she sat out here with three of the Heather Home residents for the Fourth of July fireworks. They oohed and ahhed over the display, even though one of them was blind.

Blind, like Janie will be.

Oh, Miss Stubin.

Janie, breathing hard, lowers herself to the hot cement and the tears spill out freely, the pain of being eighteen and in love with a guy who can't talk about what's happening to her, and feeling this huge weight pressing into her chest, smashing her down, holding her back, keeping her from really living like a teenage girl should be living, and she wonders, not for the first time, why all this shit is happening to her. Thinks that she made a horrible mistake, taking the job with Captain and accelerating her own blindness for the benefit of others. Wonders what it would be like if all of it had never happened to her, if she'd never read that damn green notebook, if she'd never ridden that train where it all started when she was eight. If she could actually be in control of her life, just once.

Wonders if she should really do what she's been afraid to do all this time.

Save herself and screw the rest.

"Give me a fucking break!" she shouts up to the fireworks that are no longer there. "What the fuck do I have to do to just be normal? What did I ever do to deserve this crap? Why?" She sobs. "Why?"

Also, not for the first time,
there is no answer.

5:35 P.M.

Janie picks herself up.

Wipes the dirt from her shorts.

Starts jogging home.

6:09 P.M.

She slips into the back door of Cabel's house. Exhausted and empty.

He looks up from the kitchen where's he's fixing a sandwich and blinks at her.

"Hi," she says. Stands there, her tear-stained cheeks streaked with summer road dust and sweat.

Cabel's nose twitches. "Wow. You smell disgusting," he says. "Come with me."

And then he leads her to the bathroom. Turns on the shower. Kneels down to take off her shoes and socks as she sets her glasses on the counter and takes out her ponytail. Helps her out of her sodden clothes. And then he holds the curtain aside for her. "Go on," he says. She steps in.

He watches her, admiring her curves. Reluctantly turns to go.

And then he stops.

Thinks Janie might need some extra pampering.

He slips off his T-shirt and shorts. Boxers, too. And joins her.

6:42 P.M.

"Hey, Cabe?" she says, drying her hair, feeling refreshed. Grinning. Putting all thoughts but one aside for the moment. "You wanna go get Jimmy a raincoat and we'll take care of you?"

Cabel looks at her.

Turns his head and narrows his eyes.

"Who the hell is Jimmy?"

11:21 P.M.

In the cool dark basement, she whispers, "It's not Ralph, is it?"

Cabel's quiet for a moment, as if he's thinking. "You mean like *Forever* Ralph? Uh, no."

"You've read *Forever*?" Janie is incredulous.

"There wasn't much to choose from on the hospital library cart, and *Deenie* was always checked out," Cabel says sarcastically.

"Did you like it?"

Cabel laughs softly. "Um . . . well, it wasn't the wisest thing to read for a fourteen-year-old guy with fresh skin grafts in the general area down there, if you know what I mean."

Janie stifles a sympathetic laugh and buries her face in his T-shirt. Holds him close. Feels him breathing. After a few minutes, she says, "So what, then? Pete? Clyde?"

Cabel rolls over, pretending to sleep.

"It's Fred, isn't it."

"Janie. Stop."

"You named your thing Janie?" She giggles.

Cabel groans deeply. "Go to sleep."

11:41 P.M.

She sleeps. It's delicious.

For a while.

3:03 A.M.

He dreams.

They are in Cabel's house, the two of them, snuggling up together on a couch, playing Halo, eating pizza. Having fun. There is a muffled noise in the background, someone calling out for help from the kitchen, but the two ignore it—they are too busy enjoying each other's company.

The cries for help grow louder.

"Quiet!" Cabel yells. But the calls only grow more intense. He yells again, but nothing changes. Finally he goes into the kitchen. Janie is compelled to follow.

He yells out, "Just shut up about your stupid problems! I can't take it anymore!"

There, lying in a white hospital bed in the middle of the kitchen, is a woman.

She's contorted, crippled.

Blind and emaciated.

Hideous.

It's old Janie.

The young Janie on the couch is gone.

Cabel turns to Janie in the dream. "Help me," he says.

Janie stares. Gives a slight shake of her head, even though she is compelled to try to help him. "I can't."

"Please, Janie. Help me."

She looks at him. Speechless. Shudders, and holds back the tears.

Whispers, "Maybe you should just say good-bye."

Cabel stares at her. And then he turns to the old Janie.

Reaches out with two fingers.

Closes her eyelids.

Janie struggles and pulls out of the dream.

Frozen.

Panting.

The world closing in around her again. She struggles to move. To breathe.

When she is able, Janie stumbles on numb toes across Cabe's basement floor and up the steps, out the door. Across the yards and to her tiny, stifling prison.

Lies on her side, counting her breaths, making herself feel each one, in and out. Staring at the wall.

Wondering how much longer she can hide it all.

SUNDAY

AUGUST 6, 2006, 10:10 A.M.

She stares at the wall.

And pulls herself out of bed to face another day.

Janie finds Dorothea in the kitchen, fixing her mid-morning cocktail. It's the first time Janie's seen her since they talked.

"Hey," Janie says.

Janie's mother grunts.

It's like nothing happened.

"Any word on Henry?"

"No."

"You doing okay?"

Janie's mother pauses and gives Janie a bleary look. She fakes a smile. "Just fine."

Janie tries again. "You know my cell phone number is here next to the calendar if you ever need me, right? And Cabel's is here too. He'll do anything for you, like, if I'm not around or something. You know that?"

"He's that hippie guy?"

"Yeah, Ma." Janie rolls her eyes. Cabel got his hair cut months ago.

"Cabel—what kind of name is that?"

Janie ignores her. Wishes she hadn't said anything in the first place.

"You better not get knocked up, alls I can say. A baby ruins your life." Janie's mother shuffles off to her bedroom.

Janie stares at her as she goes. Shakes her head. "Hey, thanks a lot," she calls out. She pulls out her phone and turns it on. There's a text from Cabel: *Didn't hear you leave. Where'd you go? Everything okay?*

Janie sighs. Texts back. *Just woke up early. Had some stuff to take care of.*

He replies. *You left your shoes here. Want me to bring them, or?*

Janie debates. *Yeah. Thx.*

11:30 A.M.

He's at the door. "Mind if we go for a ride?"

Janie narrows her eyes. "Where to?"

"You'll see."

Reluctantly, Janie follows him to the car.

Cabel heads out of town and down a road that leads past several cornfields, and then acre after acre of woods. He slows the car down, squinting at the occasional rusty mailbox, scanning the woods.

"What are you doing?" Janie asks.

"Looking for two-three-eight-eighty-eight."

Janie sits up and peers out her window too. She says suspiciously, "Who lives way out here in BFE?"

Cabel squints again and slows as they pass 23766. He glances in his rearview mirror and a moment later, a car zooms by, passing them. "Henry Feingold."

"What? How do you know?"

"I looked in the phone book."

"Hunh. You're smart," Janie says. Unsure. Should she be outraged or eager?

Or just ashamed that she didn't think of it first?

Another mile and Cabel turns into an overgrown two-track gravel drive. Bushes scratch the sides of the car and the track is extremely bumpy. Cabel swears under his breath.

Janie peers out the windshield. The sun beats down between the tree branches, making it a striped ride. She sees something blurry about a quarter-mile away, in a clearing. "Is that a house?"

"Yeah."

After a couple of minutes, Cabel driving agonizingly slow over the bumpy driveway, they come to a stop in front of a small, run-down cabin.

They get out of the car. In the gravel turnaround there's an old, rusty blue station wagon with wood panels. A container of sun tea steeps on the car hood.

Janie takes it all in.

Bushes surround the tiny house. A wayward string of singed roses threatens to overtake a rotting trellis. A few straggling tiger lilies are opened wide, soaking up the sun. All the other flowers are weeds. Outside the front door sits a short stack of cardboard boxes.

Cabel steps carefully through pricker bushes to the dirty window and peers inside, trying to see through the tiny opening between curtains. "Doesn't look like anybody's here."

"You shouldn't do that," Janie says. She's uncomfortable. It's hot and the air buzzes with insects. And they are invading someone's privacy. "This place is creeping me out."

Cabel examines the stack of boxes in front of the door,

looking at the return addresses. He picks one up and shakes it near his ear. Then he sets it back down on the pile and looks around. “Want to break in?” he asks with an evil grin.

“No. That’s not cool. We could get arrested!”

“Nah, who’s going to know?”

“If Captain ever found out, she’d kick our asses. She’s not going to go easy.” Janie edges toward the car. “Come on, Cabe. Seriously.”

Cabel reluctantly agrees and they get back into the car. “I don’t get it. Don’t you want to know more? The guy’s your father. Aren’t you curious?”

Janie looks out the window as Cabel turns the car around. “I’m trying not to be.”

“Because he’s dying?”

She’s lost in thought. “Yeah.” Knows that if she doesn’t invest in Henry, she can write him off as a problem solved when he dies. He’ll just be some guy whose obituary is in the paper. Not her father. “I don’t need one more thing to worry about, I guess.”

Cabel pulls the car out onto the road again and Janie glances over her shoulder one last time. All she can see are trees.

“I hope his packages don’t get all wet next time it rains,” she says.

“Does it really matter if they do?”

They ride in silence for a few minutes. And then Cabel asks, "Did you get anything from Henry's nightmare yesterday? I was afraid to ask after our little misunderstanding of doom."

Janie turns in her seat and watches Cabel drive. "It was mostly the same as before. Static. Colors. Woman in the distance and then I saw Henry in the dream too. Always sitting in that same chair. He was watching the woman."

"What was the woman doing?"

"Just standing there in the middle of a dimly lit room—it was like a school gymnasium or something. I couldn't see her face."

"He was just watching her? Sounds creepy."

"Yeah," Janie says. She watches the rows of corn whiz past in a blur. "It didn't really feel creepy, though. It felt . . . lonely. And then—" Janie stops. Thinks. "Hmm."

"What?"

"He turned and looked at me. Like he was maybe a little bit surprised that I was there. He asked me to help him."

"Other people in dreams have seen you too, right? They talk to you."

"Oh, totally. But . . . I don't know. This felt different. Like . . ." Janie searches her memories, thinking back through the dozens of dreams she'd experienced in her life. "Like in most people's dreams, I'm just there, and they accept that, and they talk to me like I'm a prop. But they don't really connect—they look at me but they don't really *see* me."

Cabel scratches the scruff on his cheek and absent-mindedly runs his fingers through his hair. "I don't get the difference."

Janie sighs. "I guess I don't either. It just felt different."

"Like the first day I saw you at the bus stop and you were the only one who would look at me, and our eyes sort of connected?" Cabel's teasing, sort of. But not really.

"Maybe. But more like when Miss Stubin looked at me when I was in her dream back in the nursing home and asked me a question. Sort of a recognition thing. Like, somehow she just knew I was a dream catcher too."

Cabel glances at Janie and then back at the road. His forehead crinkles and he tilts his head quizzically. "Wait," he says. "Wait a minute." He presses down on the brake and turns to look at Janie again. "Serious?"

Janie looks at Cabel and nods. She's been wondering it.

"Janie. Do you have any reason at all to think this dream thing could be hereditary?" The car slows and comes to a stop in the middle of the country road.

"I don't know," Janie says. She glances over her shoulder nervously. "Cabe, what are you doing?"

"Turning around," he says. He backs into a three-point turn and hits the gas. "This is important stuff. He might have some information on this little curse of yours. And we might not have another chance."

12:03 P.M.

Cabel stands at the front door of Henry's house and pulls his driver's license from his wallet. He works it into the crack of the door next to the handle and begins to move it side to side. He presses his lips together as he works, trying to get to the bolt to move aside so they can break in.

Janie watches him for a moment. Then she reaches out and grabs the door handle. Turns it. The door opens.

Cabel straightens up. "Well. Who doesn't lock their doors these days?"

"Somebody whose brain is exploding, maybe? Somebody who lives out in the middle of nowhere and has nothing good to steal? Somebody who's half-crazy? Maybe he told the paramedics not to lock it because he didn't have his keys." Janie steps into the little house, making room for Cabel to follow. "See?" she says, pointing to a key rack on the wall with one set of keys hanging from it.

It's stuffy inside. Kitchen, living area, and bed are all in the main room. A doorway in the back corner appears to lead to a bathroom. There's a radio on a bookshelf and a small TV on the kitchen counter. Hot air plunges into the room through an open, screened window at the back of the house. A thin yellow curtain flutters. Below the window is a table where an old computer sits. It appears from the coffee mug and bowl that the table serves as both an eating place and as a desk. Under the table is a three-drawer unit that looks like it once belonged to a real desk. A few papers rest on the floor as if they'd been carried there by the breeze.

Flattened cardboard boxes lean against the wall near the back door. The bed is disheveled. A nearly empty glass of water stands on a makeshift bedside table made from a cardboard box.

"Well," Janie says. "There's goes my dream of a magical surprise inheritance. Dude's poorer than us."

"That's not an easy feat," Cabel says, taking it all in. He walks over to the desk. "Unless maybe he owns this property—it could be valuable." Cabel shuffles through a few bills on the desk. "Or . . . not. Here's a canceled check that says 'rent' in the memo line."

"Damn." Janie reluctantly joins Cabel. "This feels weird, Cabe. We shouldn't be doing this."

"You'll never find out anything if you wait until after he's dead—the state will take over and the landlord's going to want a tenant who can actually pay the bills. They'll clean this place out, sell what they can to pay the hospital, and that's that."

"You sure know a lot of random shit." Janie looks around.

"Random, *useful* shit."

"I suppose." She wanders around the little house. On top of the TV there are a variety of over-the-counter pain relievers. The refrigerator is half-stocked. A quart of milk, half a loaf of pumpernickel bread, a container of bologna. One shelf alone is filled with string beans, corn on the cob, tomatoes, and raspberries. Janie glances out the window to the backyard and sees a small garden and, off to the side, wild-looking bushes dotted red.

The cupboards are mostly bare, except for a few non-matching dishes and glasses. There's a light layer of dust all around, but it's not a dirty house. In the living area, there's an old beat up La-Z-Boy recliner, an end table with a wooden lamp on it, and a large, makeshift shelving unit filled with boxes. Near it is a small bookcase. Janie pictures Henry sitting here in the evening, in the recliner, reading or watching TV in this almost-cozy house. She wonders what sort of life it was.

She walks over to the bookcase and sees worn copies of Shakespeare, Dickens. Kerouac and Hemingway and Steinbeck, too. Some books with odd lettering that looks like Hebrew. Science textbooks. Janie removes one and looks inside. Sees what must be her father's handwriting below a list of names that had been crossed out.

Henry David Feingold
University of Michigan

She squats down and pages through the textbook, reading notes in the margin. Wonders if those are his notes, or if they belonged to someone before him. The binding is broken and some of the pages are loose so Janie closes the book and returns it to the shelf.

Cabel is looking through papers on the desk. "Invoices," he says. "For all sorts of weird things. Baby clothes. Video games. Jewelry. Snow globes, for Chrissakes. Wonder where he keeps it all. Kinda weird, if you ask me."

Janie stands up and walks over to Cabel. Picks up a notebook and opens it. Inside, in neat handwriting, is a list of transactions. No two are alike. Janie puzzles over the notebook and then she goes to the front door. Pulls the packages inside and looks at the return addresses. Matches them up in the notebook.

She flips her hair behind her ear. "I think he must have a little Internet store, Cabe. He buys stuff cheap and sells it in his virtual store for a profit. So he's got a little shipping/receiving department over there." She points to the large shelving unit.

"Maybe he goes to yard sales and buys stuff too."

Janie nods. "Seems weird that he'd go to school for

science and end up doing this. I wonder if he got laid off or something?"

"Considering the state of Michigan's economy and rising unemployment rate lately, that's entirely likely."

Janie grins. "You're such a geek. I love you. I really do."

Cabel's face lights up. "Thank you."

"So . . ." Janie sets the notebook on the table and picks up a well-worn paperback copy of *Catch-22*. Pages through it, losing her train of thought. Sees a torn piece of paper used as a bookmark. Words are scribbled in pencil on the bookmark.

Morton's Fork.

That's what it says.

Janie closes the book and sets it back down on the desk. "Now what?"

"What do you want to do? I don't see any evidence that he's a dream catcher, do you?"

"No. But would you find any evidence of that in my house if you looked?"

Cabel laughs. "Uh, green notebook, the dream notes on your bedside table . . ."

"Bedside table," Janie says, tapping her bottom lip with her forefinger. She walks over to Henry's bed, but there's nothing there. Just the water glass. She even pushes aside the mattress and slips her fingers between it and the box springs, feeling for a diary or journal of some sort. "There's nothing here, Cabe. We should go."

"What about the computer?"

"No—we're not going there. Really. Let's just go. And besides, you saw the guy. He's not all gnarled and blind."

"How do you know he's not blind? You can't tell that."

"Yeah, maybe you're right," Janie says. "But his hands looked fine."

"Well . . . what did Miss Stubin say in the green notebook? Mid-thirties for the hands? He can't be much older than late thirties, forty tops, right? So maybe it just hasn't happened yet."

Janie sighs. Doesn't want to go this deep. Doesn't want to think about the green notebook anymore. She walks to the door and stands there a moment. Bangs her head lightly against it. Then she opens it, goes outside and sits in the sweltering car until Cabel comes.

"Hospital?" he says, hope in his voice, when he turns the car onto the road.

"No." Janie's voice is firm. "We're done with it, Cabe. I don't care if he was the king of dream catchers. He's probably not—he's probably just some guy who would freak out if he knew we were snooping around inside his house. I just don't want to pursue this anymore." She's tired of it all.

Cabe nods. "Okay, okay. Not another word. Promise."

7:07 P.M.

At Cabel's house, they both work out. Janie knows she's got to keep her strength up. They have a meeting with Captain on Monday, which means an assignment looms. For the first time, Janie doesn't feel very excited about it.

"Any idea what Captain will have for us?" Janie asks between presses.

"Never know with her." Cabel breathes in and blows out fiercely as he reaches the end of his arm curl reps. "Hope it's something light and easy."

"Me too," Janie says.

"We'll find out soon enough." Cabel puts his weights on the floor. "In the meantime, I can't seem to stop thinking about Henry. There's something weird about the whole situation."

Janie sets the bar in the cradle and sits up. "Thought you said you were going to let it go," she says. Teases. But the curiosity takes over. "What makes you say that, anyway?"

"Well, you said there was a connection in the dream, like you had with Miss Stubin, right? That's what got my brain going and now I can't stop it. And how odd, just the way he lives. He's a recluse. I mean, he's got that old station wagon parked in the yard, so he obviously drives, but . . ."

Janie looks sharply at Cabel. "Hmm," she says.

"Maybe it's all just a coincidence," he says.

"Probably," she says. "Like you said, he's just a recluse."

But.

10:20 P.M.

"Goodnight, sweets," Cabe murmurs in Janie's ear. They're standing on Cabel's front stoop. Janie's not about to sleep there again. It's too hard. Too hard to keep her secret.

"I love you," she says, soulfully. Means it. Means it so much.

"Love you, too."

Janie goes, arms outstretched and her fingers entwined in Cabel's until they can't reach anymore, and then she reluctantly lets her arm drop and walks slowly across the yards to her street, her house.

Lies awake on her back. And her mind shifts from Cabe to the earlier events of the day. To Henry.

12:39 A.M.

She can't stop thinking about him.

Because, what if?

And how is she supposed to know, unless . . . ?

Janie slips out of bed, puts her clothes on and grabs her phone, house key, and a snack for energy. The bus is empty except for the driver.

Thankfully, he's not asleep.

12:58 A.M.

Janie's flip-flops slap the hospital floor and echo through the otherwise quiet hallways. An orderly with an empty gurney nods to Janie as he exits the elevator. Up on the third floor, Janie pushes through the ICU door without hesitation. It's dimly lit and quiet. Janie fends off the hallway dreams and, before she opens Henry's door, goes over her plan in her mind.

She takes a deep breath and pushes open the door, closing it swiftly behind her as everything around her goes black, and then she's slammed by the colors and the outrageous static once again.

The power of the dream forces Janie to her hands and knees. The attack on her senses makes gravity ten times stronger than normal. She sways inadvertently as if to avoid the giant block walls of burning color that swing toward her in 3-D. Mentally she's trying to hear her own thoughts above the noise, and it's incredibly difficult—it's like she's in a vortex of static.

Janie's hands and feet quickly grow numb. Blindly, she turns to the right and crawls, aiming for the bathroom so that if she has to, she can get inside and close the door. As a flaming yellow block swings toward her, Janie lunges to avoid it and feels her head connect with the hospital room wall. "Concentrate!" she yells to herself. But the noise is overpowering. All she can do is slide forward on numb stumps, hoping she's even moving at all, and waiting for a flash of something, anything that will explain some of the mystery of Henry.

Janie doesn't know how much time goes by before she can't continue moving.

Before she can no longer press on, unable to fight any longer. Unable to find the bathroom, to break the connection.

It's as if she's fallen through ice, engulfed in frigid water. Numb, both body and mind. Even the noise and the colors are muted.

Things stop mattering.

She can't feel herself flopping around wildly.

Doesn't know she's losing consciousness.

Doesn't care anymore either. She just wants to give up, let the nightmare overtake her, engulf her, fill her brain and body with the endless clamor and sickening dazzle.

And it does.

Soon, everything goes black.

But then.

In Janie's own unconsciousness, the picture of a madman, a hairy, screaming madman that is her own father, slowly appears from the darkness before her.

He reaches toward her, his fingers black and bloody, his eyes deranged, unblinking. Janie is paralyzed. Her father's cold hands reach around her neck, squeezing tight, tighter, until Janie has no breath left. She's unable to move, unable to think. Forced to let her own father kill her. As his grasp tightens further around Janie's neck, Henry's face turns sickly alabaster. He strains harder and begins to shake.

Janie is dying.

She has no fight left in her.

It's over.

Just as she has given up, her father's chalky face turns to glass and shatters into a dozen pieces.

His grip around Janie's neck releases. His body disappears.

Janie falls to the ground, gasping, next to the pieces of her father's exploded face. She looks at them, sucking breath, finally able to move.

Raises herself up.

And there, instead of seeing her father in the glass,

She sees her own horrified, screaming face, reflected back at her.

Static once again.

For a very.

Very.

Long time.

Janie realizes that she might be stuck here. Forever.

2:19 A.M.

And then.

A flicker of life.

A flash of a woman's figure in a dark gymnasium, a portrait of a man on a chair . . .

And a voice.

Distant. But clear. Distinct.

Familiar.

The voice of hope in one person's ever-darkening world.

"Come back," the woman says. Her voice is sweet and young.

She turns to face Janie. Steps into the light.

Standing on strong legs, her eyes clear and bright. Her fingers, not gnarled, but long and lovely. "Janie," she says in earnest. "Janie, my dear, come back."

Janie doesn't know how to come back.

She is exhausted. Gone. Gone from this world and hovering somewhere no other living person could possibly be.

Except for Henry.

Janie's mind is flooded with the new scene, a soft and quiet scene, of a man in a chair, and a woman, now standing in the light imploring Janie to come back. The woman walks over to Henry, stands beside him. Henry turns and looks at Janie. Blinks.

"Help me," he says. "Please, please, Janie. Help me."

Janie is terrified of him. Still, there is nothing she can do but help.

It is her gift.

Her curse.

She is unable to say no.

Compelled, Janie pulls herself to attention, to full awareness, scared to death that the horrible din and burning colors will return at any moment, dreading getting anywhere near this man who turns mad and strangles her. Wishing she could gather the strength to pull herself from this nightmare now, while she has the chance. But she cannot.

Janie struggles silently to her feet in the gymnasium. With effort, she walks toward the two, her footsteps echoing. She has no idea what to do for Henry. Sees nothing that she can do to help. Really only wants to tie him up, or maybe kill him, so he doesn't have the chance to hurt her.

She stops a few feet away from them. Stares at the woman standing there, not quite believing her eyes. "It's you," she says. She feels a rush of relief. Her lip quivers. "Oh, Miss Stubin."

Miss Stubin reaches out and Janie, overwhelmed by seeing her again and incredibly weak from this nightmare, stumbles into her arms. Miss Stubin's grip is strong, full of comfort. It repairs some of Janie's strength. Janie is filled with emotion as she feels the warmth, the love in Miss Stubin's touch. "There, you're all right," Miss Stubin says.

"You," Janie says. "You're . . . I thought I wouldn't be seeing you again."

Miss Stubin smiles. "I have been quite enjoying my time with Earl since I last saw you. It's good to be whole again." She pauses, eyes twinkling. They pick up the dim rays of light coming in through the gymnasium's tiny upper windows. And then she looks toward the mute Henry, who sits ever still. "I believe I'm here for Henry . . . I think to bring him home, if you know what I mean. Sometimes I don't know myself why I'm summoned to other catchers' dreams."

Janie's eyes widen. "So, it's true. He really is one."

"Yes, apparently so."

They look at Henry, and then at each other. Silent, pondering. The dream catchers, all together in one place.

"Wow," Janie murmurs. She turns back to Miss Stubin. "Why didn't you tell me about him? You said in the green notebook that there weren't any other living dream catchers."

"I didn't know about him." She smiles. "It appears he needs your help, first, before he can come with me. I'm glad you came."

"It wasn't easy," Janie says. "His dreams are horrible."

"He hasn't many left," Miss Stubin says.

Janie presses her lips together and takes a deep breath. "He's my father. You knew that, right?"

Miss Stubin shakes her head. "I didn't know. So it's hereditary, then. I've often wondered. It's why I didn't have children."

"Did you—?" Janie's suddenly struck by a thought. "You're not related, are you? To us, I mean?"

Miss Stubin smiles warmly. "No, my dear. Wouldn't that be something?"

Janie laughs softly at the craziness of it. "Do you think

that maybe there are others out there, then? Besides me?"

Miss Stubin clasps Janie's hand and squeezes. "Knowing that Henry exists gives me hope that there are more. But dream catchers are nearly impossible to find." She chuckles. "Best thing you can do to find them is to fall asleep in public places, I guess."

Janie nods. She glances at Henry. "How am I supposed to help him?"

Miss Stubin raises an eyebrow. "I don't know, but you know what to do to find out. He's already asked you for help."

"But . . . I don't see . . . and he's not leading me anywhere." Janie looks around the near-vacant gymnasium, looking for clues, trying to figure out what she could possibly do to help Henry. Not wanting to get too close.

Finally, Janie turns to Henry and takes a deep breath, glancing at Miss Stubin briefly for support. "Hey there," she begins. Her voice shakes a little, nervous, scared, not sure what to expect. "How can I help you?"

He stares at her, a blank look on his face. "Help me," he says.

"I—I don't know how, but you can tell me."

"Help me," Henry repeats. "Help me. Help me. Help me. HELP me. HELP ME. HELP ME! HELP ME!!" Henry's voice turns to wild screams and he doesn't stop. Janie backs away, on her guard, but he doesn't come toward her. He reaches to his head and grips it, screaming and ripping chunks of hair from his scalp. His eyes bulge and his body is rigid in agony. "HELP ME!"

His screams don't end. Janie is frozen, shocked, horrified. "I don't know what to do!" she yells, but her voice is drowned out by his. Terrified, she looks for Miss Stubin, who watches intently, a little fearfully.

And then.

Miss Stubin reaches out.

Touches Henry's shoulder.

His screams stutter. Fail. His ragged breaths diminish.

Miss Stubin stares at Henry, concentrating. Focusing. Until he turns to look at her and is quiet.

Janie watches.

"Henry," Miss Stubin says gently. "This is your daughter, Janie."

Henry doesn't react. And then his face contorts.

Immediately, the scene in front of Janie crackles. Chunks of the gymnasium fall away, like pieces of a broken mirror. Bright lights appear in the holes. Janie sees it happening and her heart pounds. She shoots a frantic glance at Miss Stubin, and at her father, desperate to know if he understands, but he is holding his head again.

"I can't stay in this," Janie yells, and she gathers up all her strength, pulling out of the nightmare before the static and blinding colors overtake her again.

2:20 A.M.

All is quiet except for the ringing in Janie's ears.

Minutes pass as Janie lies facedown, unmoving, unseeing, on the clammy tile floor of the hospital room. Her head aches. When she tries to move, her muscles won't comply.

2:36 A.M.

Finally, Janie can see, though everything is dim. She grunts and, after a few tries, shoves to her feet, steadying herself against the wall, wiping her mouth. Blood comes away on her hand. She moves her tongue slowly around, noting the cut inside her cheek where she apparently bit down during the nightmare. Feels her neck, her throat, gingerly. Her stomach churns as she swallows blood-thickened saliva. Janie squints at her watch, shocked that so much time has gone by.

And then she turns to look at Henry. Runs her fingers through her tangled hair as she stares at his agonized face, frozen into the same horrible expression as in his dream when he screamed over and over again.

"What's wrong with you?" she says. Her voice is like the static in the nightmare.

She bites her bottom lip and still she watches from a distance, remembering Henry the madman. *He's unconscious. He can't hurt me.*

She doesn't believe it, so she says it aloud, to herself and to him. "You can't hurt me."

That helps a little.

She steps closer.

Next to his bed.

Her finger hovers above his hand and Janie imagines him jumping up, grabbing her with that cold death-grip. Tearing her throat out. Strangling her. Still, slowly, she lowers her hand and lays it on top of Henry's.

He doesn't move.

His hands are warm and rough.

Just like a father's hands should be.

2:43 A.M.

It's too late for the bus.

When she is able, Janie meanders her way through the hospital and down to the street. Slowly limps home in the dead of night.

MONDAY

AUGUST 7, 2006, 10:35 A.M.

A dream catcher. Her father. Just like her.

Unbelievable.

Janie slips into her running clothes and makes her way to the bus stop. Takes it to the last stop on the edge of town. And runs the rest of the way.

Things in the country are so much slower than they are in town. Janie's feet slap the pavement as she runs along, the whole world seemingly coming to a stop before her eyes. Row after row of ripe corn begs to be harvested—Janie can see the soft brown tassels go by in a blur as she runs.

Her glasses slip down on her nose from the sweat, and

she is reminded yet again that she needs to take in the sights for as long as she can. It makes her sick to think about losing all of this, so she absorbs it, one step after another, until her mind wanders again.

She hears the buzz of tree frogs and remembers how, when she was little, she used to think that the intense buzz was not an animal, but the sound of electrical wires, bustling with energy. When she learned the noise came from frogs, she didn't believe it.

Still doesn't.

After all, she's never actually seen one.

And as she sucks in stale, humid air, the faint odor of cow manure becomes common. Alongside it is the sickly sweet smell of wildflowers and the searing hint of recent road patching.

Janie's mind is clear and her purpose is sure when she reaches the long, overgrown driveway of Henry's house. She slows to a walk, trying to cool down.

Just as she reaches the clearing, her cell phone buzzes in her pocket. She ignores it, knowing it's probably Cabel. Needs to think. To do this alone. She opens the door and steps inside the house.

That eerie feeling comes over her—the one that makes her shiver and feel a little bit dizzy and sick all at the same time when being somewhere overtly quiet and extremely off-limits. Janie huffs, still winded, and the noise breaks the silence. "Talk to me, Henry, you creepy little strangler," Janie says softly. "Show me how I can help you."

She walks to the kitchen, wipes her sweaty forehead on a kitchen towel and grabs a glass from the cupboard. Turns on the faucet. The water chokes and spurts out, a lovely rust color until it run clears a moment later. Janie lets it run for a minute and then fills the glass. Drinks it, the tepid water not quite raunchy enough to make her gag.

She decides to tackle the computer first. Boots it up and realizes that it's on dial-up. Not surprising for way out here in the country, but still totally annoying. "Talk to me," she mutters again, tapping her fingers impatiently on the table.

First, she looks through his bookmarks. Immediately finds Henry's online store account and logs in, his username and password unprotected, already filled in. Janie peruses the online store, called Dottie's Place. Finds a collection of odd, unrelated items including babies and children's clothing, small electronic equipment, books, and glass figurine collectibles. She clicks on a pair of "gently worn" name-brand overalls and reads the description. Reads the words Henry chooses. Sees his intelligence and marketing ability and business savvy all rolled into the little store.

There are several auctions in progress, plus a few that have ended in the days since Henry became ill.

And then she sees his rating. 99.8% positive.

Janie doesn't recognize the feeling that wells up in her chest.

Makes her eyes water.

All she knows is that Henry Feingold has a near-perfect rating.

She's not about to let that record get tarnished.

Janie freezes the inventory. Assesses the items that were already sold and searches for them on the inventory shelves. Packs the few items up and finds the UPS slips in the drawer. Fills them out. Wonders if she needs to call for pickup, but then finds the link online in Henry's favorites. She schedules a pickup for before five p.m. Sets the boxes outside the door so she doesn't forget.

Back at the computer, Janie inhales Henry's other bookmarked pages. A political message board, a cooking website, several links to marketing professionals, a Jewish holiday website. Gardening sites.

Dreams.

And a link to a Wikipedia page about Morton's Fork.

Janie clicks on that last one.

Reads the page.

Finds out that Morton's Fork is not literally a fork. It's

a term for a dilemma of sorts. In summary: a forced choice between two equally suck-ass things.

Janie reads about it and sees a comparison to a catch-22, and she glances at the book on the table that coined the phrase. She furrows her brow. "Okay, Mister Creepy-pants," she mutters, back on the computer, typing wildly searching keywords. "What are you all about? What's your big choice?"

And then she stops typing mid-word.

She sinks back into the chair, remembering the last time she read about a catch-22. Just a few months ago, in a green spiral notebook.

Knows, of course.

It's clear what Henry chose, years ago.

He didn't have Miss Stubin to help him. To teach him.

He had no one.

12:50 P.M

The rattling, house-shaking noise of a truck breaks Janie's attention. Through the window she sees it rumbling toward her and her heart races, knowing she shouldn't be here. But then the driver raps on the door and she shouts in a friendly voice, "Hey, Henry, you gotta sign for this one! You out back?"

Janie hesitates, and then she opens the door. "Hi."

The delivery woman looks up, machine in hand. Sweat streaks her tan cheeks and she has wet stains under her arms. She wears the company brown shorts and her tan legs are covered in bug bites and bruises. She looks surprised and confused for a moment, but then says, "Hi, uh, are you eighteen? You can sign."

"I . . . yeah."

"Where's Henry? Out garage-saling? Well, obviously not, because there's his car . . . Well, you can tell him I saw a sign for a big rummage sale that the Luther'ns are putting on. Over on Washtenaw, Fridee and Saturdee." She looks uneasy.

"Henry's—he won't be able to make it. He's . . . sick. Not doing well." Janie feels her throat growing tight. "In the hospital, probably not going to make it."

The woman's jaw drops. She grips the door frame. "Oh, my heck. You're not serious. Are you . . . who are you?" She pounds a fist to her hip as if to get a hold of herself. "If I may ask, I mean—it's none of my business but Henry's been my customer for years. We're friends." She turns abruptly and stares at the woods, her fingers now fidgeting at her lips and then shoving through her mullet.

"I'm Janie. I'm his daughter," Janie says. It sounds weird.

"His daughter? He never told me he had a kid."

"I don't think he knew about me."

The woman sighs. "Well, I'm sorry about it, that's for sure. Will you tell him I wish him well?"

"Sure, I . . . he's in a coma, or something, but I'll still tell him. But—can you tell me a little bit about him? I mean, I just found out he's my dad when he got taken to the hospital, so I don't know anything. . . ." Janie swallows hard. "You want some water?"

"Naw, thanks. I got plenty in the truck." Still in a state of shock at the news, she swipes mindlessly at a mosquito. "Henry Feingold is a good guy. He don't bother anybody. He might look a little strange but he has a heart of gold. He just does his business and lives here, all alone, but he says he prefers it. He studies a lot on the computer, researching for his business and some other stuff—I think he took an online course once. Not quite sure what, but he's usually always got something interesting to talk about."

"Did he say he was feeling sick at all last week?"

"Nothing more'n his usual headaches. He'd get migraines sometimes. Never got 'em checked out, though I told him he should. Said he didn't have insurance."

"So he's had headaches for a while?"

"On and off. Is that what . . . ?" The UPS woman nods in place of saying the words.

"Yeah. Something in his brain, maybe a tumor. They don't know much, I guess."

The UPS woman looks down at the dirt. "Well. I'm real sorry. You take care. I'm . . . yeah. Heck. I'm real sorry." She picks up the packages that Janie prepared for shipping.

"Thanks," Janie says.

"If something happens, you know—if you could maybe leave me a note on the door? I come by a lot, sometimes twice a day if there's an afternoon pickup. I'd sure appreciate it. Name's Cathy with a C."

Janie nods. "I'll try. Hey, Cathy?"

"Yeah?"

Janie fidgets. "He's not, like, blind or anything. Is he?"

Cathy gives Janie a quizzical look. "No," she says. "He doesn't even wear glasses."

1:15 P.M.

Janie sits in the old La-Z-Boy, thinking it all through.

Isolation.

He lives here, he's in his late thirties, he's not blind or crippled.

"Oh, jeez," Janie says. She lets her head fall back in the chair. "What the hell am I doing? It makes perfect sense. I'm such an idiot."

Her phone won't stop buzzing.

"Hey," she says.

"Hey," Cabe says, sounding miffed. "You got something going on or what?"

"I just needed to get away," Janie says. "Why, what's so important that I can't be gone for three hours without somebody chasing me down?" Her tone is sharper than she intends. But Janie was really beginning to enjoy the quiet.

Cabel doesn't speak for a moment, and Janie cringes. "Sorry," she says. "That didn't come out right."

"Okay, well," he says. But his voice is still bristly. "I was calling to see what time you wanted me to pick you up for that meeting we have with Captain. At two."

Janie sits up in the chair. "Oh, crap!" She checks her watch. "Shit, I forgot." She glances around the room to make sure everything's in place and she careens out the door, closing it but not locking it, just as Henry left it. "I'm . . . out for a run. I gotta hightail it home and grab a quick shower. How about one fifty-five?"

"Wow, that's cutting it close. We'll be late. You want me to pick you up from where you are now and get you home faster?"

Janie starts jogging down the driveway, her muscles stiff. "No," she says. "No, I can just meet you at the police station."

"What, you're taking the bus? Captain will be pissed. I'm supposed to drive you. You know that. Come on, Janie." He sounds mad.

Janie's voice jiggles as she runs. She breathes out through pursed lips to avoid the stitch she's already getting in her side. "I know," she says. "I know."

"Where *are* you?"

She slows to a walk. "You know, Cabe, I think . . . just . . . go without me," she says. "Okay? I'm not going."

"What the—? Janie! Come on. Don't do this. I'll pick you up at one fifty-five. It'll be fine."

Janie keeps walking. "No," she says firmly. "I've got some stuff to do. I'll call her to explain. Just go."

"But—" Cabel sighs.

Janie's silent.

"Fine," he says. Hangs up without a good-bye.

Janie flips her phone shut and shoves it back in her pocket. "God," she says. "I don't know if I can do this."

She calls Captain as she walks back toward home.

"Everything okay, Hannagan?"

"Not really, sir," Janie says. Her voice quivers. "I'm not coming in today. I'm sorry."

Silence.

Janie stops walking. "I can't make it to the meeting. I—I think I made my decision."

There is the sound of her chair creaking and a soft sigh on the other end. "Okay. Well." She pauses. "Cabe?"

Janie drops to her haunches on the side of the road and squeezes her eyes shut. Bites her forefinger. Takes in a measured breath to steady her voice. "Not yet," she says. "Soon. I need a couple days to figure out what I do from here."

"Oh, Janie," Captain says.

1:34 P.M.

She stands on the road, not sure where to go now. Home, or back to Henry's. Her head tells her one thing.

But when her stomach growls, she knows the answer.

Doesn't feel right about eating her father's food. So she trudges to the bus stop. Thinking, always thinking.

She knows she's going to have to say good-bye to Cabel.

Forever.

It's just really hard to imagine doing it.

2:31 P.M.

At home, Janie fixes three sandwiches. She eats one, wraps the other two in plastic and stows them in her backpack. Dorothea makes a rare appearance, scrounging around in the refrigerator.

"You want me to make you a sandwich, Ma?" Janie says, not really wanting to. "I've got all the stuff out."

Dorothea dismisses the suggestion with a careless wave and a grunt, and grabs a can of beer instead. She shuffles back to her room.

And then the front door opens.

"Hey, Janers, you home?" It's Carrie.

Janie groans inwardly. She just wants to go back to Henry's house. "Hey, girl. What digs?"

"Nothin'." Carrie saunters into the kitchen and hoists herself up on the counter. Sticks her feet out. She's wearing flip-flops. "Check out my pedi. Aren't you so jel?"

Janie fixes her attention on Carrie's toes. "Totally! Really cute, Carrie." Janie fills up a water bottle at the tap and tosses that in her backpack too.

"You going somewhere?" Carrie looks a little disappointed.

"Yeah," Janie says.

"Cabe's?"

"No." Janie sighs. She'd been forced to lie to Carrie when on assignment during their entire senior year. Doesn't want to now. "Can I trust you to keep a secret?"

"Der."

Janie smiles. "I—I found Henry's house. I'm going to go back out there and try to learn more about him."

"Sweet!" Carrie hops off the counter. "Can I come? I'll drive."

"Uh . . ." Janie says. She wants to be alone, but after trekking out to Henry's once already today, the thought of having a ride there and back is too tempting to say no. "Sure. Can you be ready to go, like, now?"

"I'm always ready to go. I'll go start up the little diva and meet you in the driveway."

2:50 P.M.

"So," Janie says from the passenger seat of the '77 Nova. "No plans with Stu tonight?"

"No." Carrie frowns as she steers the car out of town, following Janie's directions. "Why does *everybody* ask me that whenever they see me without him?"

"Because you're almost always with him?"

"So? I am my own person too. Is that all there is to talk about? Where Stu is?"

Janie sticks her head out the window to catch the breeze on her face and hopes for no dreamers. "Are you guys fighting or something?"

"No," Carrie says.

"Okay. So . . . when does school start for you?"

Carrie brightens. "Right after Labor Day. And it's going to be a blast. Finally! I get to learn about something I actually want to learn about."

"You'll be the best in your class, Carrie. You got mad hair skillz."

"I do, don't I," she says. "Thank you." She turns her eyes from the road for a moment to look at Janie. They glimmer just a little. Maybe they're just watery from the wind. Or not.

Janie smiles, reaches her arm around Carrie's neck and gives her friend a little half-hug. Forgets that Carrie doesn't get a whole lot more encouragement at home than Janie gets.

Carrie pulls Ethel into the bumpy driveway. Ethel protests in squeaks and groans, but Carrie presses onward. "Why the heck does he live all the way out here in freaking . . . freaking Saskatchewan?" Carrie says, giggling.

Janie doesn't bother to point out that the nearest Canadian province is actually Ontario. Nor that they were going south.

Outside of the car, Janie goes immediately to the house as Carrie takes it all in—the overgrown bushes, the tiny, run-down cabin, the door left unlocked. "What, he doesn't lock it?"

"He didn't—at least not the last time he left."

"Well, yeah, I can see that. It's not like he lives in the 'hood, yadamean? Who comes way out here? It'd be a real crapshoot. People out here'd either pull a gun on you or invite you for pot roast."

Carrie yammers on.

Janie ignores.

It's all good.

3:23 P.M.

Janie goes directly to the computer. Carrie bumbles around the kitchen, snacking on raspberries from the refrigerator, but Janie doesn't pay any attention. The computer, still on since she left in such a hurry earlier, takes forever to wake back up, and another forever to get online with the dial-up access.

The dialing noise makes Carrie look over at Janie. "What are you doing on his computer, Janers? That's kinda, like, wrong, isn't it?" Carrie stands in the kitchen, hands on cupboard doors, picking up things and setting them down again.

"Nah," Janie lies. "He's my father. I'm allowed."

Carrie shrugs and moves on to the next cabinet.

Janie puzzles over Henry's shop name. "Hey, Carrie, 'Dottie' is a nickname for 'Dorothea,' isn't it?"

"How would I know?" Carrie says. And then, "Yeah, it sounds like it could be. And a hell of a lot easier to say than that mouthful."

"Yeah," Janie says, and then opens up a new window and Googles it. "Yep, it sure is."

"What?" Carrie yells, now apparently sitting on the kitchen floor. Pans rattle.

"Nothing," Janie says absently. "Just stop—whatever you're doing. You're making me nervous."

"What?" Carrie yells again.

Janie sighs. Her finger hovers over the mouse, deciding. Finally, she drops it, opening Henry's e-mail client.

Really feels like she's snooping, now.

But just can't help it.

Janie smiles, reading his kindly correspondence with his customers, trying to imagine him. Wishes she could have talked to him about all of this.

About his life.

But then a loud crash in the kitchen startles her again and she jumps up, frustrated. "Carrie, what the hell? Seriously, let's just go, okay? Jesus Christ, I can't take you anywhere!" Janie just wants to concentrate, to be able to savor these words. The interruptions are driving her crazy.

Carrie stands on the kitchen counter facing open cupboards, hanging on to a door. She peers over her shoulder looking sheepish as Janie stomps to the kitchen to survey the mess. "I love it when you call me Jesus Christ."

Janie pinches her lips together, still mad, trying not to smile.

The crash wasn't as bad as it sounded.

Mostly just empty tins.

"Look what I found," Carrie says, pulling a shoe box from the shelf. She hops to the floor. "Notes and stuff! Like a box full of memories."

"Stop! This is so not cool." Janie glances nervously out the window, as if the crash of tins in this quiet setting would bring sirens and squealing tires. "We should get out of here, anyway."

"But—" Carrie says. "Dude, you've got to check this stuff out. It's a bunch of clues to your past. The story of your dad. Aren't you totally curious?" She stares at Janie. "Come on, Janers! What kind of detective are you, anyway? You should care about this. There's some little pins and some coins and stuff, and a ring! But there's also letters. . . ."

Janie's eyes flash, but she glances at the shoe box. "No. This is too invasive. It's not . . ." her voice falters.

"Come on, Janers," whispers Carrie, her eyes shining.

Janie leans over and peeks into the box, gently moving a few things around. "No." She straightens abruptly. "And I want you to stop snooping around."

"Ugh! How boring."

"Yeah, well, we're sort of breaking the law here."

"I thought you said—"

"I know, I know. I lied."

"So we could get arrested? Oh, that's just great. You remember I've done that once already, and I'm not interested in ending up in jail again—especially *with* you! Who would bail us out?" Carrie's picking up the tins from the floor and shoving them back in the cupboard. "My parents would absolutely kill me. And so would Stu. Sheesh, Janie."

"I'm sorry—look, it's not like we're going to get caught. Nobody even knows about the guy. Plus, I'm his daughter. That might get us out of a mess. Not that there will be one. . . ." Janie sets the box of memories on the counter and hands the other cupboard items up to Carrie. She's frustrated. Wishes she hadn't brought Carrie here after all. She just wants to have some time alone to sift through things, to concentrate and figure things out.

But time is running out, Janie knows. She's got to figure out how she can help Henry, before he dies. And maybe there's a clue in the box.

Still, Janie's above stealing. Physical items, anyway.

Janie sighs, resigned. "Let's just go, Carrie."

They go.

Janie's fingers linger on the doorknob.

6:00 P.M.

She shuffles her feet up the driveway on Waverly, past the Beemer. "Hey."

Cabel looks up from his seat on an overturned bucket.

He's painting the trim around the front door. He wipes the sweat from his forehead with the sleeve of his T-shirt. "Hey," he says. His voice is cool.

"You haven't called me all afternoon."

"You don't answer when I call, so why should I bother?"

Janie nods, acknowledging that she's a jerk. "So, how was the meeting?"

He just looks at her. Those eyes. The hurt.

She knows what she needs to say. "I'm sorry, Cabe." And she is. So, so sorry.

He stands. "Okay, thank you," he says. "Would you like to tell me what's going on with you lately?"

Janie swallows hard. She rips her fingers through her hair and just looks at him. Tilts her head and presses her lips together to stop them from quivering.

She can't do it.

Can't tell him.

Can't say it. Can't say, *I'm leaving you.*

So she lies.

"It's all this stuff with Henry. And crap with my mother. I can't handle anything more right now. I need some time to get things together." She feels her eyes shift away from his. Wondering. Wondering if he can tell.

He's quiet for a moment, studying her. "All right," he

says, measured. "I get that. Is there anything I can do?" He leans over and sets down his paintbrush. Comes down the steps to her. Reaches toward her face and fixes a lock of her hair that flopped the wrong way.

"I just need some time and—and some space. For a little while. At least until something happens with Henry. Okay?" She tilts her head up. Meets his eyes again. They stand there, face-to-face, each studying the other.

Then, she steps into him. Slips her arms around his waist. His shirt is damp with sweat. "Okay?" she asks again.

He takes her in. Holds her.

Kisses the top of her head, and sighs.

7:48 P.M.

Janie, on the floor, leaning up against her bed. Thinking.

She could just go to bed early.

Tempting.

Not.

8:01 P.M.

Janie eats her sandwich on the bus. Washes it down with water. Walks the two miles from the last bus stop to Henry's house. At least it's not so hot out. And there's still plenty of light.

The sounds of the woods in the evening are louder than during the day. A mosquito flies furiously past her ear. Janie slaps her legs and arms as she walks. She's gnawed by the time she gets there, especially after going down that long, overgrown driveway.

Inside the house, it's decidedly cooler than it's ever been. A decent breeze blows in and because of the trees, the little house has been in the shade for hours.

"Ahh," Janie says when she's inside, the door clicked shut behind her. Peace and quiet. A little house all her own. Janie looks around the place and imagines what it would be like to live here, without fear of anybody's dreams.

Thinks Henry got it all just about right. To run a little Internet store, to have this serenity and nobody bothering you but Cathy the UPS driver . . . and Cathy'd never be sleeping.

She thinks about the money she's been saving for years now, including the five grand from Miss Stubin. She thinks about the scholarship. She'd lose that, if she quit her job. If she isolated herself. But isn't her eyesight worth losing a scholarship for?

Wonders if she could still pull it off on her own if she got a little Internet job.

Or.

What if she just sort of . . . inherited one?

Her skin gets goose bumps.

What if she took over for Henry—in everything?

She looks around, her mind turning. Hell, she practically ran the household already with her useless mother—she knows how to do it. Pay rent, get groceries . . . would anybody even notice, or care, if she just took over this place?

"Why not?" she whispers.

Janie takes a swig of water from her water bottle and just sits there, in the old, beat-up chair, surrounded by the sounds of night, consumed by her thoughts. Suddenly, the whole isolation option in Miss Stubin's green notebook doesn't sound so bad.

"I could totally get used to this," she says softly to—happily!—no one. "Never getting sucked into dreams again." She grins because it feels delicious.

And then she stops.

"Maybe I *could* still see Cabe," she whispers.

She imagines it, spending candlelit dinners together here, or maybe lunch if he can get away from classes. Hanging out a few hours a day . . . making out and being together. Just not during sleeping hours.

It sounds good.

For about five minutes.

And then she thinks about years to come.

There's no way they could ever live together.

There'd be no babies, no family unit, ever. Janie couldn't risk that if she intends to keep her eyesight—having a dreaming child would totally wreck her. Besides, there's no way Janie would pass this dream catcher curse along to anybody.

She's okay with that.

But what does it mean for Cabe?

His future, in a nutshell:

- live elsewhere
- spend a couple hours a day hanging out at the shack
- never marry
- never have children
- never spend a night with the woman he loves

She pictures their time together, what it would be like, day in and day out. Stagnant. Cabel coming over for an obligatory two hours while he juggles school, his house, his job.

Janie knows it would be hell for Cabe.

It would be like visiting hours at Heather Home.

They'd end up talking about crossword puzzles and the weather.

And he'd do it too. He'd stay with her. Even though it would totally wreck his entire life.

That's just the kind of guy he is.

Janie slams her fists down into the La-Z-Boy arms.

Lets her head fall back.

Whispers to the empty room,

"I can't do that."

9:30 P.M.

She looks through all Henry's things. His business records. Notes to himself, grocery lists. Pamphlets on migraines. And online, a plethora of medical websites bookmarked, along with sites that offer ways to deal with pain.

She wonders, if he'd had insurance, and if they'd caught the tumor, or aneurysm, or whatever, early . . . if she'd still have him.

But she wouldn't have met him, that way.

She thinks about him, pulling his hair out, clutching his head. The frozen look of agony on his face. Wonders if he's still in so much pain, lying helpless in the county hospital, now. Thinks about how he begged her for help. She talks to the holistic words on the screen. "I wish I knew how to help you, Henry. I guess . . . I hope you just let go soon, so you can be done with it."

Janie peels her warm, sticky thighs from the plastic kitchen chair seat and looks around the small living room. Imagines him here in this tiny, cozy house away from the noise, the people.

She walks over to the kitchen, where the box that Carrie found still sits on the countertop. Janie's tempted to go through it. Go through the letters that very nearly beckon to her in the light breeze from the open window. But.

Two things.

She doesn't want to read some intimate icky love letter written by her alcoholic, sorry excuse for a mother. And.

She doesn't want to feel sorry for Henry more than she already does.

She's had enough heartache, thanks very much. Enough trouble. Enough of just getting to know someone who understands, right before they go and die.

She'll gladly take over things here. But she's not going to love him. It's too late for that. He's too far gone. And she's got enough heartache coming just around the corner.

Janie takes a deep breath. Shakes her head. Pushes the box back into the cupboard where Carrie found it.

She tidies up the house so it looks just like it did the first time she saw it. Turns off the computer and the lamp and stands there in the dark, listening to the quietness.

Wishing for it—wishing for this kind of peace in her life. And knowing now that she can have it, once Henry dies. This place where she can let down her guard. And live. Where she doesn't have to worry about catching anybody's dream.

Something deep inside her longs for it, more than the longings for anything else. Even Cabe.

Maybe it's a survival technique.

Or maybe, as it's been all along up until she met Cabe, she's really just a loner. Will always be a loner.

It certainly looks that way.

And so she sits down again in the old chair, in the dark, in this sanctuary. Wondering what her life will hold. Wondering how she'll care for her mother, and why she even has to—maybe Dorothea needs to fend for herself from now on. Maybe Janie's just been enabling her all this time.

Living peacefully like this. Keeping her eyesight. She looks down at her fingers. They cast long shadows in the starlight from the open window. Janie wiggles her fingers and their shadows splash in her lap.

She smiles.

And though Captain will be disappointed, and will have to take the scholarship back, she knows Captain would never blame Janie for wanting to try to live a normal life. Janie knows deep down that it will all be okay.

She'll miss seeing Captain and the guys. That's sure.

"Well," she says softly to her hands, flexing her fingers and clasping them together in her lap. "It's decided. Isolation. My choice."

God, it feels good to say it out loud.

Even though it's a lot scary.

There's just one last loose end that Janie's got to tie up before she quits catching dreams altogether. One last puzzle to solve.

It seems fitting to end it this way.

Although it's bound to be the worst one of her entire life.

Janie sucks in a deep breath and lets it escape, making her lips vibrate. She's scared. More scared now to go back to the hospital than she was when she had to go to Durbin's party. More scared than when that strange boy named Cabel first fell asleep in the school library and dreamed of a monster man with knives for fingers.

But.

But.

This is also Janie's last chance to see, and say goodbye, once and for all, to Miss Stubin.

Close the door, as they say. It's fucking painful to think about.

But Janie's going to get through this, figure out how to help Henry, and get it done in one shot, even if it kills her.

Er . . .

Well, hopefully not "kills her." That would ruin everything. Yeah.

HENRY

STILL MONDAY. 10:44 P.M.

It's a long, dark walk to the bus stop. Heat lightning flashes in the sky. Thunder rumbles low and the humidity is thick. No rain, though.

Enough with the mosquitoes already.

Janie snacks on a sandwich and a PowerBar. Stocking up on energy, gearing up for a big night. Wondering if Henry is still alive, even.

11:28 P.M.

The hallways are quiet as usual and the doors are closed. Janie waves to Nurse Miguel and approaches the desk. "Anything new?"

Miguel shakes his head. "The doctor thinks it won't be long now," he says.

Janie nods. "I'm probably going to spend the night . . . just sit with him. Okay?"

"Sure thing, hon," he says. He reaches down behind the counter. "Here's a blanket in case you get cold. You probably know the chair reclines, right?"

Janie doesn't know, but she nods anyway, taking the blanket. "Thank you." She continues down the hallway to Henry's room. Stands there for a moment, taking a few deep breaths. "This is it," she says softly, and then she opens the door. Shuts it quickly behind her as she goes down.

It's different this time.

This time, Janie is flung directly into the nightmare. She's in a familiar spot as before, with Henry screaming out, "Help me! Help me!" again and again. He turns to Janie when she approaches and he continues to scream at her. A stoic Miss Stubin stands near Henry, waits patiently for it to end. Even in her divine state, if that's what it is, she looks weary.

Janie doesn't waste any time. "Henry!" she shouts. "I want to help you! I'm here to help you. But I don't know what to do. Can you show me?"

There's no stopping him.

Janie turns to Miss Stubin. "Why don't you leave?"

"I can't. Not until he's ready to come with me."

Janie groans, realizing now she's not only responsible for her hysterical, nearly dead father's peace, but her beloved Miss Stubin's happiness as well. She puts her hands over her ears. Frustrated, growing frantic because of the yelling. It's unnerving, really. And painful. Her whole body begins to ache.

Henry stands up and walks over to Janie and she steps back, tensing, worried that he'll grab her, strangle her, but he doesn't. "Help me! Help me!" He screams in her ear, making her bones rattle from the intense pitch. She moves and he follows her around. His voice is pleading. He gets on his knees and grasps Janie's hand, tugging at her, crying out. Begging for help.

His voice grows ragged, out of control.

Janie doesn't know what to do. She screams back at him, "Tell me what to do!"

Henry's cries grow even louder.

Miss Stubin waits and watches, her eyes filled with pity. "I don't think he can," she says, but Janie can't hear her.

Janie knows she can't hold on much longer. She can't move. Her physical body is gone from her, and her dream body screams out in its own pain. There's nothing she can do for Henry . . . nothing.

Nothing she can think of.

She turns to Miss Stubin. "Can you try? Like last time?"

Miss Stubin nods. She approaches Henry. When she walks, it looks like she's gliding effortlessly across the floor.

"Henry," she says. She puts her hand on his shoulder.

His screams falter.

Miss Stubin concentrates. Talks to him with her mind. Calms him.

Henry's ragged voice falls away.

Miss Stubin leads him back to his chair and beckons Janie to come.

"There," Miss Stubin says, smiling. "It's really a lot easier this way, Henry."

Henry holds up handfuls of his hair. Shows them to Janie.

Janie nods. "Your head hurts, doesn't it?"

"Yes," he says, cringing, as if talking calmly is difficult for him. "Yes, it hurts."

"I don't know what to do," Janie says. "Do you know how I can help you?"

Henry looks at Janie. He shakes his head. "I just want to die," he says. "Please. Can you help me die?"

"I don't know. I'll . . . I'll try. I can't do anything illegal. You understand?"

He nods.

"Where are we?" Janie asks. "Is this your dream? This dark gymnasium? This is it?"

Henry stands up. "This way." He beckons the other two

to follow. He pushes open the double doors that lead out of the gymnasium. They walk through, into a hallway. There are doors on both sides.

They go into the first room.

It's a synagogue.

A boy convulses in his seat. His father, next to him, reprimands him.

"It's you, the boy, isn't it?" Janie asks.

"Yes."

"A memory?"

"Sort of. That is my dream—my life, over and over."

They go to the next classroom. People are lined up outside it. Henry, Miss Stubin, and Janie squeeze past the line of people and go inside. It's a pizzeria. They walk past tables filled with people eating, laughing, to the kitchen, into the walk-in cooler. There, Henry leans in a corner with a girl. Kissing.

Janie stares. "Who is that?"

Henry looks at Janie. "That's Dottie."

"You mean Dorothea? Dorothea Hannagan?" Janie can't get over it, even though she knew there was probably some kissing involved there somewhere.

"Yes." He sighs. "The one true love of my life."

Janie wants to gag.

Miss Stubin interrupts. "Tell us what happened, Henry. Between you and Janie's mother. Will you?"

He looks tired. And it's cold in there. "There's not much to tell."

"Please, Henry," Janie says. She wants to hear him say it. Wants that validation that she's doing the right thing.

"We worked together in Chicago one summer—she was in high school, I was at U of M. In the fall, I went back to Michigan. She quit school and followed me. We lived together. It was terrible. The dreams. I had to choose—be with her, miserable, or be able to function, alone." He begins to pull at his hair again. "Oh, hell," he says. "It's coming back."

"So you just left her to fend for herself? Did you know she was pregnant?"

"I didn't know." His voice grows louder, as if he's trying to talk above the noises in his head. "Janie, I didn't know. I'm sorry. I sent her money. She wouldn't take it. I'm so sorry." He squats down, head in his hands.

"Are you glad you did it? Glad you isolated yourself?" Janie gets down on the floor by him, anxious to get answers now.

"Help me," he squeals. "Help me!" He grabs her T-shirt. "Please, Janie, Please please help me! Kill me! Please!"

Janie doesn't know what to do. Miss Stubin tries desperately to calm him, but nothing works.

"Are you glad?" Janie shouts. "Are you? Was it the best choice?"

"There is no best. It's Morton's Fork." He falls to the floor with a scream. "Help me! Oh, GOD. HELP ME!"

Janie looks at Miss Stubin in horror and sees the cracks in the scene. Pieces of the dream begin to fall away. She can hear the static in the distance. "Shit," she says. "I can't stay in this."

"Go!" Miss Stubin says.

They clasp hands for a moment. Look into each other's eyes, Janie desperately trying to communicate that she's not coming back.

Not sure if it translates.

But it's time to go, before she gets trapped here again.

Janie concentrates and with all her strength, bursts through the dream barrier.

As Janie lies on the floor, shaking, trying to move, trying to feel her skin, trying to see, all she can think about is the look on Miss Stubin's face and the complete, hopeless desperation of Henry, overcome by his own demons.

Oh.

Miss Stubin.

What an awful way to say good-bye forever.

Slowly, exhausted, Janie pulls herself to the chair next to Henry's bed. Her joints, even her teeth, ache, and she wonders just what happens to her body when she's in a nightmare like that.

But it doesn't matter now.

She is done with them.

Janie wraps herself in the blanket to help stop her body from the uncontrollable shaking. She can barely stand to look at poor Henry's twisted face. Sometime since she'd been here last, Henry pulled himself up into fetal position, hands fisted up by his head, as if to protect himself from the terrible unseen monsters that have taken him hostage. Janie reaches over to him. Touches his hand. Holds it.

She pleads with him. "Please, please just die. Please." She whispers it over and over, begging Henry to let go, begging his invisible captors to let him go. "I don't know how to help you." She buries her face in her hands. "Please, please, please . . ." The words brush the air in rhythmic patterns like willow branches shushing the waves on the shore of Fremont Lake.

But Henry doesn't die.

A half-hour ticks away on the clock. It feels beyond real in the dark, quiet room, like they are in a world cut off from everyone else. Janie snacks on the last sandwich from her backpack, trying to regain some strength, and then she starts talking to her father to help pass the time.

She tells Henry about Dorothea, choosing her words carefully so as not to say anything too negative—she knows Henry doesn't need to hear negative stuff in his condition. Janie talks about herself, too. Tells him things she's never told anybody else, like how lonely she's been.

She tells him that she's not mad at him for not knowing about her. And she talks about her secret dream-catcher life, that she is just like him. That she understands. That he's not crazy—and he's not alone. Everything comes rushing out—dream catching, her job, Miss Stubin, and Janie's plan to just stop all of the dreams and have a nice quiet life like Henry. "I'm doing it too, Henry," she says. "I'm isolating, like you. You probably didn't even know about the real choice, did you? About the blindness and the loss of your hands."

And then Janie tells Henry that she understands why he did what he did to Dottie, even though he loved her so much. She understands that horrible choice. She tells him about Cabe. How much she loves him. How good he is, how patient. How torn she is about what this isolation plan means.

How scared she is of telling him.

Saying good-bye.

It's amazing, having someone who is just like her.

Someone who understands.

Even if he's unable to respond.

Suddenly, Janie feels like she's wasted so much time these last few days, when she could have been here for Henry.

She tells him how hard it's been, discovering all this stuff in the past few days, and she cries a little.

She talks deep into the night.

Talks until she has emptied out her soul.

Henry's face doesn't change. He doesn't move at all.

When Janie is too tired to think or say another word, she drifts off, all curled up in the chair.

All is quiet.

4:51 A.M.

She dreams.

Janie's in her bedroom, sitting up in bed, disoriented. Her tongue feels dry, parched, and she wets her lips. Her tongue leaves a film on her lips—it feels gritty like sand. When Janie reaches up to wipe away the grittiness, her lips give way. Her teeth collapse and tiny pieces break off in her mouth. Crumbling. The sharp, stumpy remains cut her tongue.

Horrified, Janie spits into her hands. Bits and pieces of the crumbled teeth come out. Janie keeps spitting and more and more tooth shards pile up in her hands. Frantically, Janie looks up, unsure what to do. When she moves her eyes, everything is blurry. Filmy. Like she's trying to see in a steamed-up mirror or a waterfall. She dumps her teeth on the bed, forgotten, and wipes at her eyes, trying to clear them, trying to see. But she's blind. "I'm isolating," she cries. "I'm not supposed to go blind! No! I'm not ready!" She claws at her eyes, and then realizes that she has vertical slits—holes in her face—next to each eye. Something pokes out from each.

Janie takes hold of whatever it is and pulls.

Slivers of soap slide out from the slits.

Janie's eyes itch and burn like crazy. She swipes at them and pulls more pieces of soap out, but the pieces seem to reproduce. As she pulls out soap slivers, she runs her tongue over the jagged remains of her teeth, tasting blood. "No!" she cries.

Finally, she pulls out the last of the soap and she can see again. She looks up, relieved.

And there.

Sitting in his chair. Watching Janie with a look of calm on his face.

Henry.

Janie stares at him.

And it dawns on her, after a minute, what she should do.

"Help me. Help me, Henry."

Henry looks surprised. Obediently he stands and approaches Janie.

Janie shows him her handful of teeth. "You can help me change it, you know. Is it okay if I put these back in?"

Henry's eyes speak. They are filled with encouragement. He nods.

Janie smiles a brickle smile. Nods back. Pushes the teeth back into place as if they are Lego pieces. When she is done, she pats the bed and smiles.

Henry sits. "You're just like me," he says.

"Yes."

"I heard you—all the things you told me. I'm sorry."

"I'm glad. Glad you heard, I mean. You don't have to be sorry. You didn't know." She stares at Henry's empty chair.

He turns to her. "I think . . . I think I would have liked to know you."

Janie chokes back a sob.

He takes her hand. "I miss her. Dottie. Is she good to you? A good mother?"

She stares at his hand in hers for a long minute. Not sure what to say about that. Finally she shrugs. Says, "I turned out all right." Looks up at Henry's face.

Smiles a crooked smile through her tears.

6:10 A.M.

The door to Henry's ICU room opens.

It's the first shift nurse, checking vitals. Janie startles awake, sits up and rubs her eyes.

"Don't mind me," the nurse says, checking Henry's pulse. "You look like you could use some more sleep."

Janie smiles and stretches. She glances at Henry, remembering. It was weird, having someone in her dream for the first time.

Then she sucks in a breath, surprised, and hops to her feet to get a better look. "He's—" she says as the nurse turns to go. "He looks different. His face."

The nurse glances at Henry and checks her chart. "Does he?" She smiles, distracted. "Better, I hope."

But Janie's staring at Henry.

His posture has relaxed, his face is no longer strained, his hands are unclenched and resting gently now by his face. He looks peaceful. The agony is gone.

The nurse shrugs and leaves. Janie keeps staring, thrilled to see him looking better, hoping he's no longer experiencing the horrible nightmares. Wonders briefly if there's a chance he could pull out of it.

Knows there's a better chance he'll finally get to die.

6:21 A.M.

Janie, with a plan, goes into Henry's private bathroom and closes the door. She knows she doesn't have much strength, but closing the door is a no-brainer if she gets stuck.

She opens the door and gets sucked in. Slowly. Gently. No static, no bright walls slamming into her.

It's just a dark gymnasium, just one patch of light streaming though the high window.

The hallway's rooms are empty, now.

Miss Stubin, Henry, both gone.

All that remains is Henry's chair.

And on the chair, a note.

My dear Janie,

Much has been demanded of you. And yet, you remain stronger than you think.

Until we meet again,

Martha

P.S. Henry wishes you to consider Morton's Fork.

6:28 A.M.

Janie closes the door on her last dream.

When she is able, she escapes the dream again and trudges through the hallways and outside to the bus stop, takes the bus home, and falls into bed.

TUESDAY

AUGUST 8, 2006, 11:13 A.M.

Janie wakes up, sweating like a marathoner. Her cheek is stuck to her pillowcase. Her hair is soaking wet. It's at least 450 degrees in the house.

And she's starving.

STARVING.

She stumbles to the kitchen and stands at the refrigerator, eating whatever she can find. She presses the cold milk jug against her face to cool it before taking a long swig from it. And then she takes an ice cube and runs it all over her neck and arms. "God almighty," she mutters, grabbing a container of leftover spaghetti and meatballs. "I need air!"

Fifteen minutes later, she's in the shower, water temp set to cold. It's almost too cold, but Janie knows the minute she steps out of there, she'll start sweating again, so she keeps the setting on freezing.

When she turns off the water and steps out of the shower, she hears her mother's voice, talking on the phone. Janie freezes and listens for a minute, and then she whips a towel around herself, clutching it at her chest, and opens the bathroom door, her hair dripping all over the floor.

Dorothea, in her nightgown, hangs up the phone. Turns to look at Janie, her face haggard and old-looking. Pale, like the moon. "He's dead," she says simply. Shrugs. "It's about time." Shuffles back to her bedroom, but not before Janie sees Dorothea's lip tremble.

Janie stands in the hallway, dripping, feeling numb. "He's dead," she echoes. It's as if the sound of her voice makes it real. Janie leans back against the hallway wall and slides down until she's sitting on the floor. She tips her head back until it bumps the wall. "My dad is dead."

Still numb.

It's over.

After a few minutes, Janie stands up and marches into her mother's bedroom, not bothering to knock. Dorothea sits weeping on her bed.

"So. What do we need to do?" Janie asks. "I mean, like, funeral stuff."

"I don't know," Dorothea says. "I told them I don't want nothing to do with it. They can just handle it."

"What?" Janie feels like yelling. She moves to call the hospital herself, but then she stops. Turns back to her mother. Says in a way-too-calm voice, "Call them back and tell them that Henry is Jewish. He needs to go to a Jewish funeral home." Janie glances at Dorothea's sparse closet. "Do you even have a single decent dress, Mother? Do you?"

"What do I need a dress for?"

"For the funeral," Janie says firmly.

"I'm not going to that," Dorothea says.

"Oh, yes, you are." Janie's pissed. "You are definitely going to my father's funeral. He loved you, all these years. You might not understand why he left, but I do, and he still loves you!" Janie chokes on her mistake. "He loved you," she says. "Now go call the hospital before they do something else with him. And then call the funeral home—the hospital should be able to recommend one."

Dorothea looks confused, alarmed. "I don't know their numbers."

Janie eyes her coldly. "What are you, fucking eight years old? Look them up." She storms out of the room and slams the door. "God!" she mutters, frustrated, as she stomps down the hallway and enters her room. Still wearing a towel, Janie fishes some clothes from her dresser, tosses them on the bed, and then rakes a wide-toothed comb through her tangled, wet hair.

She hears her mother's door open. A few minutes later, Janie can hear Dorothea stammering on the phone. Janie flops back on the bed, sweating again in the heat.

Damn it.

"Henry," Janie says.

She cries for all the things that could have been.

12:40 P.M.

Janie pulls her suitcase from the closet.

Climbs up into the attic to look for boxes.

She'll have to move her stuff over slowly since she has to take the bus and walk.

Wonders briefly if the keys to Henry's station wagon are hanging somewhere obvious in his little house. And then nixes that plan. That could really look like stealing if she got pulled over. No sense getting killed right before restarting her whole life, either.

She fills her backpack with clothing and grabs the suitcase.

Heads out the door.

1:29 P.M.

Janie sets her things down in the middle of the shack and sits at Henry's desk to write a list of things to do:

- Get through funeral first
- Find rental lease and landlord address for rent payments
- Figure out if utilities are included or if I pay
- Clean house
- Study online store history to find out what sells
- Water garden!! And freeze veggies
- Switch to cable Internet if not too expensive
- Tell Captain the plan
- Tell Cabe

She stops writing and stares at the last two words.

Throws the pen at the wall. Slams her fists on the desk. Shoves the chair back so hard it flips over. Stands in the middle of the room and screams at the ceiling. "My life fucking sucks the meanest one of all! How could you force me to choose? How can you do this to me? Do you hear me? Anybody?"

She falls to her knees, covers her head with her arms, and bends forward into a ball.

Sobs rip through the house, but no one is there to hear her.

There is no comfort here.

3:57 P.M.

Janie stares out the bus window, cheek against the glass, watching Fieldridge go by.

As she walks from the bus stop to her mother's house, she calls him.

"Hey," he says.

And suddenly, Janie can't speak. A garbled sound comes from her throat instead.

"Janie, you okay?" Cabel's voice turns immediately concerned. "Where are you? Do you need help?"

Janie breathes, tries to steady her shaky voice. "I'm okay. I'm home. I'm . . . my . . . Henry died."

It's quiet on the line for a moment. "I'll be right over," he says. "Okay?"

Janie nods into the phone. "Yes, please."

And then Janie calls Carrie. Gets her voice mail. "Hey, Carrie, I just thought I should let you know that Henry died. I'll . . . I'll talk to you later."

4:43 P.M.

Cabel raps on the door. He's carrying a potted plant and a bakery box from the grocery store.

"Hey," he says. "I didn't have time to make you, like,

a casserole or whatever. But I stopped by the store and brought you this. I'm so sorry, Janers."

Janie smiles and her eyes fill up. She takes the box and the plant, sets the plant near the window. "It's really pretty," she says. "Thank you." She opens the box. "Oh, wow—doughnuts." She laughs and goes to him. Hugs him close. "You rock, Cabe."

Cabel shrugs, a little embarrassed. "I figured doughnuts are good comfort food. But I'm going to fix you ladies some dinner, too, so you don't have to mess with it."

Janie shakes her head, puzzled. "What for?"

"That's what you do when somebody dies. You bring them casseroles and KFC and shit. Charlie got all kinds of food when Dad died in the clink, and nobody even liked my dad. I was in the hospital but Charlie snuck me some . . . God, I'm rambling." Cabel shuffles his feet. "I'm just going to shut up now."

Janie hugs him tightly again. "This is really weird."

"Yeah," he says. He strokes her hair. Kisses her forehead. "I'm really sorry about Henry."

"Thanks. I mean, we all knew he was going to die. He's really just a stranger," Janie says. Lies.

"Still," Cabel says. "Anyway, he's your dad. That's gotta feel bad, no matter what."

She shrugs. "I can't . . ." she says. Doesn't want to go there. She's got other immediate things to think about now.

Like how to get her drunk, nightgown-wearing mother to a funeral.

5:59 P.M.

Instead of heating up the house even more by cooking, Cabel picks up dinner. Apparently, the scent of fried chicken and biscuits penetrates the Portal to Sorrow, as Dorothea appears and silently helps herself to the food before retreating once again.

The director from the funeral home calls. Janie first writes things down frantically, then discusses arrangement options with him. She's relieved to hear that Jews have their funerals as soon as possible. That suits her just fine. And with no relatives to contact, they set the service for the next morning at eleven.

After she hangs up, Janie whips through clothes hampers and gets some dirty laundry together for the Laundromat. She shoves the basket at Cabel, and then she remembers that she promised Cathy a note. She scribbles something on a piece of paper and hands it to Cabe, along with a roll of masking tape. "Can you drive out to Henry's and stick this on his front door?"

"No problem," he says. He heads out the door while Janie irons a dress and then wipes the dust off of a pair of ancient, rarely worn flats.

"It's not fair," she mumbles. "It's totally not."

8:10 P.M.

Cabe shows up at the front door with the laundry—fresh, clean, and almost, sort-of folded. "Note's on the door, laundry is finished."

Janie grins and takes the basket. "Thank you. You're wonderful."

Cabel grins. "Laundry's not my strongest area of expertise, but I get by. Can I keep the panties?" He grins and backs out of the house.

"Uh . . . you'll have to ask my mother." Janie laughs.

Cabe cringes. "Oof. Fuck and ugh. Hey, I'll let you get stuff done . . . and give you your space. Call me if you need me. I'll pick you guys up tomorrow for the funeral, if you want."

"Thank you," she says. "Yes, that would be great."

Janie watches him go.

WEDNESDAY

AUGUST 9, 2006, 8:46 A.M.

Cabel knocks on the door. “I’m sorry to bug you,” he says. “I’m not trying to. I know you need space. But here’s a little breakfast so you don’t have to mess with it.”

Janie bites her bottom lip. Takes the tray. “Thanks.”

“Back later.” He sprints across the yards back to his house.

Janie knocks firmly on her mother’s bedroom door.

“What now?”

“Mother? I’ve got some breakfast for you,” she says through the closed door. “Cabel made it. He’s going to be back here at ten thirty to pick us up for the funeral, so you need to be ready.”

Silence.

"Mother."

"Just set it on my dresser."

Janie enters. Dorothea Hannagan is sitting on the edge of her bed, rocking back and forth. "Are you okay?"

"Set it there and git outta here."

Janie glances at her watch, sets the plate on the dresser and leaves the room, a sinking feeling in her gut.

She hops into the shower and lets cool water wash over her. It's not as hot outside today. That'll be a relief at the funeral, standing out by the grave site in the sun.

Janie's only been to one other funeral in her life—her grandmother's in Chicago a long time ago. That one was in a church and there were lots of blue-haired strangers there. They had ham buns and sugar cookies and orange drink afterward, she remembers, and Janie ran around the church basement with a bunch of distant cousins until the old people made them stop. That's about all Janie remembers.

Janie chose a grave-site service for Henry. It's harder for people to fall asleep when they're standing around outside.

Even the drunk ones.

9:39 A.M.

She remembers now why she's not fond of dresses.

9:50 A.M.

Janie knocks tentatively on her mother's door.

There's no answer.

"Mother?"

With only forty minutes to go before Cabel picks them up, Janie's getting nervous. "Mother," she says, louder this time. *Why does everything have to be so hard?*

Finally, Janie opens the door. Dorothea is sitting on the bed, a glass of vodka in her hand. Her hair is still greasy. She's still wearing her nightgown. "Mother!"

"I'm not going." Dorothea says. "I can't go." She doubles over, wraps her arm around her stomach like it hurts, still holding the glass. "I'm sick."

"You are not sick, you're drunk. Get your ass into the shower—now."

"I can't go."

"Mother!" Janie's losing it. "God! Why do you have to do this? Why do you have to make everything so fucking hard? I'm turning the shower on and you are getting in it."

Janie stomps to the bathroom and turns on the shower. Stomps back to her mother's room and grabs the drink from Dorothea's hand. Slams it down on the dresser and it splashes all over her hand. Pulls her mother up by the arm. "Come ON! They are not going to delay this funeral for you."

"I can't go!" Dorothea says, trying to sound firm. But her frail body is no match for Janie's strength.

Janie pulls her mother to the bathroom and pushes her into the shower, still wearing her nightgown. Dorothea yells. Janie reaches in and grabs shampoo, washes her mother's hair. It's so greasy that it doesn't lather. Janie takes another handful and tries again.

Dorothea claws at Janie, also now sopping wet in her dress. Janie holds her mother's head back so the water runs over her, rinsing out the shampoo. "You ruin everything," Janie says. "I'm not going to let you ruin this. Now," Janie says as she turns the water off and grabs a towel, "Take off that ridiculous nightgown and dry yourself. I can NOT believe this is happening. I am so done with this." Janie turns abruptly and stalks off, soaking wet, to her own room to find something else suitable to wear.

All Janie can hear is some shuffling around in the bathroom. She runs a brush through her hair and fixes her soggy makeup. And then she goes to Dorothea's bedroom, takes out the dress and undergarments, and carries them to the bathroom. Finds her mother still drying off.

Janie looks at her mother, a bedraggled rat, so thin her bones poke through her skin. Her face is tired, dejected. "Come on, Ma," Janie says softly. "Let's get you dressed."

This time, Dorothea goes quietly, and in the dusty light of Dorothea's bedroom, Janie helps her mother get ready. Brushes her hair, pulls it back into a bun. Flips the light switch and puts some makeup on her. "You have nice cheekbones," Janie says. "You should wear your hair back more often."

Dorothea doesn't respond but her chin tips up a notch. She wets her lips. "I'm going to need the rest of that glass," she says quietly, "if I'm gonna get through this."

Janie looks her mother in the eye, and Dorothea's gaze drops to the floor.

"I ain't proud of that, but it's the truth." Dorothea's lip twitches.

Janie nods. "Okay." She turns as she hears the front door open and Cabel's car running in the driveway. "We'll be right there!" she calls out.

"Take your time, ladies. I'm a few minutes early," Cabe says.

Dorothea drinks the vodka in two swallows and cringes. Breathes a sigh, but it sounds more like a burden than a relief. She takes the bottle of vodka from the table by her bed and fumbles with her purse, pulling out the flask. Filling it, spilling a little, replacing the cap.

Janie doesn't say anything.

Dorothea closes her purse and turns to Janie. Janie helps her with her shoes.

"Ready?" Janie asks. "After you."

Dorothea nods. She walks unsteadily to the hallway.

Cabel smiles as the two approach. He's wearing a dark gray suit and he looks pretty freaking amazing in it. His hair is tamed and still damp, curling up just barely over his collar. "I'm very sorry about your loss, Ms. Hannagan," he says. He offers his arm to her.

Dorothea looks surprised for a minute, but she gathers her wits and takes his arm as he ushers her to the door and outside to the awaiting car. "Thank you," she says with rare dignity.

10:49 A.M.

They arrive at the cemetery early. The grave site is obvious by the pile of dirt, the suspended pine box, and the rabbi and cemetery workers around it. There are several other people standing quietly nearby as well. Cabel pulls the car to the side of the narrow road.

Janie gets out of the car and helps her mother out of the front seat. The three of them walk together as the rabbi comes to greet them.

"Good morning," he says. "I'm Rabbi Ari Greenbaum." He reaches out his hand.

Janie takes it. "I'm Janie Hannagan. This is my mother, Dorothea Hannagan, and my friend, Cabel Strumheller. I am the daughter of the deceased." She's proud she doesn't stutter through it, but she's been practicing in her mind. "Thank you for helping us with this. We . . . none of us is Jewish. Not, really, anyway. I guess." She blushes.

The rabbi smiles warmly, apparently unbothered by the news. He turns and they walk together to the grave site. Rabbi Greenbaum goes over the details of the ceremony and hands each of them a card with Psalm 23 written on it.

Dorothea stares at the words on the card. She looks up at the casket. Glares at it. Her mouth quivers but she remains quiet.

The strangers approach and stand around the grave site—several men and a few women as well. "From my congregation," the rabbi explains. "The men prepared your father's body for burial and sat with him through the night, then acted as pallbearers and carried the coffin here."

Janie looks up, grateful. Thinking this is all so very strange, but sort of beautiful, too. How thoughtful of these people to do this, and to take the time to come to the funeral of a stranger.

They stand near the grave and wait. Even the birds are quiet as they approach the heat of the day.

Janie stares into the hole. Sees a thin tree root, freshly cut, its raw, white end sticking out of the dirt. She pictures the casket at the bottom of the pit, under all that heavy dirt, the roots growing and wrapping around it, seizing it, breaking through the casket, seizing the body. She shakes her head to clear it and looks up at the blue sky instead.

Behind her, Janie hears more cars approaching. She turns to look and sees two black and whites. Sergeants Baker, Cobb, and Rabinowitz get out, dressed in uniform. Behind the cop cars is a black sedan and Captain steps out.

Charlie and Megan Strumheller are right behind, still tan from their week at the lake. And then Ethel pulls up with Carrie and Stu. Janie tears up a little. In the distance, a big, brown UPS truck rumbles up the narrow cemetery road. Janie can't believe it—all these people coming. She looks at Cabe, incredulous. "How did they know?" she whispers. He smiles and shrugs.

It's time.

The rabbi greets the tiny congregation of attendees and speaks for a moment.

And then.

"May he go to his resting place in peace," the rabbi says.

Before Janie can think, the cemetery workers lower the casket into the grave and soon everyone is looking down on her father in a box. Next to Janie, Dorothea sniffles loudly and sways. Janie grabs her mother around the shoulders and steadies her as the rabbi begins talking again.

And as Janie absorbs the ebb and flow of the rabbi's words, the musical lilt of the Psalms, a little part of her life suffocates in that pine box in the ground too.

"The Lord is my Shepherd, I shall not want." Janie is startled from her thoughts by the group around her, all reciting aloud. She hurries to find her place on the handout and reads along.

And then the rabbi asks if anybody wants to share a story about Henry.

Janie stares at the grass.

After a moment, Cathy, dressed in her standard UPS browns, clears her throat and steps forward. Janie can feel her mother stiffen.

"Who's that?" Dorothea hisses to Janie.

Janie squeezes her mother's shoulder and says nothing.

"Henry Feingold was my customer, and over the years we became good friends," Cathy says, her voice wavering. "He always had a cup of coffee to offer or a cool drink. And when he found out I like to collect snow globes, he started looking for them when he was buying things for his little Internet shop. He was a really thoughtful man, and I'm going to miss him on my route and . . . I'm grateful to you, Janie, for letting me know that he passed on so I could have a chance to say good-bye. And that's it." Cathy steps back to her spot.

"Thank you. Anyone else?"

Cabel nudges Janie. She pokes him back.

And then, and then.

Dorothea says, "I want to say something."

Janie freaks out inside.

The rabbi nods, and Dorothea takes a few unsteady steps to where she can turn around and face the crowd.

What is she going to say? Janie glances at Cabe, sees his eyes are worried too.

Dorothea's thin voice isn't easy to hear in this wide-open space.

At least, it isn't until she starts yelling.

"Henry was the father of Janie, here. The only man I ever loved. But he left me after I quit school for him, and my parents wouldn't let me back home. He was crazy and a horrible person. He ruined my life, and I'm glad he's dead!" With that, Dorothea fumbles at the zipper of her purse.

"Dear God," Cabe whispers.

The small crowd is completely shocked into silence. Janie rushes over and guides her mother back to the spot where they were standing. She feels her face boiling and red. Sweat drips down her back. She purposely averts her eyes from the guests. Mortified.

It doesn't help that Dorothea manages to get her purse open and makes only a small effort to hide that she's taking a swig from the flask.

Rabbi Greenbaum hastens to speak.

Cabe rests his hand on the small of Janie's back to comfort her. He looks down at the ground and Janie can see the amused look on his face. She feels like stomping on his foot. And pushing her mother into the grave hole. Wonders what sort of sitcom that would turn this scene into.

Janie looks up and catches the rabbi's attention. "May I say something?" she asks.

"Of course," Rabbi Greenbaum says, although he looks uncertain.

Janie stays where she's standing and just looks at the casket. "I've known my father for one week," she says. "I've never seen him move, never looked him in the eye. But in that short time, I found out a lot about him. He kept to himself, didn't bother anybody, just lived the life he was given the best way he knew how.

"He wasn't crazy," she continues.

"Was too," Dorothea mutters.

"He wasn't crazy," Janie repeats, ignoring her mother, "he just had an unusual problem that is really hard to explain to anybody who doesn't understand it." Her voice catches. She looks at her mother. "I think, and I'll always believe, that Henry Feingold was a good person. And I am not at all glad he's dead." Janie's lip quivers. It's like the numbness is suddenly wearing off. "I wish I had him back so I could get to know him." Tears trickle down her face.

When it is clear that Janie has said all that she has to say, the rabbi leads Kaddish, a prayer. Then he smiles and beckons Janie to come around the other side of the grave, guiding her to the pile of dirt. Cabel takes Dorothea by the arm and follows. There are several shovels on the ground. They each pick one up.

Janie takes a heaping shovelful of dirt and holds it over the hole in the ground. A trickle of dirt slips off and hits the casket below. She can hardly bear to turn the shovel. The rabbi murmurs something about returning to dust, and finally she turns the shovel over. The thud of the dirt on the wood hurts her stomach.

Dorothea does the same, her arms shaking, and Cabel does it too, and slowly each member of the small crowd takes a shovelful of dirt and releases it into the hole. They continue to fill it.

And that's when Dorothea loses it.

She falls to her knees, almost as if she's just now realized the truth of it. "Henry!" she cries. Her sobs turn to deep shudders. Janie just stands next to her, unable to help. Unwilling to try to stop it.

Such a mess. Janie can see it now, all the guys at the department talking about Janie's mother the drunk, the one who ruined a funeral, the one who fucked around and had an illegitimate daughter and isn't fit to do much of anything but be an embarrassment. She shakes her head, tears streaming down her cheeks as she gets more dirt.

It doesn't matter anyway.

When they are finished, the mound of fresh earth tamped off, Janie knows she has to face the guests. Cabel gets Dorothea to the car.

Janie lays her shovel on the ground. She straightens again and Captain is there.

Captain embraces Janie. Holds her. "You did well," she says. "I'm so very sorry for your loss."

"Thank you," Janie says, tears flowing fresh again. This isn't the first time Janie's cried on Captain's shoulder. "I'm so embarrassed."

"Don't be." Captain's voice is firm—it's a command. For Janie, it's nice to have somebody else running the show for a moment, at least. A relief. Captain pats Janie's back. "Will you be sitting shivah?"

Janie pulls away to look at her. "I don't think so. What's that, again?"

Captain smiles. "It's a time of mourning. It's usually a week, but whatever you decide."

Janie shakes her head. "We . . . I don't . . . I didn't even know I was half-Jewish until last week. We don't practice or anything."

Captain nods. Takes her hand. "Come by my office

when you're ready. No hurry, okay? I think we need to have a talk."

Janie nods. "Yeah, we do."

Captain squeezes Janie's hand and Janie greets the guys from the department. Janie wants to try to explain, apologize for her mother's behavior, but the guys don't let her get a word in about it. They offer condolences and by the end, they're making Janie laugh. Just like always.

It feels good.

Cathy remains by the grave until the guys have left, and then she approaches Janie. "Thank you for the note."

"He'd be glad to know you came, I think," Janie says.

"I dropped off a couple more boxes. They're sitting outside on his step. You want me to return to sender?"

Janie thinks for a moment. "Nah," she says. "I'll take care of it. I'll probably have something that needs to go out tomorrow, then, so . . ." Janie doesn't want to explain here. She'll have all the time in the world to talk to Cathy next week.

"Just request a pickup like you did last time on the Internet, okay? I'll be sure to get them." Cathy looks at her watch. "I got to get back to work. You take care. I'm real sorry."

"I think you knew him best of anyone, Cathy. I'm sorry too."

"Yeah. Yeah, thanks." Cathy looks down. She turns and walks to her truck.

Charlie and Megan embrace Janie in a group hug. "You gonna be all right, kiddo?" Charlie asks.

"Sure, she is," Megan says. "She's tough as nails. But we're here for you if you need us, right?"

Janie nods gratefully, thanking them.

And then Carrie and Stu are there, offering comfort. Stu's wearing the same shirt and outdated tie that he wore to the senior prom, and it makes Janie smile, remembering. So much has happened since then.

"I can't believe how many people came," Janie says. "Thank you. It means a lot."

Carrie grabs Janie's hand and squeezes it. "Of course we'd come, you idiot."

Janie smiles and squeezes back. "Hey," she says, "where's your ring?" and then she stops, worried.

Carrie grins and grabs Stu's hand with her free one. "No worries. We decided that we weren't quite ready for that, so I gave it back. He's keeping it safe, aren't you, honey?"

"Very," Stu says. "Thing was freaking expensive."

Janie grins. "I'm glad you guys are doing okay. Thanks again for coming, and Carrie—thanks for all you did."

"Most entertaining funeral I've ever been to," Carrie says.

Stu and Carrie wave good-bye and walk through the grass to Ethel, swinging hands. Janie watches them go. "Yeah," she says. "Way to go, Carebear."

Janie goes over to the strangers who remain in a small group, talking quietly. "Thank you very much for all you've done," Janie says.

One speaks for all of them. "No thanks necessary. It's an honor to care for the bodies of the deceased. Our sincerest condolences, my dear."

"I—thanks. Er . . ." Janie blushes. She looks around and spies the rabbi. Goes to say good-bye. Afterward, seeing no one else, Janie makes her way to the car.

"Not one single flower!" Dorothea is saying. "What kind of funeral is that?"

Cabel pats the woman on the hand. "Jews don't believe in cutting down a living thing to honor the dead, Ms. Hannagan. They don't do cut flowers."

Janie closes the door and leans her head back on the seat. It's nicely cool inside. "How d'you know that, Cabe?" she asks. "Ask-a-rabbi-dot-com?"

Cabel lifts his chin slightly and puts the car into drive. "Maybe."

4:15 P.M.

When there's a knock at the screen door, Janie rouses herself from a nap on the couch, her mother safely tucked away in her room. She fluffs her hair and grabs her glasses.

It's Rabinowitz.

"Hi. Come in," Janie says, surprised.

He's carrying a box in one hand and a basket of fruit in the other. He brings them inside and puts them on the kitchen counter. "This is to help sweeten your sorrow," he says.

Janie is overcome. "Thank you." The words seem too small to express what she is feeling.

He smiles and excuses himself. "I'm still on duty but I wanted to drop them off. I'm sorry for your loss, Janie." He waves and ducks out the door.

All of the nice.

All of it.

It only makes it harder.

4:28 P.M.

Lies back down on the couch, full of cake.

Thinks about what happens next.

Knows that soon she'll say good-bye to Cabe forever.

And that?

Despite the benefits,

Will be the hardest thing she's ever done.

6:04 P.M.

She walks up Henry's bumpy driveway, backpack on

her back, carrying a suitcase and a bag of clothes. Two forlorn boxes rest in front of the door. Janie goes inside to deposit her stuff and then pulls the boxes inside.

She rips open the first box and pulls out a baby's snowsuit. Goes over the ancient computer and turns it on. Rifles through the notebook that contains the order log, then opens the file drawer under the table. Repackages the snowsuit and writes the address on the box.

Janie opens the second box. Pulls out a bubble-wrapped package.

A snow globe.

It's not listed as an item that needs to be shipped out.

It's for Cathy, she's sure.

Paris. Janie shakes the globe and watches the golden, glittery snow swirling about the gray plastic Eiffel Tower and Notre Dame.

How stunningly tacky.

Yet totally full of a certain sort of special.

Janie smiles, wraps it up again and puts it back in the box. Writes on the box with a black marker:

TO CATHY, ONE LAST GIFT.
FROM HENRY.

Janie finishes her father's business and then she searches, and finds, the ancient rental agreement. Discovers that

Henry's been month-to-month since 1987, just mailing in a check faithfully so it arrives by the first of each month. It'll be easy continuing on from here.

Oh, she'll let the landlord know Henry passed on. But she'll make it very tempting for the landlord to accept Janie as the new tenant. She can even pay the first year in advance if she has to.

She shuts down the computer.

Pulls the sheets off the bed and puts them in the little old washing machine. Decides she's going to clean up the place and sleep here tonight.

Here, in her new home.

It's such a freaking huge relief.

MEMORIES

8:43 P.M. STILL THE FUNERAL DAY.

The first evening in her new place. Isolation, day one.

Laundry done, house dusted, sandwich eaten, grocery list made, Janie sits on her new bed with Henry's shoe box full of memories.

Inside:

- fourteen letters from Dottie
- five unopened letters to Dottie from Henry, marked "Return to Sender"
- a small, tarnished medal from a high school cross-country team
- a class ring
- two envelopes containing photographs

- a loonie and a silver dollar
- nine paper clips
- an old driver's license
- and a folded piece of paper

Gingerly, Janie takes the photographs out of the envelopes and looks through them. Snapshots of Dorothea—tons of them. Photos of the two of them, laughing. Having fun. Kissing and lying together on the beach, blissful smiles on their faces. On the big gray rocks by Lake Michigan, a sign in the background that says "Navy Pier." They look good together. Dorothea is pretty, especially when she smiles. Unbelievable.

Janie also recognizes the living room in the pictures. Henry with his feet propped up on the same coffee table, the same old curtains on the windows, Dorothea stretched out on the same old crappy couch, although it all looks nearly new in the photos. Everything's the same. Janie looks again at the photos of the happy couple.

Well, maybe not everything is the same.

Janie puts the photos in chronological order according to the red digital time stamp marked on the corner of each picture, and she imagines the courtship. The whirlwind summer of 1986 where they worked together at Lou's in Chicago, then there's a break from photos in the fall—that must have been the time they were separated, Dottie in high school and Henry at U of M. Janie peeks at the letters in the shoe box from Dorothea and sees the mail stamps on each opened envelope—all were marked from August 27 through October of that year. *Fourteen handwritten letters in two months*, Janie thinks. That's love.

The second group of photos begin in mid-November of 1986 and the last photo is stamped April 1, 1987. April Fool's Day. Go figure. Janie does the math backward from her birthday, January 9, 1988. *That's about right*, she thinks. Nine months before would have been April 9, 1987. Not much time went by after the last photo before they made a baby, and then it was splitsville.

She fingers the letters, extremely curious. Overwhelmingly curious. Dead freaking curious. She even picks up the first one and runs her index finger along the fold of the letter inside the envelope. But then she puts it down.

It's like the letters are sacred or something.

That, and eww. There's probably something gross written inside. It would be almost as bad as getting sucked into her mother's sex dream. Ick and yuck. Blurgh. Once you read something, you can't erase it from your brain.

Janie puts the letters and the photographs back into the box. She picks up the loonie and wonders how long it's been since her father visited Canada. Smiling, she sets the loonie back down next to the silver dollar and picks up the cross-country medal. She turns it over in her fingers, holding it close to her face and squinting so she can see all the little nooks and crevasses. "I'm a runner too," she says softly. "Just a different kind. The road kind." She holds the medal close and then she pins it on her backpack.

Next, Janie looks at the driver's license. It was his first one, expired long ago. His photo is hilarious and his signature is a boyish version of the one that Janie has seen around the house.

And then Janie picks up the class ring. *1985* is engraved on one side, and *LHS* is on the other. There's a tiny engraving of a runner below the letters. The ring is gold with a ruby stone and it's beautiful. Janie imagines it on Henry's finger, and then she goes back to the photographs and spies it there, on his right hand. Janie slips it on her own finger. It's way too big. But it fits her thumb. She takes it off and puts it back in the box.

Then picks it up again.

Puts it on her thumb.

Likes how it feels there.

11:10 P.M.

After going through everything but the letters once more, Janie finds the folded-up piece of paper with words printed on it. Opens it.

MORTON'S FORK

1889, in ref. to John Morton (c.1420–1500), archbishop of Canterbury, who levied forced loans under Henry VII by arguing the obviously rich could afford to pay and the obviously poor were obviously living frugally and thus had savings and could pay too.

Source: American Psychological Association (APA):

morton\'s fork. (n.d.). Online Etymology Dictionary. Retrieved from Dictionary.com website: http://dictionary.reference.com/browse/morton\'s fork

Janie reads it again. Remembers the bookmark in the book, and the one online. Remembers what the note from Miss Stubin said, about Henry wanting Janie to consider Morton's Fork.

"Yeah, I get it already, Henry. You had a choice. I know." She has considered it—about a million times. She's known it since before she even knew Henry existed. Poor Henry didn't have Miss Stubin's green notebook. Didn't even know the real choice. "I'm way ahead of you, man," she says.

Janie knows which choice sounds like the better one to her. Or she wouldn't be here.

She crumples up the paper and tosses it in the trash can.

She gives a last glance at the letters. And lets them be.

Turns out the light.

Tosses and turns, knowing that tomorrow, she's got a lot of hard explaining to do.

6:11 A.M.

She dreams.

Henry stands on a giant rock in the middle of rapids at the top of waterfall.

His hair turns into a hive of hornets. They buzz around angrily.

If he falls in, the hornets might go away, but he'll die falling down the waterfall.

If he stays on the rock, he'll be stung to death.

Janie watches him. On one bank stands Death, his long black cloak unmoving in the breeze. On the other bank is old Martha Stubin in her wheelchair. Blind, gnarled.

Henry flattens himself on the rock and tries to wash the hornets out of his hair. That only makes them furious. They begin to sting him, and he cries out, slapping at them, futile to stop them. Finally, he falls off the rock and soars over the waterfall. Plunging to his death.

Janie snaps awake and sits up with a gasp, disoriented.

Sits there, sinking back into the pillow, trying to get her heart rate back down to normal.

Thinking.

Hard.

Harder.

And then she pads over to the computer and waits in the cool dawn for it to boot up and connect to the Internet.

Looks up Morton's Fork again. *Why won't Morton's Fork just go away? Why do I keep running into this stupid concept? I know, already. Seriously. I. Get. It. I get it more than Henry ever got it.*

She finds it. Paraphrases under her breath. "A totally suck-ass choice between two equally terrible outcomes. Okay, okay. Right? I KNOW this."

She thinks about it more, in case she's missing something.

Thinks about Henry.

Henry's Morton's Fork was obvious. He chose isolation over the torture and the unpredictable nature of being sucked into dreams. That was his choice. That's what he knew.

Equally terrible.

Yes, Janie could argue that his options were equally terrible. It's a crapshoot. He could have gone either way.

She thinks of Martha Stubin. About how, when she was young, her Morton's Fork was exactly the same as Henry's, and she'd chosen the other path. She didn't know, at the time of her choice, what would happen to her. But then, she became blind and crippled.

Which adds a factor. And it makes Janie's Morton's Fork different.

Janie has the most information of all of them.

Still, this is not news. She's had all this information since the green notebook.

Equally terrible.

The term niggles at Janie's brain and she begins to pace around the little house, the wood floor cool and smooth on her bare feet.

She opens the refrigerator and stares into it, not really seeing anything inside, and thinks about her options.

Argues with herself.

Yes, it's equally terrible. Leaving Cabe and society to go live in a shack, alone? Yeah, that feels pretty terrible. As terrible as becoming blind and crippled? Sure.

Isn't it?

But what if Cabe wasn't a factor?

Isolation. Going off to live alone—hermits do it. Monks do it. People actually choose to do that. To isolate.

No one in his right mind chooses blind and crippled—not after really thinking about it, like Janie did. Martha didn't choose it—it just happened. She didn't know it would happen. No one would ever choose it.

No one.

Unless the only alternative is equally bad.

She's thinking. Thinking about Henry. How he lived. How he died. About how he grew calm, finally. After. Only after he got sucked into Janie's dream.

"There is no best," he'd said during his dream earlier. Holding his head. Pulling his hair out. But he was talking about his version of Morton's Fork. His choice. Janie knows Henry couldn't have known the true choice—he didn't know about Miss Stubin and her blindness, her hands. He still doesn't know, probably, unless she told him. After.

7:03 A.M.

Janie's brain won't let it die.

Because what if?

What if Henry's brain problem actually wasn't a real illness, like a tumor or aneurysm, that normal people have?

What if . . . what if it was a consequence?

The migraines, the pain. Pulling his hair out. As if there was so much pressure.

From not using the ability.

Pressure from not going into other people's dreams.

So much pressure, parts of his brain exploded.

"Noo-o," she says softly.

Sits there, frozen.

In shock.

And then she drops her head. Rests her cheek on the desk.

Groans.

"Shit, Henry," she says softly. She sighs and closes her eyes, and they begin to sting and burn. "You and your Morton's fucking Fork."

THE LAST DAY

THURSDAY, AUGUST 10, 2006, 7:45 A.M.

Janie still sits at Henry's desk. In shock. Denial.

But deep down, she knows it's true. It has to be. It all makes sense.

Can't believe it all comes down to a totally different choice than what she—and Miss Stubin—had thought all this time.

Not between isolation and being blind and gnarled.

But between being blind and gnarled, and isolating until your brain explodes.

"Gaaah!" Janie shouts. That's one great thing about this little house out in the middle of nowhere. She can shout and nobody calls the police.

She slumps back in the desk chair. Then slowly gets up.

Falls on the bed and just lies there, staring at the wall.

"Now what?" she whispers.

No one answers.

9:39 A.M.

She gets up. Looks around the little shack. Shakes her head.

Sorry.

So very sorry.

And now, looking at a fresh set of equally suck-ass options, a true Morton's Fork, she realizes that she has a new choice to make.

She sits cross-legged on the bed, pen and paper in hand, and lays it all out. Pros and cons. Benefits and detriments. Suck versus suck.

Miss Stubin's life, or Henry's?

Which one does Janie want?

"No regrets," Miss Stubin had said in the green notebook. But she didn't know the truth.

"There is no best," Henry had said in the dream. He didn't know either.

Janie, alone in the world, is the only one who knows the real choice.

10:11 A.M.

She calls Captain.

"Komisky. Hey, Janie, how you doing?"

"Hi, Captain—okay, I guess. You have time to talk today?"

"One sec." Janie hears Captain's fingernails clicking on her computer keyboard. "How's noon? I'll grab takeout, we can have lunch in my office. Sound good?"

"Sounds great," Janie says. She hangs up.

Feels the butterflies in her belly.

And then.

She shakes her head and starts packing.

Packing up the things that she brought over here, smashing them into her suitcase to make it all fit. Hoping to carry it all in one load.

She's going back home.

If it weren't for Cabe, she'd probably just risk it. Stay isolated. In case she's dead wrong about what really happened to Henry.

But she's pretty sure she's right.

It's a gut thing.

So.

There it is.

Janie grabs a handle shopping bag from under Henry's sink and fills it with all the stuff she couldn't fit in her suitcase. Shakes her head from time to time.

Still can't believe it.

Before she leaves, she calls Henry's landlord to let him know that Henry died. Then, she closes down Henry's online shop for good, schedules a pickup for the last remaining item, and leaves the snow globe gift outside with a sign so Cathy doesn't miss it.

She sets her suitcase down. Closes the door behind her, leaving it unlocked, just as she found it.

Takes a deep breath of country air and holds it in, lets it out slowly.

Glances at the certainly potent sun tea, still resting on the station wagon's hood.

Picks up her suitcase. And sets off.

Crunches down the gravel driveway like a homeless person, carrying all her crap.

Doesn't look back.

When she gets home, she puts her things away in her

room, and from the bag she pulls the shoe box, all the letters untouched. Janie, medal pinned to her backpack and ring on her thumb, carries the box to the kitchen and sets it on the counter next to the lure of Rabinowitz's fruit and cake.

11:56 A.M.

Janie greets the guys as she makes her way through the department to Captain's office. She stops at Rabinowitz's desk to thank him again for the sweets, but he's not there. Janie smiles and scribbles a note on a piece of scratch paper instead.

Then she knocks on Captain's door.

"Come!"

Janie enters. The smell of Chinese food makes her stomach growl. Captain is setting out paper plates and plastic forks. She opens up the food containers and smiles warmly. "How are you?"

Janie closes the door and sits. "Oh, you know," she says lightly. "Crazy as usual." She takes the napkins and peels one off the small pile, setting it next to Captain's plate.

"Help yourself," Captain says. They dish out food.

It feels awkward, the silence, just the two of them. Eating. Janie fingers the new ring on her thumb and accidentally dribbles brown sauce from chicken cashew nuts on her white tank top. Tries desperately to clean it with her napkin before it sets.

Captain reaches into her drawer—the drawer that seems to have everything anyone could possibly need—and pulls out an individual packet of Shout Wipes. Tosses it to Janie.

Janie grins and rips it open. "You have absolutely everything in that drawer. Snacks, Steri-Strips, food stain wipes, plasticware . . . what else?"

"Anything and everything a person needs in order to live for several days," Captain says. "Sewing kit for button emergencies, hair clips, toiletries, screwdriver set, SwissChamp Army Knife and no, you may not borrow it, it's the super-expensive one. Let's see, dog whistle, dog treats, police whistle, anti-venom, EpiPen, water bottles . . . and the traditional mess of rubber bands, paper clips, and outdated postage stamps. A few pennies."

Janie laughs. Relaxes. "That's amazing." Takes a bite.

"I was a boy scout." Captain's serious face never wavers.

Janie snorts, and then wonders if Captain wasn't joking. One never knows with her.

"So," Captain says. "We have a lot of catching up to do." She adds cream to her coffee. "My brilliant assessment is that your little family emergency last week had something to do with your father dying. True?"

"True," Janie says.

"Why in hell did you not tell me what was up before?"

Janie looks up sharply. "I—"

"We are family here, Hannagan. I am your family, you are my family, everybody here is a member of this family. You don't dis your family. You tell me when something big like this is happening, you hear me?"

Janie clears her throat. "I didn't want to bother you. It's not like I even knew him. Well, not really. He was unconscious the whole time."

Captain's sigh comes out like a warning blast from a steam engine. "Stop that."

"Yes, sir."

"Thank God Strumheller had sense enough to tell me about the funeral, or you would have been toast."

"Yes, sir." Janie's losing her appetite. "I'm sorry."

"Good. Now, your father. Let's talk about him. He was a dream catcher too?"

Janie's jaw drops. "How did you know?"

"You said so in your testimonial. Between the lines. You said he had issues that people wouldn't understand, but you understood, or some such thing. Normal folk wouldn't have guessed what you really meant."

Janie nods. "I didn't intend to say that—it just came out. But yeah, he was an isolated dream catcher."

"Ahh, isolated. Like what you're considering. Well,

no wonder we didn't know about him," Captain says. "How did you find out?"

"I went into his dreams."

"Oh?"

"Uh . . . yeah. Found out some interesting stuff."

"I'll bet. And how did you know his UPS driver, Ms. Hannagan? Seems a bit odd that you've never spoken to your father, but from what she said in her testimonial, you apparently had a previous conversation with this lady in brown." Captain takes a bite of her lunch. "What's that on your thumb? Looks like high school bling right out of the eighties. Mm-hmm. Don't answer that."

Janie grins. Her face turns red. "Yes, sir."

"Quite the detective you are, even when you're not on assignment."

"I guess."

"So. Have you made a decision? What we talked about? The isolation thing?"

Janie sets her fork down. "About that," she says, a concerned look on her face. "I, uh . . ."

Captain looks Janie in the eye. Says nothing.

"I was going to. I mean, I made a decision." Janie's having a terrible time saying it.

Captain's gaze doesn't waver.

"And turns out, it's not going to work out after all."

Captain leans forward. "Tell me," she says quietly, but it has an edge to it. "Come on."

Janie is confused. "What?"

"Say it. For Chrissakes, do it. Share something that goes on in that mysterious brain of yours. You don't always have to hold everything in. I'm a good listener. Really."

"What?" Janie says again, still puzzled. "I just—"

Captain nods encouragingly.

"Okay, I just pretty much found out that Martha Stubin had it wrong. My choices are different—either I become like her, or I become like him. My dad. He isolated. And his brain exploded."

Captain raises an eyebrow. "Exploded. Medical term?"

Janie laughs. "Not really."

"What else?" Captain's voice loses the edge.

"Well, so I think I'll just live at home, then. And, I guess, go to school as planned. I mean, it's a toss-up—blind and crippled in my twenties, dead from a brain explosion in my late thirties. What would you choose? I guess, because I have Cabe, I'll choose blind and crippled. If he can deal with it, that is." Janie remembers his dreams.

"Does he know any of this? Any of it at all?"

"Er . . . no."

"You know what I always say, right?"

"Talk to him. Yeah, I know."

"So do it, then!"

"Okay, okay." Janie grins.

"And once things settle down after your terrible week, and you get to feeling good about school, because you will, we'll talk about you and your job. Okay?"

"Okay." Janie sighs. It's such a relief.

They pack up the remains of the lunch.

"Before you go," Captain says, rolling her chair over to the filing cabinet and opening the middle drawer, "here's something—if it's not helpful to you, just toss it. I won't be offended." She pulls an orange photocopied paper from a file, folds it, and hands it to Janie. Stands and walks Janie to the door. "And if you ever want to talk about that, you know where to find me. Family. Don't forget."

"Okay." Janie takes the paper and smiles. "Thanks for lunch. And everything." She stands and heads for the door.

"You're welcome. Now stop bothering me." She smiles and watches Janie go.

"Yesss," Janie says as she runs up the steps to the street level. One hard conversation over. Goes outside and walks to the bus stop. She opens up the orange paper and squints, reading it.

After a moment, she folds it again slowly, thoughtfully, and puts it in her pocket.

1:43 P.M.

She takes the bus to her neighborhood stop. Nobody dreaming this afternoon.

Walks to Cabel's.

He's painting the garage door now.

Janie stands in the grass at the side of the driveway and watches him.

Thinks about all the things that have happened in the past days. The whole journey she's been on. The lows, and the lowers.

She thought she'd have to say good-bye.

Forever.

And now, she doesn't.

It should feel so good.

But there's still the matter of his dreams.

She clears her throat.

Cabel doesn't turn around. "You're quiet," he says. "Wasn't sure how long you were going to stand there."

She bites her lip.

Shoves her hands in her pockets.

He turns. Has paint on his cheek. Eyes soft and crinkly. "What's up? You okay?"

Janie stands there.

Tries to stop the quivering.

He sees it. Sets down his brush.

Goes to her. "Oh, baby," he says. Pulls her close. Holds. "What is it?"

Strokes her hair while she sobs in his shirt.

2:15 P.M.

In the grass, under the shade tree in the backyard. They talk.

About his nightmares

And her future

For a very, very long time.

4:29 P.M.

It's all so complicated.

It always is, with Janie.

It's impossible for Janie to know what will happen, no matter how hard she tries to figure it out. No matter how much Cabe convinces Janie that he had no idea he was having such disturbing dreams, and admits that maybe he is scared. But also that he really is dealing with things—he really is.

No matter how much they both promise to keep talking when shit like this comes up. Because it always will.

There's just no happily ever after in Janie's book.

But they both know there is something. Something good between them.

There is respect.

And there is depth.

Unselfishness.

An understanding between them that surpasses a hell of a lot else.

And there's that love thing.

So they decide. They decide to decide each day what things will come.

No commitments. No big plans. Just life, each day.

Making progress. Cutting the pressure.

There's enough damn pressure everywhere else.

And if it works, it works.

She knows one thing, deep down.

Knows it hard. And good.

He's the only guy she'll ever tell.

IT IS WHAT IT IS

5:25 P.M. STILL THE LAST DAY.

"Hey, can you drive me somewhere tonight?" Her cheeks are flushed. And she has a goddamned hickey. You do the math.

"Sure. Where?"

"Place out on North Maple."

Cabel tilts his head curiously but doesn't ask.

Knows she won't tell him anyway.

Smiles to himself and shakes his head a little as he goes to the stove to make dinner. "God, I freaking love you," he mutters.

6:56 P.M.

Cabel pulls up to the building. Janie peers out the

window and then checks the orange paper. "Yep, this is it." She's nervous. Not sure about this. "Can you just hang out here for about five minutes in case, you know, this isn't cool?"

"Sure, sweets. If I'm gone when you come out, just text me. I'll come right back." He gives Janie a reassuring squeeze on her thigh and kiss on the cheek. "I'll probably just head down to one of the bookstores around here. Maybe drive through campus and take a walk around."

"Okay." Janie takes a deep breath and gets out of the car. "See you." She walks, determined, to the door. Doesn't look back. Doesn't see Cabel pick up the orange paper from the seat where she left it. He reads it. Smiles.

7:01 P.M.

A dozen people mill around the room, getting coffee and chatting. Mostly adults, but a couple of people who look to be about Janie's age. Janie steps into the room, feeling awkward, not sure where to stand. Slowly she backs up to a wall and just looks around, a fake smile on her face, trying not to make eye contact.

"Welcome," says a stocky, middle-aged man as he walks up to Janie. "My name is Luciano." He holds out his hand.

Janie takes it. Shakes it. "Hi," she says.

"Glad you came. Have you been to Al-Anon before?"

"No—this is my first time."

"Don't worry. We all have something in common. Let me get this thing started." Luciano turns to the room and calls out for everyone to grab a seat at the table. Janie makes her way, and a young man offers Janie some coffee. Janie smiles gratefully and accepts, adding her traditional three creams, three sugars.

The small group quiets down and Luciano speaks. "Welcome to Al-Anon. For those who are new here, this is a support group for people who are dealing with the effects of an alcoholic on your life." He looks at the young man across the table. "Carl, would you like to lead today's meeting?"

Janie listens intently to the introduction and testimonial from a woman at the table who talks about her alcoholic, abusive father. After that, Carl leads a discussion about one of the twelve steps.

It feels good to know she's not alone.

And that Dorothea's drinking isn't Janie's fault.

When it is over, Janie takes some literature from the racks. She slips out of the room, texting Cabe that she's ready, and she goes outside into the cool evening. Thinking. Realizing a ton of stuff about her mother. And feeling, for the first time, that part of the stress of her life, part of the responsibility, has been taken away. It feels fabulous, actually.

Wonders why she never thought about doing this before.

8:31 P.M.

They tool around the U of M campus, first by car, then on foot, wandering through the parks and around the various buildings, Cabel pointing out what he knows about where things are and how to get there. It feels weird, and fun, and daunting, like a strange adventure, wandering the campus of such a huge school. Soon, they'll be a part of it all.

They stop for ice cream at Stucchi's and laugh for what feels like the first time in a long time.

When Cabel drops Janie off, she kisses him sweetly, holds him close. "I'm really happy about our agreement," she says.

"Me too." Cabe says. "So . . . tomorrow . . ." He sounds reluctant.

"Yes?"

"I need some junk for school. I suppose, against my better judgment, we should go shopping."

Janie grins. "Sweet," she says. "I'll bring a fork in case it all gets to be too much for you and you need to stab your eyeballs out."

He laughs. "It would be ironic if I went blind before you did, wouldn't it?"

They share a wry smile. A lingering, soulful kiss.

11:05 P.M.

When Cabe pulls out of the driveway, Janie walks slowly to the house and sits down on the step. Just thinks about things, and things, and things.

Like the time Cabel brought her to this step on his skateboard.

And she thinks about Miss Stubin, and how she never actually had a chance to say good-bye. She's glad for the note on the chair.

She thinks about Captain, and her eyes get misty. *Family*, she'd said.

It's good to have family like that.

Janie turns Henry's ring so it catches the glow from the streetlamp. The ruby sparkles. She makes a fist. Presses the ring to her lips. Holds it there. Then lifts it up to the sky. Says, "Hey, Henry . . ." and stops, because her throat hurts too much to go on.

Janie listens to the crickets and tree frogs—or wires—buzzing in their last days of summer, before the sounds of crunchy leaves take over once again.

She thinks about her mother in a different way. A new way, tonight. Plans on going back to another Al-Anon meeting. Might even share her own story sometime. If she feels like it. Or not. No rash decisions. No big commitments. Each day as it comes.

Janie takes a deep breath and feels the briskness of the night filling her lungs. She sits a moment more on the step, and then eases to her feet and peers into the house through the kitchen window, pushing her face against the dusty old screen, wrapping her hands around her glasses to shield against the glare from the streetlights. Streams of soft light from the window cut diagonally across the kitchen.

The box of memories is gone.

So is the cake.

Janie laughs quietly, but inside, she aches a little. For a moment, she left all this trouble behind. And now here she is again, and will be, for a while at least.

It's hard to get excited about that.

But life goes on.

Everything progresses in one direction or another. Relationships, abilities, illnesses, disabilities. Knowledge.

School. A new life where few will know her. Where few will call her narc girl. But where many will dream.

She sighs.

One day at a time. One dream at a time.

Her choice is made. For now. For today.

"This is it," she whispers to the buzzing wires. "This is really it."

The chill of the evening, the preamble to autumn, has arrived, and Janie rubs her bare arms, covered in goose bumps.

It's exhausting to think about it all. Quietly, she goes inside. Locks the door behind her. Slips off her shoes and tosses her backpack on the couch. But before Janie says a last good night tonight, she has just one more task in mind.

She pads on bare feet down the short hallway in the quiet night.

And pauses at the portal to another world.

There's just one more sorrow's dream to change.

Read ahead for an excerpt from Lisa McMann's

crash

One

My sophomore psych teacher, Mr. Polselli, says knowledge is crucial to understanding the workings of the human brain, but I swear to dog, I don't want any more knowledge about this.

Every few days I see it. Sometimes it's just a picture, like on that billboard we pass on the way to school. And other times it's moving, like on a screen. A careening truck hits a building and explodes. Then nine body bags in the snow.

It's like a movie trailer with no sound, no credits. And nobody sees it but me.

Some days after psych class I hang around by the door of Mr. Polselli's room for a minute, thinking that if I have a mental illness, he's the one who'll be able to tell me. But every time I almost mention it, it sounds too weird to say. *So, uh, Mr. Polselli, when other people see the "turn off your cell phones" screen in the movie theater, I see an extra five-second movie trailer. Er . . . and did I mention I see stills of it on the billboard by my house? You see Jose Cuervo, I see a truck hitting a building and everything exploding. Is that normal?*

The first time was in the theater on the one holiday that our parents don't make us work—Christmas Day. I poked my younger sister, Rowan. "Did you see that?"

She did this eyebrow thing that basically says she thinks I'm an idiot. "See what?"

"The explosion," I said softly.

"You're on drugs." Rowan turned to our older brother, Trey, and said, "Jules is on drugs."

Trey leaned over Rowan to look at me. "Don't do drugs," he said seriously. "Our family has enough problems."

I rolled my eyes and sat back in my seat as the real movie trailers started. "No kidding," I muttered. And I reasoned with myself. The day before I'd almost been robbed while doing a pizza delivery. Maybe I was still traumatized.

I just wanted to forget about it all.

But then on MLK Day this stupid vision thing decided to get personal.

Two

Five reasons why I, Jules Demarco, am shunned:

1. I smell like pizza
2. My parents make us drive a meatball-topped food truck to school for advertising
3. I haven't invited a friend over since second grade
4. Did I mention I smell like pizza? Like, its umami*-ness oozes from my pores
5. Everybody at school likes Sawyer Angotti's family's restaurant better

Frankly, I don't blame them. I'd shun me too.

---

*Look it up

Every January my mother says Martin Luther King Jr. weekend gives us the boost we need to pay the rent after the first two dead weeks of the year. She's superpositive about everything. It's like she forgets that every month is the same. Her attitude is probably what keeps our business alive. But if my mother, Paula, is the backbone of Demarco's Pizzeria, my father, Antonio, is the broken leg that keeps us struggling to catch up.

There's no school on MLK Day, so Trey and I are manning the meatball truck in downtown Chicago, and Rowan is working front of house in the restaurant for the lunch shift. She's jealous. But Trey and I are the oldest, so we get to decide.

The food truck is actually kind of a blast, even if it does have two giant balls on top, with endless jokes to be made. Trey and I have been cooking together since we were little—he's only sixteen months older than me. He's a senior. He's supposed to be the one driving the food truck to school because he has his truck license now, but he pays me ten bucks a week to secretly drive it so he can bum a ride from our neighbor Carter. Carter is kind of a douche, but at least his piece-of-crap Buick doesn't have a sack on its roof.

Trey drives now and we pass the billboard again.

"Hey—what was on the billboard?" I ask as nonchalantly as I can.

Trey narrows his eyes and glances at me. "Same as always. Jose Cuervo. Why?"

"Oh." I shrug like it's no big deal. "Out of the corner of my eye I thought it had changed to something new for once." Weak answer, but he accepts it. To me, the billboard is a still picture of the explosion. I look away and rub my temples as if it will make me see what everybody else sees, but it does nothing. Instead, I try to forget by focusing on my phone. I start posting all over the Internet where Demarco's Food Truck is going to be today. I'm sure some of our regulars will show up. It's becoming a sport, like storm chasing. Only they're giant meatball chasing.

Some people need a life. Including me.

We roll past Angotti's Trattoria on the way into the city—that's Sawyer's family's restaurant. Sawyer is working today too. He's outside sweeping the snow from their sidewalk. I beg for the traffic light to stay green so we can breeze past unnoticed, but it turns yellow and Trey slows the vehicle. "You could've made it," I mutter.

Trey looks at me while we sit. "What's your rush?"

I glance out the window at Sawyer, who either hasn't noticed our obnoxious food truck or is choosing to ignore it.

Trey follows my glance. "Oh," he says. "The enemy. Let's wave!"

I shrink down and pull my hat halfway over my eyes.

"Just . . . hurry," I say, even though there's nothing Trey can do. Sawyer turns around to pick up a bag of rock salt for the ice, and I can tell he catches sight of our truck. His head turns slightly so he can spy on who's driving, and then he frowns.

Trey nods coolly at Sawyer when their eyes meet, and then he faces forward as the light finally changes to green. "Do you still like him?" he asks.

Here's me, sunk down in the seat like a total loser, trying to hide, breathing a sigh of relief when we start rolling again. "Yeah," I say, totally miserable. "Do you?"

Three

Trey smiles. "Nah. That urban underground thing he's got going on is nice, and of course I'm fond of the, ah, Mediterranean complexion, but I've been over him for a while. He's too young for me. You can have him."

I laugh. "Yeah, right. Dad will love that. Maybe me hooking up with an Angotti will be the thing that puts him over the edge." I don't mention that Sawyer won't even look at me these days, so the chance of me "having" Sawyer is zero.

Sawyer Angotti is not the kind of guy most people would say is hot, but Trey and I have the same taste in men, which is sometimes convenient and sometimes a pain in the ass. Sawyer has this street casual look where he could totally be a clothes model, but if he ever told people he was one, they'd be like, "Seriously? No way." Because his most attractive features are so subtle, you know? At first glance he's really ordinary, but if you study him . . . big sigh. His vulnerable smile is what gets me—not the charming one he uses on teachers and girls and probably customers, too. I mean the warm, crooked smile that doesn't come out unless he's feeling shy or self-conscious. That one makes my stomach flip. Because for the most part, he's tough-guy metro, if such a thing exists. Arms crossed and eyebrow raised, constantly questioning the world. But I've seen his other side a million times. I've been in love with him since we played plastic cheetahs and bears together at indoor recess in first grade.

How was I supposed to know back then that Sawyer was the enemy? I didn't even know his last name. And I didn't know about the family rivalry. But the way my father interrogated me after they went to my first parent-teacher conference and found out that I "played well with others" and "had a nice friend in Sawyer Angotti," you'd have thought I'd given away great-grandfather's last weapon to the enemy. Trey says that was right around the time Dad really started acting weird.

All I knew was that I wasn't allowed to play cheetahs and bears with Sawyer anymore. I wasn't even supposed to talk to him.

But I still did, and he still did, and we would meet

under the slide and trade suckers from the candy jar each of our restaurants had by the cash register. I would bring him grape, and he always brought me butterscotch, which we never had in our restaurant. I'd do anything to get Sawyer Angotti to give me a butterscotch sucker again.

I have a notebook from sixth grade that has nine pages filled with embarrassing and overdramatic phrases like "I pine for Sawyer Angotti" and "JuleSawyer forever." I even made an *S* logo for our conjoined names in that one. Too bad it looks more like a cross between a dollar sign and an ampersand. I'd dream about us getting secretly married and never telling our parents.

And back then I'd moon around in my room after Rowan was asleep, pretending my pillow was Sawyer. Me and my Sawyer pillow would lie down on my bed, facing one another, and I'd imagine us in Bulger Park on a blanket, ignoring the tree frogs and pigeons and little crying kids. I'd touch his cheek and push his hair back, and he'd look at me with his gorgeous green eyes and that crooked, shy grin of his, and then he'd lean toward me and we'd both hold our breath without realizing it, and his lips would touch mine, and then . . . He'd be my first kiss, which I'd never forget. And no matter how much our parents tried to keep us apart, he'd never break my heart.

Oh, sigh.

But then, on the day before seventh grade started,

when it was time to visit school to check out classes and get our books, his father was there with him, and my father was there with me, and I did something terrible.

Without thinking, I smiled and waved at my friend, and he smiled back, and I bit my lip because of love and delight after not seeing him for the whole summer . . . and his father saw me. He frowned, looked up at my father, scowled, and then grabbed Sawyer's arm and pulled him away, giving my father one last heated glance. My father grumbled all the way home, issuing half-sentence threats under his breath.

And that was the end of that.

I don't know what his father said or did to him that day, but by the next day, Sawyer Angotti was no longer my friend. Whoever said seventh grade is the worst year of your life was right. Sawyer turned our friendship off like a faucet, but I can't help it—my faucet of love has a really bad leak.

Trey parks the truck as close to the Field Museum as our permit allows, figuring since the weather is actually sunny and not too freezing and windy, people might prefer to grab a quick meal from a food truck instead of eating the overpriced generic stuff inside the tourist trap.

Before we open the window for business, we set up. Trey checks the meat sauce while I grate fresh mozzarella into tiny, easily meltable nubs. It's a simple operation—our winter truck specialty is an Italian bread bowl with spicy mini meatballs, sauce, and cheese. The truth is it's delicious, even though I'm sick to death of them.

We also serve our pizza by the slice, and we're talking deep-dish Chicago-style, not that thin crap that Angotti's serves. Authentic, authschmentic. The tourists want the hearty, crusty, saucy stuff with slices of sausage the diameter of my bicep and bubbling cheese that stretches the length of your forearm. That's what we've got, and it's amazing.

Oh, but the Angotti's sauce . . . I had it once, even though in our house it's contraband. Their sauce will lay you flat, seriously. It's that good. We even have the recipe, apparently, but we can't use it because it's patented and they sell it by the jar—it's in all the local stores and some regional ones now too. My dad about had an aneurysm when that happened. Because, according to Dad, in one of his mumble-grumble fits, the Angottis had been after our recipe for generations and somehow managed to steal it from us.

So I guess that's how the whole rivalry started. From what I understand, and from what I know about Sawyer avoiding me like the plague, his parents feel the same way about us as my parents feel about them.

Trey and I pull off a really decent day of sales for the middle of January. We hightail it back home for the dinner rush so we can help Rowan out.

As we get close, we pass the billboard from the other side. I locate it in my side mirror, and it's the same as this morning. Explosion. I watch it grow small and disappear, and then close my eyes, wondering what the hell is wrong with me.

We pull into the alley and park the truck, take the stuff inside.

"Get your asses out there!" Rowan hisses as she flies through the kitchen. She gets a little anxious when people have to wait ten seconds. That kid is extremely well put together, but she carries the responsibility of practically the whole country on her shoulders.

Mom is rolling out dough. I give her a kiss on the cheek and shake the bank bag in her face to show her I'm on the way to putting it in the safe like I'm supposed to. "Pretty good day. Had a busload of twenty-four," I say.

"Fabulous!" Mom says, way too perky. She grabs a tasting utensil, reaches into a nearby pot, and forks a meatball for me. I let her shove it into my mouth when I pass her again.

"I's goo'!" I say. And really freaking hot. It burns the roof of my mouth before I can shift it between my teeth to let it cool.

Tony, the cook who has been working for our family restaurant for something like forty million years, smiles at me. “Nice work today, Julia,” he says. Tony is one of the few people I allow to call me by my birth name.

I guess my dad, Antonio, was actually named after Tony. Tony and my grandfather came to America together. I don’t really remember my grandpa much—he killed himself when I was little. Depression. A couple of years ago I accidentally found out it was suicide when I overheard Mom and Aunt Mary talking about it.

When I asked my mom about it later, she didn’t deny it—instead, she said, “But you kids don’t have any sign of depression in you, so don’t worry. You’re all fine.” Which was about the best way to make me think I’m doomed.

It’s a weird thing to find out about your family, you know? It made me feel really different for the rest of the day, and it still does now whenever I think about it. Like we’re all wondering where the depression poison will hit next, and we’re all looking at my dad. I wonder if that’s why my mother is so upbeat all the time. Maybe she thinks she can protect us with her happy shield.

Trey and I hurry to wash up, grab fresh aprons, and check in with Aunt Mary at the hostess stand. She’s seating somebody, so we take a look at the chart and see that the house is pretty full. No wonder Rowan’s freaking out.

Rowan’s fifteen and a freshman. Just as Trey is sixteen months older than me, she’s sixteen months younger. I don’t know if my parents planned it, and I don’t want to know, but there it is. I pretty much think they had us for the sole purpose of working for the family business. We started washing dishes and busing tables years ago. I'm not sure if it was legal, but it was definitely tradition.

Rowan looks relieved to see us. She's got the place under control, as usual. "Hey, baby! Go take a break," I whisper to her in passing.

"Nah, I'm good. I'll finish out my tables," she says. I glance at the clock. Technically, Rowan is supposed to quit at seven, because she's not sixteen yet—she can only work late in the summer—but, well, tradition trumps rules sometimes. Not that my parents are slave drivers or anything. They're not. This is just their life, and it's all they know.

It's a busy night because of the holiday. Busy is good. Busy means we can pay the rent, and whatever else comes up. Something always does.

By ten thirty all the customers have left. Even though Dad hasn't come down at all this evening to help out, Mom says she and Tony can handle closing up alone, and she sends Trey and me upstairs to the apartment to get some sleep.

I don't want to go up there.

Neither does Trey.

Four

Trey and I go out the back and into the door to the stairs leading up to our home above the restaurant. We pick our way up the stairs, through the narrow aisle that isn't piled with stuff. At the top, we push against the door and squeeze through the space.

Rowan has already done what she could with the kitchen. The sink is empty, the counters are clean. The kitchen is the one sacred spot, the one room where Mom won't take any garbage from anybody—literally. Because even after cooking all day, she still likes to be able to cook at home too, without having to worry that Dad's precious stacks of papers are going to combust and set the whole building on fire because they're too close to the gas stove.

Everywhere else—dining room, living room, and

hallway—is piled high around the edges with Dad's stuff. Lots of papers—recipes and hundreds of cooking magazines, mostly, and all the Chicago newspapers from the past decade. Shoe boxes, shirt boxes, and every other possible kind of box you can imagine, some filled with papers, some empty. Plastic milk crates filled with cookbooks and science books and gastronomy magazines. Bags full of greeting cards, birthday cards, sympathy cards, some written in, some brand-new, meant for good intentions that never happened. Hundreds of old videos, and a stack as high as my collarbone of old VCRs that don't work. Stereos, 8-track players, record players, tape recorders, all broken. Records and cassette tapes and CDs and games—oh my dog, the board games. Monopoly, Life, Password, Catch Phrase. Sometimes five or six duplicates, most of them with little yellowing masking-tape stickers on them that say seventy-five cents or a buck twenty-five. Insanity. Especially when somebody puts something heavy on top of a Catch Phrase and that stupid beeper goes off somewhere far below, all muffled.

We weave through it. Thankfully, Dad is nowhere to be found, either asleep or buried alive under all his crap. It's not like he's violent or mean or anything. He's just . . . unpredictable. When he's feeling good, he's in the restaurant. He's visible. He's easy to keep track of. But on the days he doesn't come down, we never know what to expect.

We climb those stairs after the end of our shift knowing he could be standing right there in the kitchen, long-faced, unshaven, having surfaced to eat something for the first time since yesterday. And rattling off the same guilt-inspired apologies, day after day after day. *I just couldn't make it down today. Not feeling up to it. I'm sorry you kids have to work so hard.* What do you say to that after the tenth time, or the hundredth?

Worse, he could be sitting in the dark living room with his hands covering his face, the blue glow from the muted TV spotlighting his depressed existence so we can't ignore it. It's probably wrong that Trey and Rowan and I all hope he stays invisible, holed up in his bedroom on days like these, but it's just easier when he's out of sight. We can pretend depressed Dad doesn't exist.

Tonight we breathe a sigh of relief. Trey heads into the cluttered bathroom, its cupboards overflowing with enough soap, shampoo, toothpaste, and toilet paper to get us through Y3K. Thank God our bedrooms are off-limits to Dad. I peek into my tidy little room and see Rowan is sleeping in her bed already, but I'm still wired from a long day. I close the door quietly and grab a glass of milk from the kitchen, then settle down in the one chair in the living room that's not full of stuff and flip on the TV. I run through the DVR list, choosing a rerun of an old Sherlock Holmes movie that I've been watching a little bit at a time over the past couple of weeks, whenever I get a chance. Somebody else must be watching it too, because it's not cued up to the last part I watched. I hit the slowest fast-forward so I can find where I left off.

Trey peeks his head in the room. "Night," he says. He dangles the keys to the meatball truck, and when I hold out my hand, he tosses them to me.

"Thanks," I say, not meaning it. I shouldn't have agreed to only ten bucks a week, but I was desperate. It's not nearly enough to pay for the humiliation of driving the giant balls. "Where's my ten bucks?"

"Isn't it only eight if one day is a holiday?" He gives me what he thinks is his adorable face and hands me a five and three ones.

"Sorry. Not in the contract." I hold my hand out for more.

"Dammit." He goes back to his room for two more dollars while Sir Henry on the TV is flitting around outside on the moors in fast mode, which looks kind of kooky.

Trey returns. "Here."

I grab the two bucks from him and shove all ten into my pocket with my tips. "Thanks. Night."

When he's gone, I stop the fast-forward, knowing I went too far, and rewind to the commercial as I slip the keys into my other pocket, then press play.

Instead of the movie that I'm expecting, I see *it* again.

It flashes by in a few seconds, and then it's gone. The truck, the building, the explosion. And then back to our regularly scheduled programming.

"Stop it," I whisper. My stomach flips and a creepy shiver runs down my neck. It makes my throat tighten. I pause the recording and sit there a minute, trying to calm down. And then I hit rewind.

Ninety-nine percent of me hopes there's nothing there but a creepy giant hound on the moor.

But there it is.

I watch it again, and I get this gnawing thing in my chest, like I'm supposed to do something about it.

"Why does this keep happening?" I mutter, and rewind it again. I hit play and it all flies by so fast, I can hardly see it. I rewind once more and this time set it to play in slow motion.

The truck is yellow. I notice it's actually a snowplow, and the snow is falling pretty hard. It's dark outside, but the streetlamps are lit. The truck is coming fast and it starts angling slightly, crossing to the wrong side and going off the road. It jumps the curb spastically and jounces over some snow piles in a big parking lot, and then I see the building—there's a large window—for a split second before the truck hits it. The building explodes shortly after contact, glass and brick shrapnel flying everywhere. The scene cuts to the body bags in the snow. I count again to make sure—definitely nine. The last frame is a close-up of three of the bags, and then it's over. I hit the pause button.

"What are you doing?"

I jump and whirl around to see Rowan standing in the doorway squinting at me, hair all disheveled. "Jeez!" I whisper, trying to calm my heartbeat. "You scared the crap out of me." I glance back at the TV with slow-motion dread, like I've just been caught looking at . . . I don't know. Porn, or something else I'm not supposed to look at. But it's paused at a sour cream commercial. I let out a breath of relief and turn my attention back to Rowan.

She shrugs. "Sorry. I thought I heard Mom come up."

"Not yet. Not for a while."

She scratches her head, the sleeve of her boy jammies wagging against her cheek. "You coming to bed soon? Or do you want me to stay up with you?"

Her sweet, sleepy disposition is one of my favorites, maybe because she can be so mellow and generous when she just wakes up. I suck in my bottom lip, thinking, and look at the remote control in my hand. "Nah, I'm coming to bed now. Just gotta brush my teeth."

She scrunches up her face and yawns. "What time is it?"

I laugh softly. "Around eleven, I guess. Eleven fifteen."

"Okay," she says, turning to go back down the hallway to our bedroom. "Night."

I look at the TV once more and close my weary eyes for a moment. Then I turn it off and stand up, setting the remote on top of the set so it doesn't get buried, and carefully pick my way to the bathroom, and on to bed. But I don't think I'll be sleeping anytime soon.

LISA McMANN

is the author of the *New York Times* bestselling Wake trilogy, *Cryer's Cross, Dead to You*, and the middle-grade dystopian fantasy series The Unwanteds. She lives with her family in the Phoenix area. Read more about Lisa and find her blog through her website at LISAMcMANN.COM or, better yet, find her on Facebook (facebook.com/mcmannfan) or follow her on Twitter (twitter.com/lisa_mcmann).